AMERICAN STARLET

AMERICAN STARLET

THE SCARLETT CROSS CHRONICLES, BOOK ONE

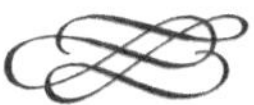

LUCY BLUE

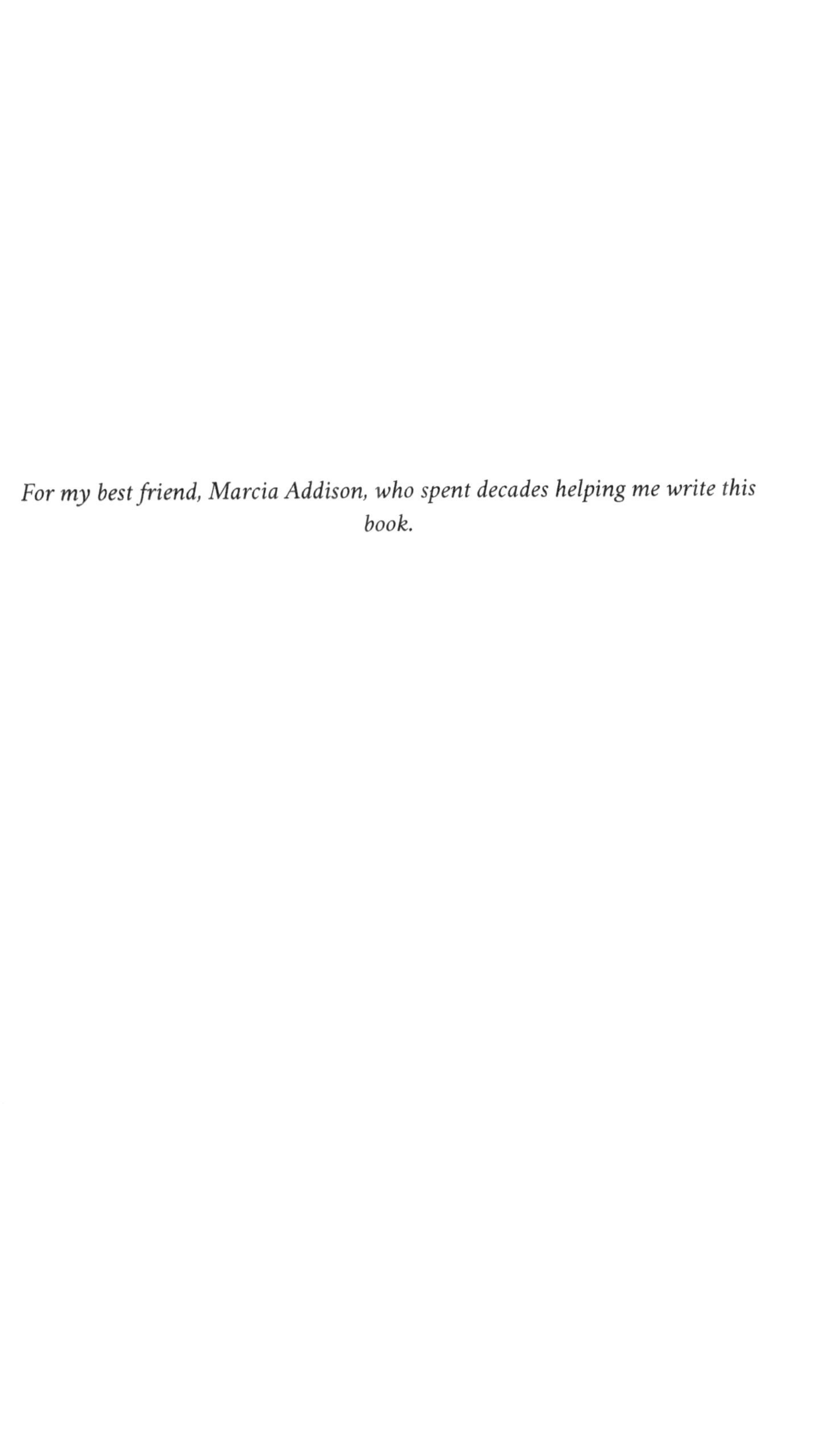

For my best friend, Marcia Addison, who spent decades helping me write this book.

CHAPTER 1

Spring 2004

Neither client had arrived, but the conference room was already buzzing. Paralegals hustled in and out, checking their PDAs and barking urgently into their headsets. One assistant was polishing the spotless black glass conference table —"That's not lemon-scented is it?" a paralegal yapped, "Miss Cross is allergic!"—while another laid out legal pads and freshly sharpened pencils. The office manager, a woman of fifty who was paid more than the CEO of most mid-sized corporations, spent at least ten minutes counting and recounting chairs.

Ten minutes before go time, a catering cart turned up with coffee, tea, water, various sodas, fruit, and pastries. "Caramel corn!" one of the paralegals snapped. "Halliwell-Brighton specifically said that Mr. Kidd would need caramel corn!" The head caterer herself rushed out to get some.

While setting up her equipment, the court reporter thought that if a transcript of this settlement conference should go astray and end up with one of the less-scrupulous media outlets, she'd be able to move to her own private island. And she'd need to, too. Nowhere else would be safe.

Promptly at ten, the three lawyers who would be representing Scarlett Cross walked in, surveyed the scene, pronounced it acceptable, and left to wait in their offices for their client to arrive. Half an hour later, the office manager ushered in the three lawyers from Halliwell-Brighton, the second-most-expensive family law firm in Los Angeles. When they'd given the room their okay, an assistant they'd brought with them went back downstairs to the limo and brought back an up-and-coming model/actress no one had thought would have the brass to come and *Gossip* magazine's three-time Juiciest Beefcake Alive, Romeo Kidd.

"Miss Cross isn't here yet," the office manager said. "We're expecting her any minute. Can I offer you anything?"

"We'll take care of it," the youngest of the three lawyers said.

"Mrs. Kidd," Romeo said. If anyone had expected him to dress up for the occasion, they were doomed to disappointment. As always, he looked like an exquisitely unmade bed. "Her name is still Mrs. Kidd."

Forty-five more minutes passed. The actress/model binged on grapes and diet soda and played a noisy game on her PDA. She tried sitting on Romeo's lap, but the oldest and scariest member of his legal team asked her very nicely but very firmly to please use a chair. Romeo scribbled on one of the legal pads, a strange little smile on his face.

At last, a wave of conversation came rolling up the hall. The door opened, and Scarlett Cross Kidd swept in with the home team of lawyers behind her and a respected Shakespearean actor at her side. "Oh good," Romeo said, standing up. "You brought a date, too."

"Actually, I'm not staying," the Shakespearean said, offering his hand. "Lovely to see you again." He and Romeo shook hands as Scarlett watched and everyone else looked on awkwardly.

"I love your work," the actress/model blurted out.

"Thanks," the Shakespearean said with a smile. "I like yours, too." He turned to Scarlett, took her hand, and kissed it. "I'll see you later."

She held on to his hand for an extra moment. "See you later."

Unlike her husband, she was perfectly dressed for the occasion in a Carolina Herrara suit, but she seemed anxious and fragile while Romeo was calm.

"Let's get started," her lead lawyer suggested as the Shakespearean left, and Scarlett took a seat directly opposite her husband. "Scarlett, can Marley get you something to drink?"

"No, thanks." One of the lawyers set a chic pink satchel on the floor at her feet. "Thank you," she said. "Sorry I'm late."

"It's okay," Romeo said. "I still like watching you make an entrance."

She smiled but didn't answer.

"So I think we've all had a chance to look over the proposals and counterproposals," Scarlett's lead lawyer began. "Let's start with real estate."

"Hang on," Romeo said. "Where's Ranhosky?"

Scarlett's team bristled as one. "Mr. Ranhosky won't be joining us," the leader said.

"Ranhosky died," Scarlett said. "Three weeks ago. It was cancer."

"Well, fuck me," Romeo said, making the model/actress snicker over her PDA. "And the San Andreas Fault didn't open up to suck him down to hell?"

"Not that I noticed," Scarlett said.

"So you're doing this without him or Daddy?" Romeo said. "Are you okay with that?"

She smiled, the flash of dazzling white teeth that had been lighting up movie screens since she was sixteen years old. "I am so okay with that."

"Let's take a look at these proposals then," Romeo's lead lawyer said, whipping out a sheaf of stapled papers. "I agree that we should start with the property settlement."

"I don't," Romeo said. "Let's start with the important stuff."

"You're not getting the kids," Scarlett said.

"I think it would be better to save the more emotionally-charged issues until after we hammer out a settlement on the property," Romeo's lawyer said.

"Delilah wants to live with me," Romeo said, talking over his lawyer.

"I don't care," Scarlett said, ignoring the lawyer, too.

"She's old enough to decide for herself."

"You think I don't know how old she is?"

"She isn't even your daughter!"

"Romeo, please!" his lawyer said, putting a hand over his. She was very pretty and shiny, like a lawyer on TV.

"Miss Cross?" Scarlett's lawyer said. He was shiny, too, but maybe not quite so pretty.

Scarlett and Romeo sat back in their chairs. The actress/model was watching them like a kid at the movies, but the lawyers all looked miserable. The court reporter was just trying to catch up.

"Fine," Romeo said. "Let's talk about the beach house. I bought it."

"You bought it for me," Scarlett said with a tight smile on her lips and sparkling tears in her eyes.

"I bought it for my wife," he said. "The woman I loved."

"It's good you said wife first," she said. "Just to clarify."

Romeo turned red. "This is ridiculous."

"This meeting is your last chance to work out these issues privately," Scarlett's lawyer said. He had gone to Harvard and sounded like a Kennedy. "If we can't come to some settlement here, we'll have no choice but to fight it out in open court. Every detail will become public."

"Let's do it," Romeo said. "I've got nothing to hide." His smile at Scarlett was chilling. "What do you think, Mrs. Kidd? Shall we let it all hang out?"

To everyone's shock, she smiled back. "It's funny you should ask."

She put the pink satchel on the table and took out a pair of thick, spiral-bound notebooks. Each one looked to have other papers stuffed between the pages at intervals, and both were obviously worn, as if they were written full. "I've been writing my memoirs," Scarlett said.

Everybody looked shocked, no one more so than her lawyers. "Oo, wicked," the actress/model said. "Can I see?"

"Eventually, maybe," Scarlett said. "That's all up to Romeo."

"Trust me, honey, you don't need to see," Romeo said. "I can tell you right now everything she wrote." He leaned back in his chair and laced his hands. "'My daddy is a saint; my brother is a genius; my husband is an asshole,'" he said in a cruel but accurate parody of Scarlett's voice. "'And I don't remember Mama.'"

They were glaring at one another with the kind of heat that had made millions at the box office, but again, Scarlett smiled. "You might be surprised."

"Wait, I'm confused," Romeo's lawyer said, addressing her counterpart, not either client. "Is this some kind of blackmail? He gives her whatever she wants, or she publishes some kind of trashy tell-all about both of them?"

"Sort of, but not exactly," Scarlett said. "And don't blame poor Alex; he knew nothing about it." She was still looking at no one but Romeo. "No one has seen what I've written but me. There aren't any other copies; it's all written in longhand except for the clippings."

"So when did you write all this?" Romeo said. She had his attention; he was leaning forward again.

"The past couple of weeks," she said. "I went to Mexico."

This seemed to mean something to him; a flicker of shock crossed his face. He watched her for another few seconds, a poker player gauging a bluff. Then he leaned back with a smile. "I think you should publish it, sweetheart," he said. "I'll read it when it comes out."

"Hang on," his lawyer said. "You can't just publish a book like this without letting Romeo read it first. We would have to insist on first approval for the entire manuscript."

Scarlett's lawyer laughed. "Dream on."

"I don't have a problem with that," Scarlett said. "Well, not a big problem. How about this?" She pushed the top notebook across the table toward Romeo. "Take the first half. It's got most of the stuff your lawyers are going to freak out about anyway, I think. Read it, sweetheart." The southern accent she'd inherited from her mother came out in the word, or maybe she was imitating him. "If, when you're finished, you still don't give a crap, fine. I'll publish, and we'll take it all to court. Like you said, we'll let it all hang out. But if you want to read the second half, you'll have to give me the beach house."

Romeo's smile was impossible to read. "You were right," he said. "You don't need Ranhosky at all."

"So what do you think, my baby?" she said. "You always said I never told you anything. Want to see how truthful I can be?"

"Oh come on," the actress/model said. "You know you have to do it."

Romeo laughed. "She's right," he said. "I guess I have to read."

CLIPPING 1

AP Wire report:

Model and Former Lover of Calvin Cross Dead in Mexico

The mutilated body of model Stella St. John was discovered early Tuesday in a hotel room in Habos San Reyes, Mexico. St. John, 24, was stabbed repeatedly in the face, neck, arms, and torso. Police state that while their investigation is on-going, their only witnesses at present are hotel employee Dolores Cruz, 56, who discovered the body, and an unidentified four-year-old child who may have seen the killer or killers as they left the scene. No suspects have been identified at this time.

St. John was best known for her runway and magazine work in Europe, where she appeared on the covers of both the French and Italian versions of Vogue, and for her former relationship with Oscar-nominated actor Calvin Cross. She was the mother of Cross' second child, a daughter named Scarlett. He also has a son, Sebastian, with longtime girlfriend Greta Strassman, the daughter of well-known playwright and political activist Arthur Strassman. Sources close to Cross indicate that Scarlett was visiting Cross and Strassman at their home in Beverly Hills at the time of her mother's murder and will remain in their custody.

St. John's remains were released by Mexican authorities to her parents, Horace and Jasmine St. John of Tupelo, Mississippi; however, a police spokesman stressed that their investigation into the brutal murder is still on-going. A private funeral is planned in Tupelo, but there has been no word on whether or not Cross will attend.

CHAPTER 2

My mother, Stella, was a fashion model. She was discovered at a movie house in Tupelo, Mississippi; she was a tall, thin girl with black hair and big blue eyes. She dropped out of high school and ran away from home three weeks before graduation and three days after the prom. She was the prom queen, and she didn't think she should miss it. She did some runway work in New York and Milan and a couple of commercials—nothing where she had to talk; she never lost the accent. I think she met my father in Europe, but I've never known for certain. He did some horror movies in Italy around the time I was conceived, and they would have likely been at some of the same parties.

Somewhere along the way, Stella got hooked on heroin and pills, probably to stay thin after she had a baby. The first place I remember being is a tiny town in Mexico where we stayed in a shithole hotel on the beach. Stella took me down to the water when we got there one late afternoon, and I remember the sunset and how beautiful she looked. This is my first clear memory. I have a framed *Vogue* cover she did that looks a lot like what I remember, or maybe I really just remember that. I've seen many photographs of her since. Anyway, I loved the ocean, and I remember asking her if we could stay there forever.

"We might," she told me, lifting me over the breakers. "I don't know where else we can go."

After that first afternoon, I went to the beach by myself. I was four years old. Stella had brought a lot of medicine in her suitcase and a wallet full of cash. Whenever I got hungry, I would take some money and walk down the beach to the tamale stand. I suspect I ate a lot of twenty-dollar tamales. Stella watched Mexican TV, shot up, and drank tequila. One time the phone rang, and she ripped the cord out of the wall and screamed. She wrapped it in a towel and hid it in the dresser.

I don't know how long we were there, but it seemed like weeks and weeks. But I don't suppose it could have been; I doubt Stella and our money could have lasted that long. One day when I came back from the tamale stand, a car was parked in front of our door, a white and yellow Volkswagon minibus. *That's a hippie car,* I can still remember thinking. Stella used to talk about hippies a lot.

The motel was right on the beach; you walked out our door and stepped onto the sand, but there was a road you had to cross to get to the ocean, just this little strip of unlined asphalt. I stood on the opposite side and stared at that hippie bus like the road was some kind of magical barrier, like as long as I stayed on the other side of the road, I couldn't be seen. I don't remember being scared, and I don't remember hearing any noises.

Finally, some guys came out of our motel room. There may have been three; there may have been four. I just know there were more than two. The only one I really saw was the driver; he came around to my side of the minibus to get in. He could have been a Mexican or just a white guy with a tan. He wasn't a hippie. His hair was dark and not really long, maybe collar-length, greasy, combed back over his ears. He was wearing motorcycle boots and jeans and a white T-shirt covered with blood. He must have seen me. Sometimes I think I remember him smiling at me or winking or saying something evil and profound. But honestly, I can't be sure.

For my whole life, I've been telling people I don't remember going inside. Subsequent events have suggested there must have been a lot of blood. I've been told Stella's face was covered with a towel when the Mexican cops arrived, but whether it was me who did it or the guys who killed her, I couldn't say. I don't even remember the cops in the room. I don't even remember the room. They tell me they found me wrapped in Stella's raincoat, sitting on the floor beside the bed where my mother's mutilated body lay. They say the woman who managed the motel called the cops because of the smell and the flies, but I don't remember that, either. Everything about that time is fuzzy. I remember a nun at the orphanage where they took me. She was crying while she gave me a bath, and I remember wondering what was wrong, why she was crying. I remember the handsome Mexican police detective giving me candy and getting me to describe the guy in the minibus. He was very nice; I think he must have been the one who called my grandparents in Tupelo.

Their coming is the next thing I remember clearly. My grandmother looked like an older, fatter Stella with a short, tight perm and orange lipstick. My grandfather looked like a background player on *Green Acres*; he came to Mexico wearing a straw cowboy hat. He looked at me one time in the orphanage and said, "She don't look nothing like Stella." Then he walked outside and lit a cigarette and never looked straight at me again. My grandmother scooped me up and started crying, hugging me tight. She smelled like hairspray and White Shoulders perfume—that's how I knew who she was. "You want to smell Mawmaw?" Stella had joked every time we went to the drugstore, letting me sniff White Shoulders. "You can buy her cheap in little bottles all over the world."

The Mexican cops wouldn't let them take me back to Tupelo because they said I was a witness. So they took a room in another shithole motel to wait. This one had a porch across the back with big rocking chairs and a hammock. My grandfather would lie in the hammock and read a Zane Gray western and bitch about the heat. My grandmother rocked me in a rocker. She cried and talked about Stella and sang songs about Jesus and the Rapture. Any time I try to imagine what it must be like to be a fetus in the womb, I think of her lap and that rocker. Every day the handsome cop would come to question me, and I would tell him again about the guys in the minibus, but Mawmaw wouldn't let him give me candy. She said it was dirty, that there was no telling where it might have come from. The handsome cop just smiled.

Then one day we were sitting there when the cop pulled up, and a shiny black limousine pulled up beside him. My grandmother hugged me tight, and my grandfather stood up out of the hammock. The cop got out first and called up to us, "It's okay, baby; don't be scared." I swear, if I could find that Mexican cop today, I'd give him a million dollars.

The back door of the limousine opened, and two men got out: a lawyer with a briefcase and my father. He was wearing a white dress shirt unbuttoned halfway down his chest with faded jeans, and his golden hair looked like a mane down to his shoulders. "Sweet Jesus," my grandfather muttered, and I thought he must be right.

My grandfather went down to meet them in the parking lot, and my grandmother

rocked harder and started singing again. The men talked; my father shook my grandfather's hand. The lawyer opened his briefcase on the hood of the limousine, and my grandmother stood up. "You stay right here," she told me and went down to join them. They argued, my grandparents and the lawyer—both of the men were against my grandmother, I think. The Mexican cop smiled at me and waved, then turned away and lit a cigarette. He just stood there smoking and watching the ocean the rest of the time they talked.

My father came up to the steps and sat down, and I saw he wasn't wearing any shoes. His feet were perfectly clean, as clean as Stella's had always been. "Your name is Scarlett, isn't it?" he asked me, and I told him yeah, it was. "I used to have a little sister who looked almost exactly like you."

"What happened to her?"

"She died of polio. She caught it in a swimming pool."

I liked that he told me the truth, and I thought he was beautiful, even better looking than the cop, as beautiful as Stella. "My mom is dead," I told him. "She's murdered."

"That's what I heard."

"I didn't see it happen."

"I heard that, too." He looked out at my grandparents, still arguing in the parking lot—my grandmother was crying. "Scarlett, I think I must be your father." He took my hand, and I sat down beside him. "Do you want to come and live with me?"

"Where do you live?" Mawmaw had been saying we would go to Tupelo, but I didn't want to. Stella had told me Tupelo was where the devil went to shit, and I believed her. Otherwise, why would we have ever come here?

"I live in Beverly Hills with the movie stars." He turned my hand palm up in his and spread the fingers. "I'm a movie star."

My grandfather was signing something for the lawyer while my grandmother cried, hugging herself and shaking her head. "Is it nice?"

"It's one of the nicest places in the world. People come from all over to live

there." He twisted a lock of my hair around his finger. "I have a big house with a little house behind it."

"Did Stella ever go there?"

"No. I didn't have it when I knew Stella. Is that what you called her, Stella?"

"Most of the time. Sometimes Mama, but not much." He smelled like the ocean and shaving cream and laundry detergent. "What's your name?"

"Calvin. But you could call me Daddy if you wanted to. Your brother, Sebastian, does." He picked me up and set me on his lap. "Sebastian is four years old."

"I'm four."

"I know." He kissed me on the temple. "His mother's name is Greta."

"Is she your wife?"

He laughed a little and squeezed me. "No, sweetpea. I don't have a wife. But she and Sebastian live with me." He folded his hands over mine. "Do you want to come and live with us?"

All the time before that moment, I never remember crying. Even when my grandmother kept sobbing and sobbing for Stella, I never shed a tear. It just didn't seem right to cry. But in that moment, looking at my father, I started crying, my whole body shaking as I screamed with grief. He held me close and kissed me, and I loved him with all my heart.

And for the record, in spite of everything that's happened since, I still do.

CLIPPING 2

Excerpt from "Riding a New Range: The Western Boom in the New American Cinema;"
  Cinephilia magazine

The weirdest and most interesting of the nouveau western films of the 1970s is The Canyon, *starring established movie idol Calvin Cross and directed by gonzo auteur Wallace Cole. Rarely has such an edgy, ironic, and ultimately evil-hearted movie been such a box office hit.*

When production began, Cross was already a studio darling, a major draw in both romantic comedies and the kind of sweeping dramas so beloved of critics and audiences alike. He was—and is—an actor of rare intelligence and sensitivity, but unlike many of his equally gifted peers, he had what one producer called "a face for Technicolor." By contrast, nobody expected Cole to even finish the movie. He was too strange, too abrasive; his scripts were just too plain weird. Legend has it he had been shopping the script for The Canyon *to studios since the mid-1950s when he had worked as a staff writer for television. One can only imagine what the Gunsmoke crowd must have made of it. But in this story of an angry, racist Confederate veteran with a taste for rape and bloody vengeance, Cross saw an opportunity to use both his beauty and his brains in service to a truly original story. He approached Cole about the project, and Cole was quick to agree.*

The film opens with an unnamed damsel in distress running across an open field of grass. She is lovely, raven-haired, just starting to weep. The camera sweeps back from her face and away to find Cross, ruggedly handsome on horseback, riding hellbent for leather, blue eyes steely with resolve. We assume he means to rescue her, of course. When the camera pulls back again, our eyes automatically search the horizon for some outlaw or savage about to receive his just comeuppance from our hero.

Then Cross' character, Holt, rides the lady down and yanks her over his saddle. He's not the hero; he's the threat. Within minutes, he has forced his attentions upon her (quite graphically, even for 1975), and she and the audience understand that he "bought her fair and square." The damsel is played by an actress named Dorothy Andrews (who is now, incidentally, producer Dorothy Andrews Cole and an ex-wife of the director), and she does a fine job, evolving over the first half of the picture from this tearful victim to passionate lover and finally to Holt's willing and capable partner in crime. But somehow, the audience's sympathies lie entirely with Holt. Through one despicable act after another, Cross' performance and the black humor of Cole's script make us love him without ever trying, just as the Lady (the only name ever given for Andrews' character) does.

Eventually the Lady is killed, quite lawfully, by the unluckiest sheriff's deputy in the history of the West, and Holt goes on his final rampage. Watching him wreak bloody vengeance on a posse that was only doing right, we applaud him. Somehow it feels like he's avenging us.

Remarkably, The Canyon was a critical and financial smash, garnering four Oscar nominations and two wins, one for Cross and one for the cinematographer. Wallace Cole has yet to repeat this kind of success, directing only two more films so far, both ambitious failures. But Calvin Cross remains one of the pre-eminent leading men of our time.

CHAPTER 3

When I met him and he took me home, my father had been living with Greta Strassman for five years. Greta was a supposedly promising writer from New York who had yet to publish or even finish so much as a dirty limerick. Her father was a famous pinko playwright and stage director; her dead mother had been a poet. She and Calvin had recently moved onto an estate on Mulholland Drive. Calvin and the ever-shifting circus of his entourage lived in the main house, a big, fake Tudor he called and still calls Castle Asshole. Greta and her mostly untouched typewriter lived in the guesthouse on the other side of the pool with their son, my half-brother, Sebastian, who was exactly thirty-six days older than me. Apparently when my dad was in Italy fucking my mother, Greta had had better things to do.

When we got to Beverly Hills, we walked straight through his empty house to the pool where Greta and Sebastian were waiting. He led me outside by the hand, and I was shaking all over. I had spent most of the last forty-eight hours in his arms while his lawyer made all the arrangements and booked us a private flight home. I was still wearing the clothes my grandmother had put on me two days before in Mexico. My hair had not been washed or even combed. My feet were bare. "Hi guys," Calvin called as we stepped into the blinding L.A. sun. "We're home."

Greta was lying on a chaise, reading a book. She's very classic-looking now, all sharp angles and perfect planes, but at that time, she was still kind of juicy with a bit of padding on her hips and the slightest hint of a belly over the top of her two-piece suit. "Hi," she said, standing up to kiss Cal on the lips. "This must be Scarlett."

I didn't say anything, just stared up at her, thinking she wasn't as pretty as Stella. I looked past her to Sebastian, who was standing on the steps of the shallow end of the pool with his chin level with the surface of the water, staring back at me with the biggest, bluest eyes I had ever seen.

"Isn't she beautiful?" Cal said, picking me up. I wrapped my arms around his neck and held on tight.

"Of course she is." Greta smiled at me. "Hi, sweetie." She held out her arms to me. I didn't want to go to her, but it never occurred to me that I could refuse. Calvin handed me over, and she held me close. "I'm Greta," she said, kissing my cheek. Over her shoulder, I could see Sebastian, still staring. He stuck out his tongue at me, and I stuck mine out back. He grinned, and I smiled, too.

Cal touched my cheek but spoke to Greta. "She can stay with me."

She shifted me in her arms so I was facing her. "Of course she can't." She was looking at me closely, her eyes searching my face, and I stared back. After a moment, she smiled. "Poor baby," she said, hugging me close again. "It's going to be fine."

Sebastian sprang up from the pool with a splash. "Daddy, look at me!" He ran up the steps and along the slippery edge so fast he was a blur of pink skin, golden hair, and blue bathing suit.

"Sebastian, no!" Greta said, almost dropping me to grab for him, but he was too fast for her. Dodging her grasp, he launched himself into the deep end, feet still flailing as he hit the water. She set me on my feet so fast I almost fell over, rushing for the edge. "Cal, get him!"

Sebastian surfaced almost before I'd gotten my balance, dog-paddling like mad and grinning ear to ear.

Our father hadn't moved. "All right!" he said, applauding, and I clapped, too. "Scarlett, meet your brother, the Frog Prince of Beverly Hills." He went over, bent down, and scooped Sebastian out of the pool. I followed as he hugged him close, sopping wet, and kissed him on the cheek. "Sebastian, this is Scarlett." Greta was still just standing there, her hand pressed to her chest.

"Hey," Sebastian said, reaching down from our father's arms to me, and I clasped his hand in mine. And we've been together ever since.

Greta continued to pretend to care about me for the next nine years. She took me to her house and put me in the bathtub and dressed me in Sebastian's clothes like it was the most natural thing in the world. Over the course of the next seven days, she brought in a decorator to do me up a pink princess bedroom of my very own with a white canopy bed, bought me a whole new wardrobe of my own, got my hair cut in a little girl's bob, and filled the shelves in my room with toys. She took me and Sebastian with her wherever she went and introduced me to her friends and her hairdresser and her personal shoppers as "my little girl, Scarlett." By the end of that first week, I had been completely incorporated into her life as if I had always been there and Stella had never been real.

Every night, Calvin came home to our little house for dinner and played with me and Sebastian until it was time to go to bed. He and Greta would tuck me in together, and if I woke up crying in the night, Calvin was the one who would come in. He would climb in bed with me and hold me close and let me cry and never ask me questions, and I would fall back to sleep in his arms.

But then Calvin went back to work. The first few nights were fine. He had explained to me that he would be gone for a few weeks but that Greta loved me and would take care of me. And she did take care of me at least, and I assumed the love came with it. Certainly, I was better tended than I had ever been with Stella.

Then one night I woke up screaming. To her credit, Greta tried to comfort me. She came into my room and turned on the light and picked me up and sat down on the bed to hold me. She rocked me back and forth and promised everything was fine. But when I wouldn't just stop crying, she started to ask me what was wrong. She kept on asking and asking me to tell her why I was crying, what I had dreamed about, why I was afraid. And every time she asked, I got more scared until I was thrashing like a wild thing in her arms, biting and clawing to get away. "Scarlett, stop it!" she cried, and I saw blood on her arms and her face from where I had clawed at both our skin. I screamed even harder and louder, the whole world as I saw it turning red.

The next thing I knew was Calvin's voice coming through the phone receiver the housekeeper was holding to my ear. "Scarlett," he was saying over and over again. "Scarlett, honey, it's okay. You're all right, baby, stop."

"Daddy!" Greta was holding my arms pinned to my sides and half lying on top of me on the bed to keep me still. "Daddy, I'm scared!" I cried into the phone, suddenly able to make words again. "Come home!" In my mind, I could see myself breaking free of Greta and running away from the house, down the driveway in my nightgown, running for the street. "Please, come pick me up!"

"Hush, baby, shhhh," he was saying. "It's all right." The sound of his voice was acting like a drug on me, making me do what he said, but I felt cold. "Baby, you know I can't come home right now." A knot was forming in my stomach, making me feel sick. "I have promised these people I will do this job, and I have to finish." Greta was hurting me, she was holding me so tight. "But I promise I will come home just as soon as I possibly can. Okay?"

"Okay." I hadn't meant to answer him, but I had. I recognized the voice as mine. I looked up and saw the housekeeper was holding a bottle of antiseptic. Greta loosened her hold and took the phone, still holding it against my ear.

"When I get home, we'll go somewhere," Daddy was saying. "Just you and me if you want. Won't that be fun?" He sounded just the same as always, the same voice as in Mexico. But this time he wouldn't come.

"Yes." The housekeeper was dabbing antiseptic on my scratches, and I let her, barely feeling the sting.

"Be thinking about the place you would most want to go." He was smiling now, I could hear it. "You just had a bad dream, sweetpea," he was saying. "But you're okay now. You're awake."

"I'm awake." He was lying, and he wanted me to lie. I looked down at Greta's arm and saw a bead of blood starting to clot on a scratch, shiny as a licked red lollipop. I closed my eyes and pushed her arm away.

"That's my girl," Daddy was saying. "I love you." I heard a slight catch in his voice. "Daddy loves you very much."

"I love you." My eyes were still shut tight.

"Let me talk to Greta." I looked up at Sebastian's mother. She was watching me with a strange look on her face, as if I were something scary she had suddenly discovered, like a spider in a dresser drawer. "I'll see you very soon."

"He wants to talk to you." She stared at me a moment longer before she took the phone. She carried it away from the bed, and the housekeeper took her place at my side. She took off my blood-stained nightgown and started putting on a fresh one. I could barely hear Greta speaking softly and urgently into the phone. "Calvin, she needs help!" The housekeeper picked me up out of the bed to change it, and I let her, compliant as a doll.

By the time she was done, Greta was off the phone. She was standing by the door, smoking a cigarette, something I had never seen her do before. Her arms and cheek were still smeared with blood, and the cigarette was shaking.

"I'm sorry, Greta," I said. "I . . . I had a bad dream."

She turned her back on me to put out the cigarette in a saucer from my tea set on the dresser. "It's okay." When she turned back around, she was smiling. "It's over." She came and kissed me on the cheek, her lips perfectly dry and cool. "The past is past, sweetie," she said, smiling down at me. But little as I was, I could still see the horror in her eyes. "All that matters is the now." She pulled the covers up to my chin, and she and the housekeeper left me, leaving the door ajar.

I stared at the crack for a long time, the dim light from the hallway coming in. Suddenly a shadow crossed the light, and I almost screamed again. I had to put both hands over my mouth to keep the noise from coming out. *Bad dream,* I thought inside my head. Just a bad dream.

The door swung open, and I saw Sebastian standing in the light. He was carrying his stuffed dog, a present from Daddy he never slept without. "Scoot over," he said, turning on the bedside light—Sebastian needed a nightlight. He climbed into the bed beside me, putting his head beside mine on the pillow. He smiled at me, and I smiled back. I reached out and took him by the hand.

"Night night, sleep tight," I said, the same thing Stella had said to me every night when she put me to bed. "Don't let the bed bugs bite."

He snorted. "Don't be ridiculous." He snuggled close to me, the stuffed dog smashed between us, his hand still clasped in mine. "We do not have bugs."

Most of the time we were fairly normal kids; we went to a posh but perfectly ordinary private school; we made decent grades; we had a lot of friends. Sebastian played little league baseball; I took gymnastics and dance. But our father was a movie star. He never let us doubt for a moment that he loved us, and when we saw him, he gave us his absolute, undivided attention. But we didn't see him much. He worked a lot in those days, spending months at a time on location, and even when he was in L.A., his time was pretty booked. There were places he had to go and people he had to see to maintain who he was as both an artist and an image. And Sebastian and I understood that, because Greta explained it to us.

Sometimes Greta would go visit him on location and leave us at home with the housekeeper, but never for more than a week or so at a time. On very rare occasions, she would take us with her. I remember Christmas in London the year we were seven while Cal played a World War II POW at Pinewood, and we spent my tenth birthday in Cairo with him while he shot a heist picture in the desert. But those visits were big, unusual events that broke into the routine Greta made for us at home, and as time went on, seeing Cal at home became the same. Cal was a supernatural being who lived out in the world and kept a church on the other side of our swimming pool. Sometimes we visited him; sometimes he visited us. But we lived with Greta. It never occurred to me or Sebastian to expect him to act like a father. If Greta wanted him to act like a husband, she never let on to us.

Then came his first flop and Dolci Guiliana. Sebastian and I were thirteen years old. Cal had just come home from his location shoot in Europe and was visiting our house. Sebastian and I were doing homework together at the kitchen table—eighth grade, Algebra I; I can still remember the juice stain on the book. Greta was making dinner, and Calvin was sitting on the counter, drinking a glass of wine and watching her, teasing her like always. At first she was smiling, laughing, but even I could see she was a little preoccupied, not as happy as she usually was on his first night home. Sebastian was antsy, too, I remember—he was already reading *Variety* every day, preparing for his own brilliant career in the movies, and he had probably seen the tabloids, too. Me, I didn't have a clue what was coming; I thought everything was fine. Daddy was home; all was right with the world.

"I've found an apartment in New York," Greta said, chopping mushrooms by the sink.

"What's in New York?" my father asked, perfectly cheerful. But Sebastian froze across from me, his pencil poised over his notebook.

"My apartment," she said, her voice casual but with a tiny tremor. "I've decided to move back east." Greta always spoke of New York City as "back," her native soil to which she must someday, like Dracula, return. "I'm leaving you, Cal."

"Oh yeah? How's that?" he asked, still almost laughing, like he thought she was making a joke. Now, as a grown woman who has had the unparalleled pleasure of being involved with a man other women find irresistible, I have no choice but to see things from her point of view. But at that moment, I was utterly shocked that she could dare to threaten him this way. I looked at Sebastian, eyes wide. *Did you know?* I mouthed to him, and he shook his head, frowning.

"What did you think I would do?" she asked, putting down the knife to face him. "Did you think I would just pretend I didn't know what was happening, that we'd just keep pretending that you love me?"

"I do love you," he protested, and my heart went out to him completely. He sounded horrified, and she just sounded mean.

"Do you?" she asked. Her voice was so calm that she might have been firing the maid.

"Of course!" He reached for her, and she stepped back, jerking away from his touch. "Greta, what are you doing?" He glanced over at me and Sebastian, both of us rapt and appalled. "We should talk about this in private."

"Why?" she asked. "You don't honestly think they don't know, do you?"

"I don't," I said, and Calvin put the last nail in his coffin when he laughed. Greta looked at me with such pure, cold fury that I felt the blood rush to my face.

Calvin didn't seem to notice. "Why don't you two go upstairs?" he suggested, smiling at me and putting a hand on my shoulder. "Go ahead."

Sebastian pushed his chair back first, nearly in tears, watching our father. "It will be all right," Calvin promised. "Go on."

We did as we were told and left, but we stopped on the landing, out of sight but still well within earshot of everything they said. I would have gone all the way up, but Sebastian grabbed my wrist and dragged me down to sit beside him on the stairs. "He cheated," he hissed in my ear. "It's all over the papers. He…he fucked the girl from the movie." He stumbled over the obscenity, and when I looked at him, wide-eyed, he was blushing. We both knew what the word meant by then, of course, but neither of us had ever dreamed of actually saying it before—Greta would never have allowed it.

"Okay, tell me what's going on?" Calvin was saying at the same time, and I don't know what shocked me more, what Sebastian had said or the sudden change in the tone of my father's voice. He sounded like a stranger, someone angry and impatient, a man I'd never met. "What the fuck, Greta?"

"I think it's pretty simple, Calvin," she answered. She sounded angry, too, but not hurt, and certainly not surprised. This angry Calvin was apparently no stranger to her. "I've had enough. I'm done."

"Don't be stupid."

"That, my darling, is exactly what I'm trying not to be." They sounded like a soap opera playing on a TV in another room. "Do you have any idea what it's like for me, knowing that as soon as you walk out of this house, you…what am I supposed to do? How am I supposed to handle it? It's one thing when the only people who know are the people you work with. I mean, yeah, I have to see them all the time, but at least they have the decency to pretend nothing is going on and to let me pretend I don't know."

"Greta, stop it."

"But how am I supposed to ignore this? It's EVERYWHERE, Calvin. EVERYBODY knows you had an affair with this girl—house-wives in Idaho are talking about it; it's on the fucking NEWS, for Christ's sake."

"It's not an affair, Greta. I can't have an affair; I'm not married."

Sebastian gasped and clutched my wrist so tightly my bones cracked and my hand went numb. "You're absolutely right," Greta was saying, and there were tears in her voice. "You're not."

There was a moment of terrible silence. Then Calvin said, "Oh shit, honey," like he'd just heard himself, like someone else had been speaking through him when he hurt her. Bless him, that's my father in a single moment, his entire character. He never, ever means to hurt anyone; he's always so terribly sorry.

"No, don't," she said, and we could hear them moving, hear something slide off the counter to the floor with a crash

"I didn't mean it."

"Obviously, you did."

"No," he was protesting; his voice had gone soft, as if he had moved close to her. "Baby, it's nothing, I swear. I swear." She said something else we couldn't hear, a soft, womanly sound, and beside me, Sebastian closed his eyes, his mouth moving as if in silent prayer. "It doesn't mean anything. It's been blown completely out of proportion." We heard him kiss her, heard her breathing hard, like she was crying.

"Please, forgive me, baby. Please…I'm so sorry. You and the kids are my life." Sebastian and I looked at each other and smiled, both of us with tears streaming down our cheeks. It would be okay.

"Bullshit." There was no more softness in her voice and no more tears. "You don't have a life, Calvin," she said. "You don't want one. You have art." She was moving away from him; her voice was getting louder as she moved closer to us. "Sebastian is already enrolled in a private school in New York. You'll have to hire a nanny for Scarlett." Sebastian and I both gasped at that. "You'll enjoy that."

"Hilarious," Calvin retorted, but he was obviously shaken. The angry stranger had come back, and now he sounded scared, too. "You're not taking my son from me, Greta."

"Your son?" she repeated. "In what way would you call him yours? What exactly have you ever done to make him anything but mine? He's a pet to you, a prop, a toy for you to play with when you don't have anything better to do. Play with Scarlett. She needs you. We don't." Sebastian was openly crying now, still quiet, but shaking with sobs, and I pulled him close to me. "We fly out first thing in the morning."

And so they did. The next morning before the sun was up, the chauffeur put their bags into a limo, and they left. Sebastian screamed and cried at his mother all night long, begging her to reconsider. Calvin was gone; he had left right after the fight, left our house, left the grounds, his car roaring out of the driveway like a dragon.

Greta and I never spoke. When Cal first left, and Sebastian and I first went back into the kitchen, I intended to say something to her, to ask her not to go. But she looked at me and said nothing, and I couldn't speak. Because I understood. At some point between the time I had left for school that morning and the time she had told Cal she was leaving, I had stopped being real to her any more. She had said Cal thought Sebastian was a pet, a toy; she was wrong. But I was a toy to her, a doll her lover had brought home from Mexico for her to play with. But now she was leaving, leaving Calvin, leaving that life behind. So she didn't want me anymore.

When it was time for them to leave, Sebastian and I hugged each other so tight, my arms ached. "Tell Daddy I don't believe her," he said, the same thing he'd been saying to me all night. "Tell him I love him, and I know he loves me back."

"I'll tell him every day," I promised. *But I won't see him every day,* I thought. *I'll be by myself.* "But he already knows."

CHAPTER 5

When they had gone, I just stood there in the kitchen, paralyzed, listening to the car roll down the driveway and out of the gates. I didn't know what to do next. I was still standing there half an hour later when the housekeeper came in. "They left already?" she asked me as she put her purse down on the table.

"At seven." *Greta must have told her before she told Daddy,* I thought. "Their flight is at eight." I looked at the clock, my imagination following Sebastian through the airport. "I don't want to go to school."

"No," the housekeeper agreed, touching my cheek. "Not today." She gave me a hug. It's weird; in all the years she was our housekeeper, that's the only time I ever remember her touching me. "I'll call the school. You go back to bed."

"Okay." But I didn't. I went out the back door and across the back yard in my nightgown and bare feet. I couldn't go to bed, couldn't go to sleep. I kept thinking what it was going to be like to wake up in the house with Greta and Sebastian gone.

I had been inside my father's house before, of course, many times. But I had never gone in by myself with no particular purpose. His cook was in the kitchen, and I could tell she was trying not to look surprised when I came in. "Good morning, miss."

"Good morning." She was cutting a cantaloupe into cubes.

"Are you hungry?" There was coffee brewing in a shiny machine on the counter, but I saw no sign of any cups. The room was all shiny black stone and dull, buffed stainless steel with all the props for cooking and eating tucked away somewhere out of sight. It could have been an autopsy lab as easily as a kitchen. "Can I make you some breakfast?"

"No, thank you." I knew better than to ask her where my father was. At eight in the morning, he was either still out or sleeping. I smiled at her and went through the swinging doors that led to the rest of the house, half-expecting her to stop me. But she didn't, of course.

I went through the living room to the front hall where the Picasso was hanging and stopped to look at it. It's a cubist piece called "Harlequin," and it's beautiful, at least eight feet tall and three feet across without its heavy frame. I didn't know anything about the cubist imagery at that point, but Cal had told me it was a picture of a clown. "A really expensive Emmett Kelly print," I had heard him say it was to someone else. But I didn't see the figure as a clown at all. Even broken by a prism into triangles and squares, he was lithe and handsome, a lover preparing to bow, Prince Charming in a parti-colored suit.

I flipped on the light above it and just stared at it for a long time, trying to puzzle out the face, but I couldn't. It was like Picasso had painted him in a thousand different poses all at once. But I did see a long, thin splash of crimson I had barely registered before, one narrow, triangular shard of a truer red than any other in the painting. Moving closer, I tried to make it into a rose he was sweeping to his breast before offering it to a girl—that was the image my imagination wanted. But it wasn't right.

"He's bleeding." I said it out loud even though I thought I was alone.

"You think so?" My father was sitting on the stairs. I had no idea how long he might have been watching me. "I think so, too." He looked terrible. I hardly recognized him as my beautiful movie star father. The glamour that had always surrounded him from the very first time I had seen him had vanished. He hadn't shaved, and he was wearing a plush but ratty black bathrobe over faded, saggy jeans, and grayish-white socks on his feet.

"They left," I said. He motioned me closer, and I sat down on a step below the one where he was sitting.

"I heard the car," he answered as he stroked my hair. From so close, I could smell the whiskey on him, not just on his breath but rising like a vapor from his skin and clinging to his clothes. I started shaking because I knew what that smell meant. He smelled like Stella had just before she died. "My poor baby," he said as I laid my head against his leg, and my heart beat faster. I had been Stella's poor baby. She had held me close and told me she knew what a shit mama she was and asked how Jesus could give such a sweet baby girl to such a piece of shit.

"I'm all right, Daddy," I lied.

"I know." But he was lying, too. "I really fucked it up for you, didn't I, sweetpea?" He touched my chin and turned my face up to his, his beautiful face haggard with sorrow and regret. "I'm sorry." He hugged me close, his voice and shoulders trembling with tears. "I'm so sorry."

"It's not your fault, I swear to God." I was desperate to comfort him. I felt like Castle Asshole might start crumbling around us any minute, like the world might be coming to an end. "Sebastian didn't want to leave, I promise. Greta made him go. I hate her."

"Hey, no." He drew back to look at me, and I was comforted to see his eyes were lucid even through his tears. "Nobody gets to hate Greta. Greta loves you."

"No, she doesn't," I said, and I could see in his eyes that he knew it was true.

"It's okay, baby." He put his hand on my head and leaned down to kiss my cheek. "She just wanted to leave."

"If she loved me, she wouldn't have." My real mama didn't leave me, I thought. She took me with her, no matter what, until somebody cut her up, cut her heart out to take her away.

"She left me, baby, and I deserve it," he said. "I couldn't stop her."

He sounded calmer, I realized, like my daddy again. The crisis had passed.

"I'm just as glad." I wasn't. I was still terrified. But I wanted to feel what I had heard in Greta's voice, that bitter resignation that had made her seem so strong. "If she doesn't want me, I don't want her."

He hugged me close with one arm and gave me a kiss on the top of the head. "Well, I want you," he promised. "I want you a lot."

"I want you, too," I said, snuggling close against him. "I wouldn't have let her take me with her even if she had wanted to."

"Neither would I," he promised. "I just worry, sweetpea. I mean, you're growing up; you're going to need a woman in the house to… you know…tell you stuff, help you with stuff."

"I'll be fine." I couldn't stand the thought of him worrying about me or being afraid for me. I couldn't stand for the terrible, crushing sadness to come back into his voice, not if I could stop it. "Greta already told me all about all that stuff, and I already started…trust me, I'll be fine."

"Really?" He looked down at me, turning my face up to his. "I guess you could always ask the housekeeper if there was something you didn't want to talk to me about."

"Absolutely," I said. "It's totally okay, Daddy." I made myself smile my very best smile. "You never have to worry about me."

"I love you, sweetpea, more than anything else in the world." He hugged me close. "My beautiful miracle girl."

I wonder now if he knew I was lying and just let me go on and do it, or if he really believed me. Not that it really matters. I know that even though I knew he could be a liar when he needed to be, in that moment, I believed him, so much that I felt bad for Sebastian, who loved him so much. Even though I knew he'd still be leaving me to live his life, and I'd still have to figure out how to keep my own life running on my own, I believed that he loved me and wanted me, just like he said. And that, for the moment, was enough. Greta couldn't forgive him, but I could. I was still his little girl; I could forgive him anything.

CLIPPING 3

from *The Rude Guy's Guide to the Movies*

*Lionheart *1/2: The good news? Not nearly as bad as its reputation might lead you to believe. The bad news? It's still pretty fucking bad. Calvin Cross wrapped up his unironic heartthrob period with this deeply uncomfortable portrayal of the English crusader king Richard the Lionhearted (yeah, let that one sink in for a second) in this monster-budget bio-pic. Everything looks fantastic—reports at the time set the costume budget alone at upwards of $20 million—but no amount of gorgeous can compensate for a story that's just plain ludicrous or a performance from Cross that will inspire giggles from all but his most loyal fan-girls—his weirdly awful English accent alone is enough to make those of us who admire him cringe. Italian sex kitten Dolci Guiliana plays Richard's Muslim princess lover (WTF?!?!?) with the face of a marble statue of the Virgin Mary and the animation level to match. Their sex scenes do have a certain soft-core porno appeal rarely seen since the R-rated heyday of the early 1980s—these are pretty, pretty people. My suggestion? Skip ahead to those, and give the plot a miss.*

CHAPTER 6

So that's how I ended up with a house of my own at the age of thirteen. I spent the first few weeks after Greta and Sebastian left in a constant state of abject terror any time I wasn't with my father. The whole first week I slept on the couch in the den, afraid to go upstairs after the housekeeper went home every night for fear someone might break in, and I wouldn't know it until it was too late to run. That was silly since we lived in a compound behind an electronic gate with cameras and a guard. But knowing my history up to that point, I don't think it was entirely unreasonable.

The housekeeper came back every morning; she bought the groceries and cooked all my meals and did my laundry the same way that she always had. Cal's business manager made sure all my bills were paid. The driver took me wherever I needed or wanted to go. After three days, I went back to school because I had a vague notion of the truant officer from old *Our Gang* shorts I had seen, and besides, what else did I have to do?

But school, like everything else, had definitely changed, or rather, I guess, I had. For months, I didn't buy any new clothes or shoes because I didn't have a clue what I should buy. Truth be told, that first day after Greta and Sebastian left, I went to my closet and put together half a dozen outfits that I remembered Stella putting out for me, and I wore them over and over. I didn't get my hair trimmed; I cut my nails down to the quick with clippers and let the polish chip away. When the little girl make-up and perfume Greta had bought me ran out, I raided the cabinets in her bathroom for samples and swag she had left behind, grown-up colors and textures I couldn't begin to use properly. I just put on everything in the kit with whatever applicator seemed appropriate.

By Thanksgiving, my so-called friends had stopped calling me completely. "You've gotten to be a real bitch, Scarlett," my best friend, Chloe, said the last time I went to her house to visit after school. I don't even remember why she said it, but she was probably right. I had developed a sarcastic chip on my shoulder from answering questions about where Sebastian had gone. No one cared, apparently, that I was still around. Very few of my classmates dared to be openly hostile to me; my dad was too rich and too famous. Most of their parents were either in the movie industry already or trying desperately to be. But nobody sought me out. The week before Christmas break, the faculty advisor of the cheerleading squad suggested that maybe I'd be happier if I quit. "You just don't seem committed any more, Scarlett," she said sadly, patting my hand. "The other girls feel you don't care."

"I care," I said because I knew I was supposed to say it, but of course it wasn't true. I had never cared, exactly, and now it just seemed stupid. Everything at school seemed pointless and unreal; reality was my empty house.

I wrote Sebastian every night, and he called me at least twice a week. He loved his new school. He'd made a whole gang of disreputable new friends who apparently did nothing but go to the movies and sniff glue in Central Park. I lied about what I was doing, and he at least pretended to believe me. If he was in contact with his old L.A. friends and knew better, he never let on.

For the next year or so, that was my life. Looking back on that time now, it seems weird that no adult noticed anything was wrong, that none of my teachers or the parents of the other kids I had known

bothered to check up on me at all. You'd think my changing so drasti-
cally so quickly would have at least made somebody think I was on
drugs. Maybe they all figured that as Calvin's daughter, of course I
was on drugs. Or maybe they thought something even worse was
going on, and they didn't want to know anything about it. Or maybe
really no one noticed. I would like to think that if I had been in their
position, I would notice, and I would care, and I would have the tits to
investigate. But hell, who knows?

Greta had let Sebastian start auditioning almost as soon as they
landed in New York. I think that was the only way she kept him
from going off the deep end completely. He started getting commercials almost immediately. He did one for bubble gum about six
months after they moved that aired so often, even I got sick of it.
Over the next year, he did a couple of guest spots on two different
TV crime dramas—loud-mouth jock victim in one, angel-faced
psycho killer in the other. Both got great reviews; he could have
gone straight into films right then if Greta had let him. His official
age listed on his resume was 16, almost two full years older than his
real age by then. But Greta was determined that he stay in normal
high school and even more determined that he stay in New York. So
he ended up doing a play instead, a revival of one of his grandfather's classics.

It was only scheduled to run for two weeks, and I really wanted to
go to the opening. But Calvin couldn't get away that week, and
nobody came up with any kind of plan for me to go without him. So
we went for closing night instead. We flew east on the redeye, first-
class with all the seats around us empty—me, Calvin, Calvin's latest
assistant, Cory, and Calvin's latest girlfriend, a tall, blonde fashion
model from Kansas who thought everything was, "oh my god, so
awesome!"

Everybody else was asleep as soon as the wheels left the tarmac.
Cory had given Calvin and Awesome sleeping pills with their first-
class complimentary champagne. But I was much too excited to sleep.
Sebastian and I hadn't seen one another in more than a year. We had
been on the phone with one another for hours the night before, plan-

ning every minute of my forty-eight hours in New York. I hadn't felt so happy since he and Greta had left L.A.

We landed at Kennedy around seven a.m., and I just assumed we'd go straight to Greta's apartment. I was in no great rush to see Greta, but that was where we'd find Sebastian. But the limo took us straight to the Plaza Hotel. "Daddy, what's going on?" I said, catching him as we were going in. "Aren't we going to see Sebastian?"

"Sure we are, sweetpea." A couple of photographers were lurking on the sidewalk, and they managed to fire off a few shots before the doormen shooed them away. Awesome draped her long, willowy arms around Calvin's neck and leaned her golden head on his shoulder, posing. Calvin hugged her with one arm, barely seeming to notice. "But we're beat." He started moving again, the rest of us following in his wake. Cory was directing the limo driver and bellhops with the luggage as we passed into the lobby.

'I'm not tired," I told Calvin.

"Oh, to be young," Awesome said. She might have been as old as twenty-five, but I doubt it.

Calvin just smiled. "We need to get some sleep, sweetpea," he said, petting my cheek. The manager had come out from behind the registration desk, followed closely by an assistant carrying a manila envelope. Cory met them before they got to us, friendly and pleasant but firm. "We'll all see Sebastian tonight."

"Tonight?" I echoed, but he had already turned away. Cory had the manila envelope—a bundle of room keys.

"Cory, get Scarlett settled," Calvin said, taking a key. "Make sure she knows how to call room service." He winked at me then stepped into the elevator with Awesome; the two of them were wrapped around one another like eels before the doors were closed.

"Cory, I want to go see Sebastian," I said. Half a dozen people with big gray vacuum cleaners were just finishing up the carpet in the lobby, and people were starting to drift in from the street.

"Come on, honey, give me a break," he answered. Now that Calvin was gone, he looked exhausted. "Here's your key; your luggage should be in your room. Do you need me to walk you up?"

I had stayed in a big hotel before; I had even stayed in the Plaza. But that had been with Greta and Sebastian. We had stayed in a big suite, and Sebastian and I had shared a room. And we'd had a professional babysitter whenever Greta went out to shop or have lunch with friends. "No, it's okay," I said, taking the key. "I'll be okay."

As soon as I was upstairs behind the locked door of my room, I called Sebastian on the number that only rang in his bedroom. "Hello?" he answered on the first ring. He sounded just as wide awake as I was.

"We're here!" I could have jumped up and down with joy at the sound of his voice. I would have sworn he even sounded closer.

"Excellent!" He sounded just as excited. "Are you in the car? When are you getting here?"

"We're at the Plaza. Daddy…he's exhausted." All of a sudden it hit me how disappointed he would be, how much it would hurt his feelings to know Cal preferred to bang some model before he came to see him. "He was working right up to when we got on the plane." It was a lie, but I wasn't the least bit ashamed to tell it. "So he's getting a nap."

"Oh." I doubt my brother was fooled. He knew our father as well as I did, at that point probably better. But like me, he appreciated the effort of a loving fib, and unlike me then, he knew how to bounce back. "Okay, whatever. Where do you want to meet me?"

"What?"

"The Four O'Clock Diner is pretty much the halfway point. Just take the subway to Columbus Circle, and I'll meet you at the station. Wait for me on the sidewalk."

"'Bastian, I can't take the subway by myself." The very idea made me feel light-headed. All those strangers, all those maps; all that big, scary, empty world full of people who could just as easily want to kill me as not.

"Oh, for fuck's sake." He had gotten a lot more comfy with that word; I had noticed it on the phone with him before. "Fine, just take a cab. I'll give you the address."

I didn't really want to do that either, but I couldn't stand the thought of waiting all day in an empty hotel room to see him. "Why don't you come over here?" I suggested. "We can order room service, just hang out like we used to. It'll be fun."

He didn't answer for a few seconds, but when he did, he sounded sweet, not laughing any more or impatient. "Just meet me in the lobby," he said. "I'm coming to get you."

CHAPTER 7

An hour later, we were tucked into a booth at a busy New York diner, eating pancakes. Sebastian looked wonderful; I couldn't stop smiling at him. He didn't look like a kid any more—he could have been any age from fifteen to twenty-five. His blonde hair had grown out shaggy and soft, and his skin was flawless like our father's. It was chilly out, late October, and he was wearing a leather motorcycle jacket over his jeans and plain white tee-shirt. Every female who saw him, regardless of age, stopped to look again. "What's with you, psycho?" he asked, laughing with me as I giggled at another one who turned all the way around to look.

"Nothing," I said, still snickering. "You're just gorgeous."

"Oh, shut up," he said, throwing the crust of his toast at me. "What do you want to do today?"

Be with you, I wanted to say. *Feel like myself again.* "I don't know," I said instead. "Whatever."

"My sister the Hollywood princess." He was grinning at me, blue eyes twinkling. "Spread the greatest city in the world at her feet, and all she can say is, 'whatever.'" He put a handful of cash on the check and drained the last dregs of his soda. "Come on, let's go to the museum."

Two trains and a long walk through Central Park later, we were at the Metropolitan Museum of Art. One of my favorite books takes place in the rococo furniture section, so we went there first, then the Egyptian tomb and the medieval castle stuff, all like different movie sets where all the props were real. We ate lunch in the cafeteria, spaghetti and salad and milk and a huge chocolate cupcake each— school food like we'd eaten together every day before Greta took him away. I was in heaven. Everywhere we went, he talked—about his school, about the play, about the other actors, about his crazy grandfather the director whom he seemed to worship almost as much as he did Calvin. He even knew all kinds of stuff about the art. He said his school took field trips there almost every month. It was a very progressive school, he said, for arty kids, the kids of famous actors and writers and artists, and very, very rich kids who had been kicked out of other schools for bad behavior.

After lunch, we went to Sebastian's favorite section, European Paintings. We walked hand in hand down the galleries, and he told me what his teachers had told him about the artists. People smiled at us as we walked past them, and I smiled back, unafraid.

We stopped in a section with only one painting hanging in it, a huge, dark, overwhelming canvas of a dense, detailed forest. We sat down on the bench in front of it, and for a long time, we were both silent, just looking at it. "This one is my favorite," he finally said, still holding my hand.

I wasn't sure I liked it at all. "Who painted it?" It was too dark, too full and too empty at the same time, a million little branches and brambles with no rhyme or reason to it.

"I don't know." My brother's eyes were searching the image, completely focused, reading some secret message there. "I don't want to know."

I searched the image, too, trying to see what he saw. Finally just off the center, I found a tiny stain of light in the midst of the darkness—a fire, I realized. There were two little slashes of color beside it, maybe figures, two little people huddled together by the fire. But the perspective was too distant to be sure. They could have been living or dead or nothing at all. The fire could have been nothing but a mud puddle in the path reflecting moonlight.

"Hey bitch!" a voice called from behind us. "Why weren't you in school?"

I stiffened, horrified, but Sebastian smiled. "Hey bitch, I'm famous," he fired back, standing up. "I go to school when I feel like it." The spell of the painting was broken.

"Commie bastard," the boy who was speaking said, coming up to us. He was tall and lanky with pale white skin and jet-black hair that drooped over his forehead and brushed the bridge of his long, patrician nose. He was holding the hand of a short, comfortably rounded girl with reddish brown hair pulled back in a headband. Both of them were wearing school uniforms and carrying backpacks.

"Sissy, meet Henry Wharton, famous New York asshole," Sebastian said, grinning at his friends. "And his lovely girlfriend, Saint Emily Van Ryker." The girl let go of her boyfriend's hand to shake mine. "Guys, this is my sister, Scarlett."

"Nice to meet you," Emily and I both said, exchanging shy smiles.

"Jesus, 'Bastian," Henry said. "This proves they dropped you on your face as a baby." He shook my hand, too. "Your sister is gorgeous."

"Back off, you pervert," Sebastian said, but it was easy to see he was pleased. "Come on, let's go to the park."

"They just got here," I protested. I would rather have had Sebastian all to myself for the rest of the day, but he seemed so happy to see his friends, I couldn't fuss. "They don't want to waste their tickets."

"It's okay," Emily said. "Our parents...well..." She was actually blushing. "They're members of the museum. So we don't need tickets."

"Wow." I was impressed. Calvin was crazy rich with fine art hanging all over Castle Asshole, even in the bathroom. But this seemed like a whole different world of access and privilege, a whole different level of wealth. "That must be amazing."

"Sure," Emily said. "I guess." She tossed Sebastian her backpack and linked her arm through mine. "Sebastian's right." She gave Henry an adoring smile. "Let's go."

In the park, the boys played pick-up football with a dozen or so others, some from their school, some not. Emily and I sat on the hill above them with the other girls and watched. "Henry's really good," I said as her boyfriend scored another touchdown.

"Oh yeah." He was running in a circle, crowing, arms up, and Sebastian, who was on the other team, crashed into him, knocking them both to the ground, laughing and swearing. "Sebastian, too."

"He always wanted to play at school, but Greta wouldn't let him," I said. Some of the other boys had joined the fray; the others were standing around waiting, looking mildly pissed.

"She won't let him here, either," she said. She had taken a book out of her bag, but she didn't open it. "Your mother is kind of a weird duck, isn't she?"

"Greta's not my mother." Most of the girls were wearing school uniforms and plain, dark anoraks or parkas. Suddenly, my quilted purple velvet coat and designer boots seemed painfully conspicuous.

"Oh god, I'm sorry." She obviously meant it; she was blushing again. "Sebastian always calls you his twin, so I thought she must be."

I smiled. "We're almost the same age, and we do have the same dad." My golden twin had just thrown a touchdown pass and was roaring in triumph as one of his teammates lifted him into the air. "But my mom was different." I hooted and applauded, and he waved. "She died when I was four."

"Oh…yeah, we've all got crazy families, too." Henry loped by and dropped his gloves in her lap, and she blew him a kiss. "Henry's already had three stepmothers, and he's getting a new one in the spring."

"Wow." Since Greta had left him, Calvin had switched girlfriends so often, I had stopped learning their names. "Does he like her?" I asked, making conversation. "The new one, I mean?"

"I guess." An awkwardness had settled over us; I could see her fingering the pages of her book as if she were itching to open it. "Sebastian said you're a cheerleader at your school."

"I was." I was cold; I wanted my brother to come back and take me back to the Plaza.

"I bet you were great," Emily said. "You look like a cheerleader, so beautiful." I looked at her, and she snickered, embarrassed. "I guess it was really lame, though, huh?" she said. "That was why you quit."

"It was okay." I suddenly realized she was more nervous about talking to me than I was talking to her. "But I wasn't very good at it," I confessed. "They actually asked me to quit."

"Really?" She seemed relieved. "Still, at least you made the squad." She stuffed her book into her bag. "I tried out twice and never made it." She smiled and shrugged. "It's the glasses, I guess." She took off the very flattering tortoise shell glasses she was wearing and gave them a look of contempt. "I don't really look like the cheerleader type."

She didn't, but neither did any of these other girls around us, these New York girls who all looked like they belonged here. "You're really, really pretty," I said, meaning it.

"It's okay," she said, putting her glasses back on. "I wish I could stand to wear contacts, but they drive me crazy. But my dad says I can get my nose done when I turn seventeen, before I go to college."

"What's wrong with your nose?" It looked fine to me.

"Oh please," she said, wrinkling it. "It's huge, and my eyes are tiny. I look like a pig."

"What?" I couldn't believe she could say something so stupid. "You do not look like a pig," I promised. "Or any other farm animal."

"You're sweet." She gave my hand a squeeze. "I'm glad you finally came to visit."

I squeezed back. "Me too."

Soon after that, Sebastian had to go home and shower for the theatre. "I shouldn't have played today," he told me in the cab on the way back to the hotel. "But I really wanted you to meet Henry and Emily." He put his arm around me and hugged me close. "Aren't they great?"

I snuggled close. "They're amazing," I promised. "I really love them both."

"I miss you." He kissed the top of my head. "I'm so glad you're here."

CHAPTER 8

Cory was waiting for me in the lobby when Sebastian dropped me off. "Dear god, honey, where have you been?" he demanded as soon as he saw me. "You scared me to death." The house detective who'd been waiting with him smiled and shook his head at me before he walked away.

"I was with Sebastian," I said. "Was Daddy worried?"

"No, thank god, he's still sleeping," Cory said. "Mira's upstairs in your room. She wanted to take you shopping. If he asks later, can you tell him that's where you were?"

"Of course." I was pretty sure nobody had ever specifically told Cory he was responsible for me, no more than my housekeeper or chauffeur back in Beverly Hills had ever been told. But if something bad had happened to me, he'd have been in big trouble just the same. "I'm sorry, Cory."

"It's okay, sweetie." He smiled, obviously relieved. "Go on upstairs and get ready. We're leaving in ninety minutes."

Awesome was in my room, unpacking what looked like at least a dozen shopping bags on the bed. "There you are, sneaky!" she said as I came in. "Are you okay?"

"I'm fine," I said. "What is all this stuff?"

She laughed. "I went a little crazy." She unfolded a pair of designer jeans. "I had to guess your size, so these will probably have to be tailored." She held them up. "But aren't they awesome?"

They were very expensive, the height of magazine fashion, with silver glitter encrusting the weave of the black denim and legs pegged so tightly, I wasn't sure I could get into them. "They are," I made myself say. Somehow, I knew girls like Emily would slit their wrists before they would wear jeans like that. "Totally awesome."

She smiled, satisfied. "Where were you, anyway?" she asked, going back to unpacking. "Or is it a secret?"

"I was with Sebastian." She must have completely cleaned out Fifth Avenue for candy-colored tee-shirts, most of them ripped at the neck or sleeves or both. "Thank you for all this stuff. It's really sweet of you." *Back home, girls from the Valley would drool over this stuff,* I thought. At my own school, I'd be crucified in it. "And thanks for not telling Daddy I was gone." I could only assume she and Cory had already worked out my alibi.

"Oh honey, no problem," she said. "I love to shop." She pulled out a high-end, brand new version of a black leather motorcycle jacket like Sebastian's, only this one had lots of extra silver chains and a pink and black zebra print lining. "And I used to be a teenager, too, you know."

Yeah, I thought, *last month.* "Still," I said out loud. "Thanks a lot."

"You're welcome." She put down the jacket and hugged me. I allowed it for a few seconds then pulled away as firmly as I thought I could without hurting her feelings. "So was he mad?" she asked me as I let her go.

"Who?" I pretended to be interested in the tee-shirts, unfolding each one, looking at it, then folding it back.

"Your brother," she said. "Because your dad wasn't with you." She smiled as I unfolded a particularly hideous flesh pink one with a line drawing of a bikini babe in sunglasses on it. "Isn't that cute?" The sunglasses were studded with little rhinestones.

"Oh yeah." I folded it back up. "But no, he was fine." Actually, I thought, Sebastian hadn't really mentioned our father all day. "We don't really get mad much at Daddy." Suddenly I couldn't stand to be around her one more minute. "Listen, would it be okay if I was by myself for a little while? We went to the park, and I really need a shower."

"Oh sure." She seemed surprised and a little disappointed. "You can just go through the rest of this stuff. Maybe there'll be something you want to wear to the play tonight."

"Yeah, I'm sure there will be." This time I made myself hug her. Poor girl, she really was trying to be nice. She didn't know I was way past being won over. "Thanks again."

As it turned out, she had managed to pick me out a really nice black jersey knit ballerina dress. She had even gotten me cute high-heeled shoes and a black lace push-up bra and panty set to go with it —my very first. The only bras I had that came close to fitting me were a couple of cheap white ones the housekeeper had slipped into my drawer. I was falling out of the little training bras Greta had gotten me. But this one was completely different, this was a grown-up hottie's bra. It changed my look in the clingy black dress completely. For once, I didn't look like a china doll or a little girl playing dress-up in some grown-up lady's clothes. I looked like a young woman.

Cory came down to my room and got me when it was almost time to leave for the play. "Oh my god!" Awesome screamed as soon as I walked into her and Calvin's suite. "You look gorgeous! Cal, doesn't she look gorgeous?"

"Of course she does." My father was smiling, sort of, but I could tell he wasn't really happy. "Where'd you get that dress?"

"We got it this afternoon," Awesome said, completely oblivious. "Doesn't she look grown-up in it?" Before he could answer, she was turning me around. "How are the shoes? Those heels are pretty high."

"I think I'll be okay." I was watching my father's face and feeling a little sick. "Daddy, I can change. It won't take but a minute."

"No, sweetpea, it's fine." He touched my cheek. "Mira's right; you look beautiful."

The play was amazing. After everything I had heard from Greta over the years about Sebastian's grandfather and his "importance to the American theatre," I had expected to be bored during all the parts when Sebastian wasn't on stage, but I wasn't. Everybody was great, and my gorgeous twin was just phenomenal. He was dressed just like Henry had been that day in the park in a disheveled private prep school uniform, and I noticed he had picked up some of Henry's mannerisms, too—the hip-cocked, slouchy way he stood, the way he tossed his hair back when he wanted to see the person he was talking to. But where Henry seemed lazy and bored, Sebastian's character was edgy and sad, the laconic gestures a thin cover-up for a kid going crazy inside. At the end, when he came out for curtain call, the crowd went crazy, and he took a solo bow, blushing and embarrassed and pleased. Daddy howled his approval, and Sebastian finally looked in our direction for the first time all night and burst into happy tears.

We went backstage as soon as the crowd started to clear. Sebastian was in his dressing room with what looked like at least two dozen people, including Greta standing beside him with her hand on his back. An old man that I assumed was his grandfather was standing on his other side, gesturing with his plastic champagne flute.

As soon as Sebastian saw us, he yelled out, "Daddy!" and broke away from Greta to push his way through the crowd. Everyone was smiling as Daddy gathered him up in a bear hug.

"You were so good," I heard Daddy say softly in my brother's ear. "I'm so proud of you." Sebastian was crying again, clinging so tight, and I hugged him, too, leaning against his back. "So proud." Sebastian turned his head enough to kiss my cheek, but he didn't let go of Daddy, and I totally understood.

After not nearly long enough, I felt a hand on my shoulder and heard Greta's voice say, "Hello, Calvin." I drew back completely. Sebastian turned slightly, but Daddy kept an arm around his shoulders. "It's nice you were finally able to come."

"Tonight was our best performance," Sebastian said. "Gramps was just saying that."

"You were wonderful, son," she said. "All of you were." She looked at me, a smile that only seemed a little forced on her face. "Hi, Scarlett. You look lovely."

"Thanks." Awesome was huddled near the doorway with Cory, looking uncomfortable. "Mira helped me pick out a dress."

Greta barely flinched. "It's lovely." She looked different, calmer and more put together, if that was possible. She was wearing twice as much make-up as she had in California, so much that the stark contrast between her pale skin and her black hair and eyes made her look sort of Egyptian. "Are you all coming to the party? I know it would mean the world to Sebastian."

"Please come," Sebastian said. "I want you to meet everybody." Earlier that day when it had been just us kids, my brother had seemed so grown up he'd scared me a little. But now, with Daddy there, he was back to being a kid.

"Of course we're coming," Daddy said, kissing Sebastian's cheek. "We wouldn't miss it for the world."

CHAPTER 9

The party was a total bust as far as I was concerned. Sebastian and I were the only kids there. Everybody else was a stuffy New York theatre person or a freak some group of theatre people had adopted as a pet for the week. The only good part about it was getting to see where Sebastian lived. It was kind of a loft and kind of not, a fairly spacious, fairly new apartment designed to look old and vaguely industrial, with lots of exposed brick on the walls and big pipes and ducts along the ceiling. The walls in the main living area were lined with bookshelves, and Greta's typewriter was set up on a desk behind a half-wall of glass bricks. I wondered if anybody besides the maid who dusted it had touched it since she came to New York.

I tried walking around with Sebastian for a while, but everybody wanted to talk to him, and nobody even pretended to talk to me. Plus Greta kept hovering over him like a mother hen. Plus my feet were killing me. The only person who looked as miserable as I felt was Awesome. She was hanging limply at the end of Calvin's arm while he talked to Sebastian's grandfather like they were the best of friends. She looked so bored, I felt sorry for her and took her a fresh glass of wine.

"Oh, you sweet thing," she said, taking it without letting go of

Calvin's hand. Apparently she had been with him long enough to know if she moved or let go, some other chick would slip up to take her place. "How are you holding up?"

"My feet kinda hurt," I admitted.

"Oh god, I'm sorry," she said. "I should have told you to bring extra shoes. If you take those off, your feet will swell up and you won't be able to get them back on." She looked down at her own feet, which were at least three sizes bigger than mine. "Mine are as bad as yours, but my shoes are bigger, and they're broken in. Do you want them?"

"No, it's okay." Calvin glanced over and smiled at me, and I smiled back. "If it gets too bad, I'll borrow some slippers from Sebastian."

Just then Calvin said something funny, and she turned back to him to laugh and forgot about me completely. I decided to go to the bathroom just to give myself something to do.

Greta's medicine cabinet put her old stash back home to shame. In addition to the sleeping pills, diet pills, and mild sedatives I remembered from her old routine back home, there were lots of exciting new pills with names I only vaguely recognized from movies and TV —Valium, Lithium, Percocet. No wonder she looked like a stone sarcophagus; it was a miracle she could move at all.

Sebastian was waiting for me in the hallway when I came out. "Are you okay?" he asked. "Are you sick?"

"I'm fine, silly." He was so beautiful tonight, I thought, as beautiful as Daddy. He looked shockingly like Calvin, actually. He had that same golden boy glow. "You were incredible in the play," I told him. "You are really, really talented."

"Thanks, sissy." He took my hand, and I realized he was shaking. "Come on, let me show you my room."

"Okay." I squeezed his hand and let him lead me down the hall.

I expected his bedroom to look just the same as his old room at home, but it was completely different, with a big platform bed and a desk and shelves made of tubular steel and glass—very, very modern for the time. The only things I recognized were his Johnny Rotten poster and his battered cedar chest of drawers. "Hey, can I borrow some slippers?" I asked him. "My feet are killing me."

"Sure, psycho," he said, laughing. "Look in the closet." He let me go and opened up his chest of drawers. "What are you wearing those crazy shoes for, anyway?"

"They came with the dress," I said defensively, rummaging through the messy pile of shoes in the bottom of his closet. "You don't like them?"

"You look amazing," he said. "Too good, actually. Greta's freaking out."

I came out with a pair of ratty moccasins. "Greta? What's her problem?"

"Oh, you know Her Highness." He was sitting on the bed rolling a joint. "Her magic mirror probably gave her bad news." He licked the edge of the paper and sealed it off. "If she gives you an apple, don't eat it."

"'Bastian, what are you doing?" I was deeply shocked and absolutely horrified. I knew exactly what he was doing, of course—I had watched my mother do it before I could talk. "Stop it!" I tried to snatch the joint out of his hand, but he jerked away.

"You stop it!" He held it out of my reach. "Jesus, what's wrong with you?"

"You can't do that," I insisted. "It's bad. You'll get hurt." I knew Calvin smoked weed and worse all the time, but I guess I thought he could handle it or that it was out of my control. Sebastian seemed fragile, like Stella, and he was my brother, a kid like me.

"It's okay." He didn't sound okay. "I do this all the time." He straightened out the joint where we had bent it in the struggle and lit it with trembling hands.

"I hate drugs." I knew he would call me a baby, but I didn't care.

"Yeah, well, you don't have to live with Greta." He took a long drag, holding it, and I watched his whole body relax, the same way Stella's had, first with pot, then with needles. "Not any more, anyway."

"What did she do to you?" With blinding clarity, I suddenly knew it was all Greta's fault, not just in general but specifically, this moment. "Tell me what she said."

"Oh, you know Greta." He leaned back on the pillows. "She told me

I shouldn't make too much of Daddy coming to see me or anything he said, that it was probably all just bullshit." He took another toke. "'You know your father,'" he said in a spookily accurate impression of Greta's voice. "'He just wants everybody to love him, so he tells them what they want to hear.'"

"That's not true." I wanted to rip her heart out. "You know that's not true."

"I know." He laughed, but it was shaky, wounded laughter. "She's just a cow. He doesn't want her anymore, so she wants me to hate him. I get that, sissy, I promise." He took another toke, his eyes sliding away from mine. "Don't be mad at me, okay?"

"You know I'm not mad." I watched, helpless, as he took one more toke before stubbing it out in an ashtray. "He loves you, you know."

"Of course I know." He put the whole ashtray in his dresser drawer, along with the rest of his paraphernalia.

"He'd take you back to L.A. if she'd let him." He looked at me, and I saw tears in his eyes. "I promise you he would."

I could tell he really wanted to believe me, but he wasn't sure he could. "Come on," he said, holding out his hand and putting on a brave, beautiful smile. "We better go back to the party."

"You go ahead." I squeezed his hand. "I need to stop and pee first."

I went back into Greta's tiny, pristine bathroom and locked the door behind me. I opened up the medicine cabinet and took out every bottle of pills, lining them up on the counter. I poured each one into the toilet and flushed, over and over, until every single pill was gone. I couldn't make her give up Sebastian, but I could give her at least one night of hell. I put the empty bottles back in the cabinet, lined up precisely the way she'd had them, and went back to the party.

The next day was absolutely perfect. Awesome went off to do look see appointments with designers, and Calvin signed Sebastian out of school for the whole day. He took us both shopping and bought us each a state-of-the-art stereo, and then he took us to the Hard Rock Café for lunch. Sting, my almost-ultimate rock star crush at the time, second only to Bono, was there having lunch with some long-haired guy in a suit, and he actually stopped by our table to say hi on his way to the bar.

After lunch, we took a cab out to the Village to a massive record store Sebastian loved, and Daddy let us buy whatever we wanted, records and tee-shirts and posters for our bedroom walls. That night he took us and Awesome to a Broadway musical and Sardi's afterwards; it was so much fun. He even let us both have a few sips of champagne to celebrate.

Sebastian spent the night at the Plaza with me. Calvin called Greta and just told her he'd be home after school the next day and hung up the phone before she could protest. "Sleep well, my darlings," he said, kissing us each good night. "Don't stay up too late." We ordered ice cream and French fries from room service and piled up in bed watching TV and talking until we passed out.

The next morning was awful. We had breakfast together in Calvin's suite. Awesome was on the phone, making everybody she knew in L.A. aware of her ETA back on the coast, and the TV was on, playing some morning show. Sebastian was wearing his school uniform. Calvin kept trying to make cheerful conversation, and we kept answering him and trying to smile. But it was obvious we were miserable. We took Sebastian to school in a limo on our way to the airport. I kissed him good-bye and so did Daddy, and Awesome hugged him, and he was smiling, cracking jokes as he waved and shut the door and sprinted up the sidewalk.

But as soon as we'd pulled away from the curb, I felt tears stinging my eyes. Ten blocks later, I was bawling like a baby.

"I know, sweetpea," Calvin said, putting his arm around me. "I miss him, too. But we'll see him soon, I promise."

"It isn't that." Awesome had drawn a little away from us to stare out the window. "I mean, it is; I do miss him. I just hate leaving him with that bitch."

"Greta?" he said. "Baby, don't say bitch—"

"But she is, Daddy!" All I could think about was what she'd be like when Sebastian got home to her that night with no rehearsal to go to, no way to escape. "She lies to him all the time. She told him you don't really love him. She tells him that all the time." I had rarely seen my father really angry. His life was too charmed for him to get upset very often. But his blue eyes were dark with rage now. "She even told him you probably didn't even think he was all that good in the play, that you were just saying that because you knew that's what he wanted to hear."

"Sebastian told you this?" he asked, looking into my eyes. I nodded. He punched the button on the intercom. "Turn around," he told the driver.

"Wait, what?" Awesome said. "We'll miss our flight!"

"Take us back to the school," Calvin told the driver, patting Awesome's hand to shut her up. She looked ready to protest, but he just smiled at her. "It will be okay."

The woman at the school reception desk didn't want to pull Sebastian out of homeroom, but the headmaster came out of his office as soon as Calvin started talking and told her to not be silly. Sebastian came in a few minutes later, looking confused and a little scared. "Daddy?" He looked back and forth between us. "What's going on?"

"Come here." Daddy said, pulling him into a hug. "You know what the happiest day of my life was? The absolute, very best?"

"No," Sebastian said, hugging him back.

"The day your mother told me we were going to have you." He drew back and framed my brother's face in his hands. "You and your sister are the best things that have ever happened or that ever could happen. You're my miracles, both of you."

"I know, Daddy." I could see in his face that he finally did. Tears were spilling down his cheeks.

"It kills me that your mom took you away from me." He stepped back and beckoned me into the circle. "But I am so proud of you," he went on, holding on to us both. "I watched you on stage the other night, and I couldn't believe you could really be my kid. You blew me away." I took Sebastian's hand, and Calvin smiled. "Don't ever, ever let anybody tell you I don't love you." He looked at me. "Either of you."

"We won't," we both said at once, squeezing one another's hands.

"I'm a shitty dad, I know," he said. "But I would die for you, I swear."

"We know, Daddy," I said, letting Sebastian go to throw my arms around Calvin.

"You are not a shitty dad," Sebastian said, hugging him, too.

<hr>

Later in the car, Awesome was pouting, but I felt happier and safer than I had since Greta and Sebastian had moved to New York. "Hey, Daddy?" I took his hand. "I think you're perfect."

He didn't say anything. He just smiled and pulled me close, hugging me tight all the way to the airport.

CLIPPING 4

From *The Gothamite*

Did Broadway need a weirdly updated revival of George Strassman's seminal 1950s masterwork, Fear of High Places? *Most probably not. Does the world need to see the performance of Strassman's 15-year-old grandson, Sebastian Cross, in the lead? Most assuredly yes, we do.*

The story of a privileged prep school track star finding his social conscience and embracing his inner beatnik with tragic results for his stolid, Upper West Side family, Fear *was Strassman's first hit, winning him a Tony and a Pulitzer Prize when it debuted in 1958. Since that time, it has become a community theatre and high school staple,* Catcher in the Rye *for the drama camp set. But in this new production, the action has been transported through time from the moral rigidity of the 50s to the economic excess of today. Father, originally written as being vaguely "in business" is now starkly defined as a Wall Street stockbroker, complete with Brooks Brothers pinstripes and a red power tie. Mother's interest in church charities has become an obsession with art. These transformations, enacted ably by stage veterans John Kindle and Mariah Stait, feel a bit creaky at the joints—a snide remark about Jesus from the original has been re-targeted at Keith*

Haring, rather a stretch—but Strassman's own social conscience as regards adults remains as sharp as ever, and he mostly makes it work.

The real worry comes in updating Kip, the adolescent anti-hero at the center of the play. Apartheid and MTV are perfectly acceptable concerns for today's youth, but they rather pale in comparison to the civil rights movement and Thelonious Monk. Strassman was still in his thirties when he first wrote Fear; *now in his sixties, he's lost his hipster edge.*

Luckily, he has a grandson. I don't mean to belabor the relationship—young Cross would be a perfect choice even if his grandfather sold shoes in Dubuque. But it gives this production what it needs the most—a reason to exist. This familiar chestnut becomes something new, a rite of passage, a passing of the torch from one generation of artists to another. Strassman himself has taken on the role of Nate, the sharp-tongued bum—pardon me, homeless man; these are the 80s, after all—who first shakes Kip's world view, and his obvious pride in his young co-actor gives this pivotal scene a burnished gleam.

And well, he should be proud. Cross is already a ubiquitous face of the MTV generation, instantly recognizable from commercials and numerous TV roles. But with this performance, he proves he's actually an actor. He begins the play arrogant and charming, a winning child, then slowly crumbles into madness as he grows into a man. Cross marks this fall with the simplest gestures—a sudden howl of frustration at a phone that won't ring, a tentative reaching out toward Father's oblivious back—that make us ache for this character in a way we haven't in decades. We know this story; we should be immune to it by now. But this young man won't allow it. There is heartbreak in Sebastian Cross, and triumph, too. This son of a movie star and grandson of a playwright may someday outshine them all.

CHAPTER 10

The trip to New York was a wake-up call for my father, I think. He suddenly became a lot more aware of what was going on in my day to day life. He hired a stylist to take me shopping for "age-appropriate" clothes every month or so and to make sure I kept my hair done. He even started taking me with him whenever he went away on location. Sometimes I even got to be in the movie, usually as a background extra, but a few times with actual lines. I learned what life was like on a movie set, how to feed myself from craft services, how to make friends with the techies without getting anybody in trouble; how to stay out of everybody's way when work was getting done. I liked it much, much better on the set than I did at home and would have been happy to live there all year long.

Unfortunately, I wasn't getting anything like a normal education. By the time I turned fifteen, I was almost a full school year behind. Calvin's business manager suggested he take me out of public school and put me into the very exclusive Catholic academy for girls his own daughters attended. They tested me and decided I was still a seventh-grader, so like magic I was a twelve again, complete with a brand-new birth certificate. I didn't care. I loved my new school. We wore uniforms, so clothes were no longer a problem. I did wear some make-up, but I had to sneak it, and compared to the other little girls "my age," just knowing how to put on eyeliner made me seem madly sophisticated. As a fifteen-year-old, I might have been a total flop, but as a twelve-year-old, I was awesome. I even started doing well academically. Algebra and Nathaniel Hawthorne made so much more sense the second time around. I was still horribly lonely; Catholic school girls "my age" didn't go out at night. But during the day I had friends, and I spent most of my vacations with my father. So for the next year or so, I was pretty much content.

The summer after I turned sixteen, Greta got married to a playwright old enough to be her father. While she was in Europe on her honeymoon with her new husband, Sebastian came to California to stay with me and network. Calvin was on location in Australia, so he wasn't there to help introduce him around. Luckily, Sebastian didn't need him. He set up an appointment with our father's agent who signed him on the spot, and by the end of the first week, he was a fixture on the Sunset Strip, partying with an older actor he had met in a class in New York. I almost never saw him; I was back to living by myself.

But on one particular night, he dragged me along with him to this big party in Malibu, probably because I knew the host, a producer named Lewis Moore. He had a reputation as a real asshole, but he had produced a couple of Daddy's latest movies, and he had always been quite nice to me. He met us at the door when we came in, said, "Scarlett!" sweeping me up in a big hug. Then I introduced him to Sebastian, and he forgot I was alive. Within five minutes, he had taken my brother by the arm and steered him to the other side of the room to introduce him to a hot new director who was apparently casting a hot new movie full of hot new young guy talent. Looking around, I realized the entire party must have been for that explicit purpose because there certainly weren't very many young girls hanging around, and as young and stupid as I was, I still knew that was weird. Even being barely sixteen and passing for two years younger, I was already well accustomed to sticking to my father's elbow at parties to keep from getting hit on. But here, no one seemed to notice me at all. There were plenty of women, but they were all older and impossibly chic, and they looked at me like I'd beamed in from another planet. Getting a glass of wine from the bar, I walked past a trio of these lovelies, all looking me up and down, and I felt like a rag doll in my sweet little dress. "Hi," I said, and one of them actually laughed as they all three turned away.

"Bitch," I said, making a face at the bartender, and he grinned.

"Not to worry, sweetheart," he said, handing me my drink. "You'll drop a house on her yet."

After an hour of alternating between answering questions about Cal and being ignored entirely, I had had enough. Sebastian was still deep in conversation with Hot Director and another Hot Young Prospect, so I decided I'd just call myself a cab. I couldn't drive; I didn't have a license yet. So I went upstairs and started opening random doors, looking for a phone. It was a little like a fun house with a different wacky horror in each room—two people snorting coke together in here; one of the chic old bitches blowing a Hot Young Prospect in there. But I had been to enough parties to be no more than mildly shocked until I found Romeo.

The room was dark when I opened the door, so I thought it was empty and walked in. I gave the dimmer switch the tiniest turn and had made it halfway into the room before I registered what I was seeing right in front of me—a naked boy handcuffed to the bed. "Oh shit!" I exclaimed, because honestly, what else would you say? "Sorry." I turned around, cheeks blazing with embarrassment, and headed for the door.

"Wait!" He sounded young, like my age. "Please?" I froze and heard him rattling the handcuffs. "A little help?" His voice broke, and I turned around slowly—he was laughing. "Please?" He had the sweetest smile I had ever seen.

"What?" I held my hand up in front of my face, fingers splayed, so I could sort of see and sort of not. He was skinny as a rail and white with dark hair. I had never seen a naked guy before, and my eyes were drawn to his cock as if by magnetic force. "What are you doing?" I gathered my wits and tossed a cashmere throw from the nearby chaise over his middle so I could make myself look him in the face.

"Not much," he said, smiling at me. I was trembling, but he seemed perfectly calm. His wrists were handcuffed to the headboard, and what looked like they must have been his clothes were folded neatly on an Asian lacquered chest across the room. "How's the party?"

"Horrible." I laughed, too. I couldn't call it boring any more. "I'm sorry…is there some point to what you're doing or not doing? Do you really need help?"

"Oh yeah." He had a thick southern accent. *Like Stella's,* I thought. "Don't I look like it?"

"But how did you get there?" I felt like I had fallen down the rabbit hole, but hey, at least I was dressed for it. I was definitely intrigued.

"Does it matter?" he asked. "I'm being held against my will."

"Oh my god!" I moved forward, reaching for the phone, interest turning instantly to alarm. Here I was being all amused, and this poor kid had been kidnapped. "I'll call 911."

"Oh shit—honey, no!" I froze again, receiver in hand. "Don't call the cops; it's not like that." I just stood there, gaping at him. "The guy who owns this house paid me to have sex with him before the party," he explained.

"Oh," I answered, mouth and eyes completely round, no doubt.

"But when I said I had to leave, he thought it would be funny to make me stay." He was explaining it all very matter-of-factly, but I thought I could detect him blushing just a little bit. "But my boss is expecting me back. Do you understand?"

"Yes," I said scornfully. "I'm not five." But of course, if he hadn't spelled it out for me in little words, I probably never would have caught on. This was way outside my comfort zone. *But he seems so nice!* I almost said about the guy who was keeping him cuffed for a laugh, but I managed to bite it back. And this boy didn't look anything like my admittedly uninformed notion of a boy-whore. He just looked like a boy I might see at the mall, cute and funny, not sleazy or slick. But hell, why would he lie? "So fine," I said, hanging up the phone and trying to pretend I dealt with this sort of thing every day of my life. "Where are the keys?"

"In his pocket," he said. "Now you see the problem."

"Fine." I made up my mind what to do in about three seconds. I doubted very much if our host would still think his joke was funny if I announced it to his guests. "I'll be right back."

"Wait!" He looked worried for the first time since I had come in. "What are you going to do?"

"I'm going downstairs to ask him for the key," I said. "And if he doesn't give it to me, I'm going to tell everybody you're up here and threaten to call the police."

"You can't do that." He was smiling at me like he couldn't quite believe I was real.

"Then what exactly—?"

"Unscrew those knobs on the headboard," he said. "Then you can take the slat out, and we can slip the cuffs up and over."

"But you'll still be in handcuffs," I pointed out.

"If you can get me up, I can get out of the cuffs." His eyes met mine as I reached the bed, and I swear I felt a shiver, that somehow I knew I was looking into at my...something—destiny? True love? Eternal torment? Whatever—I was lost. "Will you try?"

I took a deep breath. "Oh hell," I grumbled. "Why not?" I kicked off my shoes and climbed onto the bed, a huge California king. "At least you're not insulting me or ignoring me like those bitches downstairs."

"Definitely not." The knobs I had to unscrew were directly over his head, so I was kneeling on the mattress right beside him, my knee touching his shoulder. "You're my angel."

"Yeah, right," I said, but I smiled. Unscrewing the first knob wasn't easy, I discovered. I had to use both hands and all my strength, and I could still barely make it turn. "I'm Scarlett, by the way."

"Hi, Scarlett. I'm Romeo."

I stopped to look at him. "Stop shitting me."

"I'm not," he said, laughing. "Swear to God, my name is Romeo." His smile was the most gorgeous thing I had ever seen, I thought. "So what are you doing here?" he asked me, teasing. "You seem so nice."

"I am nice." I got the first knob off at last and leaned further over him to start on the second. "Nice enough to help my brother get a part by coming with him to this stupid party."

"Who's your brother?" He sounded a little breathless, and when I looked down at him, he smiled again, the sweet, angelic grin that would someday set the whole world's hearts a-flutter.

"Sebastian Cross." The second knob wasn't budging. "Our father is Calvin Cross."

"Wow." As far as I noticed, he never skipped a beat. Ever the gentleman, he was trying to shift over so I could get closer and get a better grip. "Lucky y'all."

"Yeah, we think so." I was loving his accent. "Where are you from, Romeo?"

"I was born in Philadelphia, but I grew up in Savannah, Georgia." I tried to just work the slat the cuffs were hooked around loose without taking off the second knob, but it was impossible. I sat back on my heels, trying to decide if I'd have better luck working from the other side of the bed. "Are you giving up?" he asked me.

"No." Steeling my courage, I hitched up my skirt. "Don't take this personally." I threw a leg over him, straddling his chest.

"No problem," he said, laughing. "This just keeps on getting better."

I smiled, too. "Yeah, right." I went back to trying to unscrew the knob. "My mama was from Tupelo, Mississippi." It still wasn't budging. "You kind of sound like her."

"So do you, I bet." Being so close to him, it was impossible not to notice how he smelled, not clean, exactly, but good—animal and alive. He had one tiny zit on the edge of his upper lip; otherwise his face was perfect. His breath smelled smoky and spicy—clove cigarettes, which I recognized from Sebastian. "Does your mama know where you are now?"

"I guess, if you believe in heaven. She's dead." I braced the heels of my hands under the knob and tried to just pop the damned thing off. "She was murdered when I was four years old."

"Holy shit." He sounded genuinely regretful, which was sweet, I thought. "So do you believe in heaven?"

Before I could answer, the door opened. Sebastian did exactly what I had done; he took two steps into the room, saw what was happening on the bed, and froze. "Scarlett?" The difference was, after those first three seconds, he started laughing his ass off. "Well, pardon me!" He started to leave.

"Sebastian, get back here!" I struggled off of Romeo and the bed, trying to not to clock him in the head or fall on his face while I did it. "Help us!"

"Who needs helping?" he asked, closing the door again and coming back.

I explained the situation as succinctly as possible. Romeo, I noticed, didn't say a word. "You're stronger than me," I finished. "Come unscrew this knob so we can get out of here."

I could tell it was taking all the kindness my brother could muster not to make a crack on that one, but somehow, he held it back. "Okey-dokey." He came over to the bed, pausing on the way to give me a one-armed hug. "Hey," he said to Romeo.

"Hey," Romeo answered. He didn't seem as amused as he had when I had come in, but he still didn't seem particularly embarrassed.

Sebastian made a token effort to loosen the knob. "Not gonna happen," he decided, stepping back. "Wait here."

"What are you going to do?" I said, following him to the door.

"I'm going to get a key," he said.

"No, I already thought of that," I protested. "We can't tell the dude who has the key that Romeo is leaving."

"I didn't say I was going to get THE key; I said I was going to get A key." He kissed me on the forehead. "I'll be right back, I promise."

"He's kind of a criminal genius," I said, going back to the bed when he was gone. "He'll figure it out."

"It's okay," Romeo said. "You don't have to stay."

"I don't mind."

'It's not like I'm in danger or anything."

"Sure you are." I snickered. "What if the house caught on fire?"

He grinned. "That would be bad."

"Exactly." I shifted a corner of the throw to cover him up more. "I can't risk it."

"I told you, you're an angel."

Sebastian came back in, brandishing a key. "Worship me for my brilliance!"

"Where did you get that?" I asked, impressed.

"Security guard." He winked at Romeo and started working on the cuffs. "All handcuff keys work on all handcuffs." He snapped them open. "Just like that." Romeo sat up, rubbing his wrist.

"Thanks," he said. "I've got to split, but thank you both."

"Get dressed," Sebastian cut him off. "We'll drive you." He acted like he was going to just stand there and watch Romeo get dressed, so I grabbed his arm and turned him around.

"Pervert," I said softly, suddenly annoyed. I didn't know why, but I was sort of pissed with him. He had solved the problem, and he was ready to go; I should have been relieved. But I wasn't. I felt like something wonderful and important had been snatched away from me, and Sebastian had done it. "How do you know about handcuff keys?" I demanded, still trying to speak softly so Romeo wouldn't hear. "What are y'all doing for fun in New York?"

"Sacrificing virgins," he retorted. "Why do you think I'm always after you to visit?" I heard Romeo snicker behind us, and I looked over my shoulder. He was now wearing ragged jeans and a tee-shirt and was sitting on the foot of the bed, putting on his boots. "My sister goes to Catholic school," Sebastian informed him. "She's not allowed to play with boys."

"Shut up," I warned him.

"So you're a real novelty for her," he went on, relentless.

"She's a natural," Romeo said, smiling at me like we were the ones with a secret. "But seriously, I've got to go."

Sebastian was looking at me strangely, a weird little half-smile on his face. "Here," he said, tossing his car keys to Romeo. "Drive my baby sister home."

Romeo was obviously shocked. "Dude, I'd love to, but I can't." On his feet, he was a head taller than me, and dressed he was a little intimidating, dangerous in a way he hadn't been when he was help-less. "I mean, I've got to check in, and what about your car?"

"Bring it to me at the Rainbow after you drop Scarlett." Suddenly, I got it—they had met before. Just what exactly was my brother getting up to when he left me alone every night? He reached into his pocket and held out a folded packet of money. "And bring me a surprise." Romeo looked wary, glancing at me, but he took the cash, and Sebastian smiled. "You kids have fun."

"Right." Romeo smiled at me. "Come on. Let's go."

CHAPTER 11

Getting out of the house wasn't hard, but it was interesting. Our host looked up and saw us just as we got to the bottom of the stairs. "Come on," I said, taking Romeo's hand and giving his thwarted captor the very first cool kitty stare of my life. "Let's go." We held hands on the front steps while the valet brought the car, and he opened my door himself.

"Your brother is crazy," he said as he slid behind the wheel.

"Yeah," I said. "He tries."

As we turned onto the Pacific Coast Highway, headed back to the city, I realized I was almost perfectly happy. Sebastian was right; I was a Catholic schoolgirl of the entirely non-naughty type. I had never even been on a date. Yet here I was, riding down the coastline in a hot black convertible with the cutest boy I had ever seen. And apparently, he was a professional.

"Hey, Romeo?"

He smiled, his eyes on the road. "Yes, Scarlett?" He drove much better than Sebastian, I thought. My brother had pitched a fit for this particular car because of the way it looked and he looked in it, but he drove it like he thought it might leap out from under him at any moment, riding the brakes, grinding the clutch, then roaring forward in spastic spurts of speed. Romeo shifted like it was as easy as breathing, and while he was attentive, his hands on the wheel were relaxed.

"How were you supposed to get home in the first place?" I asked him.

"The dude was supposed to give me cab fare back." He didn't seem fussed by my questions, accelerating smoothly until the cool night air was whipping through our hair. "I was actually just supposed to be making a delivery." He glanced back at his blind spot and switched lanes. "But he asked me if I wanted to make some extra money, and I did."

"Ah." I was shocked, no question. But it was a sort of thrilling kind of shocked. "What were you delivering?"

He looked at me, surprised for a second, then his face went deadpan blank. "Balloons," he answered. "I was delivering balloons."

I blinked at him for a second, half-believing he was serious. Then we both laughed. "Okay, that was stupid." I looked out at the lights glittering like stars along the cliffs below us and the creamy shadows of the surf beyond. The sky was perfectly clear, and an orange half-moon hung over the ocean—just gorgeous. I felt like I was dreaming, or, better yet, had fallen into a movie, a night too exciting to be real. On the ride out with Sebastian, I had barely noticed the view. We had been too busy bickering over the radio. "Are you gay?" I asked, trying to sound as casual as possible.

"Not by nature, no." I looked at him and found him looking back, and he winked. "Okay, my turn. How old are you?"

"Sixteen." *He thinks I'm an idiot,* I thought. "How old are you?"

"Seventeen." He slowed down and switched lanes again, dropping in behind a white Mercedes. "I just realized, I think I saw you in a movie once."

"Oh yeah?"

"Yeah. A western your dad was in."

"Oh god...yeah." The only western part I'd ever done was as a pioneer kid with pigtails; I had been fourteen playing about nine. I'm short; I played kid parts until I was old enough to buy hard liquor.

"You were cute."

"Thanks." My one big scene had consisted of almost being run down in the street in front of the one-room schoolhouse by the carriage of the evil cattle baron. I think I got two takes because the first time, I tripped and dropped my lunch pail.

"You were!" he insisted, teasing me.

"Yeah, you're sweet." This was not the image I wanted to project just then—prepubescent urchin. Catholic school virgin was quite bad enough. "So are you an actor?" I asked, just to change the subject. "Is that why you moved to L.A.?"

"My sister wants to be in the movies," he said, sobering at once. "I came out here to be with her." I was shocked to see we were making the turn at Santa Monica, more than halfway home. He must have been flying, and I had barely noticed. "I need to make a stop before I take you home," he said. "Do you mind?"

"Of course not." I was in no big hurry to get home. I was pretty sure that once he let me out, I'd never see him again. But even so, when we got to the city and turned off toward Inglewood instead of Beverly Hills, I got a little nervous. He seemed sweet, and he was beautiful, but he was still the closest thing to a dangerous character I had ever known. As the houses around us got seedier and seedier, I had a vision of a headline: "Daughter of Hollywood Icon Found Dead." They'd probably even do a sidebar about Stella.

He stopped in front of a paint-peeled wreck that had been a Craftsman cottage in another life. The weedy front yard was enclosed behind a chain link fence, and a motorcycle was parked on the porch. A late-model Lincoln was parked out front, too, nose to nose with us. Romeo pushed the button to raise the roof and rolled up his window. "I'll be right back," he promised as I rolled mine up, too, quickly. "Don't get out of the car, okay?"

"No problem." I wanted to tell him he couldn't leave me there, that I wanted to go home that second, but I didn't want him to think I was a baby.

A tall, fat black dude got out of the passenger side of the Lincoln as soon as Romeo got out, and he stopped him at the gate. They talked briefly, and the black dude looked back at me, smiling. He waved, and, nonplussed, I waved back. Romeo didn't look back at me; I could see every muscle in his rangy body was drawn taut. He went through the gate and into the house, and the black dude followed.

After less than five minutes, Romeo came back out of the house alone, walking fast. I leaned over and unlocked his door, and he got in, carrying a small brown paper bag. "What's that?" I asked as he tossed it into the floor of the tiny back seat.

"Your brother's surprise." He threw the car into reverse and did a U-turn into the street, making a Honda Civic coming toward us run a tire up on the sidewalk to get out of the way. I braced against the window frame, but I didn't make a sound, and he looked over at me and smiled. "So tell me where you live."

So I told him. I wanted to ask him who the black dude was and why we had stopped there and was that where he lived and what was in the bag, but all of those questions seemed rude. So I asked him again what everybody in Los Angeles eventually asks everybody else. "So are you an actor, too?" He raced through a yellow light on a left turn, steering one-handed but checking both mirrors. "You're good-looking enough." This was the standard line, too, but in his case, I absolutely meant it.

"Thanks." He smiled at me, the same relaxed smile from the moment we met, but it wasn't hard to tell he wanted to get us the fuck away from here as soon as possible. "I'm not, though. I haven't really thought about it."

"You really should." I wanted to say I could help him, get Calvin to hook him up with an agent, but I wasn't sure that was true. People in my world did that sort of thing all the time, but at that point, I was still a background player. I didn't know how to make things happen.

"So is that what you want to be?" We were back in a part of the city I knew, and I half-consciously relaxed. "Permanently, I mean?"

"An actress?" I rolled down my window again, and he pushed the button to lower the top. "I don't know." No one had ever asked me what I wanted to be when I grew up before. I don't think anyone ever thought about me as a grown-up, even me. "I guess I never thought about it, either." We passed the sign going into Beverly Hills, and I pointed him to the turn. "My brother is the real actor, him and our dad, of course."

He stopped at the gate, and I got out to put in the security code, waving at the camera in case the security guy at Castle Asshole was still awake and watching. "Bear off to the left," I said, getting back in. "I'm the little house in back."

He drove all the way up to my back door and stopped. "Mission accomplished," he said, putting the car in park.

"Yeah, I guess so." I was so not ready to watch him drive away. "You want to come in for a minute?" I asked because I thought that was what people asked.

"Yes, of course." He sounded weirdly formal, so grown-up, and the way he was looking at me suddenly was making my toes curl up. He leaned over and kissed me on the cheek. "Are you sure you want me to?"

"Well, yeah." I was tingling all over, but I faked a perfect nonchalance—all those years of watching Sebastian were paying off, I guess. "Come on."

We went in through the kitchen, me leading him by the hand. "Do we need to be quiet?" he asked as I turned on the lights.

"No. Why?" There were dishes in the sink and pans on the counter where Sebastian and I had made slice and bake cookies that afternoon, and I made myself resist the urge to whisk them into the dishwasher. "We're the only ones here." *Was that stupid?* I thought. No...for whatever reason, I knew he wouldn't hurt me.

"You live in this house all by yourself?" He didn't seem impressed; he seemed appalled.

"Sure," I said, laughing. "Well, Sebastian is living here with me now." He moved closer to me and gave my hand a little tug to pull me closer. "Do you and Sebastian know each other?"

He smiled. "No." He touched his nose to mine—an Eskimo kiss, my daddy always called it. "Not really."

"Not really?" I echoed, breathless, every muscle tense. "I thought you acted like maybe you did." He stopped me talking with a kiss, the first grown-up kiss of my life. I shivered all over and sighed, and he put his arms around me. The way he felt, the way he smelled, it was all making me feel drunk. I felt like I might faint. Unfortunately…

"Wait." I braced a hand against his chest. His heart was beating so hard I could feel it through his shirt, and my knees went weak to feel it. "I'm so sorry." I laughed, blushing, embarrassed. "I have to go to the bathroom."

He smiled. "Okay." He kissed me again, barely brushing his mouth against mine before he let me go.

I made myself walk slowly until I got to the stairs then broke into a sprint—the downstairs toilet wouldn't do. I kicked off my heels on my way through the bedroom and barely made it. (It's a sad truth of my life that I have never once entered an interlude of romance that I didn't have to pee.) Then I took a fifteen-second bird bath in the sink and brushed my teeth. Then I wiped up the water I had splashed on the counter. Then I fluffed my hair, still windblown from the car. I considered changing clothes, but that seemed stupid. I faced my reflection, took a deep breath, closed my eyes, and said a prayer that the nuns at school would have fainted to hear (*dear God, let me do this right*), then turned off the light and headed back downstairs.

Romeo had found the stereo. I found him standing in the living room, listening to music. "Hey," I said, going in. "You want something to drink?"

"Not really." He took my hand and drew me into a slow dance.

"I love this song." I had never danced with anyone before except my father, but it was surprisingly easy. He tucked our joined hands against his chest and pressed me close with his other hand at my waist.

"Me too." He kissed me, slipping his tongue inside my mouth this time, and I closed my eyes, clinging to him. *What do I do?* I thought desperately. Then he drew back ever so slightly, and I knew. I went after him, kissing him this time. I wanted to touch his face, so I did, drawing back to run my fingertips along his jaw, barely prickly with stubble, willing him to kiss me again, and he did, hotter and deeper than before.

"I want to go upstairs," I said, looking into his eyes. "I want to show you my room."

"Okay." He lifted my hand to his lips like Prince Charming in a fairy tale. "Whatever you want."

I led him up the stairs to my bedroom, shaking so much I could barely walk. I had outgrown my original canopy bed years ago, but the walls were still powder-puff pink with cream-colored trim, and my dollhouse still stood on a long, low table by the window. He let go of my hand to walk over to it as I closed the door. "Do you still play with this?"

"Sometimes." He picked up one of the dolls, a princess with messy blonde hair. "When nobody else is around I play with it." I wanted him to come back and kiss me some more, but I didn't know how to ask.

"It's pretty." He put down the doll and came back to me, taking me back into his arms. "You really are a princess." Before I could answer, he had kissed me, and I couldn't speak. He framed my face in his hand and kissed my forehead, my eyelids, my cheeks, and for some stupid reason, I had tears in my eyes, spilling down my cheeks. I grabbed the bottom of his tee-shirt and pushed it up over his stomach, fighting to get it off of him, to jump forward past whatever it was that was making me sad to whatever came after. He yanked the shirt over his head and tossed it away, letting me touch his stomach and side while he kissed my shoulder. His skin felt smooth and warm, and the dark brown line of hair on his stomach was soft.

"Sebastian was right," I said softly, not sure I should say anything. "I'm not...I don't know anything."

He touched my chin and turned my face up to his. "Trust me, baby. You're doing fine." As he kissed my mouth, I slid a hand under the sagging waistband of his jeans, tracing the curve of his hipbone. His breath caught short as my hand slid lower, and I giggled into the kiss, thrilled beyond belief. He was delicate, but hard, pure muscle over bone. "Don't be scared," he whispered in my ear. "It's okay, I promise."

"I trust you." His mouth moved to my throat, kissing then biting, his arms around my waist as he walked me backward to the bed. I felt a chill along my spine and realized he'd unzipped my dress; now he was sliding it off of my shoulders. I let go of him to step out of it then stood there, trembling, letting him see me in my underwear. He smiled, shaking his head.

"You're beautiful." He put his hands on my bare waist, making me shiver. "You're perfect." He let me go to kick out of his boots, an awkward little dance that made me laugh, then drew me close to him. I draped my arms around his neck—we matched up perfectly. The way he looked into my eyes was hotter than his kisses. I let myself fall backward on the bed, still holding him, and he came with me, kissing me. But when I moved to wrap my arms around him, he pulled away, kissing his way down my stomach. I wanted to ask what he was doing, but no words came out, only a sigh. Kneeling between my legs, he slid my underpants down over my hips, and I couldn't help blushing. But when he bent closer, I forgot to be embarrassed. I cried out, clutching the bedspread in my fists, my hips rising of their own accord. I thought I must be dying, it felt so good.

Then he stopped, moving up to kiss my mouth, and I threw my arms around his neck, arching under him, twining my leg around him. Then he was moving again, unfastening my bra and bending to my breast. I made myself focus to touch him, raking my fingers through his hair. I clutched a handful of his hair and drew him up to kiss me. As soon as I had his mouth on mine, I slid my arms around him, holding him to me, and he took the hint. Brushing my lips with his once more, he lifted his head and looked into my eyes. I held my breath, held on to him…then he was there. It felt strange, so intimate; I couldn't pull away; I couldn't hide. This boy, this stranger was inside me.

He kissed my cheek and whispered something, words I couldn't catch, but the sound was soothing, making me feel safe. I closed my eyes, tears spilling down my cheeks again, but I wasn't sad or happy. All I felt was him. He caught my wrists and pinned them to the bed, his cheek pressed to mine, saying my name over and over, saying I was beautiful, his precious baby, his angel. I arched up to meet him, the final sweet wave breaking over me, and I cried out, begging him never to stop. Just as my coming started to subside, he started moving faster still, and the wave broke again as he came, too, spilling inside me. A condom, I thought, too blissful to panic. We were supposed to use a condom.

I looked up at him to say this aloud, but as soon as our eyes met, I started crying, stupid, childish crying like he had hurt me, like my heart was breaking. "I'm sorry," I said through the tears, shaking all over. I could feel him sliding out of me, and somehow that made me cry harder. "I'm okay, I swear."

"I know, my baby," he promised, kissing my cheek "I know." He rolled onto his side and wrestled the covers from underneath us. "Come here; it's okay." He drew me back against him, cuddling me close. "It's okay," he repeated, kissing my cheek.

I fell asleep cradled in his arms, the sweetest sleep I could remember. When I woke up the next morning, he was gone, of course. So were all my credit cards and a couple of hundred dollars from my purse. I waited three days to report the cards stolen, and I never told Sebastian what had happened. Romeo had turned up at the Rainbow with his car and his bag full of drugs, just as they had agreed, and when he asked, I told him Romeo had dropped me off at home. I felt no need to tell him anymore. I thought it was money well spent.

CLIPPING 5

from *The Gothamite*

Room Four, *opening Friday, is not a bad movie. It's a perfectly competent thriller, a standard tale of one good cop in a nest of corruption, much better written and photographed than most. It has style to burn, grit and edge and car chases and gore and a soupçon of awkward and angsty romance— everything this kind of entertainment needs to keep a reasonably undemanding audience on the edge of its adequately comfy seat for a little under two hours. If it starred some newcomer out of left field, a professional wrestler making his acting debut or a longtime character actor from TV, critics would likely be falling over themselves to praise its protean charms, myself included.*

But it doesn't. It stars Calvin Cross.

It would be grotesquely unfair to judge this film by Cross' last project, last year's disastrous Lionheart, *but at least that was an ambitious failure. Cross ought to be able to play Tom Countryman, the good cop at the center of this story, in his sleep, and frankly, he almost does. His performance is measured, stalwart, but ultimately unexciting, giving the viewer little to do but reflect on how far the mighty have apparently fallen. By working so hard to be understated and disappear completely in this less-than-original role (a generous assessment that disallows the possibility that Cross just simply didn't care), this popular and well-regarded movie star stands out like the proverbial sore thumb. His glamour works against him and against the movie as a whole. At no point did I feel like I was watching a real policeman in real peril or even a plausible archetype for justice in our time. All I could see was this film icon slumming, an all-star dropping back to punt.*

Room Four will likely perform well at the box office and be hailed as a return to form for Cross on those terms. But I for one was sadly disappointed.

CHAPTER 12

About six months after Romeo made me a woman, I finally got my big break in the movies. Calvin had come home and gone again, this time to Brazil on vacation with some girl, and I had started my freshman year of high school. Sebastian had gotten the part in *The House* and gone off to Europe to film it. I was looking forward to Christmas coming up at the end of the month; Cal had promised we would all be together, at least for a couple of days. I hadn't seen or heard from Romeo at all and didn't really expect to do, but I thought about him all the time.

I came home from school early one afternoon because field hockey practice had been canceled (and no, I'm not kidding), and I found my house empty and my cupboards bare. The housekeeper had gone to the store. Craving chocolate, I decided to go up to Castle Asshole and raid my father's stash—he's as much of a sugar addict as I am. I was vaguely aware that he had a houseguest, some famous Danish director, but this was hardly unusual. He always had somebody staying at the house, whether he was home or not. They rarely if ever took any notice of me. Some of them probably never even realized I lived across the pool or even that I existed. So I never expected to see this guy or even stopped to consider him at all. I just wanted candy.

So I was in my father's kitchen, rummaging through the pantry when I heard someone come through the swinging door behind me. "How did you get in here?" a thickly-accented voice asked. "Are you looking for drugs?"

"I live here, and I'm looking for Milk Duds." I turned around with my most winsome, Catholic schoolgirl smile. "The drugs are in the living room in the coffee table drawer."

He just blinked at me for a moment, then laughed, a deep, rich laugh like thunder. "Of course. You must be the little girl." He was at least twenty years older than Calvin, very tall, but slightly stooped, with white hair swept back from his brow.

"Scarlett. Yeah, that's me." I took my box of Milk Duds and a big bar of semi-sweet, just to get me through my homework. "Sorry to disturb you."

"Wait." The Great Dane was smiling at me like he thought I was adorable. "Please, stay. Let me get you some milk."

"Sure." I was a lonely kid, and people very rarely took an interest in me when my father wasn't around. Besides, it never occurred to me he could be anything but harmless. He was supposed to be a genius, and he seemed like a very nice old man. He poured me a glass of milk, and we sat down at the bar together.

"You wear this for school, I take it?" he said. "This uniform?"

"Yeah, I go to Catholic school." I opened my candy and offered it to him, but he shook his head with a small smile. "But we're not Catholic or anything. It's just a really good school."

"And safe, I would imagine." He took out a pack of cigarettes and offered it to me, but I shook my head, too. "I'm sure your father worries about you very much."

"I suppose." Truth be told, I doubted that profoundly. Calvin had fallen back into leaving me on my own and didn't seem to worry about it in the slightest. But that was none of this guy's business. "So you're a director?"

"I am." He lit his cigarette. "I am here trying to finish a script."

"How's it coming?" I asked around a mouthful of sticky candy.

"Not very well, I'm afraid." My hand was lying on the bar, and he reached out very casually and picked it up. "I don't find California very conducive to serious work, I'm afraid." He touched the ragged tips of my nails with their chipped, baby pink polish. "There are too many distractions."

"So why don't you leave?" I wasn't at all comfortable with this total stranger touching me, but there didn't seem to be any way to make him stop without being rude.

"My producers won't allow it." He drew my hand deeper into his grasp, the pad of his thumb at the center of my palm. "I have promised them a script, and they will not hear of my leaving until it is finished."

"It sounds like you better get on the stick." I took my hand back to eat more chocolate.

"Indeed." He took a long draw on his cigarette, studying me, amused. "You know, little one, I met your mother once."

"Really?" Now he had my attention. I never met anyone who had known Stella, and I was desperate for information about her, any sort of detail that might fill in the blanks in my own memory.

He nodded. "Yes. She was exquisite and quite bright—funny like you." He touched my cheek just barely with the backs of his fingers for no more than a few seconds. "We only spoke for a few minutes, but I was quite struck by her."

I had never really thought of my mother as bright or funny before, but of course she had been; thinking back, I knew she had been. And I liked it very much that he had said so. "I barely remember her," I admitted. "I was just a baby when she died."

"A terrible thing," he said, his deeply-lined face showing what looked like genuine sadness. "An abomination." My hair was pulled back, and he drew a loose strand down along my jaw. "Thank God your father was able to find you."

"I do." He had very pale gray eyes, I noticed, that seemed both piercing and very, very kind. "My daddy is my angel."

He shook his head, smiling. "Beautiful child."

The back door suddenly opened, and Daddy's cook came in, her arms full of shopping bags. Her eyes widened at the sight of us, me and this old man sitting together so intimately at the bar, and I drew back from him, my face going hot. But the Dane just smiled.

"Here she is," he said as if I had come there looking for the cook in the first place. "This little one is hungry."

"I'm sorry, Scarlett." She hurried to put down her bags. "I'll make you something."

"No, it's fine." I got up from my stool. "I found what I was looking for." I held out a hand to the Dane. "It was nice to meet you."

"Likewise," he said, shaking it and making a little bow from the waist. "Very much indeed."

I was shocked as hell after Christmas when Calvin told me the Dane wanted me to screen test for a part in his new film. "Why?" I asked him. We were sitting at the kitchen table at my house, eating tacos. "Daddy, I don't know shit about acting. Sebastian is the actor."

"Sebastian is brilliant, but this character is a girl," he interrupted, laughing. "My daughter, as a matter of fact." The kitchen looked like the staff of a fast food joint had gone psycho with the ingredients. We had cooked together, and there were bits of veggies and globs of meat and cheese splattered everywhere. "Convenient, huh?" He faked a frown. "And don't say shit." He grinned and took another messy bite.

"Well, yeah, but what if I suck?" Believe me, I was not being disingenuous. The Dane's movies were the real deal; I had no idea in the world that I could be anything but awful.

"That's why you're doing the screen test." He took his napkin and wiped a smear of sauce off my chin. "Trust me, you won't suck." I still wasn't convinced, and it must have shown on my face. "Come on, do it for me."

Like I could ever refuse him. "Okay." I took a big, messy bite of my own, a glob of sour cream hitting my plate. *Behold the actress,* I thought. "But don't say I didn't warn you."

So I did the screen test, also known as a torture of the damned. The Dane and his people had set it up at a tiny little studio in Burbank no bigger than a public toilet and almost as inviting. They had done me up like an extra from Oliver Twist, complete with a heavy wool coat sized for a grown man and a wool-felt military cap with ear flaps.

My tits, such as they were, were smashed flat under enough swaddling to bind down a gorilla. My face was smeared half an inch thick with greasepaint and fake grime. Then they focused two huge, blazing lights straight down on my face, so not only was I melting; I was blind. But worst of all, I didn't have a fucking clue what they wanted me to do.

"Do you understand the speech, Scarlett?" the Great Dane spoke from somewhere beyond the lights. The kindly old man I had met in Calvin's kitchen had become a disembodied voice that was all business.

"I think so." My character was a German war orphan in Berlin after World War II. "I memorized it last night." I was sweating and itching all over, and I knew I looked ridiculous. "But I don't think I can do it right." I wanted him or, even better, Calvin, to reassure me, but for a long time, no one said anything, like they were waiting for me to explain.

Then finally the Dane said, "Why don't you think you can do it, little one?"

I could hear the cameras whirring—he was already filming me looking like an idiot. "Because I'm not German, for one thing," I said, fighting back tears of embarrassment and frustration. "I can't do the accent."

"The accent is nothing," he said brusquely with no sympathy at all. "Just say the words." I heard Cal start to say something, but the Dane shushed him, hissing like a dragon. "Tell me what happened to your mother. How did she die?"

"Me, or the girl in the movie?" But he didn't answer. So I did the speech.

"We were in the basement of the church." I knew I was doing it wrong, that I should be crying or something, but I mostly just sounded pissed off. "Everyone from our block of flats was there." I hadn't even known what a block of flats was. I had asked my father in the car on the way over. "As soon as we heard the first bomb in the distance, one of the sisters made all of the children sit in a circle and pray." I thought of the nun who had cried over me in Mexico. "My mother was talking with a man on the other side of the room, flirting with him. They were sharing a cigarette." In my mind, I saw Stella smoking a cigarette as she put on her make-up to go out. "She was wearing a red dress." I looked up into the light, waiting for the Dane to stop me, to tell me I sucked or to start over. But he didn't say anything, and the camera whirred on. "She was laughing with her head thrown back, and a bomb crashed through the ceiling and exploded. There was smoke, and things breaking and flying in the air, and I couldn't see her anymore." I knew I should be trying harder, that my father was probably disappointed in me. But I was so scared and uncomfortable and embarrassed, all I could do was keep going and pray to be done. "When the bombs stopped, only the children were alive," I recited, not trying in the slightest to emote.

"And your mother?" Cal's voice spoke from inside the light. He sounded weird, like a stranger, and that made me feel even worse.

"I didn't see her." I'm sorry! I tried to tell him with my eyes, wanting to cry. "I saw her red shoe." That was the end of the speech, and I heard the camera stop, but for a long time, no one said anything. "Do I have to do it again?"

The Great Dane stepped out of the light. "No, little one." He was smiling; the kindly old stranger was back. Cal didn't say anything. He didn't even look me in the face. He just hugged me tight and kissed me on top of the head. I was absolutely positive I had been horrible, and I was even more sure when he sent me home by myself. I cried in the car all the way.

But later, after they came back to Castle Asshole, my father sent his assistant to get me, and they made me watch it back. I sat beside Cal in his screening room, my eyes shut tight as the screen burst into light, my cheeks flaming as I heard myself start talking—"I don't think I can do it right." I bit the corner of my lip until I tasted blood, dying to run away. Then suddenly I heard the beginning of the speech, but it didn't sound like me at all. My eyes flew open, and I froze.

There was my face on the screen in close-up, six feet across. "Oh my God," I whispered, breathless with shock. I was beautiful. I didn't even hear what the girl I was watching was saying; I was too enraptured by her face. My eyes looked huge and brilliant blue—Stella's eyes. My skin was transformed by the glare of the lights into a surface too fine to be real, purest porcelain made flesh. The grimy, gloppy make-up that had looked diseased when I saw it in the mirror had somehow given me the same graceful planes of shadow on my cheeks and brow that Cal had. "Daddy, look at me." Tears glittered in the movie-girl's lashes like diamonds, my tears of humiliation transformed by the magic of the camera to her tears of grief. "I look so pretty."

"I see you," he said, kissing me, and I heard the Dane chuckle behind us. "Welcome to the movies."

CHAPTER 13

And so, I was an actress, and we went to Germany. My part, Josephine, wasn't really that big; the star was definitely Calvin. He was supposed to be an American playboy who had partied in Berlin before the war with this gorgeous boho chick, and when he comes back after the war as some kind of diplomat/spy guy, he encounters this kid that he finally realizes is his daughter. Josephine is part of a group of orphans who support the Soviet Russians against the Americans. She meets the hero guy when she tries to throw a rock through his windshield, and he almost runs her over. The movie switches back and forth in time frames, and at the end, he decides that the way to make up for every bad thing he's ever done is to take this kid back to the land of opportunity, to rescue her. But of course, it's too late. She and a bunch of her little commie pals have staged a terrorist attack on the American barracks, and she's been shot. She dies in her father's arms; he's shattered—it's all very Great Dane. Me, I just worried about my German accent.

If I had known it before I started, I might have worried even more over the fact I was supposed to be playing twelve years old. The first night we got there, straight off of the plane, I had to go to the studio for a hair, make-up, and costume test, and Jenna, the dresser chick, insisted on taping down my tits again, this time with duct tape. "Is this completely necessary?" I asked her, too crabby to be shy.

"Oh yeah," she said, laughing. She was pulling my arm through the sleeve of my blouse, dressing me like no one had since Stella. "You're a little bit too bombshell for twelve." She buttoned the blouse and adjusted the collar. "You're a bit bombshell for fourteen, actually."

"Thanks." It had never occurred to me that all of these people would, like the people at school, assume I was really fourteen, not almost seventeen. I just assumed my father had told them the truth. But apparently, he hadn't, and I decided I didn't care.

Once I was dressed and made up, my driver/nanny, Wolfie, an aspiring filmmaker of twenty-one with a cute little blonde goatee, sat with me off to the side of the set to wait while they finished testing the last of many, many wardrobe changes for the girl who was playing my mother, a German soap opera actress named Bette Haust. As we were sitting down, she was bitching because they had darkened her hair. "I look like a vampire, but fat," she complained, pushing her heavy curls up on either side of her head and making a face at the camera.

"Trust me, honey," my father said, sitting in his own chair beside the Dane to watch. "You do not look fat."

"She's pretty," I said to Wolfie, leaning over to whisper.

"You think not?" she said to my father. She posed, one hip cocked forward like a pin-up. She was wearing a red dress. *She's going to die in that,* I thought, remembering my monologue. *I wonder if they'll show it?* "Maybe not for an American." She had just the sort of German accent I wanted, crisp but feminine.

"Oh, yah, very pretty," Wolfie said, leaning close to whisper back. "But as an actress, she is shit."

Watching her try to make a series of poses as the Great Dane called them out, I had to admit he had a point. Every movement was stiff and rather clumsy, but she didn't seem the least bit embarrassed. She behaved as if it were all some big joke, like she might bust out laughing at any moment, even when she was supposed to look terribly sad.

"I don't think she's that bad," I said, mesmerized by her even so. At the Dane's direction, my father had stepped into the light to pose with her. She turned and caught his shirt front in both hands and threw her head back like the girl on the cover of a romance novel. Daddy laughed. He obviously didn't think she was that bad, either.

"Tell me something beautiful," she said to him, a line from the script.

"You," my father answered, his scripted reply, and suddenly he was serious, and the very air around them changed. "You are beautiful." I had seen most of my father's movies, but I had never been so close on set when he was acting a love scene before. Watching him pretend to want this pretty, funny German girl, I blushed hot from the roots of my hair to my toenails. "I love you," he told her, leaning closer, and I closed my eyes quickly as they kissed.

Bette laughed and said something in German, and Wolfie laughed, too. "That's enough," the Great Dane said, sounding both tired and amused. "You're done." He looked back at me. "Your turn, little one."

"But who is this?" Bette said, letting go of my father as I walked onto the set.

"I'm Scarlett." I offered her my hand. "I think I play your daughter."

"So grown-up," she marveled to Cal as she shook my hand, though she couldn't have been many days over twenty-five herself. "And so pretty."

"We think so," Cal said, winking at me, and I smiled.

"You guys look beautiful," I told them, and it was true. They looked perfect together, Cal so blonde and golden and Bette so pale against her ebony hair.

"Thank you," she said, smiling as she really looked at me for the first time. A dimple appeared in her round little chin. *My God*, I thought. *She looks like Stella.*

"Come, come," the Great Dane said impatiently. "Let us see this little one so she can go to bed."

He ran me through my own paces, and I made the faces he wanted without thinking about it—frown, angry; laugh, smile, be glad; turn around as if you mean to run away; open your arms to be embraced.

"You see?" the Dane said to Bette, who had changed her clothes and come back to watch me. "Like this—and this is a little child." She said something in German that I could tell was not very nice, but she smiled at me and winked.

Luckily, my make-up was too plain to need much tweaking, and I only had two costumes—the jumper and blouse I was wearing, with and without the horrible coat and hat I'd worn for my screen test, and a nightgown. But it was still almost dawn before I was finally done. "Come, little one," the Dane said, getting up and holding out his hand as they started breaking down the cameras. I looked around, but my father was nowhere to be seen. "It is all right." He took my hand and smiled. "I just want to see you in the light."

As he led me through the canyon of dark sets, my vision started to blur, and suddenly my scalp felt cold and light. It was more than twenty-four hours since we had left New York, and I hadn't eaten so much as breath mint since I had picked at my dinner on the plane. Just as we were passing what looked like the stage of a nightclub hung with silver streamers, I swayed once and crashed to the floor.

I came around a few seconds later to find him bending over him, his light gray eyes full of concern. "Are you high?" he asked me.

'No." I tried to sit up, but my head was still swimming.

"Hungry?" He laid a hand against my cheek with surprising gentleness. "Thirsty?"

"Yes," I said, nodding, my stomach rolling over.

"Here." He caught me under the arms and hoisted me to sitting up. "Wait here." He disappeared into the darkness. I could hear them breaking down equipment and see lights going off in the distance, and I wondered where my father was and if he was worried. Just as I was deciding to try to get up and go look for him, the Dane came back, his hands full of food—a sandwich and a brownie wrapped in plastic and a cardboard carton of milk. "Start with this," he said, crouching beside me and handing me the sandwich. It was cold corned beef with some sort of pickle relish, and ordinarily I would have turned up my nose at it. But just then, it was delicious. "Better?" he said when I had swallowed a few bites.

"Yes." I took a long swig of milk, wiping my mouth with the back of my hand.

"You have to tell Wolfie when you get hungry," he said, his tone crisp but kind. "That is his job." He stood up and offered me his hand again. "Now come."

He led me to a huge, yellow-painted metal door at the outside edge of the soundstage and pushed it open, shocking me with the sudden light of dawn. Outside our cave, it was morning. I stepped out on an ordinary street in the warehouse district of West Berlin, all ugly gray concrete and beautiful gray light. In the distance, I could see the skyline of the prettier sections of the city, spires with angels and saints. A truck rumbled past us down the alley, so close I had to step back almost into the Dane's arms.

"Careful," he said, catching my elbow. He turned me to face him and studied my face as if I might have been a doll, something completely unaware or uncaring as she was being studied.

"So why did you pick me?" I asked him, more to break the silence than anything else. I was feeling kind of dizzy again, and very sleepy; I wanted to go home. "For the screen test, I mean."

He frowned slightly. "Why should I not?" He took hold of my chin and turned my face up to the morning light. "Oh yes." He smiled. "I think you can do well."

CHAPTER 14

Filming the movie was tough, but it was fun, more fun that I had ever had in my life. Being with Calvin, working with him, was sheer bliss, and I was completely fascinated by Bette. The Great Dane let me watch the filming of anything I wasn't in, a sort of crash course, and most of the basics; I learned by watching her. She made a lot of careless mechanical mistakes like missing her marks or dropping lines. But when she was on (usually in love scenes with Cal, it must be said), she found a devastating, bone-marrow level of truth that was exhilarating to watch. I admired her tremendously, and I let her know it, so she liked me back. She played with me like a little sister, even taking me shopping on our days off and helping me pick clothes that I actually liked. "Who cares what anybody else will say?" she would demand when I would waffle. "If you think you look pretty, you do."

One afternoon she took me with her to lunch at her mother's apartment in the oldest section of Berlin. Her mother was a film actress, too, a famous beauty, now retired, and she lived in this tiny, over-decorated little flat that was absolutely crawling with cats. She gave us lunch—fish fingers and pierogies, still half-frozen, and a luke-warm soda from the bottle, and Bette showed me her old room.

"She never changes anything," she explained, closing the door. It reminded me of my own room at home, a little girl's room. The bed was made with linens covered with cartoon rainbows, and the walls were covered with posters, including one of my father dressed as an existential cowboy from one of his earliest movies. "Everything is the same as it was before I left." She reached under the bed and took out a little wooden box. "You see?" She opened it and started rolling a joint.

"It's great." Opposite Cal's cowboy poster was an even bigger one of David Bowie, a space alien with bright magenta hair.

"You think so?" she said, amused. "Look in the closet; see if there is anything you like."

I pulled out a pair of tattered jeans that made me think of Romeo. "I like these." They were hanging beside an aged ivory lace blouse with tiny pearl buttons that looked like it might have belonged to a Victorian hooker. "And this."

"Try it on." She lit up and took a long drag as I stripped out of my clothes. "How old are you, Magenta?" she asked, holding the smoke in her lungs as she talked. Magenta was my nickname; I couldn't make her give it up.

"How old do I look?" The jeans were a little snug, but I was able to wiggle into them, holding my breath to get them zipped.

"Older than fourteen." She let out the smoke in a rush. "So how old?"

"Older than fourteen." I slipped the blouse over my head. "I never said I was fourteen." I turned to face her. "How do I look?"

"Very sexy." She held out the joint to me, but I shook my head. "The old man thinks you are fourteen, you know."

"I know. Everybody does." I looked at my reflection in the sticker-framed mirror on her dresser. "I don't know why."

"Because that's how old your father told them you were, goosey-girl." I met her eyes in the reflection, shocked, and she laughed. "Who else?"

"Why would he do that?" I asked scornfully.

"I don't know. How old are you?" She got up and knelt behind me on the bed. "Here, hold this." She gave me the joint and started brushing my hair.

"I'm sixteen." She pulled it up into a loose chignon that made me look even older.

"That would be why. The father of a fourteen-year-old baby is much, much younger than the father of a sixteen-year-old woman." She pinned it into place with a pair of ivory chopsticks.

"My father doesn't care about that," I scoffed. "He's beautiful."

"He is," she agreed. "But he's an actor." She took the joint back and sat back on her heels to admire her handiwork. "Trust me, Magenta," she said, smiling. "He cares." She took another drag, holding it casually between her ring and middle fingers like a regular cigarette. My soon-to-be-ex-husband is the only other person I've ever seen smoke a joint with that absolute confidence. It's a pretty sexy trick. "But I won't tell anyone." She let out the smoke again. "Let the old man have his fantasy."

I had no clue what she meant, and I didn't care to ask. I let the matter drop completely, still not convinced she was right. But she had definitely given me something to think about.

A few nights after that, I found out just exactly how well she was getting to know my father. I was supposed to have been out all night shooting. The Dane filmed most of my scenes on location with natural light, and there were several sequences where my character was supposed to be running the streets with her orphan gang after dark. So his great concession to our youth was to schedule all the shots with nothing but kids for one long night. Unfortunately, it was late winter in Berlin, and it started sleeting. At first, he didn't care, but by three o'clock, it had gotten so bad that the weather was ruining the shots, so he called it off and sent everybody home. I didn't even bother to change out of my costume. Wolfie wrapped me in a blanket and stuffed me into the car, wet and shivering, to drive me back to the hotel.

As we were walking from the elevator to the suite, we heard music. "Come on," Wolfie said, taking my arm to turn me back toward the elevator. "We will go and find you some supper."

"What, are you kidding?" I protested. "I'm tired, and I'm cold. I'm going to bed." We had gotten to my door, and it was obvious the music was coming from the suite, but I didn't care. I figured my father was still up, studying his lines for the next day.

Wolfie looked like he wanted to argue with me, but he didn't. "Go to sleep quick," he said, ruffling my hair before he turned away and headed down the hall.

The door of the suite led into a dark, narrow hallway that opened out on the left to an archway into the parlor and turned sharply to the right to the doors for both bedrooms. The music was coming from the left, so I turned that way first, my mouth open to speak.

But I didn't say anything. Bette and Cal were dancing. All the lights were out except for the little red equalizer lights on the stereo, and the drapes were open. The lights of the city were reflected in the windows and sparkling in the sleet—very beautiful. But the view outside was nothing special compared to my father and his girl. Cal's shirt was untucked and unbuttoned down the front, and Bette was wearing a black lace half-slip and matching bra. As I watched, stunned silent, they kissed.

As luck would have it, Bette saw me first. She took a stumbling step back from Cal, bracing him away with one red-nailed hand on his bare chest, and he turned his head and saw me, too. "Hey, sweet-pea," he said. Bette looked concerned, even embarrassed, but my father was perfectly at ease. "How was the shoot?" He turned away from me, back to her, and smiled, one hand on the back of her neck, still buried in her hair.

"Wet," I answered. "And cold. We had to stop." Bette's eyes met mine over his shoulder. She looked like she felt bad for me.

"Are you all right?" she asked me.

"Sure," I answered. "Wolfie got me a blanket."

"Good," my father said, drawing her hand up around his neck again. "Wolfie's a prince."

"I guess." I was so jealous I could have screamed, but I couldn't say anything—what could I say? "Good night."

"Good night, sweetpea." I had started down the hall when he added. "I love you."

I stopped and looked back at him, smiling. "I love you, too."

Bette left the shoot before the wrap party, heading to the Bahamas on vacation. "I need a little sunshine," she had told me, kissing me good-bye. "Be a good girl, Magenta."

The wrap party for *The Little Match Girl* was my first ever and the last one I ever enjoyed. We actually finished principal photography the day before my birthday, so I had a huge cake at the party, and everyone sang to me in German. And later I danced with one of the boys who played one of the other orphans, Vincent. He had dark hair and blue eyes and perfectly arched eyebrows and a perfectly straight nose and a strong, emphatic jaw, and he was very, very serious about acting. "I will miss you, Scarlett," he said to me in his adorable accent, his arms around me, my hands locked behind his neck.

"I will miss you, too." Truth be told, we had barely spoken before, but it was the wrap party. Suddenly everyone who was a mere acquaintance the week before feels like your last chance for perfect happiness on the brink of being lost forever. He bent and kissed me softly on the mouth, and I thought of my Romeo. What was he doing now? I thought. Was he safe? Did he remember me at all?

"No, you won't," Vincent was saying. "You will go home to California and forget that I exist."

"I promise I won't," I said. "I will never, ever forget you." And allow me to point out, please, that I haven't.

An hour later, all the other kids but me had gone. Cal had been beside me when I blew out my candles, but I hadn't seen him since. The lights over the party had been turned down until they were almost as dim as the rest of the soundstage, and people were dancing close and talking in groups. I moved among them, stopping to hug and be hugged every few steps. But I still couldn't find my father. On the far side of the light, I could see the Dane, sitting in his director's chair with several of the younger members of the cast and crew gathered at his feet, listening to him talk—Wolfie was among them. I caught his eye and waved, and he waved back, grinning at me for a moment before he turned back to the master.

I made my way down the corridor between the trailers. People here weren't so eager to acknowledge me. Standing close together, they would barely glance up as I passed, their eyes sliding away from mine before I could speak to them if they bothered to notice me at all. Cal's trailer was the last and best one in the line, and I could see his lights were on. Silly me, I figured he was missing Bette and had slipped away from the crowd.

The door was slightly ajar, so I didn't even bother to knock. I had opened my mouth to call his name as I went inside, but luckily, I stopped before I spoke, paralyzed by what I saw. Cal was kicked back in a chair, his legs stretched long in front of him and his head laid back while Jenna, the dresser, knelt before him, giving him a blow job. Her back was to the door, and his eyes were closed.

I knew exactly what was happening, of course. I had seen it happen to other people before. But nothing could have prepared my worshipful, adolescent brain for the crass reality of this, six feet in front of me. My father, the god of my idolatry, was being serviced— there was just no other word for it—by a girl I knew adored him whom I further knew he didn't care about in the slightest.

It's one thing to know your father is a hound. It's quite another to see it.

I held my breath and backed out of the trailer, my hand slipping from the doorknob, clammy with sweat. I kept backing slowly down the steps, careful not to make so much as a creak. Then I swallowed, took a deep breath, squared my shoulders, and prepared to turn around, to walk back to the party.

And backed into the Dane.

"Shhh," he whispered, catching me gently by the elbow. "Come."

He led me across the soundstage through the abandoned sets, away from the party and the trailers to his office, a little room made from collapsible walls with a desk and a long conference table. Wolfie was inside, leaning against the conference table, smoking a cigarette. "Hey, cupcake," he said to me, standing up as we came in. "Are you—?"

Before he could finish, the Dane spoke to him sharply in German, making him blush under the golden fuzz of his beard. He answered him, also in German, frowning. He seemed nervous, edgy, as if he'd been waiting for us and expecting the Dane to be pissed. The Dane was still holding me by the elbow. "Her papa is still here," the Dane said in English. "Get out."

I could tell Wolfie didn't want to go. I also knew from listening to him talk about it for weeks that he worshipped the Dane, that his dearest ambition was to work for him as something more important than a driver. "I'm okay," I said. And by the way, I totally believed it. It never occurred to me that I was in any sort of peril at all, not from this sweet old man who was making me a star. "My dad will drive me home."

"Right," Wolfie said, smiling at me. He reached out and chucked me on the cheek. "I will see you."

Then he left, closing the door behind him.

I don't remember what the Dane said to me then, though I suppose he must have said something. Maybe he mentioned my father, asked me what I had seen in his trailer that had upset me, or told me I had done well in the film. I remember him pouring himself a drink and drinking half of it in one gulp. Then he was just looking at me, no expression on his face, his pale gray eyes lit up with something I didn't recognize yet. I think I said, "What?" I might have even laughed.

Then he was kissing me. It wasn't a first kiss; there was nothing tentative about it. He kissed me like I belonged to him, grabbing me up in his wiry, old man's arms and pushing his tongue in my mouth. I was fighting back, but it wasn't fighting like I was angry or scared—I was pushing against him like maybe he didn't realize that I didn't want this, like I was trying to have some kind of reasonable argument with him, my palms planted against his chest, pushing as hard as I could but nothing else, not kicking or biting or trying to scream. I was just so fucking shocked; I couldn't believe this was happening, that he could possibly think that this was okay, that he would dare to do it if he knew it wasn't. He shoved me back against the table, and it skidded underneath me with an ugly, scraping noise of metal on concrete, script pages sliding to the floor, and that's when I finally got scared. He put a hand under my skirt, and I started hitting him, slapping at him first then balling up my fist and pounding on him, his head and shoulders, whatever I could reach, but he barely seemed to notice. He turned me around and heaved me completely up on the table, his arm around my waist, then grabbed my wrist and twisted my arm behind my back, so that hard it hurt badly; I saw stars. I don't remember saying anything or screaming for help or crying. I remember him talking and talking, all in Danish, how rough his cheek felt rubbing against mine and the smell of his breath, tobacco, and red wine. I heard something—the door opening again.

Then suddenly he was gone, snatched away from me, his hands clutching at me, wrenching my arm as he was pulled away. I heard another scrape and a crash, and the Dane was shouting, furious, in German, and someone else was shouting back, sounding almost in tears. I turned around to find Wolfie holding the Dane by the shoulder and the throat, pinning him against the wall. The Dane's pants were down around his ankles; I could see his skinny, old man's legs and the shadow of his sex under the tail of his shirt. I closed my eyes, feeling sick. Wolfie was still shouting, crying, but the Dane had stopped. I started crying, sliding down from the table to the floor, my hands over my face.

"It's all right, cupcake," Wolfie was saying. "Come on." He touched my arm, and I shuddered, jerking away from me. "Come on," he said, sounding almost as young as me. "Let me take you home."

I was sitting bare-assed on the concrete floor, I realized. Face burning hot with shame, I opened my eyes, staring at the floor as I let Wolfie help me to my feet.

"Forgive me, little one." The Dane was standing with his back to us at his desk, fastening his pants. He sounded exhausted and terribly sad.

"It's all right," Wolfie said again, putting his arm around me. He was holding my underpants out to me, not looking at them. I took them and stepped into them, stumbling, but Wolfie held me up.

We walked out of the office, me leaning heavily against his side.

But as soon as I heard the music from the party, I felt sick again. All the birthday cake I had eaten before was coming back up. I turned the other way and ran like hell for the big yellow door at the back, shoving it open and falling through it to the alley, puking as I went.

"Scarlett!" Wolfie came running after me. He caught me by the shoulders before I fell into my own puke and held on to me until I was done. "Come on." He put his arm around my shoulders again and led me to his car, parked at the end of the alley. He didn't ask me if I was all right. He didn't say he was sorry, but I knew he was. We both cried silently all the way back to the hotel.

He pulled up to a stop in front of the doors and threw the car into park like he always did, ready to walk me up. "No," I said, opening the door. "I can go by myself." I couldn't look at him anymore. Part of me wanted to grab hold of him and thank him over and over for saving me. But part of me never wanted to look him in the eyes again.

I went upstairs and got into a boiling hot shower, clothes and all, and scrubbed. I thought I could smell the Dane all over me, seeping out of my skin. Then I took my clothes off and sat down in the tub, letting the water rain down on me until I stopped crying and the tub was full. I was still there when I heard my father come in, long enough later that the water had turned cold.

"Daddy?" I called out, then instantly regretted it. I couldn't talk to him. What could I tell him? And how could I talk to him and not tell him anything?

"Scarlett?" He sounded wide awake and happy. "What are you doing still up?"

"I'm in the tub." I heard him just outside the door. "I just wanted to say good night."

"Good night, sweetpea." He gave the door a little slap and started to walk away.

"Daddy!" I heard a little sliver of hysteria in my voice, and I gritted my teeth, willing it back. "I love you."

"I love you, too." I hadn't been entirely successful; I could hear him pause, concerned. "Are you okay?"

"Yes." If I told him, he would have to do something, but what could he do that would help? *The past is past,* I thought, remembering Greta. *All that matters is the now.* "I'm fine. Just sleepy."

"Right." I could tell he was just on the other side of the door. "You know, I'm really proud of you and the work you've done on the movie," he said. "You did a really good job." The door vibrated a little; he was touching it. "Did you have a good time?"

"I did." I made myself think about the good stuff, watching Daddy work and shopping with Bette and kissing Vincent on the dance floor. There was so much good stuff that had happened, so much to focus on. Five minutes couldn't ruin it, not if I just didn't think about it anymore. I could decide to just forget it had happened, then everything would be okay. "I had a really good time."

CLIPPING 6

from "In the News," a monthly column in *Popcorn* magazine

Tony-nominated stage actor Sebastian Cross has been cast in the lead role in the big-screen adaptation of Harold Branch's best-selling novel, The House. *Producer Lewis Moore optioned the novel for his new Open Hallways Pictures studio last year, beating out several more established studios for the hot property and kicking off months of speculation as to the cast. "We've seen every actor in Hollywood who thinks he can look eighteen," Moore confided with typical tact. "But Sebastian is eighteen, plus he's got the chops to pull it off. We're all very excited." Pulitzer Prize winner Branch is adapting the novel with Moore, and music video wunderkind Dewey Kimble is attached to direct.*

Cross, the son of actor Calvin Cross and writer-producer Greta Strassman, was nominated for a Tony last year for his performance in the revival of the classic Fear of High Places. *Early gossip indicated that his father might also appear in the new film in a supporting role, but reports that Calvin Cross is currently developing another script with Danish auteur Aksel Jorgen make this unlikely. Shooting is scheduled to begin in October with a release date tentatively set for the spring.*

CHAPTER 15

In the gap between principle photography on *The Little Match Girl* and the release date in November, I finished my sophomore year in high school and got cast with Sebastian in a teen slasher flick called *The Funhouse*. The director was Wallace Cole, a once-brilliant burnout we had known since we were babies, and Calvin was one of the producers. Sebastian and I played clean-cut kids whose father had died, leaving them with a sexy wicked stepmother who owns an amusement park on the beach called Batholdy Park. The park is run by this clan of gypsy white trash, and both of our characters fall in love with gypsies, even though we're part of the preppie crowd—I got to be sixteen in this one, at least. In a twist on the usual theme, I hold out on my gypsy and get slaughtered; Sebastian fucks his in the second reel, and they live, because Wicked Stepmom is a 300-year-old monster who bathes in virgin blood.

We started out shooting on location at the beach; two weeks of night shoots. In my first scenes, I was supposed to be meeting my gypsy for the first time underneath the boardwalk. He tries to lure me away on his motorcycle, but my brother, Sebastian, our hero, scares him and his gypsy biker friends away. The sexy gypsy was being played by Kevin Heath, a little shithead TV actor who thought he was a way bigger deal than he was. He was all pissed off that Sebastian had the lead, and the first half a dozen takes he and I did together on our first night of shooting were just a catastrophe. Cole finally shut down the set-up altogether. "Is your guy ready with the bike?" he asked the stunt coordinator at the end of take 7 without even bothering to call "Cut."

"Hey, I can do the fucking bike," Shithead insisted, pushing past me to get to the director. This was another major bone of contention. Kevin the Shithead imagined himself to be a real Easy Rider, but his bosses at the TV network were worried he'd break his neck, so they'd made the producers of the movie sign a contract saying he wouldn't be doing any stunts.

"You're not insured," Cole snarled around his burning stub of a cigar without sparing him a glance. The techies had already started breaking down the lights, and one of the PAs had brought me a soda. "Shut up and get out of the way."

"This is bullshit!" Shithead declaimed, knocking over a lighting tree as he stormed off to his trailer, his own assistant scurrying in his wake.

"Okay, pussycat, come over here," Cole said, motioning to me. "You're going to be over here under the boardwalk when you hear the motorcycles coming down the beach." He walked me through it, his arm around my shoulders. "You look out around the piling, Snow White in the forest, dig? And the beam of one of the headlights is going to catch you in the face, pow. You're gorgeous, but you're scared. The lead bike breaks out of the pack, roars once around you, and skids to a stop, and you flinch, but you don't back down. Can you do that?"

"Sure," I said, nodding, sipping soda through a straw.

"Good girl." He was looking at the air in front of us, already watching it happen. "So you're facing him down; you're scared; you're blind from the light. Then he switches it off, and there he is. Prince Charming." I snickered, and he grinned, giving me a squeeze. "Let's do it." He let me go and started yelling at the techies, who had barely had time to get started on the set-up. "Come on, come on! What the hell are we doing?"

An hour or so later, we were ready. I had been standing off to one side, watching the stunt biker practice hitting his mark, still wearing his helmet. He was really good, I realized. There was no way Shithead would have been able to match his easy, graceful control, even just sitting on the bike. Once everything else was set, the stunt coordinator sent him back down the beach, and when he got to the other bikers, he took off his helmet. He had long black hair just like Shithead. Sebastian called down to me from the boardwalk above where the trailers were, and I waved to him as I moved to my mark.

The scene went just the way Cole had blocked it. I heard the bikes; I came out between the pilings; the light hit me just right; the one bike roared up in a spray of sand; the light went out; and I saw him. "Hey," I said, blowing my line and positively blooming with delight. "It's you." It was my Romeo.

"Hey," he answered back, both of us grinning like idiots.

"Cut!" Cole yelled as I moved in and gave him a hug.

Once Cole was done bellowing at us for wasting a shot, we did three more takes, hanging out on the set to chat in between. I told him I had been in Germany, and he told me he was taking classes at Stella Adler. "I'm taking your advice, I guess," he said. "I'm trying to be an actor." In the year since I had seen him last, he had lost most of the Southern accent I had liked so much, and he looked much healthier. His face was fuller, though I'd still have called him thin. His hair was just as long, but now he had an expensive bad-boy-with-a-product-addiction haircut, probably to match Kevin the Shithead.

"Good for you," I said, beaming at him. I suppose it seems stupid for me to have been so happy to see the gigolo drug dealer who had deflowered me and stolen my wallet, but sorry, I was thrilled. "Stella Adler is great. Sebastian takes classes there sometimes."

"So I hear," he said. "You look beautiful."

I looked down at my ungodly costume, khaki camp shorts and a pink-and-white striped sleeveless shirt. "I look ridiculous," I said, laughing, embarrassed and pleased. "But thanks."

When it was time to move on, Shithead refused to come out of his trailer, so I did my close-ups for the scene with Romeo. "Just stand there and read with her," Cole told him. "Give her something to look at." I noticed he sent an AD off between two takes, and twenty minutes later, she came back with one of the executive producers who went into a little low-talking conference with Cole while the lights were moved again. But I was too psyched to be with Romeo to really wonder why.

"How long have you been doing stunt work?" I asked him.

"This is my first job," he answered. He tried to hand the script pages he'd been given to read with me back to a passing PA, but she waved him off. "My teacher is Cole's ex-wife." He grinned. "I think she gave up an alimony payment to get him to use me."

"You ride really well." I remembered watching him drive Sebastian's roadster along the cliffs from Malibu. I wanted to ask him if he remembered that, if he remembered our being together. I wanted very much to touch him. "I feel a lot better, actually," I said instead. "I was worried I might have to ride with that Shithead who's playing the part."

"Don't worry." He reached out and took my hand lightly in his like it was the most natural thing in the world. "I'll take care of you."

We finished my close-ups, but Shithead still wasn't ready, so they hustled together a set-up for the featured players in the biker gang. "Do you have lines?" I asked Romeo.

"Yeah," he answered, watching the techies. He obviously found the whole process of movie-making fascinating. He'd been studying everybody all night from Cole down to the grips, soaking it all in. "A couple, I think. But not in this scene."

"Do you die?" Everybody had been asking everybody else this same question all night. It was our version of "what's your major?" at the freshman mixer, I suppose.

"Not on camera," he answered with a grin. "I'm part of the pile of corpses they find at the end."

"Lovely." Sebastian was coming down the sandy steps from the boardwalk, and we both waved. "Aren't they using dummies?"

"They haven't decided yet." We walked toward Sebastian, leaving the set-up behind.

"Your heart's desire is pitching a fit," my brother informed me as he reached us, meaning Shithead. He had been teasing me about him since I'd gotten the part; I fucking hated his TV show. "He keeps saying he's going to quit."

"I wish he would," I answered. "'Bastian, do you remember Romeo?"

"Of course." He gave Romeo a hug. Sebastian has always been a hugger. "Congratulations on your first gig."

"Thanks." Romeo glanced over at me and smiled. "I was telling Scarlett, I'm pretty well fucked. I don't have a clue what's going on."

"That sounds pretty much perfect," Sebastian promised him. "Trust me; you'll be fine."

"Hey, Motorcycle Kid," Cole called from behind us. "Let's go!"

"Coming!" He gave my hand a squeeze. "I'll see you."

"Yeah, I know." I watched him run off to join the other bikers, a big, goofy grin on my face.

"Oh dear," Sebastian said with a theatrical sigh.

"What?" I said, wiping my grin away.

"He's cute," he said, putting an arm around my shoulders. "But he's a bad, bad boy."

"Not anymore," I protested. "He's taking classes at Stella Adler."

"So I hear," he answered. "Care to guess how he's paying for it?"

"Shut up, Sebastian."

"He isn't," he explained. "His sister pays. With the big coin she's making as a porn star." I drew back to gape at him. "Oh yes," he said, obviously enjoying my reaction. "From what I understand, she's running a very profitable little cottage industry out of a house in the valley."

I watched an AD hide Romeo in the back of the pack of bikers for a medium shot. As Shithead's stunt double, he wouldn't get more than a few seconds of face time on camera; it was a bottom feeder gig. "So what?" I said, pretending to be blasé, like I had drinks with porn stars every night of the week.

"So nothing, I suppose," Sebastian said. "I just think it's interesting, that's all. And seriously, from what I hear, your Romeo could probably have won a scholarship if he'd had to. He's supposed to be pretty good."

"He is, actually," I said, making an effort to sound nonchalant. "He read with me before." Kevin the Shithead and his assistant had finally re-emerged and were coming down the steps toward us. A group of fans had gathered behind a barricade on the beach, and as soon as they saw him, they went nuts. He smiled for the first time that night and went over to sign autographs. "So you're my brother, tell me the truth," I asked. "Do you think I have a shot?"

"With Romeo?" He looked surprised, but only for a moment. "Of course you do, stupid. You're a dish." He tweaked my nose, and I swatted at him. "And it's pretty obvious he likes you. Did he remember you from before?"

"Yeah, he did." I felt warm and happy all over. "Do you really think he likes me?"

"No, I was lying," he said sarcastically. "Seriously, though..." He turned away slightly to watch the filming. "Don't you think he might be a little bit much for you, at least for your first boyfriend?" He grinned, glancing up at the rides on the boardwalk. "Maybe you should take a couple of turns on the merry-go-round before you try the rollercoaster."

"I think I'll be all right." Sebastian, like our father, always assumed that nothing ever happened to me unless he was around to see it, that I was a total innocent. And just like with our father, I let him keep on believing it.

"Just be careful," he said, not convinced. "Oh, and by the way, princess, Fiona likes him, too."

My mood plummeted like I really was riding a rollercoaster. "What?" I looked at him, appalled. "Shit...are you kidding?" Fiona Fleming was the female lead, Sebastian's love interest in the movie, and far and away the coolest, best connected kid in the cast. She had been working since she was four years old, the oldest and most successful of a huge clan of professional moppets. She was dark and exotic and bitterly hilarious, and everybody loved her, even me. Or at least I had until now. If she wanted Romeo, I knew I was well and truly fucked.

"She caught a look at him the first night of filming, yeah. She's the one who gave me the scoop on him and his sister," Sebastian said. "But so what?"

"So I can't compete with her," I answered, shaking my head in disgust. The bikers were doing doughnuts in the sand, and Shithead was watching, obviously jealous.

"What?" Sebastian turned back to me. "Please tell me you're kidding." I snorted, trying for a jaded laugh. "Have you seen you?"

"Yes," I said. "And I've seen Fiona, too." He was my brother, and he was sweet, and I loved him. But I wasn't stupid.

"Yeah, me too." For once, there was no teasing in his tone. "Look, I'm still not all aquiver at the idea of you hooking up with this dude, but if you want him, you can have him."

"Yeah, right," I said, heavy with gloom.

"Yeah, right." The executive producer had finally spotted Kevin and pointed him out to Cole, and now the techies were hustling to put our scene back together. Romeo was walking the bike back into position. "Fiona wishes she looked like you."

"No, she doesn't." Romeo was trying to show Shithead how to hold up the bike, but Shithead wasn't having it, waving him off. "Did she really say she liked him?"

"Yeah, she did. I believe her exact words were, 'I gotta get me some of that.'" He sounded disgusted, but I knew that was for my benefit. He thought Fiona was cool as all hell. "But she doesn't have to be right —I know she hasn't gotten any yet."

"She likes you, too," I said, struck with sudden inspiration. "I mean she really likes you, not just to fuck. If she was with you…"

"Not a chance, little sister, not even for you," he said, cutting me off. "Fiona is most profoundly not my type."

"Great," I grumbled. Romeo was walking off with the rest of the bikers. He turned back to wave to me and Sebastian, and we waved back.

"Scarlett?" a PA said, appearing at my elbow. "Sorry." She smiled shyly at Sebastian, and he smiled back and winked. "They're ready for you again."

"Right," I said, giving my brother a hug and a kiss. "I'm coming."

We shot the long and medium shots of me and Shithead, then Sebastian came in for his medium stuff with us, then his close-ups. Then, instead of shooting Shithead's close-ups like everyone expected, Cole used the last hour of dark to bring the bikers back to do establishing close-ups of their faces, and I noticed that, rather than hiding Romeo in the back, he shot about twice as many of him as he did of anyone else. Plus he kept giving him very specific emotional reactions to do, even though he had no lines in the scene. Meanwhile, Shithead was laying an egg. He didn't dare leave the set again, but he prowled around the edges, bitching under his breath and generally making an ass of himself.

Just as the sun was about to start to come up, Burnout had them set up one last long shot where the bikers would peel out down the beach and leave me standing with my brother. They hadn't shot a single close-up of Shithead, and trust me, he had noticed. He went into an intense whispered conference with his assistant, and the executive producer hurried over to join them. But Cole didn't even seem to notice.

"Hey, Hotshot," he called as the cameras were rolled into position. "I thought you wanted to ride the bike." Another stunt biker had already taken Romeo's position in the back of the pack so he could double for Shithead, but the stunt coordinator moved in and waved him away. "Come on," Cole said, waving Shithead in. "Let's do it."

To be fair, Shithead had obviously ridden a motorbike before. Sneering slightly at Romeo, he mounted up and walked it backward into position just fine. But as soon as he cranked up, it was obvious he couldn't handle the sand. He couldn't hold the bike up in the turn, even in first gear. He spun out and nearly lost it through two failed takes, then spilled completely on the third.

"Holy shit!" the executive producer shrieked, running forward with the medic and Shithead's assistant in her wake, and the crowd of spectators went wild.

"Look," Sebastian said, nudging me and pointing to Cole. "He's smiling."

"Cut!" Cole yelled through his bullhorn, cheerful as a kid on Christmas. "Okay, that's it for tonight." They had lifted the bike off of Shithead, who was remarkably calm, considering.

"I think he's okay," the medic called, kneeling beside him and feeling down his leg.

"Praise Jesus," Cole said, lighting his cigar.

"What a dick," Sebastian said, laughing. "I love it."

The shoot was breaking up; we were surrounded by people on the move. The stunt coordinator was talking to the bikers, but I noticed Romeo was looking back at me. When he saw me looking, he smiled, and I started toward him, leading Sebastian by the hand.

Then I heard someone else call his name. Fiona was tripping lightly down the steps from the boardwalk, ignoring the pleas of the crowd for autographs like she didn't even notice they were there. She got to Romeo first and threw her arms around his neck. I couldn't hear what she was saying, but she was laughing, her body pressed to his. And he was smiling.

"Come on," Sebastian said, trying to tug me on. I had stopped dead. "Don't be a pussy."

"I'm tired." I waved once more to Romeo, and he waved back, but Fiona was in his arms. "Come on. I want to go home."

CHAPTER 16

We went home and slept, then came back late that afternoon to watch the dailies. Cole and his crew had taken over the old movie palace on the boardwalk as a screening room, and people had gotten into the habit of coming in to watch. On the days when we had shot big crowd scenes, the place would be more than half full, and craft services would even do popcorn. Other times it would be almost empty but for Cole and whatever techies might need to see the shots. I had just started, so this was my first visit, but Sebastian came every day, and he said Romeo did, too. When we got there, he and Fiona were already sitting in a row halfway back. "Hey!" Fiona said, turning in her seat. "Come sit with us!" So we did, Sebastian sitting between me and Fiona, Romeo sitting on Fiona's other side.

The first few minutes were of Sebastian and Fiona, the two of them walking down the deserted boardwalk and into the empty amusement park. Compared to the lushness of what I had already seen from *Match Girl*, this footage looked like home movies, garish and grainy, lit as if by neon. But even uncut, even a know-nothing like me could see the lurid excitement of it, the genius in the way it moved. The centerpiece of the set-up was a long, twisty tracking shot that followed and circled Sebastian and Fiona as they passed under the rollercoaster, the two of them coming together and pulling apart as the camera stalked them. "It looks good," I heard Cole say from a few rows in front of us. "It's good."

Then suddenly we were watching me under the boardwalk. Sebastian wolf-whistled, and Fiona hooted, reaching across him to give my arm a squeeze. "All right, pipe down," Cole ordered, but he didn't sound displeased. Like always, I was struck by how different I looked on film. The harsh light made me look more real than real; in close-up, you could see every freckle. But there was still a glamour there, a weird glow that seemed entirely separate from me, that came from the camera alone.

"So pretty," Fiona said softly. "You guys look so much alike." And it was true. In real life, Sebastian and I barely resemble one another at all, but on film, we could easily be twins. I can't explain it. The movies are magic.

Light splashed over a corner of the screen as the door behind us opened and closed. "Hey," Sebastian murmured, nudging Fiona with his elbow as he looked back over his shoulder. "What did I tell you?"

A pair of suits were skulking down the aisle, one of them carrying a briefcase. "Son of a bitch," Fiona whispered, laughing, as they slid into seats directly behind Cole. The one with the briefcase opened it up and started riffling papers while the other leaned forward to speak softly but urgently into the director's ear. Briefcase found what he was looking for and passed it to his buddy, who passed it forward to the executive producer sitting on Cole's right. And just at that moment, Romeo appeared on the screen.

"Wow," Sebastian said softly, and you could hear other people whispering the same thing all around the theatre. The camera didn't just love him. It wanted to buy him a house and have his babies. My own heart flipped over, and a big, goofy grin broke out on my face. I heard my own voice from the film and saw the beautiful boy-face on the screen react, and I laughed out loud. Half the time I had thought we were shooting my close-ups, Cole had been shooting Romeo. The angle jumped back to a medium shot on both of us, and watching, you could feel how much the girl on the screen wanted the boy, so much so I felt my face getting hot.

"You guys have great chemistry," Sebastian said, his mouth close to my ear, his arm around my shoulders. Fiona, I noticed, was quiet.

"Shut up!" Cole suddenly exploded. We all jumped, but he was yelling at the suits. He tossed their magic papers back over his shoulder at them, and the producers on either side of him leaned in. Even though I couldn't hear exactly what they were saying, it was obvious there was some begging going on.

The footage switched again, this time to Kevin the Shithead. He really was a handsome kid. He knew how to work the camera, and his line readings were a lot more polished than Romeo's. And that, in essence, was the problem. For whatever reason, Romeo looked, moved, and sounded like a street kid. Shithead looked, moved, and sounded like a street kid on TV. By the time we got to him wiping out on the motorcycle, the argument was over. Even the suits had sat back in their seats and surrendered.

So that's how a big chunk of budget ended up buying Shithead out of his contract and Romeo got the second male lead. We got the official word later that day while Sebastian and I were shooting a scene with Theresa Swann, the gorgeous actress who played our wicked stepmother. When we came off the set, Romeo was waiting in the parking lot on his own motorcycle. "Congratulations!" I said, hugging him. "I'm so glad."

"Thanks." He hugged me back tight before he let me go. "I'm glad, too."

"It's great, man," Sebastian said, giving Romeo's shoulder a squeeze. "You're going to be awesome." He gave me a quick grin. "Hey, you know what? I left my…something in the make-up trailer." He winked. "Ro, keep my kid sister company a second. I'll be right back."

I blushed bright red as my brother ran back toward the set. "He's subtle, isn't he?"

Romeo was smiling. "He's great."

"Yeah, he is." Suddenly I felt shy. The last time I'd been alone with him, we'd been naked. "Anyway, I can't believe I get to have you as my boyfriend—in the movie, I mean." I would have dearly loved to sink under the asphalt and disappear.

"I can't believe I get to be your boyfriend." He was holding my hand. "How'd I get so lucky?"

"It's not luck." I shivered, happy down to my toes. "You're really, really talented."

"So are you." I was looking straight into his eyes, and just as suddenly I didn't feel shy at all. "I saw the trailer for your Germany movie today before work," he said. "Holy shit, angel." He was so beautiful just looking at him made me dizzy, and I saw a sadness in his eyes that made me want to wrap myself around him and never let him go. "You were amazing."

"Really?" Hearing him say it made me tingle all over. "You really liked it?"

"Yeah, I did," he said, laughing. "I can't wait to see the movie."

"They made me look really young, though," I said. "I'm only supposed to be about twelve, I think."

"Yeah, I couldn't believe it was filmed after we…" This time, he was the one who blushed, and it was adorable. "After we met."

"Yeah, they had to tape my boobs down and everything." Lord, I was such a goof. "I hated it."

"I bet." He looked serious. "Listen, it's a weird time to bring it up, but I wanted to talk to you about that night when we met, to tell you…I'm going to pay you back. I'm so sorry."

"It's totally okay," I hurried to assure hm. "I understand you needed the money."

"Those guys you saw at the house—my sister, Amy, owed them a shitload of money," he said. "But that's all over now, the drugs and everything. Amy's clean, and I don't have to take care of her anymore."

"Ro, it's okay." I put my hands on either side of his face, making him look at me. "Absolutely, positively, unequivocally okay. Okay?"

He smiled. "Okay." He took my hand and kissed the wrist. "But there's something else I think I might need to tell you."

"There he is!" Fiona's voice interrupted. She was coming toward us across the parking lot with Sebastian trailing behind her. "Wallace

Cole's amazing new discovery." She nudged me aside with perfect grace and hugged Romeo. "The next big thing," she finished with a grin, kissing him on the lips.

"We should celebrate," Sebastian said. He put his arm around my shoulders and squeezed. "Come on, Fiona, ride with us. I've got the Mercedes."

"That's okay," she said. "Romeo can take me on the bike."

I knew that was my cue. I could have said, "He can't; he's taking me." Or Romeo could have said, "I can't; I'm taking Scarlett." But he didn't. So I didn't either.

"Awesome," I said instead. My eyes met Romeo's for barely a moment before I looked away. "We'll meet you at the Whiskey."

CHAPTER 17

That's what it was for the next three weeks as we filmed the movie—me wanting Romeo, me believing that Fiona was fucking him. Sebastian kept insisting that she wasn't, that Romeo was holding her off, but after that first night at the Whiskey, I couldn't make myself believe him. Everywhere we went, she was all over him, and he didn't seem to mind. It was sickening, and I was miserable, but I was too much of a wimp to even try to do anything about it. I couldn't even get mad at Romeo, though I hated Fiona's guts a little bit more every day. But I pretended I didn't care at all, that I was happy, that everything was hunky-dory fine.

The only time I could let the real me out was on the set. The only time I wasn't acting was when I was acting. I filled the stereotypical teen-age virgin I was playing with all the spooky, twisted adolescent yearning for my biker beloved that I didn't dare to show for real. Cole adored it. He told me every day—hell, every take—that I was perfect. But I could tell Sebastian was worried. He knew me too well to be fooled, and he knew I wasn't eating or sleeping, that I was completely wretched. "Just tell him you like him," he kept pleading. "He'll dump Fiona like a rock."

"I can't," I kept answering. "Leave me alone." I knew he was just being my big brother, that Romeo couldn't want me, not if Fiona wanted him. But finally, one early morning after a sleepless night, I heard my brother come in downstairs from a night shoot and decided to ask for his help.

My brother was in the living room, eating cereal and milk from a mixing bowl and watching old cartoons. "Hey bubba," I said, sitting down on the sofa beside him. There was a cold beer open on the coffee table in front of him and an open pack of cigarettes. "How was your shoot?"

"Useless." He took a big bite of cereal, his eyes focused on the TV screen. "Fiona was all fucked up. She and Romeo had some kind of big fight, and he roared off on his motorcycle, and she was just for shit. We blew so many takes, we ended up losing the light—or losing the dark, I mean."

"Ugh." I tried to sound sympathetic, but of course I was secretly thrilled. "How was Cole?"

"How do you think? He went bananas." He took a swallow of his beer, making me flinch. "Harry suggested we shoot day for night, and Cole threatened to fire him." Harry had been Cole's go-to cinematographer since before Sebastian and I were born. He was the closest thing our psycho director had to a best friend.

"What did Harry do?" I pulled the cashmere throw off the back of the sofa and wrapped it around me.

"He told Cole to fuck off and left." He went back to his cereal. "So the producer sent everybody home."

"Lovely." I would have been more worried if Cole's tantrums hadn't closed down the set twice already since filming started. "Fiona is such a bitch."

"No, she isn't." Sebastian didn't sound mad, just tired. "She's the only one being honest. She likes Ro, and she's acting like she likes Ro, and she doesn't care who knows it. Meanwhile, you just keep standing around making the big sad eyes like a little lost puppy."

"I do not!" I tried not to notice how much that had sounded like a yelp.

"You do so." He was still watching cartoons, not looking at me.

"And Romeo, poor bastard, is so confused he doesn't know what to think. He's just trying to keep everybody happy and not fuck up the first real job he's ever had."

"I can't believe you think this is all my fault." I didn't want to think about how anybody else was feeling; I was too wrapped up in my own luscious pain. "You really do like Fiona, don't you?"

"You know I do," he said. "You used to like her, too, remember?"

"She's great," I agreed. "She is; she really is." I grabbed his arm. "Please, bubba, please please please please please, just try to like her like a girlfriend. Just ask her out, just kiss her or something. You'll like it—she's gorgeous."

"Sissy, stop being stupid--"

"I'm not," I insisted. "You're right; she's awesome..."

"Sissy..."

"And you're gorgeous, and she likes you so much..."

"Just stop..."

"You guys would be great together..."

"I can't..."

"You can! Please, Sebastian, for me..."

"Scarlett, goddamnit, I can't!" He slammed his bowl down, sloshing milk across the coffee table. "I can't date Fiona. I can't want Fiona, not even for you." He finally looked at me, and I saw his eyes were rimmed in red. "Sissy, I'm gay."

I won't lie. I was shocked. "You're what?" No, I was horrified. "Are you serious?" It wasn't that I had any problem with anybody being gay, including my own darling brother. But I couldn't believe that I didn't know already, that he had this big, scary secret he hadn't told me, that he was separated from me by this incredibly important thing that I knew nothing about. I felt myself go pale; I actually felt faint.

"No, I'm kidding," he said, being sarcastic, hurt in his eyes.

At that moment, I got over my stupid self. All I wanted was to protect him from my shock, to do anything, swallow any hurt feelings I might have had that he'd kept it from me, deny any hint that I might feel anything but happy to hear about it now. He was my Sebastian, my twin, the other half of me. How could I look at him and see anything but perfection? I pulled him close and squeezed him tight and said, "Why didn't you tell me?"

"I don't know." He squeezed me back, and I heard tears in his voice. "I was scared, I guess." I stroked his hair. "I couldn't handle it if you freaked out or stopped talking to me."

"Oh yeah, like that could happen. Who else am I supposed to talk to?" I kissed his cheek. "Why should I care if you're gay? I wouldn't fuck you even if you weren't."

"Nice," he grumbled, giving me a pinch. He sat back, and we looked at one another, and we were okay again.

"So are you with somebody now?" I tried to picture what Sebastian's boyfriend would be like. He would have to be someone amazing.

"No." He picked up his cigarettes from the coffee table. "I was, but I'm not." He lit up and inhaled deeply, letting out the smoke in a cloud. "That's why I left New York." He sounded casual, but I knew better. I could hear him covering up some kind of pain. "I had a pretty dramatic break-up, very basic cable."

"What happened?" *What kind of idiot would let him go?* was what I really thought.

"It was this guy I knew from school, Henry. I think you met him once."

"Yeah." I remembered Henry. I remembered not being particularly impressed. I had wondered why Sebastian seemed to like him so much. "Didn't he have a girlfriend?"

"Emily, yeah." He took another drag off his cigarette. "Sweet precious mealy-mouthed little Emily whose daddy owns half of Wall Street. She was just for show, to keep his parents off his back."

"Did she know that?" I had liked her. She was the only one of Sebastian's New York friends who had actually talked to me.

"Is she your brother?" he shot back.

"Of course not." I took his hand that wasn't holding the cigarette. "You know I'm on your side."

He smiled at me, squeezing my hand. "I know. We were together for months, me and Henry, and it was great; I was happy; he was happy. But he got scared. He was applying to colleges, and his dad is this big jock." He scrubbed a tear from his cheek with the heel of his hand, the cigarette still burning between his fingers. "When he told me it was over, I freaked out. I loved him so much."

I took the cigarette and stubbed it out. "My poor baby bubba."

"It's okay." His brave smile told me it wasn't. I was his sister; I knew when his heart was broken. "I mean, it was months ago. I told him I'd tell people he was gay, and he panicked. We fought, but it wasn't that bad. We didn't hurt one another that bad, and we ended up fucking afterwards." He wasn't looking at me, but when he said this, he glanced at my face, gauging my reaction.

"So did you make up?" I said, making sure my expression didn't change.

"I thought we were going to." He took my hand and squeezed it again. "Then a couple of days later, Emily's brother jumped me in the boy's room at school."

"Oh my god—Sebastian…"

"He called me a faggot." I saw something in his eyes then that I'd never seen there before, sister or not, a hard, cold rage. I hated it; I hated the bastard who had inspired it; I hated Henry for breaking his heart. "I knew he really meant to hurt me. He was a lot bigger than me."

"Sebastian!" I was much more appalled by this than I was that he was gay. How could something like this have happened to him, and he not tell me about it? How dare anybody try to hurt him?

He laughed, short and shaky. "So I hurt him first. I grabbed a mop out of the janitor's bucket and beat the living shit out of him."

"Good for you," I said.

"I told him if he came after me again, I'd rip his head off and fuck it on the podium at morning chapel," he finished, snickering again.

"Good for you," I said again.

"Yeah, well, the school didn't think so," he said, but he looked straight at me and smiled. "They called my mother, and she flipped completely out, of course. She couldn't even look at me. She told me it was my problem, that she washed her hands of it."

"Oh my god…" I could just hear Greta saying it. *This is too ugly; you are not my problem anymore.*

"So I called Ranhosky." Ranhosky had been our father's lawyer since before we were born, and his friend much longer than that. He was the one who paid my bills and hired my servants and checked up on me at school. I had never spent much time with him, but I knew he and Sebastian had talked a fair amount since Sebastian moved to New York. "I told him everything," he said, putting an arm around my shoulders and pulling me close. "I begged him not to tell Daddy, and he didn't. He came to New York and got my money released from my trust somehow and fixed it."

"So what did Greta do then?" I asked, nestled against his shoulder.

"Nothing," he said. "She acted like she didn't know anything about it, like it hadn't happened. Except that she stopped talking to me or looking at me." I could feel him shaking, but his voice was steady and scornful. "Like I care."

"Of course you care, stupid." I hugged him, my arms around his waist.

"I didn't even tell her I was leaving when I came out here this time." He kissed the top of my head. "But you notice she hasn't called to check on me yet."

"Bitch." I had my own reasons for hating Greta, but this was worse. She was Sebastian's mother; he was supposed to be her everything. She had taken him away from our father, away from me, because she said she needed to keep him with her, to keep him safe. "What about Henry?" He didn't say anything for so long, I drew back and looked at him. "What did he say?"

"Nothing." He was still shaking, worse than before. "I tried to call him, but he wouldn't answer. I even tried a couple of times from out here, but somebody had changed all his numbers, even the number at his parents' place." He laughed, but it sounded like a sob. "This other guy we knew sent me a letter. He said Henry had changed schools, that he and Emily had both gone away."

"Oh honey…" I hugged him close and held him so tightly my arms ached. "It's going to be okay."

He squeezed me back. "Of course it is." I could hear the Sebastian I knew through his tears. "I'm going to be a big movie star, and so are you, and so is Romeo, and you guys are going to fall madly in love and have a bunch of babies, and it's all going to be awesome."

"I love you." I put my head on his shoulder. "Right now, I just love you."

CHAPTER 18

In the movie, mine and Romeo's characters finally become a couple at this big bonfire on the beach, a crowd scene with virtually everybody in the cast in it at some point. We worked on the sequence every night for a week, and the scene with me and Romeo took one whole night by itself. Cole wanted to film it in one long tracking shot the same way he'd shot 'Bastian and Fiona for the beginning of the movie, the camera-wolf stalking her prey. So everything had to be perfect—the movement of the camera on the track, the extras partying around the fire in the background, the boom mike over our heads. Our remembering our lines and hitting our marks was the least of it, or so it seemed. A hundred different people were working their asses off around us. All we had to do was fall in love.

When the scene started, I was moving around the edge of the crowd, looking for my brother. The party was mostly schoolkids, but there were gypsies scattered around. Some drunk guy in a football jersey came stumbling past me and almost knocked me down, but Romeo's character caught me.

"Thanks," I said, smiling up at him like he was the greatest thing ever.

"What are you doing here?" He wasn't supposed to be glad to see me. "You shouldn't be here." He was still holding on to me, and he looked like he wanted to kiss me, and I'm sure it was obvious how much I wanted to kiss him. Then he let me go.

"I'm just looking for my brother," I said. "My stepmother said he would be here."

"Don't listen to her." The barest trace of the vaguely Eastern European accent all the older gypsy characters were putting on crept into his speech. "Whatever she tells you, it's a lie."

"So he isn't here?" I kind of hated that my character was so stupid. Cole called her innocent. I called her dumb as a box of wet mice.

"He's here, somewhere. With Natasha." Natasha was Fiona's character.

"Hey, cutie, come on," another guy, a frat-boy-looking dude, said, coming into the shot and making a grab for my hand. "Come dance with me!" It was his only line.

"Get away from her!" Romeo pushed him away with a little more force than was probably necessary. "Leave her alone." The other kid wandered away looking pissed.

"He was just asking me to dance, Marco." I knew I probably sounded too flirtatious, too knowing. Cole would probably make us do it again. "Do you want to dance with me?" I remembered dancing with him in my living room at home and the first time he really kissed me.

"We need to get you out of here," he said, looking straight into my eyes. The camera was moving around us, watching us both in turn; we had to be perfectly on mark. But you never would have known, watching him, that he knew there was a camera there at all. "You're not safe."

"Would I be safe with you?" I couldn't stop myself from touching him, putting both hands on his chest, or from ad-libbing the line that came into my head. "Will you keep me safe?"

"Always."

His answer was an ad lib, too, and so was the kiss. He grabbed my wrists and yanked me close so fast I lost my balance. I fell against him as his mouth came down on mine, and he held me up. I slumped against him, forgetting the camera, forgetting everything but the taste of his mouth and the way he felt holding me. *Now,* I thought, *this moment. This is what I want.*

"Cut!" Cole was loud, but he didn't sound unhappy. "Save some spit for the next take." We stepped apart, barely making eye contact. "Okay, let's go again," Cole said. "Keep the new lines; I like it."

"I'm sorry," Romeo said to me as the techies scrambled to reset the scene.

"Don't be; I'm the one who blew the line." One of the P.A.s handed me a bottle of water. "Wait, can I get a soda instead?"

She smiled. "Sure, be right back."

"You didn't blow it," Romeo said. A make-up assistant was putting powder on his forehead. "You made it better." She stepped back, fluffed his hair over it, then went away. "I meant kissing you like that," he finished.

"I liked it." I could feel myself blushing, but I smiled. "You made it better, too."

"All right, what's the hold up?" Cole was shouting. If he'd had one of those old-fashioned megaphones, I swear we would have all been deaf. "Let's go again."

We did take after take through the night, and at first it was great. There was nothing I wanted to be doing more than spending the night kissing Romeo. But then we started bleeding into the time for one of Sebastian and Fiona's set-ups, and Fiona came out to the set to watch while they were waiting. After every take, she would dance out on the set and give Romeo her own big fat kiss, squeezing his ass or whispering something in his ear. Once I even saw her reach down and fondle his crotch before I could turn away. Finally, Cole yelled at her and told her to get the fuck off the set and stay off until she was called.

"I'm sorry," Romeo said to me as they were resetting the cameras.

"For what?" For a little while, I had forgotten that she was his real girlfriend, that he and I were just playing pretend. But I remembered now.

"For Fiona." He looked embarrassed; even I could see that. But

Cole was the one who had told her to go away, not him. So even if she had embarrassed him, he must have liked it. "She just…"

"Please, God, it's fine." I couldn't look him in the eye for more than a few seconds at a time, but otherwise, I thought I was doing pretty well. "I get it; she's a dish." I took another sip. "And she can totally help you."

"Help me?" he repeated.

"Well, yeah." Now I couldn't look him in the eye at all. "I mean, she's a pretty big deal, and she knows fucking everybody. You'll meet people with her, and when you go out, you'll be photographed."

"Is that what you think?" He had taken a step closer to me and leaned in, his face barely inches from mine. "You think if I'm with her, it's because of what she can do for my career?"

"No," I said, barely able to breathe. He sounded hurt and angry, and while I hated it, I liked it, too, liked that I could hurt him. "She's beautiful, and she's funny…" I paused, giving him time to disagree, but of course he didn't. "But there's nothing wrong with taking advantage of the other thing if it's there. What's that expression? It's as easy to fall in love with a famous woman as a nobody?"

He was staring at me, obviously aghast. "Do you really think this way? You're just a kid."

"I'm the same age you are, Romeo, and everybody thinks this way," I cut him off. "If you really want to be an actor, you better get used to it." He shook his head, swearing under his breath. "And sorry for saying it, sweetie, but you're a funny one to be playing so naïve."

His eyes met mine, and he smiled, bitter and beautiful. "Good shot."

"I'm sorry." I was so furious with him for picking Fiona over me I could have punched him, even though I knew she was the only logical choice. I wanted him to want me for reasons that weren't logical, reasons that no one else could see. I wanted him to want me for qualities I couldn't define or even know I had. "I'm not trying to be mean."

"Whatever, angel," he said, starting to turn away.

"Romeo, wait." Angel was what he had called me in bed; I couldn't stand him calling me that now, couldn't stand for him to think I was awful. "Tell me what I'm supposed to say," I said, holding on to his arm. "Am I supposed to be jealous?" He was looking me straight in the eyes again, and I shivered as I smiled. "I can totally be jealous."

He smiled back, and this time it looked real. "Don't hurt yourself." He touched my cheek, and I felt a tingle to my toes. "You know, I do like Fiona, but…it's not…" He laughed, turning his head away. "Whatever."

"It's okay," I said, interrupting him. "You don't have to tell me anything." I felt physical pain in my chest as I made myself finish. "It really isn't any of my business."

"Let's go, let's go," Cole shouted. "Just one more tonight."

We did one more take. The others had felt natural and fun, but this one was awkward and angry and painful. I think it's the one that ended up in the movie.

CHAPTER 19

It's probably hard to believe it, but this conversation with Romeo had no negative effect whatsoever on our chemistry at work. In my case, I think it helped. With the cameras rolling and lines from a script in my mouth, I could do and say and feel everything inside of me for him that I couldn't express anywhere else. The only problem was that, eventually, I had to watch his character die.

We had been shooting our death sequence for about a week, and we were almost done. We had done the beginning—us making out (pure bliss and exquisite agony for me), him pushing for more, and me saying no and running away into the dark, scary funhouse. And we had filmed the end—me running through a maze of mirrors with the killer in pursuit and almost, but not quite, making it outside. We had gotten my actual moment of death in two takes at the very end of a long shooting day, no muss, no fuss at all. Now all that was left was the pivot in the middle—me finding Romeo in a pool of his own blood, watching him die, seeing the killer, and running away.

In most slasher flicks, they would have used a Romeo dummy. He would have been dead as rock and fake as silicon when I found him. I would have let out a single scream, seen the maniac, and run like a hell —a sequence of ninety seconds. But we were working for Wallace

Cole. So the slaughtered body was a real live boy, soaked in stage blood with a slash wound in his throat that could have fooled a doctor standing half a foot away—the guy who designed and made it has since won four Oscars, one for directing a feature of his own. And Romeo wasn't supposed to be dead yet when I found him. He was supposed to be alive and trying desperately to warn me about the maniac behind me through his ruined throat, then die in my arms.

I sat in a folding chair just off set for two hours waiting while they tested and retested the pump apparatus that made him gush blood from his throat and his mouth when he tried to speak—they wouldn't let me leave in case they got it. "We need to get this one in one, pussycat," Cole confided to me. The crew was setting up a second camera so they could shoot both of our close-ups at once. "If this thing works, it won't work more than once."

"Don't worry," I said, wondering vaguely why my scalp was tingling and my hands felt cold. "We'll get it."

"That's my girl." He gave me a pat on the head, and I flinched. "Let's go."

Romeo and I didn't speak before the take. Good little acting student that he was, he was probably "in the moment." Me, I was having an out-of-body experience. As soon as I looked down at him, I felt so dizzy and sick I thought I might pass out. I closed my eyes and got down on my knees beside him, my opening position for the shot. *Not real,* I chanted silently inside my head. *Not Stella.* I heard the dragonfly buzz of the light meter close beside my cheek, and I felt someone touching my hair, making it match the last shot where I had fallen to my knees. "None of this is real." I realized my lips were moving, that I had spoken aloud. I opened my eyes and found Romeo looking up at me, a question in his eyes. But he was dead; except he wasn't. Except maybe he was.

"The Funhouse, scene 94, take one," the clapper operator said, calling the scene.

"Roll camera," Cole said. I could hear the blood pump churning behind Romeo's shoulder. "And...action."

"Marco," I made myself say, my first line. "Marco, oh my God." The camera was so close, I thought I might bump my forehead on it as I leaned over him. "Oh my God." I touched his face, real tears choking me and running down my cheeks. His eyes were so beautiful, looking up at me. He opened his mouth and tried to speak, and blood gushed from his lips and throat on cue, a trickling fountain of blood from the wound that pumped in weak spurts, barely spattering my mouth. "No," I said, crying, forgetting the script. "I can't." I kissed him, tasting candy blood. "Please..." I nuzzled my cheek against his and felt the tension leave his body, felt him die. Drawing back, I saw the life fade from his eyes. I didn't remember where I was or what I was supposed to be doing. I felt possessed by someone else, someone too little and scared to understand what was happening. I dropped my head to his shoulder and sobbed, clutching him to me, begging incoherently for something to save him, for him to come back. My camera was tracking backward as the camera behind me moved aside out of the shot, but I noticed this in a weird, vague, disconnected way, like I was watching from across the room.

"Scarlett." Cole's voice came to me like something in a dream. "See the killer."

No, I thought, head down, still clinging desperately to Romeo. *I don't want to see him. If I see him, he'll have to kill me, too.*

"Scarlett," Cole said again. He wasn't scolding me; his voice was very gentle. "Now. It's time."

I raised my head and looked at the camera, but I didn't see it. "No." The camera came closer, but I was still seeing something—someone— else. "Get away." I heard the whirring of the camera and the buzz of the lights. *Not real,* I thought again, but I wasn't sure quite what or which I meant. "No!" I screamed aloud, springing to my feet. Turning on my heel, I staggered then ran from the shot.

"Cut!" Cole called, triumphant. 'Let's set up for the long shot." A production assistant came forward with a blanket to wrap around my shoulders, and I realized I was shaking. "We'll use the doubles," Cole said, looking at me. "Good work, kids."

"We should do it again," I said. I felt frozen, like a zombie. Romeo was sitting up, but he was covered with techies disengaging the pump.

I met his eyes with mine for barely a moment, then looked back at Cole. "Just one more time, to be sure."

"No, pussycat, we got it." He smiled at me. "It's good."

I clutched the blanket more tightly around me and headed for the trailer I shared with Fiona and two other girls, locking the door behind me so I couldn't be disturbed. I grabbed the phone and dropped to my hands and knees on the floor, my energy exhausted before I could get to a chair. I made myself sit up and punched the number I had for my father, fighting tears. "This is Scarlett," I said calmly to the voice that answered. "I need to speak to Calvin."

There was a pause as I heard the rumble of a muffled conversation. Then the voice came back, kind, friendly, and completely unfamiliar. "Scarlett, he's kind of in the middle of something," he said. "Can he call you back?"

A scream rose in my throat, so strong I had to put my hand over my mouth to hold it back.

"Scarlett?" the voice repeated. "Are you there?" I still couldn't answer. "Are you all right?"

I closed my eyes and forced myself to breathe. "I'm here." I still sounded shaky, so I took another breath. "I'm fine." I was clutching the receiver so tightly my hand hurt, so I forced it to relax. "I'm on the set," I said, making myself smile. "Tell him I'll call him back."

"Great," the voice said, smiling back. "I'll tell him."

I tried to hang up, but the receiver was stuck to my hand, sticky with corn syrup blood. "I'll take a shower," I decided, barely noticing I was talking out loud. I peeled the receiver out of my hand very carefully and set it on the floor, then yanked the cord out of the wall with a single jerk. I went into the bathroom and turned on the water, and as I did it, I was vaguely aware of someone knocking on the trailer door. But I ignored it.

I was wearing a camisole shirt. I reached down to take it off and realized it was completely plastered to my skin with drying blood. Trembling again, I looked up and caught sight of my reflection in the mirror. My face was covered from the nose down in red like a veil. My hands were thick with it to the elbows. Even my legs, bare under shorts, were spattered with droplets of red. I suddenly realized I had seen this before, that I wasn't me. It wasn't me who was supposed to be dying, covered in blood. I was smelling something that couldn't be real, the smell of rotten meat. I balled up both fists and smashed them hard into the mirror, shattering my reflection. A man's face swam before my eyes for barely a moment, a ghost from a past I had made myself forget. I hit the jagged glass again and barely felt it slice into the fleshy heel of my hand. Looking down, I saw the scar that had been on my wrist most of my life, the one I never acknowledged that I had, the cut my father had pretended wasn't there when he found me. Someone was calling my name, but I could barely hear them over the buzzing of hallucinated flies. My throat hurts, I realized. I was screaming. But I couldn't hear it. I crumpled to the floor, my stomach heaving, reality just gone.

I heard a crash and footsteps, and then Romeo was there. I saw him see me, saw shock in his eyes, saw his lips form words, but I couldn't hear him. It was like I was split into two people again, one crazy as a shithouse rat, the other standing off to the side, just watching. The Watcher wanted to tell him not to worry, that I would be all right. But Crazy wouldn't let her. He was putting his arms around me, and I pressed my face against his throat, now whole and warm and real. I breathed in the warm, clean smell of him and tried hard to pull it together. He was holding me, the thing I wanted most in all the world, and I was blowing it, screaming like a lunatic. He dragged me to my feet and into the shower, still holding me close. As the hot water streamed over me, the two halves of me started coming together again. I started to be aware of things that were real, the stinging pain in my bleeding hand and the feel of his arms around me. I stopped screaming and started crying instead, my hands like claws clutching at his shirt. "I'm sorry," I kept saying, humiliated and hurting and still so scared that I was shaking all over.

"For what?" He sounded on the point of tears himself, and his southern accent was back. "Come on now." He tried to steer me out of the shower again. "We need to get you to the nurse."

"No!" I knew they would think I was crazy. It would be like

when I was a little kid, like when Greta kept trying to put me in therapy. They would try to make me talk about Stella and everything else. They would give me pills that might even make me want to talk. I had heard enough about people having breakdowns to know what would happen, and I knew I couldn't stand it. I might even slip up and talk about the Dane. They would have to tell Calvin, and he would think he had failed me. It would be like when Greta left us, only worse. I was barely seventeen, but I already had so many secrets I was choking on them, so many lies to protect. "I can't," I told him, fighting to get away from him. As much as I wanted him to hold me, I couldn't let him take me to the nurse. "Let me go!"

"All right, honey, hang on." He didn't let go of me, but he stopped trying to make me move. "I won't make you do anything you don't want to do, baby, I promise." He kissed me, soft little kisses all over my face. "But you're hurt."

"I'll be okay, I promise." Looking up into his eyes, I think I knew he loved me. That's the way I remember it, looking up at him and knowing he was mine. "I don't want to be crazy," I confessed to him, as much truth as I could possibly have told. "I just want to go home and be safe."

Bless him, he looked so horribly confused. "Scarlett..."

Before he could say any more, I kissed him. I pushed him back into the shower and lunged for him like I was drowning, which, honestly, I kind of was. He didn't fight my kiss, far from it. But when I took hold of the hem of his T-shirt and started pulling it up his stomach, he caught my hands and tried to stop me. He dragged his mouth away from mine and said, "Wait."

"I don't want to." I leaned in and kissed his throat open-mouthed then slid down to my knees in front of him, the hot water still pouring down on both of us. I pushed his T-shirt up again and kissed his stomach, the soft, wet line of hair down from his navel to the soaking denim of his fly. I didn't know what I was doing—I mean, I knew what, of course. I just didn't know how to do it. But I wanted him, to feel how we were both alive, to feel the way I had felt that night before

Berlin when I had fallen asleep in his arms. I fumbled the buttons open on his fly, and blood from my hand stained his jeans.

He caught my hands and stepped back out of the shower then fell to his knees, too, pulling me close to kiss my mouth. I climbed out from under the water, my mouth still feeding desperately on his as I crawled over him, the two of us falling slowly to the floor with me on top. We fucked there on the floor in a sopping, bloody puddle of our clothes, and I came like a rocket, everything I felt and couldn't say exploding in sex instead of words. When it was over, tears were streaming down my cheeks, but I was happy. I felt like everything that had hurt or scared me ever had been washed out of me, gone forever. I've heard people describe the sensation of shooting up heroin, and it always makes me think of sex with Romeo.

"Don't cry, sweetheart," he said, kissing my tears away. He sat up and held me on his lap, and I draped my arms around his neck, so sleepy I could barely hold my eyes open. The shower was still pouring, probably cold as ice, but we ignored it. He took my hand and turned it up so he could see the cut.

"It was just an accident," I promised. "I didn't do it on purpose."

He turned my face up to his, searching my eyes with his like he wasn't sure he could believe me. Then he kissed me softly on the mouth. "Is there anyone at home for you?"

"No." *Is Fiona waiting somewhere?* I thought. "Sebastian is out of town."

"It's okay." He wrapped his arms around me, pressing me close. "I'll take you home." He kissed the top of my head. "I won't leave you anymore."

CHAPTER 20

The studio held the wrap party for *The Funhouse* at the
Roosevelt Hotel in Hollywood. But it wasn't so much a
party for the people who'd finished filming as a publicity
stunt to let the crowds and the paparazzi on Sunset Boulevard get
their first gawp at the fresh meat in the cast. Sebastian and I arrived
together in the back of a chauffeured limousine, and even though
there was no official red carpet, the sidewalk was lined with photographers. Sebastian jumped out like an old pro, but I hung back. I had
walked carpets with my father dozens of times, but I had always been
in the background. Nobody had ever cared if they got my picture
before.

"Come on, Sissy." Sebastian gave me his hand and helped me out of
the car. A pair of studio handlers came hurrying over to flank us.
They didn't even speak to us, just started herding us down the aisle.

I had just caught sight of Romeo ahead of us when for the first
time in my life a photographer shouted, "Scarlett!" Romeo turned
around, and our eyes met at the exact same second the flash went off.
Two seconds later, I was surrounded by flashing lights and the shouts
of strangers calling my name and giving me directions. "Look this
way! Turn around! Come on, honey, smile!"

I tried to get a tighter hold on my brother, but he was moving back, giving me room to pose. I felt panicked, turning in a jerky circle like a doll on a broken music box, trying to hear what they were saying. I turned and saw Romeo again, and he smiled.

I smiled back. I consciously relaxed my shoulders and turned back toward the cameras. "That's it!" one of the photographers shouted, and I turned my smile on him. I was still terrified, but I wasn't paralyzed any more. I did a silly little twirl to make the frilly skirt of my party dress swirl out then stopped and laughed. The flashes went off even faster. Photographers from further down the line were moving in to focus on me, jostling for position. I reached for Sebastian again, drawing him close to me and cuddling up to his side, laying my head on his shoulder.

"Scarlett!" I heard Fiona's voice right behind me. I barely had time to turn around before she had caught me up in a hug like I was her long-lost sister. "Look at you!" She drew back and framed my face in her hands. The photographers went wild. "You look beautiful." She touched her forehead to mine, a lipstick-safe kiss.

"So do you." She took my hand and turned to the photographers with a dazzling smile of her own. She did look beautiful; her funky and fabulous Betsey Johnson made my blue off the rack look like a little girl's birthday party frock. "You always do."

"Romeo!" she called, letting go of me to run to him. She hugged him the same way she had hugged me, and Sebastian nudged me from behind, urging me forward. Romeo caught my eye over Fiona's shoulder and winked, making me laugh.

"Hey Scarlett!" I heard my name again over the general roar, this time coming from the crowd of photographers. "Scarlett!" A tall, skinny man in a white dress shirt buttoned all the way up had pushed his way to the front of the pack. He had a press badge sticking out of his pocket and a camera hanging around his neck. He saw me see him and raised the camera. "Do you remember your mom?"

"Yes." His flash went off. "Of course I do."

One of the studio handlers moved in front of me, blocking his shot. The other one touched me on the elbow. "Come on, Miss Cross," she said into my ear. "It's time to go inside."

"What?" I felt a little faint. "Who was that guy?"

"Never mind," the handler said. She was trying to nudge me along, but my feet were planted.

"Why did he ask about Stella?" I wanted to see his face again—something about him was familiar.

"Hey sweetheart." Romeo took my hand, gracefully brushing the handler aside. "You okay?"

"Yeah...no...I'm not sure." Clinging to his hand, I pushed the other handler out of the way to look for the weird photographer, but he was gone. I looked up at Romeo. "I guess I'm okay."

He squeezed my hand. "Let's go inside."

As we walked through the lobby, I saw Sebastian talking to a smiling older couple dressed in casual dinner clothes—tourists staying at the Roosevelt, no doubt. I waved as we walked by, and he waved back. Fiona was doing an interview just outside the doors to the pool bar where they were holding the party. The whole patio was crawling with reporters. "I see more press than actors," Romeo said. "And there are barely any crew guys here at all."

"I know, right?" I was glad I still had a grip on his arm. I had never been interviewed before and wasn't keen on it now. "Sebastian said in the car it would probably be like this. They're really pushing to sell the movie."

"Yeah." He didn't sound any more enthused than I felt, and he was keeping a pretty firm grip on my arm, too. "I reckon we're the product."

"Just the commercial." I had been hearing about the reality of being a movie star since I was four years old; I had just never thought about it as something that applied to me. "But all we have to do is be beautiful." I smiled up at him. "Trust me, you've got it covered."

"Hey, you." He turned and wrapped his arms around me, and I giggled, sliding my arms around his neck. He pushed me behind a potted palm and kissed me. I could hear cameras hissing and see lights flashing even with my eyes closed, but I couldn't have cared less.

"Hey kids!" Sebastian appeared out of nowhere, reaching past Romeo to pull me back out into the open. Fiona was right behind him. "No fair lurking in the shadows. We have to circulate and be charming." Cole's voice suddenly rose over the noise of the crowd—he was ranting at someone on the other side of the patio. "Or we could just go watch the train wreck," Sebastian snickered.

"Oh god," Fiona moaned.

"Relax," Romeo said. He and Sebastian were both grinning; they both thought Cole was a stitch. "He's just giving them a show."

One of the producers, a friend of Calvin's that Sebastian and I had known since we were babies, came hurrying up to us, looking frazzled. "Wanna help me save an idiot's life?" she said, her cheeks flushed pink in spite of the chilly breeze coming off the pool.

Sebastian kissed her cheek. "Relax, honey." In that moment, he looked and sounded exactly like our father. "Cole's just being himself."

"That's what I'm afraid of." She took my hand and squeezed it, and her palm was sweaty. "Come distract him, kids, won't you?"

"Yeah, of course," I said. I reached for Romeo, but Fiona blocked me.

"You and Sebastian go ahead," she said. "I've got some people I want Romeo to meet."

I didn't like it, but there wasn't much I could do without causing a scene. "I'll see you later," I told Romeo. He had just enough time to smile and wink at me before the producer whisked me away.

An hour later, I was finally able to wriggle free of a conversation between Cole and a friend of his who wanted him to do a think piece on how kids today were basically selfish assholes or some such crap. The actress playing the wicked stepmother was on the dance floor with Sebastian, laughing and looking as young and beautiful as any of us. I didn't see Romeo or Fiona anywhere.

I caught one of the other girls in the cast. "Hey, Stacy, have you seen Romeo?"

She blushed like I'd caught her in a lie before she even opened her mouth. "I don't...he was here a minute ago, but I don't know." She looked over my shoulder toward the bar. "You want to get a drink?"

"Sure." A photographer stepped in front of us, and we stopped to pose like best friends forever, arms around one another's waists. She was in heels; my head barely reached her shoulder. The photographer thanked us, and we headed for the bar.

"Two colas," Stacy told the bartender. "Diet for me."

"Not diet for me," I said.

"Lucky you," Stacy said. The bartender poured our drinks, and we took them. "It must be good genes."

"I guess." Truth be told, I hadn't learned yet that I was supposed to be constantly worrying about what I ate and drank. "Thanks, Stacy. I'm going to go find Romeo."

"Scarlett, wait." She caught my arm. "Just...he'll be back in a minute, okay?"

I liked Stacy. We had done some scenes together, and I thought she was talented and fun. But I also knew she pretty well worshipped Fiona. "What's going on?" I asked her. "Is he with Fiona?"

"Scarlett..."

"Did they leave?"

"No, of course not."

"But they are together."

"Scarlett, honey, just chill." People were starting to look at us. "It's no big deal, all right? You can't get so worked up about everything."

"I am not worked up." I was, but I was trying hard to hide it. "If Romeo wants to be somewhere with Fiona, he can be."

"He doesn't," she said. "That's the whole issue; he doesn't. She had to practically drag him out of here." I could see from her face she was wishing she had stayed out of the whole thing. "Look, Scar, I like you, and I know you're just a kid, and you didn't do it on purpose. But you totally fucked Fiona over on this Romeo thing. She feels like an idiot."

"I didn't!" But I had. What's worse, I knew I had, had known it when I was doing it. Worst of all, I knew some part of me had done it on purpose, that the meanest little slice of me had wanted Romeo out of jealousy as much as love, at least at the beginning of the shoot. But I wouldn't dare admit it to Stacy.

"You won, all right? And nobody blames you." She put her arm around my waist again and steered me back toward the cameras at the center of the party. "You can afford to be generous."

Later, a few of us went to a smaller club down the Strip for a more private party. This was where the cast with most of the crew were really celebrating the end of the shoot. Romeo was already there when Sebastian and I got there, sitting in a back booth with a couple of guys from the house band. They were deep in conversation when I walked up, but Romeo reached out and took my hand and kissed it. "Hey sweetheart," he said as I slid in beside him, kissing me softly on the lips. "You want a drink?"

"I'm okay." I liked the feeling of sliding into his life as it was happening without causing a fuss, like I had always been there, like I belonged. "Sebastian is getting me a beer."

He kissed my cheek and put his arm around me, dragging me deeper into the booth. I stayed that way for more than an hour, drowsing against his shoulder, sipping my beer, barely talking but happy. Other people came and went, the band, the bouncer, techies from the movie shoot, Sebastian and some guy he and Romeo both knew from acting class. Nobody ignored me; everybody spoke to me. But nobody seemed to expect anything from me or to wonder why I was there. And it was bliss.

Finally, just as the band was starting their last set well after midnight, I looked up and realized Romeo and I were alone. "Hey," I said, smiling at him. "Fancy meeting you here."

He smiled and kissed me, pulling me closer. "Fancy that." I had kicked off my heels at some point, and my legs were curled under me on the booth's vinyl bench. He blew out the candle on the table, putting us completely in the shadows. "God, you're beautiful."

"You too." I kissed him, climbing into his lap as gracefully as I could in the narrow booth. His mouth tasted sweet like whiskey. I wanted to melt into that kiss and forget everything else, to turn my brain off completely. But my jealous, nitpicky bitch of a brain refused to shut up. I drew back and touched his face. "I need to ask you something stupid."

He laughed. "Okay." He settled his hands on my hips. "Go ahead."

"At the party...at the Roosevelt..." My party dress was bunched halfway up my thighs. "I lost you for a little while." I scooted even closer, my hands laced behind his neck, and I felt him shiver. "Stacy said you had gone off with Fiona." *Scar, you're so stupid,* I thought. *What difference does it make?* I kissed the side of his neck. "Is that true?"

"I was with Fiona." He ran his hands up my thighs, pushing up my skirt even further. "She said she needed to talk to me."

"About what?" He caressed my ass around my thong, and I put my head on his shoulder, sliding my arms around him. "You don't have to tell me. I'm sorry." He felt so good, so perfect, I couldn't believe I was letting myself screw it up. "I don't want to be jealous."

"Angel, it's okay." He kissed my neck, my shoulder. "She wanted to explain why I'd be better off with her instead of you."

"That bitch!" I didn't move, but I yelped like I'd been scalded. I had suspected as much, but still, I was shocked to hear him say it.

He laughed. "Hey, she said exactly what you said before, that she was a big star and being with her would do great things for my career." He slid down the spaghetti strap of my dress.

I stopped him, catching his hand. "And what did you say?"

He looked into my eyes, and he didn't smile. "I said my career could go fuck itself." I laughed, and then he smiled. "What do you think I said?"

I thought for a second. I wanted to tell him the truth, to answer from my heart and not my fearful, fucked up head. "I think you told her you love me."

"I did." He kissed me. "I do." He cradled my cheek in his palm. "I told her she was a pretty, sexy girl, but that you're my angel. And whatever happens, as long as you want me, nothing is going to make me give you up."

"I love you." I wrapped my arms around him and held on to him with all my might. "I love you so much."

"I love you." This time I slid my own strap down, holding him as he brushed kisses down my collarbone, shivering to feel his warm breath on my skin. The club was almost empty; no one was watching us. I reached down and unzipped his pants.

"I love this song," I said softly in his ear though I barely knew what the band was playing. "Don't you?"

He snickered. "It's growing on me, yeah." His cock curved up hard in my grip. His was the only one I had ever touched, but I was learning its habits, learning what it liked. "Come here." He hooked two fingers in the leg hole of my panties and twisted. The lace dug into my flesh for barely a second, then it snapped. "Can you be quiet?"

"I can try." I grabbed a stack of napkins from the table and dropped it in his lap between us, then went back to stroking his cock. His fingertips played along the tender edges of my cleft, and I buried my face against the side of his neck, smothering a gasp. We both snickered breathlessly as I said, "I can try harder."

"You're perfect." He kissed my cheek as his finger found my clitoris, gasping himself as my grip tightened. The people so close by made it better, of course, urgent and intense. I leaned into his touch, matching my rhythm to his. My body longed for him; the shape of his cock in my hand made me remember the way he felt inside me. I came with a tiny sigh, and his arm around me crushed me closer, holding me still. He kissed me, his tongue pushing deep, and I felt his cock jerk in my hand, erupting into the napkins, the sudden, earthy smell of his coming making me spike again, crying out against his mouth. The band built to a climax of their own, the music drowning us out. I clung to him and thought nothing could be more perfect.

CLIPPING 7

An excerpt from "Bloody Murder! Director Wallace Cole on movies, madness, and these kids today." From *Infamy* magazine.

In the crazy genius world of 1970s film, Wallace Cole was a psycho among psychos. His gory epics of the Old and New West set a new standard in both shock and lyricism for American movies.

Then he went nuts. For almost a decade, Cole didn't just disappear from the Hollywood scene; he seemed to have disappeared from the planet. Now he's back with his take on that most tired of drive-in movie tropes—the teen scream slasher flick. The Funhouse, *set to open next month, tells the story of a beachside carnival haunted by a specter hungry for virgin blood and stars some of the hottest new names in Hollywood. And after this conversation with Cole, we're all kind of dying to see it.*

IF: So what makes your slasher flick better than the million or so crummy others we've all seen before?

WC:See, I'd love to be mad at you, man, but I can't because you're right. Most of those movies are shit. They start out with a script some studio hack used to wipe his ass back in 1958 then just change it around based on whatever set they can rent cheap that week—hey, my kid's summer camp is closing down, let's make a fucking movie! They hire a bunch of two-bit fashion models for the way they look, then they just stick'em together and hack'em to bits. And they film it like they might be selling toothpaste, no style whatsoever —and that's if they even bother to get a cinematographer who knows which way to point the camera in the first place.

IF:But yours is different?

WC:You bet your ass, Cochise. I've got a script written by a kid I met at AA, Billy Creel, the most twisted little motherfucker I ever met in my life. I love it; I didn't change a word of it.

IF:Your cast definitely sounds interesting, too.

WC:Ah, see, that's where it all happens, isn't it? Let me tell you how that went down. I went to the studio, and I already had my main cast, or most of it—I knew who I wanted. They went along for the most part—hell, why wouldn't they? I had already signed up Fiona [Fleming], who won a fucking Oscar when she was, what, six? [She was nine.] My old running buddy Calvin Cross is one of the producers, and I've got both his kids in it, and they're both...you know, just crazy, just brilliant, better than their old man.

But then the damned suits try to stick me with this TV kid, this Kevin Heath. And you know, it's all about chemistry; it's all about the juice between the characters. And this kid, he's in there doing Kookie or Fonzie or whatever the fuck, and it's just pathetic, and the kid opposite him knows it's pathetic, you can see it in her eyes. So I tell the suits, let me try something. I snatch a kid out of the background, a stunt driver, and put him in with this actress, this little Scarlett Cross, who's been giving him the eye all night, and all of a sudden, ka-boom, baby! We've got a scene. Romeo Kidd is his name, his actual name on his birth certificate. Can you believe it?

IF:Scarlett Cross has been getting some serious buzz from her work with Aksel Jorgen.

WC:Oh yeah, she's...people are going to have a powerful reaction to little Scarlett, I think.

IF:She's a little young for your movie, though, right? I heard that, too.

WC:Hey, she plays the baby sister; it's fine. But yeah, she was definitely the youngest member of the cast, and everybody was very aware of that, very careful. But I'll tell you...that's an old soul, man. Old and...okay, the mother, her mother, was murdered when she was still a baby, right? And the kid was there when it happened. Who knows what she saw? Who knows what a thing like that does to a kid? There are moments in this movie, this fucked-up little popcorn horror show, where the camera is on her, on that face, and she's got that thousand-mile stare, and you just know she's been there. Trust me, man, she'll break your heart. And her brother, Sebastian, same thing. You look at these kids, all of these kids, you listen to them, and you realize, holy fuck, they're just fucked up. I mean, they never had a chance, man. Think about it. We thought we were rebels, we thought we were cracking open the universe. But our parents were Ward and June Cleaver. We started out in the 50s; we were raised by the suits. These kids, the ones trying to find out where they're at now? They're ours, man. They were raised by us.

CHAPTER 21

In September, I went back to high school. *The Funhouse* was scheduled for release in late October, the Friday before Halloween. Fiona and Sebastian did a lot of press for it that whole month, magazine covers and stuff, but nobody really mentioned me or Romeo until Cole did an interview with *Infamy*, a semi-arty film and culture monthly out of New York. Sebastian read it out to me and Romeo in his best Cole impression, making us laugh until we cried. We were in the living room of my little guesthouse at Castle Asshole, Sebastian in a side chair, me and Romeo piled up together on the couch. It was pouring rain outside on a Saturday, and I was feeling cozy and content. I could totally ignore any upsetting details in what Cole had told his interviewer—like at the Roosevelt, he was giving them a show.

"Daddy is going to stroke out when he reads this," Sebastian said when he was done. "Cole is insane—after everything Dad did to help him get the movie made, I can't believe he would say all that stuff."

"Why not?" Romeo said. He laced his fingers with mine. "It's true, isn't it? Or most of it?"

"Oh yeah," Sebastian said, snickering. "We are all deeply fucked up."

"What I want to know is why everybody keeps talking about how much younger I am than everybody else," I said. "I'm not. Sebastian is only four months older than me, and you're only nine months older."

"Maybe so," Romeo said. "But your official bio from the studio says you're only fifteen." He grinned. "Believe me, Amy has pointed this out." Amy was his sister, the porn star. Technically he still lived with her, but these days, when I wasn't in school, he spent most of his time with me. "I've been wondering about that though. You and Sebastian were born the same year, but you have different moms."

"Yeppers," Sebastian said, snickering again as he flipped through the magazine.

"Calvin must have been taking his vitamins," Romeo said. He didn't sound impressed.

"Sebastian's mom was his actual girlfriend," I explained. "I think my mom, Stella, must have been a one-night stand."

Sebastian made a noise. "Hmmmm…not exactly." Suddenly my brother wasn't laughing any more. "Come on." He got up, tossing the magazine aside. "I need to show you guys something."

He took us upstairs to Greta's old bedroom. It was still furnished the way she'd left it down to the sheets on the bed and a sexy dress she had always hated that Calvin had loved hanging in the closet. "Don't be mad," Sebastian said. He took down a painting from the wall behind the bed. Behind it was a safe I had never known existed. "We weren't supposed to know this was here." He entered the combination like he'd known it all his life.

"What's in there?" I asked. I was holding Romeo's hand, and I pulled him closer.

"Stuff about you." He opened the door. "Mom took all my stuff with her when we left." He pulled out a thick stack of clear plastic bags full of papers. "Here," he said, handing me part of the stack. "Have a look."

"Hey 'Bastian," Romeo said. I sat down on the bed and opened the bag on top. "If you weren't supposed to know this was here, how do you know the combination?"

"I used to have to open it for Mommy Dearest," Sebastian said. My bag was full of school stuff—report cards, certificates, art projects—the kind of stuff normal parents put on the refrigerator. I pulled out a pink construction paper Valentine I had made for Greta in second grade. "I love you, Mommy!" it read in crayon over a big, blue heart. I tore it carefully into quarters and dropped it back into the bag.

"She would want to look at stuff after she took her sleeping pill at night, and she would be too stoned to work the lock," Sebastian explained, opening another bag. "Hey, look at this. I've never seen any of this." He handed me the bag. "Daddy must have put it in here since we moved out."

The bag was full of envelopes, all sealed, all addressed to me, all postmarked and return addressed from Tupelo, Mississippi. "What the hell?" I said, flipping through them. They dated from before I started school all the way up to that year. One big manila envelope was barely seven months old. I pulled out a smaller envelope at random and opened it.

It was a birthday card. The front read "To a Special Granddaughter Who's Thirteen" in gilded script. Underneath the writing was a picture of a girl in an old-fashioned dress and bonnet, swinging on a swing. I opened it, and a crisp ten-dollar bill fluttered out. The printed message was the usual crap, nothing I remember, but it was signed "Much love, Grandmama and Granddaddy St. John." On the page opposite was a larger note in the same handwriting.

"Your Granddaddy thinks it's foolish to send you money," it read. "But I don't know what you might like, and I know every girl needs something. So you buy whatever you want and remember that we love you very, very much. You are and ALWAYS WILL BE our most precious baby girl."

Where the devil goes to shit, I thought, Stella's voice inside my head. Thirteen was the year Stella and Sebastian had left us. My first year in the house alone.

"Can I see?" Romeo said, putting a hand on my shoulder.

"Of course." I handed him the card.

"Here it is," Sebastian said. "This is the one you want." He handed me another pouch.

"This is so sweet," Romeo said as I took it. "Your grandmother sounds so sweet. Do you see her very often?"

"Never," I said. "I haven't seen or talked to her since I was four." I had a brief vision of a soft-looking woman with an orange perm who had held me in her lap and cried and had smelled like White Shoulders perfume. "What is this?" I asked Sebastian.

"Just look." He was watching me, eyes bright.

This bag was much more tattered than the others, and the papers inside of it were creased and stained at the edges like they'd been taken out and held a lot. On top was my original birth certificate, a big, heavy, embossed certificate with my little black hand and foot-prints at the corners. Scarlett Amanda Cross, eight pounds, four ounces, nineteen inches long, white female, was born to Stella St. John Cross and Calvin Luther Cross in Tupelo, Mississippi, at 12:14 a.m. on February 14, 1968. "Stella St. John Cross?" I read aloud, confused.

"Oh yeah," Sebastian said. He was opening another one of my old birthday cards. "That was always Mom's favorite part. Keep reading."

I put the birth certificate aside and found a marriage license. Calvin Luther Cross had married Stella Ann St. John on February 13, 1968, less than a day before their little bundle arrived. The license was signed by the Reverend John Clements of the 1st Calvary Baptist Church of Tupelo. "Wow..." I tried to picture it, Stella with her belly swollen, ready to pop, and Daddy in his white shirt and bare feet at the altar of some crappy little church, my mummified little cowboy of a grandfather and orange-headed grandmother looking on.

"Congratulations," Sebastian said, still reading cards. "You're legitimate."

"What? Oh...yeah." It took me a minute to realize what he meant. "Just barely." I could hardly believe any of it was real. For a few seconds, I thought Sebastian must have made it all up, had the papers faked as some sick kind of joke. But I knew he hadn't, that he wouldn't. My father had known Stella, had known about me, had married her. So why hadn't he stayed with us? How had we ended up alone in that shithole in Mexico? Why had Stella been so scared? Why did she have to die? I looked into my brother's eyes, so like his mother's, and I thought I knew the answer.

"Look at this," Romeo said. He had opened the big, new envelope from my grandmother. "They sent you a Bible." He handed it to me.

It was bound in fake white leather with gold lettering, Holy Bible written large in the center, then, in tiny letters in the corner, "Presented by 1st Calvary Baptist Church."

"There's a note from your grandmamma," Romeo said, holding it out. "You want to see it?"

"Not really, thanks." There was an inscription written inside. "Presented to Miss Scarlett Cross on the occasion of her 17th birthday. 'When I was a child, I spoke as a child, I understood as a child, I thought as a child: but when I became a man, I put away childish things.' 1 Corinthians 13:11."

"Oh cool," Sebastian said.

"I guess." My hands were shaking. Stella had died alone in filth, scared and doped out of her mind with only me for company. Stella had been my father's wife.

"You should keep it," Romeo said. "We should call your grandmother to thank her."

"Oh, I wouldn't go that far," Sebastian said, laughing. "From what I hear, they're ass-scratching trailer trash."

"No," Romeo said. Even in my own weird state of mind, I could hear the angry edge in my boyfriend's voice. "These are nice people. Trust me, I come from ass-scratching trailer trash."

"They're fine," I said. "I mean I guess they're all right." My grandmother had sobbed over me the whole week or so I had spent with her, sobbing for Stella, I had always supposed. My grandfather had barely even looked at me at all. "It doesn't matter." I stuffed the Bible and the one birthday card I had opened into the bag with my mother's marriage license and my birth certificate.

"Sweetheart, it matters," Romeo said. Suddenly I hated the way he was looking at me, the pity I saw in his eyes. "They love you."

"They don't know me," I said, trying not to sound bitter. "They knew Stella, and I guess they must have loved her." *But they let her leave home and get in trouble,* I couldn't help thinking. *They let her run away and die.*

"The important thing is, you are definitely seventeen years old," Sebastian said. "And now you can prove it."

"You're right," I said. I took Romeo's hand. "That is the important thing."

CHAPTER 22

The *Funhouse* came out Halloween weekend and absolutely exploded. Every teen-ager in America seemed to see it opening night, and most of them apparently went back on Saturday. In less than forty-eight hours, Sebastian, Romeo, and I went from being mostly anonymous to the paparazzi's latest hot get. Fiona had been a star for years already; she already had her little flock of buzzards that followed her everywhere. Sebastian was used to being recognized in New York because of his stage work, and for a couple of years, people in airports had been spotting him as that kid from the bubblegum commercials. But nobody had ever known me as anything but Calvin Cross' daughter; if I wasn't with Daddy, nobody had ever noticed me before. And Romeo had always been a handsome stranger; people had only looked at him because he was so cute.

But now, ka-boom! Our faces were everywhere, and the photographers were everywhere we went, feeding that machine. My father's lawyer, Mr. Ranhosky, even hired me and Sebastian a pair of bodyguards for the first few weeks of the insanity. Mike and Sam spent most of their time hanging out in the guest house kitchen, ready to shadow us every time we left the house. Romeo bought a wardrobe of dark hoodies and took a lot of cabs—every time he took out his motorcycle, someone would nearly run him off the road. We all stopped going out to clubs together and hung out at the guest house instead. Sebastian hated being cooped up, and Romeo hated the attention. But I was in a state of total bliss. I came home from school every day—a wild chase in a limo with Mike and/or Sam beside me—to my darling brother and my dearest love, and everything was perfect. Romeo had passed the GED high school equivalency test the year before, and he was a brainiac, a huge help with my homework. He and Sebastian and I played games and watched TV together, and almost every night, I fell asleep cuddled in Romeo's arms. I couldn't have been happier.

By Thanksgiving, things with the vultures had calmed down a lot. The new TV season was in full swing with all its hot new faces, and the Oscar bait movies were starting to come out. The serious thespians were coming back to town to promote their flicks and get their faces seen, and interest in the cast of the autumn's hot popcorn flick fell off. We were not heartbroken. Sebastian and I managed a trip to the grocery store to pick up a turkey without seeing a single photographer. The housekeeper wrote out careful instructions for me, and I managed to cook a pretty respectable holiday feast. Sebastian bought a huge pumpkin caramel cheesecake from the deli, and several of our friends from the movie came over, including Romeo, and we had the most traditional Thanksgiving of our lives. We even watched football. My father wasn't there, of course, but he called that morning during the parade. When Sebastian told him I was up to my armpits in turkey butt, he laughed and said he loved us and wished us luck and would see us at Christmas in Berlin.

Sebastian's big Oscar bait movie, *The House*—the part he'd charmed his way into the night Romeo and I met—opened the first week in December to rave reviews. *The Little Match Girl* was set to premiere in Berlin the week before Christmas. Sebastian and I were going to fly over to meet Daddy for the opening and have Christmas there. Romeo was going to Savannah with Amy to visit their mom as briefly as possible, and then he was flying to Vancouver to film a couple of pilots and audition for a mini-series while we were away. He was actually leaving two days earlier than we were, and the day before he left, he was all I was thinking about.

It was about three that afternoon. Sebastian was outside in the pool, and Romeo and I were hanging out together in my bedroom. Bette Haust, the German actress who had played my mom in *Match Girl*, had sent me a good luck present for the premiere—a whole box full of sexy underwear.

I was standing in front of my full-length mirror, checking out how I looked in a black lace corset and garter belt combination that would have made Madonna drool with envy. Romeo was lying on the bed fully dressed, watching me. "I don't know," I said, watching his face in the mirror and trying not to smile. "I don't think it's me."

He tilted his head back against the headboard to give me a long, appraising look. "Yeah," he said, "that might be a little bit too grown up for you." He pulled the open box toward him on the bed and started going through it. "You got any Underoos in here?"

"Excuse me?"

"Strawberry Shortcake would be just about right, I think."

"Oh, you think so?" I threw a pair of lacy panties I had already tried on at him.

"You better behave," he warned me, laughing as I moved closer to throw a pillow at him. "Don't make me spank you."

"Don't you wish you could?" I taunted him, giggling as he got up from the bed.

"You better know I can." He lunged for me, and I shrieked with delight, running for the door.

He chased me all the way down the stairs into the kitchen where the housekeeper was rinsing dishes at the sink. "Get away from me!" I said, laughing and pushing her out of the way to grab the sprayer. "Stop or I'll shoot!" He kept coming, and I sprayed him with water, both of us laughing. Then he grabbed me, and I surrendered, melting into his kiss.

"Scarlett," the housekeeper scolded me a lot more softly than I would have expected. "*Chica*, stop."

I opened my eyes and saw her worried face. Breaking the kiss, I turned around and found my father standing just inside the door. He looked like someone had just hit him with a plank. "Daddy!" I said, too stupid not to be glad to see him. Romeo was still holding my hand; otherwise, I probably would have run to his arms. "You're home." The look on his face was slowly sinking in, and my skin began to prickle and turn hot.

"Who are you?" Calvin asked Romeo, his gaze moving away from me with an obvious effort.

"Daddy, this is Romeo," I said. "He's an actor. He was in *The Funhouse* with me and Sebastian." I was embarrassed, but it hadn't occurred to me that I couldn't just explain and make everything okay, that the joke might not just be on me. "We were just playing." I let go of Romeo's hand and took a step toward my father, and he actually recoiled. "He's my boyfriend." I looked back at Romeo. "I guess."

"I am," Romeo said. To my surprise, he looked just as furious as Calvin.

"No," Calvin answered him, and his voice was shaking. "You are not."

Sebastian came through the back door, took one look at me, went pale, and started stripping out of the robe he was wearing over his bathing suit. "Here," he said, putting it around me to cover me up.

"Get out," Calvin said to Romeo like he hadn't seen Sebastian at all.

"Daddy, no," I said, struggling to get my arms into the robe.

"Right now, or I'm calling the cops," he went on like he hadn't heard me.

"Daddy, please, it's okay," I insisted. Sebastian tried to hold me with him, but I took hold of Romeo's arm. "Please, just listen…"

"Shut up!" my father roared at me, shocking me to the core. Tears immediately welled up in my eyes, and he must have seen it. "Just stop talking, sweetpea," he said more gently, but the damage was done. He had never yelled at me that way before. I had never felt him being truly angry with me before. I was his baby, his miracle girl.

"It's okay," Romeo said softly in my ear. "Don't worry." He kissed my cheek. "Don't cry, angel. It'll be fine."

The housekeeper was still standing frozen at the sink, and Calvin turned to her. "Carolina, call 911."

"No!" Sebastian and I said in unison; Romeo didn't say anything.

"Dad, he's going," Sebastian added. "Dude, just go."

For a moment, I thought Romeo would refuse. Then he nodded, giving Sebastian's shoulder a squeeze. He kissed my hand, his eyes still on my father. Then he left.

After he was gone, the rest of us just stood there: my father, pale and furious; Sebastian, pale and scared; the housekeeper looking like she'd rather be anywhere else in the universe but there. Me, I was just frozen, half-expecting to wake up from a dream. It didn't seem possible that I could have crashed from being so happy to being so miserable in less than ten minutes. My father was glaring at me like he wasn't even sure he knew me, and a sob rose in my throat. For a few scary seconds, I considered running after Romeo.

"Daddy," I said instead, moving toward my father, trembling with tears. "Daddy, I'm so sorry."

Those were the magic words. "Come here, sweetpea." He gathered me close in his arms, squeezing me so tightly it hurt. "It's all right," he promised, sounding near tears. "It's not your fault." He stroked my hair and let me cry, just like he had when I was a little girl.

"Daddy, she's okay," Sebastian said. "Romeo is a sweet guy."

"What were you thinking?" Calvin demanded, turning on him with me still in his arms. "Why would you bring a kid like that around your sister?"

Sebastian looked like he'd been slapped. "Daddy, Sebastian didn't bring him home," I hurried to say. "I did." Was he going to punish me? I suddenly thought, aghast. The girls at my school were always getting punished for having boyfriends in the house when their parents were away, but Calvin was always away. He didn't even live with me, and even if he had, it wouldn't have made any difference; he still wouldn't have been there. "They didn't even know each other before the movie," I told him.

"She's your little sister," Calvin went on like he hadn't heard me. "You have to look out for her. I let her do that movie with you because you said you would take care of her."

"I did. I do," Sebastian insisted, in tears, and I think that moment could have been my turning point in my relationship with Calvin if I had let it. Seeing Daddy mad at me made me sob with remorse. Seeing him mad at Sebastian pissed me off. Sebastian worshipped Cal. The idea that he might be angry or disappointed in him was devastating, I knew, the worst thing he could possibly imagine. "I try to take care of her, Daddy, I promise," he said, and I hated hearing the pleading in his voice. As far as I was concerned, Sebastian had always, always tried to take care of me, even when Calvin and his stupid cow of a girlfriend had put an entire continent between us. For Cal to say otherwise now was grotesquely unfair, so much so that I couldn't ignore it. For the first time in my life, I was ready to confront my father, not just about being mean to my brother but about Stella, me, everything. Why couldn't he love us? Why did he always have to abandon us? Why did he have to be such a selfish prick?

Then he smiled that magical smile that lit up movie screens all over the world. "I know you do," he said, drawing Sebastian into our hug. "It's okay." He kissed each of us on the cheek. "Everything's going to be fine." They were squeezing me tight between them, and for once, I didn't feel safe; I felt like I could barely breathe. "I love you both so much." I could hear the edge of tears in his voice, and I couldn't stop myself from believing him. "You know that, right?"

"We know, Daddy," Sebastian said without a moment's hesitation, still crying himself. "Of course we know."

I wasn't crying, not this time. "Of course," I echoed, squeezing them back. I thought again about those papers Sebastian had shown me, the marriage license and the birth certificate. I had them stowed away in my underwear drawer. I thought about going and getting them, showing them to Calvin, making him explain. But I didn't. I think I was afraid of what he might say. And I think I knew even then that I would need them.

"Let's go get some lunch," Calvin said, kissing us both again. "Get dressed and meet me at the house in ten minutes."

I wanted to call Romeo right then, but Sebastian immediately hustled me upstairs. By the time I was dressed, my brother was waiting, so all I could do was grab my purse and go with him.

CHAPTER 23

Daddy took us to the Ivy, and we had lunch out on the patio where all the photographers could see us. As soon as we had ordered, I excused myself and went to the ladies' room. I had to call Romeo, to find out if he was okay, to tell him that I was okay.

I went out into the little hallway between the toilets and the dining room, looking for a pay phone. A couple of girls who looked to be about my own age walked up to me.

"Excuse me," one said while the other giggled. "Are you Scarlett Cross?"

I needed this like heat rash, but I wasn't famous or jaded enough yet to not think I needed to be nice. "I am, yeah," I said, smiling. "Hi."

"Hi," the first girl said. The giggler looked to have been struck dumb. "I'm April, and this is my friend, Kimmy. Could we maybe get a picture with you?" She was holding up a camera.

One of the hostesses came hurrying over. "I'm so sorry, Miss Cross," she said, putting herself between me and the sightseers.

"No, it's okay." I put a hand on her arm. "Could I use your phone?"

"Of course," the hostess said. "There's one at the hostess station."

"Could I maybe use one in the back?" The hostess station was clearly visible from the table where my father and brother were waiting.

"If you want," the hostess said.

"Awesome." I took April's camera and handed it to the hostess. "Would you mind getting our picture?"

"Of course not," the hostess said, though I was obviously trying her patience. The girls hunkered in around me, and I gave them my best happy Hollywood princess smile. "There you go." She caught my eye as she handed back the camera, and I gave her a more private smile and a wink, making her smile back.

"Oh god, thank you," April said.

"Yes," Kimmy said. "Thank you so much."

"No problem." With a last smile and wave, I followed the hostess into the kitchen to a phone on the wall.

"Let me know if you need anything else," she said.

"I will," I said, already dialing. "Thanks so much."

After one ring, a woman's voice answered. "Hello?"

"Is this Amy?" I had never spoken to Romeo's sister, but I thought it must be her.

"Yes."

"Hi Amy, it's Scarlett. Is Ro—is he there?"

"No, he's not." I knew Amy was not a fan of our relationship. He'd told me she worried I'd get him into trouble somehow, but he had always laughed about it. "He's leaving for Vancouver tonight instead of tomorrow, but I'm sure he'll call you when he gets back." Her southern accent was more pronounced than her brother's. She sounded more like Stella than he did.

"When is he leaving?" I didn't want to freak out in front of the kitchen staff at the Ivy, but my heart had started racing, and I felt a little sick.

"I'll tell him you called," she said, hanging up.

Sebastian's face appeared in the porthole in the door as I was deciding whether to call her back. When he came in, I saw April and

Kimmy still loitering in the hallway, obviously enthralled. "Whatcha doing?" he said with an exaggerated smile.

"Trying to call...you know."

"Right." He took my arm and pulled me out of the kitchen.

"Can we get a picture with you?" Kimmy blurted out as we came out.

"Sure," Sebastian said, giving me a quick, frown-y big brother look. "Then we've got to get back to our table."

I could barely sit still through the rest of our lunch, and as soon as we got home, I started trying to call Romeo, but I couldn't get an answer. Finally, I dialed a number I wouldn't even have guessed I knew by heart until now when I really needed it. "Hello?" Fiona's voice said after a couple of rings.

"Hey Fiona." I didn't know what I was going to say until I was saying it. "It's Scarlett. I need your help."

"Scarlett." There was a pause; I could hear she had put her hand over the microphone. Then she came back. "Okay. I know what happened." Another pause. "I'm coming to pick you up."

She showed up less than an hour later in her little black Mini Cooper. Sebastian was still out, and I hadn't seen any sign of my father since lunch. I ran out and jumped in the car.

"Thanks, Fiona." She was wearing a baseball cap and sunglasses, and her hair was pulled back in a ponytail. "I didn't know who else to call."

"This is stupid." She pulled out on Mulholland, and a black car pulled in behind her—her vultures. "I am the stupidest woman alive." She checked her rearview mirror and shot them the bird.

"Did Romeo call you?" I didn't know what else to say. She was keeping a steady, sensible speed, both hands on the wheel, facing forward, no expression. I tried to do the same, face forward, expression blank—nothing that would give them a saleable photo.

"He did." She checked her mirror again. The paparazzi had fallen back. "He needed me to ask a friend of mine to let him use a private jet to get out of Los Angeles tonight." She pulled on to the freeway, headed toward the airport. "Do you love him?" She was accelerating, and with the wind noise and the rattle and buzz of the Mini, I wasn't sure I'd heard what she said.

"What?"

"I said do you love him?" She was gripping the steering wheel so tightly her knuckles were white. "He loves you so much, he's out of his fucking mind, but what about you? How much do you love him?"

All the clichés came to mind—more than anything; with all my heart; I would die for him. But those were all just words, shit you could learn from a script. "I love him as much as I love Sebastian," I said. "And I love Sebastian more than I love me."

"What about your dad?" She took her eyes off the road just long enough to look at me. "Do you love him more than Daddy?"

I had been asking myself that same question all day long. I kept thinking about our very first conversation when he came to Mexico to rescue me. He had told me that from that moment on, I would be his little girl, and for the past thirteen years, that's exactly what I had been. Even when he had left me alone for months at a time, I had never forgotten the relief of his coming to rescue me. In that moment in Mexico, I couldn't have imagined ever loving anybody as much as I loved him. But now I couldn't be so sure. It was easy to imagine being away from my father; I had always been away from him, one way or another. The idea of being away from Romeo was a fresher, sharper pain, easier to access, easier to feel.

"Yeah," I told Fiona. "I think I do."

We lost the paparazzi at the airport when Fiona pulled off the main road into a private airfield. "Watch for number sixty-three," she said, slowing to a crawl.

I pointed. "There it is."

Romeo was standing on the tarmac near a sparkling white Gulfstream with the sun setting behind him—a perfectly framed shot. As soon as Fiona stopped the car, I sprinted to his arms.

"I'm so sorry," I was saying as he kissed me. "Baby, I'm so sorry."

"It's okay," he said, crushing me close.

"I had no idea he would come home," I said. "I didn't know he was going to freak out."

"It doesn't matter," he promised. He kept kissing me all over my face and throat.

"He dragged us out of the house to lunch," I said. "I couldn't even call you." All I could think about was how close I'd come to losing him; all I could do was touch him to prove to myself he was real. "Then Amy said you were leaving tonight for Vancouver."

"Come with me." He held my face in both hands, looking down into my eyes. "Get on the plane with me right now."

"I don't have any of my stuff." I couldn't believe he was serious.

"It doesn't matter." His dark brown eyes were avid, excited. "We'll get you new stuff." He kissed my forehead, and I slipped my arms around him. "I can take care of you."

"I know you can." I said it, but I didn't mean it. I didn't know that at all, and I was terrified. "But what about Sebastian? What about my movie? I'm supposed to go to Germany." I had my passport in my purse; legally, I could go to Canada. But the very idea scared me silly. "All of those people worked so hard. If I just disappear right before the movie opens, that's all anybody will talk about." I could barely stand to look him in the eye, he looked so shocked, so hurt. He had obviously thought I would say yes, that I would go with him without a moment's hesitation. It made sense that he would think that. Everything I had said to him, everything I had done since *The Funhouse* had shown him how much I needed him and wanted him, how desperate I was for us to be together. All of it had been real; all of it had been true. So why was I so scared? "I love you." I put my arms around him, holding him close and hiding my face from him at the same time. "I can't lose you. I can't." I squeezed him tight. "But I can't just run away." I wanted him. The very idea of losing him made me want to die. But I couldn't imagine just abandoning my life, as lonely and fucked up as it was. It was all I knew.

"I love you." He sounded sad but resigned, as if maybe he wasn't so shocked after all. "Don't let them tell you that I don't." He made me look at him again. "Promise me."

"I promise." I felt so relieved, I hardly knew what I was saying. I didn't have to run away; he wasn't mad at me; he still loved me. "Nobody is going to keep us apart." I wanted so much to believe it. I wanted to keep everything, to be everything, Daddy's sweetpea and Romeo's angel, too. "By the time you get back from Vancouver and I get back from Germany, Calvin will have forgotten all about being mad at us." Calling my father by his first name made this feel more true. "It will be okay."

He smiled, but his eyes were sad. "Just stay safe." He pulled me close, cradling my head against his shoulder.

"I will." Paralyzing fear had been replaced by an ache deep in my chest. Feeling his arms around me, I suddenly wanted to do it, to run away with him and never look back. Nobody since Stella died had ever held me this way or wanted me this much. But I was a child. As neglected as I had always been, I had always been safe. And in my mind, Romeo was a child, too. I couldn't take care of myself; how could he take care of me? "We'll see one another as soon as we get back," I said. "We'll be together soon."

"We will." He kissed me. "I promise you we will."

After he was gone, Fiona and I stood together on the tarmac and watched his plane take off. "I'm going to Vancouver tomorrow," she said as the noise of the jet faded away. "I'm filming a miniseries over the holidays, and I got Romeo a part in it."

I could tell from her tone she was trying to upset me, and it was working great. "That's awesome," I said. "What is it?"

"You're not even worried, are you?" I couldn't tell if she was angry or just amused. "Why should you be, right?"

Okay, I thought, *enough.* I felt bad enough already; the last thing I needed was more of Fiona's bullshit. "Fiona, you asked me if I love Romeo, and I told you the truth, that yeah, I do, completely. But what about you?" I was exhausted, worried, confused, heartbroken, and scared to death. Every time I thought about the future, I didn't know whether to scream or cry. I didn't have the energy to play out some dumb soap opera cat fight drama with her. "Are you in love with

Romeo? Is this going to be a thing we do for the rest of our lives, you acting all wounded and mysterious and treating me like I'm some stupid bitch who doesn't deserve him?"

"You don't deserve him." She didn't sound cool or superior any more. "He's not some cute boy toy, some heartthrob. He's an amazing actor; he could be one of the great actors of his generation if he tried, better than me or Sebastian, better than you, even."

"You think I don't know that?" I had no doubt at all that Romeo was a better actor than me—I thought they all were better than me. How dare she make this speech at me? "I'm the one who's worked opposite him."

"You're the one who's distracting him, making him into some fucked up version of your knight in shining armor." She had obviously given this some thought. She had her big speech all prepared. "You've made him think you're this tragic, broken, little princess locked up in a tower, and he's got to rescue you."

"Oh shut up," I said, not because I thought she was wrong but because I didn't want to hear it, especially not from her.

"And he loves it," she went on. "He dearly loves playing the hero for you. It's all he cares about. That's what he loves so much, Scarlett, not you."

"God, you are so full of shit." She wasn't. Even then I knew she wasn't, and I hated her for it. "You're the one who treated him like a piece of ass from the first day you met him."

"Yes, I did," she said, surprising me. "I didn't know him then. I hadn't seen him work. I hadn't seen what he could be if he could just focus on being an actor."

"Why would you think I wouldn't want him to focus on being an actor?" We were all alone now in the weird orange glow of the airport at twilight. Even the ground crew for Romeo's plane was gone. "I love him. I want him to succeed."

"It's not what you want, Scarlett." The wind was picking up, and the sky was clouding over. "It's what you are. You're a child, a fucked up, broken child, and if you ask him to, Romeo will waste the rest of his life trying to fix you. And even if that weren't true, even if you could pull it together and grow up, your father wouldn't let you."

"Leave my father out of your bullshit theories, Fiona." I had never wanted so much to slap anybody in my life. "You don't know anything about my father."

"I know I had to call in a favor from an ex to get Romeo out of town before your father could have him arrested for statutory rape," she said. "I know he was ready to throw away his whole career to take you with him. If you know your daddy so much better than I do, you tell me, what do you think he would have done if you had gone?"

I didn't even want to think about that; I refused to think about it. "But I didn't go." I was sure she must be lying or at least exaggerating to be dramatic. My father had been upset when he first came home and found me messing around in my underwear with Romeo; why wouldn't he be? But I couldn't imagine him calling the cops. He was Calvin Cross, for pity's sake, the original hipster, the golden god of the anti-establishment. It didn't make sense.

"No, thank god, you didn't," she said.

"Fuck you, Fiona."

"I'm sorry, all right?" Rain was starting to spatter around us. I couldn't tell if the glimmer on her cheeks was tears or raindrops, and I didn't care. "I know you haven't really done anything wrong. I know you really care about him."

"I don't care about him. I love him."

"But I'm going to do everything I can while we're in Canada without you to change his mind." She put her hand on my arm like she was a big sister giving Baby a hard truth. "You're bad for him, Scarlett."

"Don't touch me." It was raining for real now, drenching us both. "You're pathetic, Fiona." Something had clicked inside me, just in that moment, just as she touched my arm. I didn't even sound like myself. I sounded like someone harder, stronger, someone with the faintest edge of a small-town Mississippi drawl. "You just want him, and he doesn't want you, so you've built up this whole big drama in your head to try to explain it."

"That's not true." But I could hear in her voice that she was afraid that it was, that she was just as scared of her bullshit as I was of mine.

"So go ahead." I had no idea how I'd get home unless she drove me. We were hell and gone from the main terminal. "Do whatever you think might work. Get him a job; tell him I'm poison; give him a lap dance if you feel like it. I couldn't care less because it won't matter." It felt true; it felt right; I believed it. "Romeo loves me."

I could see from her face, she believed it, too. "Just get in the car," she said. "I promised him I'd get you home."

If I had been the tough cookie I was pretending to be, I would have refused. I would have hitched a ride with the paparazzi before I got back in her Mini. But I wasn't that girl, not yet. "Okay," I said instead. "Thanks for the ride."

When I got home, I found my father in the kitchen of the guesthouse, making tacos. "Hey, sweetpea," he said, smiling like every little thing was fine. How many times had I come home from school praying with all my heart to find him here this way? It was the dream of my childhood; I had longed for it the way normal kids long for Santa to show up on Christmas. "Where have you been?"

"With Fiona." I thought again about what Fiona had said about him wanting to have Romeo arrested. It seemed even crazier with him standing in front of me. But he had said he would, hadn't he? Standing right here? "We were doing some last-minute shopping before Berlin." I had never lied to him before; it made me feel sick.

"I'm guessing you didn't find anything." He didn't sound like he was interrogating me at all, more teasing.

"I didn't, but she found some stuff." If anybody was checking the security camera at the gate, they would have seen it was Fiona's car. My story would hold up. "Presents for her little sisters." I suddenly noticed mine and Sebastian's suitcases sitting by the door. "What's going on?"

"We're taking the red eye to New York tonight and going on to Berlin in the morning." He took a pan of tortilla shells out of the oven. "Your brother packed for you, so you probably want to make sure he got everything." He put down his oven mitt to hug me, kissing the top of my head. "Go tell him dinner is ready."

The last time Calvin had made us dinner in this house, we had been about ten years old. I had missed it so much, had cried for it, ached to have him and Sebastian here with me, to be a normal kid, to not be so alone. Why couldn't I be happy about it now? "Okay." I hugged him tight. "I'll go get Sebastian."

CLIPPING 8

From "This Week at the Movies" column in *The New American Standard*

"And a little child shall lead them"

The Little Match Girl, *opening in selected cities December 25, represents a welcome return to form for two cinematic icons, writer-director Aksel Jorgen and star Calvin Cross. But it's the astonishing debut performance of 14-year-old Scarlett Cross that steals the show and makes the movie.*

Little Miss Cross plays Josephine, an orphan running wild in the ravaged streets of post-war Berlin. From the first moment she appears, fifteen minutes in, pelting her potential savior's car with rocks, she is the movie's heart and soul. An explosive combination of pathos, humor, and rage, she holds the audience in thrall in a way actresses more than twice her age with decades of experience could well envy. Her chemistry with her real-life father is warm and palpable, and unlike other father-daughter acting pairings I could mention, never plays like a stunt.

Indeed, Cross' performance here reminds us what a glorious actor he can be beneath his movie star façade. Perfectly cast as a veteran returning to the city of his dissipated youth, he gives this seemingly-iconic hero, known simply as "the American," shades of dark complexity and flashes of near-brutal intelligence. Rumor has it Jorgen wrote the role with Cross in mind, and it shows.

Jorgen is absolutely in command here for the first time in years. Every element—casting, art direction, time frame, and performance—serves the story as a whole to the smallest detail, and the cumulative effect is devastating. He indulges his recent habit of framing and lighting his actors like Renaissance saints, but in this case, it works, serving the tragic arc of his story and the shocking beauty of his actors to perfection. After a series of missteps over the past five years, the master has finally returned.

Other standout performances include German actress Bette Haust as Josephine's mother in Weimer-era flashbacks and Austrian child star Vincent Bugatti as the leader of an orphan gang.

Not to be missed.

CHAPTER 24

I hadn't let myself think about the Great Dane since the night of the wrap party. Like my mother's murder, he was something I squashed down in a tiny, locked corner of my brain and forgot. But walking up the red carpet for the premiere hand in hand with Sebastian, I looked up, and suddenly he was there. My father reached him first, and just as they were shaking hands, a photographer shouted, "Scarlett!" My eyes met the Dane's at the exact same second the flash went off. I saw that picture in the papers the next morning. I looked like I'd seen a ghost.

But someone was there to save me. "Magenta!" I turned to find Bette right behind me, gorgeous as ever, her dark hair dyed gloriously blonde.

"Bette!" I threw my arms around her and hugged her. "My god, your hair!"

"It's madness," she said, hugging me back. "I wanted to look like Hollywood." She drew back and framed my face in her hands. "You look beautiful." She took my hand and turned back to the crowd with a dazzling smile of her own.

Calvin joined us, the two of them touching cheeks for barely a moment. He said something to her I couldn't hear, and she laughed.

"Sebastian," I called, motioning him forward. "Bette, this is my brother." The picture that made all the papers the next day was of the four of us, all smiling, Bette and Sebastian shaking hands. In the background, you could see the Dane, just watching.

I barely remember watching the actual movie. I think I was pleased. I've seen it so many times since then it's hard to remember my first impression of it. I do remember looking over at Sebastian when it was over and seeing tears in his eyes and on his face. "You were perfect," he told me, squeezing my hand.

The studio had set up a press conference for afterwards in a banquet hall at the hotel across the street with a party to follow in the ballroom next door. I tried to sit next to Bette, but a publicist I didn't know hustled me into a chair between my father and the Dane. Calvin leaned over to me as they were hooking up our microphones. "I'm so proud of you."

"Thanks, Daddy." I tried to hug him, but the sound guy was on the floor between us, doing something with the wires. Then suddenly the lights came on, like the sun being switched on directly in front of my face, and we were starting.

The first questions were all directed at Calvin, who was charming and funny and thoughtful and smart. He described the movie in ways that had never even occurred to me. Pretty quickly he tossed the ball over to the Dane, who was serious and intense and European, his answers all just long-winded and complex enough to make him seem aged and brilliant, a cinematic legend in the flesh. I just sat there listening, trying to look as interested as possible, but I slowly realized that the sound of his voice was making me feel sick.

"Scarlett?" A woman on the front row had to say my name twice before I looked at her. "Alice Brown from *Popcorn*," she said, smiling at me kindly, and I smiled back. Most of their smiles looked like sharks grinning up from a swimming pool at us, but hers was pretty and real. She wasn't very old, Bette's age, maybe, and she was wearing a cute dress, not jeans and a tee-shirt. "You were very good," she said.

"Thanks very much," I answered.

"What's your question, Alice?" the big boss publicist asked with a shark smile of his own.

"What's next, Scarlett?" she asked, unruffled. "Do you have another project lined up?"

"Yeah…yes." The Dane was looking at me again, smiling, and I tried to concentrate on my father on my other side, to smell his cologne and remember he was there. I ached for Romeo. "My brother and I were in a horror movie last fall in America called *The Funhouse.*" Everyone laughed like it was adorable that I thought they might not have heard of it. "It's really good," I finished.

"It very much is," she said. "What about after that?"

"I don't really know," I said.

"I am hoping Scarlett will be joining me in Italy," the Dane said. He put his hand over mine on the table, and I felt my whole body ice over again, worse than it had on the red carpet. "I have written a role in my next film with her most specifically in mind."

"No," I said without thinking. "I can't." I was talking too loud, or maybe it just sounded that way to me.

"I think Scarlett is more interested in high school than anything else at the moment," my father said, still charming, but he took my other frozen hand under the table.

"I suppose we will have to negotiate," the Dane said, laughing, and the sharks chuckled with him. But Alice Brown, I noticed, didn't smile.

Someone asked Bette about her hair, and she went into an explanation that soon had the crowd in stitches. There were only a couple of questions after that, none of them directed at me. Then it was supposed to be over. The publicist called time, and people started moving.

"Hey Scarlett!" someone called out from the back, a tall, skinny man in a white dress shirt buttoned all the way up. I recognized him; he was the one who had asked me about Stella at the wrap party for *The Funhouse.* "Do you remember your mom?" he asked.

"Who is that?" my father asked the publicist, scowling, angry.

"Yes." My mike had already been turned off, so I leaned over to the standing mike in front of Bette, whose dress was too filmy for a clip-on. "Yes," I repeated. "Of course I do. Who are you?"

"And that's really it, folks," the publicist said, reaching past me to turn off the mike. Two security guards were already hustling the white shirt guy out the back door. "If you'll join us in the ballroom, we'll be doing pictures there."

The press filed out the back, and the publicist's drones led us out a side door into a dark, steel, and concrete hallway. A long hair and make-up station had been set up so we could be primped back to gorgeous before we went into the ballroom. One of my father's two handlers, the girl, handed him a lit cigarette and a drink. "Thank God," he said. He took one long swallow of the drink and handed it back. "Scarlett, sweetpea, come here."

"Sure." He took me off to one side, away from the chatter. "What is it, Daddy?"

He smiled. "I know you're mad as hell at me." This was the first mention he'd made of our fight since it happened, and it knocked me off balance.

"No, I'm not," I promised.

"It's okay." He gave me a hug that lasted barely a second, and the hot ash on his cigarette barely brushed my bare back. "You think you're in love, and it's hard to see past that. But you're just a baby, baby. You've got to trust me."

"I do trust you," I said, though in that moment, that wasn't really true. He didn't even sound like himself to me; he sounded like an actor playing the part of my father, and not doing such a hot job.

"Italy is going to be so good for you." A stylist was hovering nearby with a comb to fluff my hair, and he stepped back to let her get to me. "You'll have a ball."

"Daddy, I don't want to go to Italy," I said. The publicist was herding people toward the door.

"We'll talk about it later." Another stylist was running her finger-tips through his hair, making it fall more softly over his forehead, and the handler-girl took back the cigarette. "Come on; they're ready for us."

If I had stopped him then, if I had told him exactly why I didn't want to go to Italy, maybe things would have been different. Maybe I could have even found the words to explain to him about Romeo, about how and why I was way beyond a schoolgirl crush. But I couldn't. For reasons that I hope will become clear before I finish writing out this long, sordid story of my life, there are some things I have never been able to make myself tell, even to save myself or keep hold of someone I love more than my life. When it comes to the really bad stuff, I've been under a gag order from my own brain since I was four years old.

So I didn't tell my father what had almost happened to me the night of the wrap party. I didn't tell him why I was terrified. I went into the ballroom with him and posed for pictures, smiling. In several, I even posed with the Dane.

Calvin had told us we would fly back to New York for Christmas, but we lingered in Berlin until well into January. We moved out of the hotel and into an apartment in the Friedenau suburb, and that's where we celebrated Christmas. Calvin bought me and Sebastian each a painting as our big gift. "You're old enough now to start collecting," he said as we tore into the packages. "These should get you started."

Sebastian's was a Picasso Harlequin very much like the one that hung in the front entryway of Castle Asshole. This one was smaller, but just as beautiful and probably just as rare. "This is real?" Sebastian said.

"It better be," Calvin said, smiling. "Do you like it?"

"Are you kidding?" Sebastian got up and climbed over the wreckage of wrapping to hug him. "Thank you so much."

Mine was a Degas, a ballerina with my exact shade of honey blonde hair. "As soon as I saw her, I thought of you, sweetpea," Calvin said. "Look, Sebastian, at the look on her face—doesn't she look like your sister?"

"She really does," Sebastian said, laughing. "It's kind of creepy, actually."

"Very funny," I said, sticking my tongue out at him. But truth be told, the ballerina creeped me out a little bit, too. She did look like me, though actually she looked more like Josephine, my character in *Match Girl*. With her flat little chest and rounded little arms, she looked maybe twelve or thirteen years old.

"Do you like it?" Calvin said.

"Of course I do." It was an amazing present and a very loving thought; I was being stupid. "It's beautiful, Daddy. I love it." I got up and hugged him, too.

CHAPTER 25

We stayed in Berlin another two weeks until the nominations came out for the Golden Globes. Calvin and Jorgen were both nominated, of course; the studio had been running awards campaigns for both of them since Thanksgiving. The big shock was that Bette and I were both nominated for best supporting actress in a drama. Plus Sebastian got a nomination of his own for best supporting actor in a drama for *The House*.

We all celebrated together with a champagne breakfast in Berlin, then three days later, me, Sebastian, and Calvin all flew back to L.A. I had never seen my father look so happy. The whole world had fallen back in love with him again. Walking through the airport in New York, we could barely move for all the photographers; our bodyguards were hard pressed to clear a path without causing a lawsuit.

I was happy, too, for reasons that had nothing to do with awards or paparazzi. Romeo was finally back in L.A., too. I had called him on a pay phone at the airport in New York, and while I would be getting home too late to see him that night, we had made plans to hook up the next day. I could hardly wait. We'd have to be careful, I knew, and it would probably end up with a fight with my father eventually. But maybe by then he'd be so blissed out with awards season and everything else, he wouldn't care so much. I still didn't know what I was going to do to get out of going to Italy, but that didn't seem to matter, either. All I cared about was that within twenty-four hours, I would be back in Romeo's arms, and this time apart would start feeling like a dream.

I hadn't slept at all on either flight, but I dropped off like a rock in the backseat of the limo as soon as we were back home in L.A. The next thing I knew after the airport was my father picking me up like I might have been four years old again to carry me inside. "Hey, sweetpea," he said, kissing my cheek as I nestled my head against his shoulder. "We're home."

I looked up and saw the Picasso and realized we were at Castle Asshole, Calvin's house. "What are we doing here?" I said, the words coming out in a yawn as he carried me up the stairs.

"You and your brother are staying here with me now." One of the bodyguards was leading the way, carrying my luggage. "Is that okay?"

"Yeah, of course it is." He carried me into a bedroom with freshly-painted walls of Tiffany blue. The bed and dresser were new, but my same old chest of drawers was there, and my dollhouse was set up in the corner. "But how come?"

He set me down on the white eyelet duvet on the bed and pulled off my shoes. "When you were little kids, Greta thought you shouldn't be exposed to some of the stuff that went on up here." He pulled a floral-print quilt over me. "But I'm old and tired now; things have gotten pretty quiet around these parts." He kissed my forehead. "I think you'll be safe."

"You're not old." This felt like an important conversation, but I was so sleepy, and the bed was so soft, I couldn't hold my eyes open. "You're beautiful."

"Thanks, my sweetpea." He kissed me again. "Go to sleep."

I woke up eight hours later, stiff and uncomfortable from sleeping in my clothes. I checked the clock—10:30 a.m. on a glorious California day. I got up and opened the curtains, basking in the sunshine after my month in wintry Berlin. Below me, a mimosa tree was blooming brilliant pink against the pure, sparkling blue of the pool. The bedroom might be new, but I was home.

I had a couple of hours before I was supposed to meet Romeo. I took a long, hot shower and washed my hair. I put on my favorite outfit, a short dress and sandals, and swiped on just enough lip gloss to look put together.

Downstairs in the breakfast nook, I found Mike the Bodyguard drinking coffee and reading the morning paper. "Hey princess," he said when I came in. "How was Germany?"

"Cold but nice." I liked Mike; I was glad to see him back. He was one of the ones Ranhosky had hired for me and Sebastian when *Funhouse* first hit, but he hadn't gone to Europe with us. "How was your Christmas? Did your kids like the motorbikes?"

"Oh yeah, they loved them. My ex, not so much."

"Uh oh."

A woman's voice from behind me interrupted. "Miss Cross?" I turned and found a handsome, middle-aged woman in casual slacks and a white blouse. "Hi," she said. "I'm Ivy, your father's new housekeeper."

"Hi Ivy." I shook her hand. "Nice to meet you." Calvin had always had a housekeeper, but none of them ever stayed very long, and most of them were day help and wore uniforms. This Ivy person looked like the manager of a really expensive spa. "Where's my dad?"

"He has gone to Carmel for the weekend." She pulled out a PDA and consulted the screen. "He said to tell you and your brother he'd be home on Monday. You have a stylist coming over this afternoon at three to look at dresses for the Golden Globes, and Mr. Ranhosky is waiting to see you on the terrace."

"I won't be here at three; I have an appointment." It was just like Calvin to suddenly decide to take off for Carmel, and even though I was a little surprised that he would just disappear this way, it simpli-fied my own plans a lot. "Mike, after I talk to Mr. Ranhosky, can you drive me someplace?"

"Sure, princess." He gave Ivy a look that told me he didn't like her very much.

Ivy either didn't care or didn't notice. "I'll bring you out some breakfast," she said. "Cereal? Toast?"

"Just some juice would be great." I was so excited about meeting Romeo, I wasn't sure I could eat. "Thanks, Ivy."

I had never seen Mr. Ranhosky when he wasn't dressed in a dark suit and tie, and this time was no exception. When I went out on the terrace, he was sitting at a table under an umbrella with his briefcase open in front of him. "Hi, Mr. Ranhosky," I said, giving him a hug. "Happy new year."

"Happy new year to you." He was a nice man, and I liked him, but I had always suspected I made him a little uncomfortable. I didn't think he talked to kids very much; he always sounded like he was trying to sound like Captain Kangaroo. "And congratulations on your Golden Globe nomination."

"Thanks." I sat down across from him just as Ivy came out with the orange juice for me and a carafe of coffee for him. I gave her a smile of thanks as she set it down and poured him a cup. "So what's going on?"

He took a sip of his coffee then took a breath as if he were bracing himself. "Scarlett, honey, I need to talk to you about your boyfriend." He took a file out of his briefcase. "Your dad is really concerned, and he asked me to do a little research."

"I don't...what?" He had taken me completely by surprise; it had never once occurred to me that he could be there because of Romeo.

"Your friend has a considerable criminal record," he said, handing me the file. "Drugs, petty theft, solicitation—do you even know what that means, Scarlett?"

"Of course I do." I looked at the printout, making myself focus on it. "This is all from when he was a kid—his juvenile record," I said. "How did you get this?" My father had played enough lawyers and cops in my life for me to know juvenile records were supposed to be sealed.

"You knew about this?" he asked, obviously shocked.

"Of course." Truth be told, I hadn't had a clue that Romeo had ever actually been arrested, but I was determined not to let him know that.

"Good God," Ranhosky said, reaching for his coffee.

"But he's not doing any of that stuff anymore," I said, handing back the file. "He's an actor, and he's really good."

"I heard that, too." He smiled. "But he'll have a hard time pursuing an acting career in prison, honey."

I couldn't believe he was serious; it felt like we were playing a bad scene in a movie. "I told you; he hasn't done anything."

"Scarlett, sweetheart, he has." He leaned forward, and I saw sympathy in his eyes. "I have source who tells me your friend was supplying drugs to half the cast of *The Funhouse*."

"That's insane," I insisted, but I had to look away as I said it. It was common knowledge on the set that Romeo could get the best dope. I knew it because of Sebastian. I was also pretty sure he hadn't made any money on the transactions he'd done on the set; he was just the go-between.

"My source could become a witness for the police with one phone call," Ranhosky went on.

"A phone call from you." I took a swallow from my juice and wished I had a big girl drink instead, something with a healthy shot of vodka. "Why are you doing this?" Stupid, baby tears were burning in my eyes. "Why can't you just leave us alone?"

"Honey, your dad is terrified you're going to get hurt," he said. "He has to protect you; you know that."

"My dad?" I interrupted. "Has my father seen this stuff?" I choked on the very idea of Calvin reading through that file. "Did you tell him what your source said?"

"Honey, I didn't have a choice."

"Oh my god…"

"Scarlett, now, just listen to me for a second." I had started to get up from my chair, but he stopped me, leaning forward to put a hand on my knee. "This is not the end of the world, not for your friend and certainly not for you." My freaking out seemed to have calmed him down; he sounded much more at ease. "He's got great buzz as an actor, and there's no reason in the world we can't help him with that —your dad included. Nobody wants to ruin his life. We just aren't willing to let him ruin yours."

"He's not ruining my life," I insisted, shaking my head. "He loves me."

"Scarlett, honey, you're just kids." He reached around the table and folded my hands between his. "Please, kiddo, you're going to have to trust me on this one." I looked up and saw real concern in his eyes, a deep belief that what he was saying was true and right and all for my own good. "You're not stupid, Scarlett. I see your report cards, remember? This is not your whole life."

"You don't know what my whole life is," I said, tears running down my face.

"You're going to go to college someday, maybe even someplace back East, the Ivy League. You're going to see the real world. You're going to meet real people." He smiled at me for a moment, looking into my face like a dad on a TV drama, then he let me go. "Let me take care of Romeo," he said, handing me his handkerchief. "In a good way, I promise."

"What is it you want me to do?" I said, wiping my eyes.

"You don't have to do anything," he promised. "I've already talked to his sister, and she agrees that you two being together right now would be a terrible mistake for both of you. She's going to talk to him, just like I'm talking to you now."

"Are we paying her?" I asked. It sounded stupid, like something from a soap opera, but so did this whole situation.

"Don't worry about it, honey," he said, which meant yes. "Your father has a lot of influence in this town. Your friend is going to be glad this happened, I promise." He smiled again. "And you will be, too."

I knew that wasn't true. Romeo didn't want or need my father's influence. He loved me; he wanted me; he knew how much I needed him. I thought about the last time I had seen him, standing on the tarmac beside a plane, ready to take me away and to hell with the consequences.

"And if we're not glad?" I said. "What happens if we say no and keep seeing each other? Will you call the cops?" I couldn't let that happen. Even if it meant the unthinkable, even if I never saw Romeo again, I couldn't let him go to jail.

"You won't be able to keep seeing each other, dear," he said. "I doubt very much if you'll ever hear directly from him again." He said he had talked to Romeo's sister. Was she telling him this same thing, that I was never going to call him again? Would he believe her? "If I'm wrong, if you do see him again, that's it, kiddo. After you finish your next project in Italy, you'll stay in Europe and go to boarding school until it's time for you to go to college. And your boyfriend will go to jail. Just his being here with you in the guest house overnight will be enough to arrest him, search his house, search his car, question all of his friends. With his record, I doubt his sister would be able to find a lawyer who could keep him out of prison. Is that what you want? Is it worth it?"

"You know it's not." Suddenly, I felt cold in spite of all that California sunshine.

"It's going to be okay," he said.

"Okay." He got up to go, but I just sat there. He kissed me on the cheek, but I didn't respond. He didn't comment; he just left.

I was still sitting there an hour later when Sebastian came outside for his wake-up swim. "What are you doing back already?" he asked.

"I didn't go." Ivy the Housekeeper had brought me breakfast after all, eggs and bacon and toast and strawberries, but I hadn't touched it. The eggs looked like something dead congealing in the sun, and the smell was making me sick. "I can't see him."

"What?" He squatted down in front of me to look into my eyes. "What are you talking about?"

"I can't see Romeo." I was trembling all over. "If I see him, Ranhosky will get him sent to prison." He touched my hand, and I fell forward into his arms. "Bastian, what am I going to do?"

I told him everything Ranhosky had said, and he just listened, sitting across from me, holding my hand. "I can't let that happen to him," I finished. "Ever since we met, Romeo has been trying to take care of me, trying to make me feel safe. And he does so good, and I love him, and I need him."

"I know you do." He squeezed my hand between his.

"But I can't do this to him, even if he wanted to let me." And I knew he would. I knew if I called Romeo, he would tell me it didn't matter, that it was worth the risk. He would say we could run away from everything, from Ranhosky and my father and the police, from our lives, from our careers. That as long as we were together, nothing else mattered. But as much as I loved him, I couldn't believe that was true. "I have to let him go."

"You do." My brother kissed my forehead. "I'll go talk to him." He stood up. "I'll go right now."

He left, and I met with the stylist and picked a dress for the Golden Globes. I was pleasant, accommodating, fun to be around. She and her glam squad left three hours later thinking I was a living doll. But I wasn't a doll. I was a zombie.

Sebastian came back home just as it was getting dark. I was upstairs in my new room, hiding out from Ivy, missing the privacy of the guest house so much it hurt. My new television was on, playing some sitcom, but I was looking at my new painting, the Degas ballerina girl, hanging on the wall.

"Did you find him?" I asked as my brother came in.

"I did." He sat down beside me on the bed. "He's really upset, but I told him what you said, and he is absolutely not mad at you."

"Good." The smart bits of my brain thought it might have been easier if he were furious with me, if he thought I was just dumping him. But the rest of me knew that would be too horrible for either of us to survive.

Sebastian looked almost as miserable as I felt. "Sissy, you don't know," he said. "I haven't..." He took my hands. "He does love you, but honestly, I think this will be better."

"Don't say that." I clutched his hands, willing him to look at me. "Don't you ever, ever say that, Sebastian."

"Scar, there's stuff you don't understand about Romeo."

"I understand, and I love him, and I need you to be on my side!" If Sebastian abandoned me, I really would be lost.

"Always." His eyes filled with tears. "Always always always."

"Good." I choked back tears of my own. "Did you tell him I can't see him anymore?" He nodded. "Did you make him understand?"

"I think so, but he didn't want to." He brushed my hair back from my face. "He said he would stay away until you call him, but if you call, he will be there."

"Okay."

Sebastian put his arm around my shoulders, and I buried my face in his chest. "It's okay, Sissy." He kissed the top of my head. "It will be okay."

From *Jeune Fille* magazine

I am relieved to report that unlike her alter-egos in the Golden Globe-nomi-nated The Little Match Girl *or the horror smash* The Funhouse, *actress Scarlett Cross, 16, is a healthy, happy teen-ager. We met in the garden of the Beverly Hills mansion of her movie star dad and co-star, Calvin Cross, but the actress herself would have looked equally at home at any shopping mall in the country. She turned up scrupulously on time, still dressed in the uniform of the exclusive Catholic high school she attends.*

"You look like an ad for wholesome American youth," I told her as she flopped into the chair across from mine, tossing her calfskin bookbag aside to reach for a glass of iced tea.

"Is that bad?" she asked, laughing. "It's not very sexy, is it?"

On the contrary, kid...

JF:How was school?

SC:Oh God...boring. But fine; I had a chemistry test that kicked my behind, but that was not unexpected. How are you?

JF:I'm great. Thanks for asking. Do you usually make good grades?

SC:[laughing] No. Well...good grades in English and history, okay grades in social studies, bad, bad grades in math and science. Being out to work, I think I've kind of lost the thread. But I have a tutor; I'll make it back.

JF:So school is a priority?

SC:Sure. [grabbing a handful of cookies from the plate set between us and crunching happily away] Why wouldn't it be?

JF:Well, your father is a high school dropout.

SC:Yeah, but my dad is amazingly talented. He knew he was going to be an actor. He didn't need school. And he's extremely well-read—he's self-educated, I'd say.

JF: You seem to have inherited some of that family talent. Everybody says you'll be nominated for the Oscar for your very first real speaking role...

SC:Oh God...

JF:Not to mention having the number one movie in the country for six weeks for your second.

SC:[shaking her head] Match Girl *could so be a fluke. I mean, I'm really grateful and flattered, but come on. I got the part in the first place at least partly because of who I am, and I got to act with my dad, who is brilliant and generous and oh yeah, loves me and bent over backwards to help me do well. As far as* The Funhouse *goes, the success it has had has very little to do with me personally; I'm not even in it all that much. So I'm not giving up my day job just yet.*

JF: Don't sell yourself short—hasn't anybody told you? You're a phenomenon!

SC:Yeah, right. Come back in five years, and we'll see.

JF:So where do you see yourself in five years? Will you still be acting?

SC:I hope so. But that won't really be up to me, will it?

JF:College?

SC:I don't know. I mean, I'd like to—my dad and I have talked about it, certainly.

JF:What about boys?

SC:What about them? Boys are good. I vote yes for boys.

JF:Any boy in particular?

SC:No, I feel pretty good about the whole concept.

JF: No boyfriend?

SC:What, now? No.

JF:Really? What about Romeo Kidd? You two seem pretty cozy in all those paparazzi photos.

SC:We're just friends. [giggles] Seriously, I like him, and I hope he likes me, but it's not romantic. We just have fun hanging out.

JF:Good for you. Good luck, kiddo—see you in five years!

CHAPTER 26

Zombie Scarlett took me over pretty well completely over the next few weeks. I went to school and did a lot of extra homework and took a lot of make-up tests to catch me up for the time I had lost in Berlin. I did my first solo interview for a major magazine. I went on a late-night talk show with Calvin to talk about *Match Girl*; together the two of us told a funny story about how a drunken hobo had interrupted the filming of my death scene in the basement of a ruined office block. "I saw him first, just kind of rising up out of the dark," I explained. "My eyes must have gotten really big or something…"

"They were huge," Calvin interrupted. "She looked completely awe-struck by what she was seeing, and I'm thinking, holy crap, my kid is talented!"

"So you thought she was just acting?" the host said.

"Yes!" Calvin said, laughing.

"Yeah, he did," I said, laughing too. "Then this poor guy—who obviously has no clue we're even there, much less filming a movie—starts singing."

"Scared the living hell out of me," Calvin said.

"And I started laughing," I said. "Which freaked the poor guy completely out, of course. I didn't think they were ever going to get him calmed down and out of there." The host and the audience were all laughing. "Finally, he recognized Daddy, thank heavens, and we were able to convince him to get out of the shot. But I think he ended up hanging around to watch the filming for the rest of the night."

"He did," Calvin said. "I was glad—he broke the tension for me." He had gotten serious again. "I hated that scene." He smiled at me. "It's no fun watching your kid die, even in a movie."

The audience said, "Awwww," and he hugged me, and we were a hit. After it was over, we barely said good-bye to one another before I got in one car and he got in another. I went home to do my homework, and he went out somewhere. He hadn't really been home to stay since he'd left Ranhosky to deal with me and my Romeo problem and gone off to Carmel. But our act on the talk show played great; box office for the next weekend went through the roof.

Through all of this, I felt numb. I was acting, playing the part of the fresh-faced American starlet. It was exhausting, but it was a relief, too. It gave me something to distract me from the misery of being the real me. Because that poor girl wanted to curl up and die. Romeo was as good as his word. He didn't try to call me, and somehow I stopped myself from calling him. I knew he was in L.A. Paparazzi photos of him showed up in the tabloids nearly every week, coming out of a coffee shop or going to the gym. Once I caught a glimpse of him in a promo for the mini-series he had shot in Canada, and I cried all night long. But I kept being who I was supposed to be, and I didn't call. I felt sick to my stomach pretty much all the time, but that made sense—swallowing that much misery would make anybody want to throw up. Some days I barely ate anything at all. Other days I felt ravenous and binged on junk food. But nobody but Sebastian ever seemed to notice. The weeks went by, and Calvin never once mentioned my talk with Ranhosky, and I didn't have the strength or the courage to bring it up myself.

The day of the Golden Globes ceremony, the studio sent a stylist to Castle Asshole to help me dress up in another dress that smashed my boobs flat and made me look like a child. Sebastian met me in the hallway, Prince Charming in Armani, and we walked hand in hand downstairs. I knew Calvin was in the house getting ready, too, but I hadn't seen him or spoken to him in more than a week.

The Great Dane was sitting at the kitchen bar in the exact same spot he had sat the afternoon we met. "Hello, little one," he said, smiling at me. "You look very beautiful."

"Hello, sir," Sebastian said, dropping my hand to shake the Dane's. "It's so good to see you again." The Dane was smiling at him kindly, indulgently, and I wanted to scream, *Don't you touch him!* But I couldn't seem to move. "I'm Sebastian, by the way, in case you don't remember."

"Of course I remember," the Dane said, clasping my brother's hand in both of his. "I am a great admirer of your work, Sebastian."

My brother flushed with such obvious pleasure, I could easily have cried. "Thank you," he said, beaming.

"Hey Scarlett." I turned at the sound of another unexpected but familiar voice. Fiona had just come through the kitchen door that led to the rest of the house, looking smoking hot in a slinky, sequined gown. "Don't you look nice?"

"What are you doing here?" I demanded. I felt like the ground was crumbling under my feet. "Sebastian is my date."

Calvin came in behind Fiona and put an arm around her waist. "Calm down, sweetpea," he said, laughing, lighting up the room. He was dazzling, a golden god as always, like he had just that moment stepped out of a movie screen into the kitchen. "Fiona's with me." She turned to smile at him, and he kissed her softly on the lips.

I could feel things snapping inside my head like the lines of a sail snapping loose in a storm. "I have to pee before we go," I heard myself saying. I pushed past my father and Fiona, barely seeing them. "I'll be right back."

I stumbled up the stairs past the Harlequin painting to the first bathroom out of earshot. I had barely closed the door behind me and fallen to my knees before I was throwing up.

I heard Sebastian's voice calling my name, coming closer, up the stairs. "Hey, Scarlett?" I sat down against the bathroom cabinet with my skirt twisted under me. "Scarlett?" he repeated, knocking on the door. "Are you okay?"

"I'm fine," I called, wiping my mouth.

He opened the door without waiting any longer, and as soon as he saw me, his expression clicked over from annoyance to alarm. "Sissy, what's the matter?"

"She's the source," I said. "Ranhosky's source. It's Fiona."

He squatted down beside me. "What are you talking about?"

"Ranhosky told me that he had a source who would testify that Romeo sold drugs on the set of *Funhouse*," I said. "That's how he would be able to have him arrested; that's how he was able to make me break up with him. It's Fiona."

"Scarlett, no," Sebastian said. "That's crazy."

"Is it?" I said. "Fiona hates me."

"She does not hate you."

"She would do anything to keep me and Romeo apart. And now she's with Daddy—doesn't that seem a little weird to you?" The very idea made me want to throw up all over again.

"Very weird, yes," he said. "But Fiona would never, ever do anything to hurt Romeo. Swear to God, Sissy; you're wrong about this."

I knew that I wasn't. I also knew I would never convince my brother. For all his tough talk, he was still just a kid. He wanted the world to be what he wanted it to be, and he refused to see anything else. He couldn't help me. He was one more person I needed to protect.

"Okay," I said, making myself smile. "You're right. It just threw me, that's all."

"God, yeah," he said, laughing. "Me too." He stood up and offered me a hand, and I let him help me up. "Are you okay?"

"Oh yeah." My legs felt like water underneath me. "I guess I'm more freaked out about the awards than I thought I was."

He pulled me into a hug. "Trust me, precious, I know exactly what you mean." He held me tight, and I forced myself not to tense up in his arms. "God, honey, you're shaking." He drew back and looked at me, considering. "Okay," he decided. "Big brother is going to fix this." He opened up the medicine cabinet. "Let's see." He rummaged through the contents until he found the bottle he wanted. "Here," he said, dropping a pill into my open hand. "Just don't tell Daddy."

I looked down at the pill in my palm. I recognized what it was. Greta's therapist had tried to prescribe these for me when I was twelve, but Calvin had refused to let me take them—another lost memory floating back to the surface. I remembered Stella taking something similar, Stella sitting on the bathroom floor just the way I had been a few moments before. I didn't want to be her; I had spent my whole life trying so hard not to be her. But I couldn't stand it. I was losing everything; I was trapped. Somehow, I had to get away.

"I won't tell," I promised. I took the pill with lukewarm water sucked out of the tap, then straightened up and smiled. "Thanks, bubba."

CHAPTER 27

By the time our limo pulled into the line to let us out at the red carpet, I felt like I was dreaming. Nothing around me seemed real. I wasn't dizzy or sick, just a little light-headed, but nothing anyone was saying made the slightest bit of sense. I heard myself talking, and no one else seemed to notice anything was wrong. But it was like I was watching myself in a movie—no. It was like I was imagining the whole thing, musing over a possibility instead of living through it. Everything seemed changeable at any moment, and nothing seemed to matter. I held on to Sebastian's hand, and he kept smiling at me, and I kept smiling back. But his attention was still almost completely focused on the Dane, and that was bad. I definitely didn't like it. But it wasn't really real, I thought, so it didn't really matter. I looked over once as we walked down the carpet and saw my father kissing Fiona on the lips. I burst out laughing as the flashes went off all around us. That could not be real. Sebastian looked at me and said something I didn't realize I'd understood.

"I'm fine," the doll that was my body answered him. The Dane was watching me, I suddenly realized, the wise, speculative look he wore behind the camera on his face. But he wasn't real either. I stuck out my tongue at him and laughed. "This is fun," I said to Sebastian, meaning the pill he had given me.

"Yeah," he answered. Fiona was looking adoringly at my father while he answered some journalist's question. "It is."

Once we were inside the theatre, the illusion of a dream was even stronger. Reality couldn't possibly contain so many pretty people in such a tiny, overcrowded space. I clung to my brother's hand and let him lead me, smiling and waving or kissing everyone who called my name and recognizing no one. Then I saw a discreet little sign on the wall.

"Hey, wait up," I said, jerking Sebastian to a stop. "I need to go pee."

I must have spoken too loudly; several people turned to look at me. I smiled sweetly at them all. "Are you okay?" Sebastian asked me. "Are you sick?"

"Nope." I giggled. "Wait…yep and nope." His grip had tightened on my hand, and I shook it. "Let go. I'm going to wet my pants."

He was frowning, and I laughed. "Hang on," he said, pulling me closer, his free hand on my back. "Let me just find Fiona to go with you."

"No!" I jerked away from him. "I just have to pee, Sebastian, Jesus Christ." I brushed a kiss across his cheek. "I'll see you at the table."

I walked into the weird quiet of the ladies' room, and my euphoria snuffed out like a candle's flame. I staggered on my heels, feeling disoriented. "May I help you, miss?" a voice said—an attendant sitting in the corner. She was smiling with her mouth, but her eyes were dead as a doll's. "Is there something you require?"

"No." I felt exhausted, as if all the life had been sucked out of me at once. There was a long couch along one wall, and I took a step toward it, thinking I would lie down and, if I was lucky, die.

"Scarlett?" One of the stalls had opened, and Bette had stepped out. "Little Magenta!" She swept me up in a warm, bosomy hug that smelled like flowers.

I clung to her like I was drowning. "It's so good to see you," I said, near tears. I still couldn't quite remember why I was so upset, but I knew I was.

"You disappeared so fastly from the premiere," she scolded in her sexy German accent. "We never got to talk at all." She drew back and looked into my face, first smiling, then frowning as she saw me. "Magenta, what is the matter?"

"I think I'm sort of freaking out," I confided. *I'm dreaming,* I suddenly remembered. *This is all a nightmare...but Dream Bette will help me.*

"Dear God, are you drunk?" She gave the attendant a look before drawing me into the stall. "What have you had?" She put her hands on either side of my face, and I closed my eyes, smiling. Her hands felt so good, so cool. "Magenta, answer me!"

"Just some champagne." I was calming down, feeling better. "I'll be all right."

"Where is your father?" She gave me a tiny slap, barely a pat, and I opened my eyes. "Where is Calvin? Does he know you're drunk?"

"I'm not drunk," I insisted, frowning. *Who was she to fuss at me this way?* I thought. *She's not my mother.* That struck me as hilarious, and I started laughing. "He's at the table with his new girlfriend. She's a bitch...okay, maybe not really." My laughter sounded horrible, I realized. Maybe I was crying after all. "Maybe I'm a bitch."

"No," Bette said, stroking my hair. "You are not a bitch, little one, I promise." She wiped the corner of my mouth with the pad of her thumb and kissed me on the forehead. "Come, let's go sit down."

Our table was only two rows back from the stage and nearly dead center. Even I knew what that meant. Somebody thought somebody with us was going to win. Sebastian was sitting beside the Dane, of course, still hanging on his every word. Cal was on the Dane's other side with Fiona beside him, her arm twined through his as she leaned in to listen, too. There were a couple of studio people I didn't really know and a tall, pale man in a sparkling blue rockabilly jacket and a high black pompadour haircut. He stood up, smiling, as Bette and I reached the table, and she kissed him.

"Magenta, this is Tomas," she said, smiling. "He used to be my producer; now he is my fiancé."

"Congratulations," I said, grinning, thrilled beyond measure and reason for them. "Calvin, dig it—Bette is engaged!'

I had never called my father by his first name to his face before, and I could tell it stunned him. He just stared at me for a moment, a weird light in his eyes. Then he snapped back to the moment and smiled. "Bette! Jesus!" he said, standing up and leaving Fiona to come and hug her tight. Watching them, I started laughing. All I could see was Berlin, the sight of them dancing in front of the window, the lights of the city and the snowflakes falling in the colored light. All these little movie scenes inside my head, so pretty and horrible, perfectly lit, and none of them meant anything at all. I sank into the chair beside Sebastian and poured myself a full glass of champagne.

"Sissy," he whispered urgently, putting a hand on my arm. "Are you all right?"

I suddenly remembered something Stella used to say, quoting her father, who had fought in World War II. "Oh yeah." I took a long swallow of my drink, the bubbles tickling my nose. "Situation normal…all fucked up."

The next two hours were a blur. The Dane won, as everybody knew he would, best director of the year. I stood up and applauded with the rest, just glad to see him walk away from the table. I barely heard his speech, but at one point, Sebastian reached over and squeezed my hand, and everyone at the table was smiling at me. "He thanked you for being his muse," Sebastian whispered in my ear.

"Oh gross," I said, not quite a whisper back. "I'm going to puke." But I smiled back at the others just the same.

Sebastian kept a hold on my hand through the next award, best supporting actor in a drama, the category he was nominated in. His hand was ice cold and shaking, I suddenly realized. I turned toward him, putting my other hand over his and leaning close. He leaned in also, and he kissed my cheek as the nominees were read. His lips were icy, too.

Then they read out the name of the winner—somebody else. "Oh thank God," he mumbled against my ear, squeezing my hands in his. "Thank you, Jesus." He let me go to applaud, and I clapped with him.

I felt eyes on me, and I turned toward the stage. The Dane was standing in the wings just outside the blinding light of the stage, watching and smiling at me and my brother. I turned my head away from him and reached past my own glass of champagne to take the half-drunk Scotch of the producer on my left. Closing my eyes, I drained it. A comforting warmth spread through me as the taste glowed on my tongue, and I smiled, sinking back into my dreamy trance.

"Scarlett," Sebastian said urgently, taking my hand again. The winner of his category had finished his speech and was being played off the stage by the orchestra. "This is you." I stared at him blankly. "Your category," he pressed on. "You need to pay attention; you might win."

I laughed. "Yeah, right." No one in the world expected that. The nominees were me, Bette, a producer's new wife, a three-time winner, and a former siren of the '60s who was up for playing the evil dowager duchess in a Merchant-Ivory flick. More importantly, as far as I was concerned, Sebastian hadn't won. I didn't stand a chance. I set my empty glass down and smiled across the table at Bette, who winked back. We didn't stand a snowball's chance in Vegas.

Then the actor at the podium called my name.

At first, I didn't react, thinking he was just reading out the nominees. Then I realized people were looking at me and applauding. I turned toward my smiling brother and fell into his arms. He kissed my cheek and started pushing me away. "Go," he said when I tried to hold on to him. "You have to go."

I stood up as Calvin came around the table, and I grabbed him next, dissolving into tears. *Don't make me go,* I wanted to beg him; *go for me; this is a mistake.* But he was kissing me and pointing me toward the stage. I started walking, one foot moving mechanically in front of the other until I reached the stage, stumbling a little on the steps. I turned into the blinding lights, wide-eyed, crying, completely at a loss. The extremely tall, skinny English actor who had called my name was smiling down at me, polite and barely interested as he put the trophy in my hands. I let out a little hiccup as I gripped it, and he raised an eyebrow before leaning in to hug me.

"Breathe," he ordered in a whisper. "Thank the Foreign Press."

"Yes," I was whispering back, my knees weak with gratitude.

"Your father, your brother, the people who worked on the film." He drew back, the polite smile still on his face, but his eyes now sparkling with mischief, and I smiled back.

"Thank you," I said to him out loud, and the mike picked it up—the opening of my speech. I turned toward the audience, startled, and everyone laughed, and I felt myself smile. "I'm…I want to thank the Hollywood Foreign Press." My voice sounded like a stranger on a TV in another room, and I could only see the faces of the people at the very front. The '60s siren I had beaten was smiling up at me with brittle cheer. "And my father." I couldn't see Calvin, but I could imagine him, smiling, so beautiful, so proud. "I love you so much, Daddy." I was crying again, but now I had control of it. "And Sebastian, thank you. And everyone who worked on the film…Wolfie." My handler's face was the first one to pop into my head, Wolfie crying as he drove me home after the wrap party. "You're amazing, Wolfie, wherever you are," I said. "You're going to be a great director."

Saying the word made me look toward the wings. The Dane was still standing there, much closer now. He smiled at me, but I did not smile back. "And Bette," I said, turning back to the mike. "Who is brilliant, and all of the other nominees." I could see the conductor raising his baton, ready for me to be done, and I started to step back and walk away. Then I thought of something else, something important that I never got the chance to say. "And Stella," I said suddenly, leaning close to the mike so it was loud. "My beautiful mama." My throat was closing up, and I was trembling, but I was determined I would get it out. "I miss you so much, and I love you." I was crying harder now. "And I wish so much that you were here." I held up the trophy, and I saw the '60s siren weeping. "This is for you."

The band started playing as soon as I started turning away. The scarecrow-looking English actor whose name I wished I had paid attention to took hold of my elbow. I smiled at him again and let him lead me off the stage.

CHAPTER 28

Miss Golden Globes, the pretty thing in charge of showing people how to get on and off the stage, was a girl I knew from junior high school. She had been on the cheer squad that had kicked me off. "Hey Scarlett," she said, smiling. The last time she had said my name, she had asked me if I was on drugs, which suddenly struck me as hilarious. "Congratulations."

I smiled back at her. "Thanks." A giggle escaped me. "You look beautiful."

"Congratulations, little one." The Great Dane was suddenly beside me. Before I could react, he had swept me up into a hug.

I made a hissing, snarling sound and shoved him backward. Miss Golden Globes had already turned her globes back toward the stage, but there was another chick standing there, waiting to lead me to the press. She was watching us, obviously curious, and I felt sick. I pushed past her to the fire exit, shoving it open and stumbling out onto a concrete dock, barely making it to the railing before I started throwing up, my vomit spattering across the asphalt of the parking lot below.

"Scarlett!" The Dane had followed me. I could feel his shadow moving over me as I leaned over the rail in the glare of the floodlights overhead.

"No!" I said, still snarling as I whipped my head around. "Touch me again, and I'll kill you." I turned back to the railing and vomited again, powerless to stop it.

The Dane muttered something weakly in what I could only assume was Danish. He lurched slowly back from me and sat down on the dirty concrete steps in his beautiful tuxedo. My stomach empty, I stepped back from the railing. I was still clutching my award.

"What have I done?" he said softly in English. "Sweet god…sweet child, what have I done to you?" His eyes touched my face for barely a moment before he looked away. "Little one, you must listen to me." His face was ashen as he gazed across the parking lot. "I never meant to frighten you. I know that you are just a child, that you cannot understand." He was trembling, and I wanted badly to bash his head in with my Golden Globe. "But I love you, little one, more deeply than you can imagine in my own way. I would cherish you with all my heart. We could do great things." He looked back at me, his soft gray eyes shining. "You could be brilliant, little one," he said. "If you would let me, I could make you so."

I wiped my mouth with the back of my hand. The smell of my vomit was like the stink of whiskey on his breath in that office in Berlin. "You didn't frighten me, you stupid bastard." My voice sounded like someone else. "You make me sick." I was learning how to act. "Let me tell you a secret, Gramps. My father lied. I'm seventeen years old, almost eighteen now. And I wasn't a virgin when we met. You may have tried to fuck your share of babies in your time, but sorry, I wasn't one of them." His mouth dropped open, the light fading out of his eyes. "I'm with someone, you pathetic old fool." His reaction was like another, better drug than the pill Sebastian had given me, making me feel powerful and thrilled. "You can't believe how gorgeous my lover is. He's beautiful and young, like me, and I knew him already when I met you." He lunged to his feet, and I took a step backward, but I didn't stop talking. "I was already sleeping with him before you ever even met me, you bastard." His knuckles were white as he caught hold of the railing. "When I told him what you did to me, we laughed," I said, the lie coming out of me like nothing. I had been lying all my life. "He feels sorry for you, Gramps. He said it was cruel of me not to tell you the truth." I smiled. "So now I have."

He raised a trembling hand. "Stop it," he begged, barely louder than a whisper. Stop it—I had begged him that before Wolfie pulled him away.

"I don't need you to make me anything," I finished, glaring straight into his face. "My father and I made your stupid movie a success. You were washed up when my father rescued you." I took a step toward him, and he actually recoiled. "If you ever put a single, filthy hand on me or my brother again, I'll scream rape in every paper on the planet. They will lock you up and throw away the key." He crumpled to his knees in front of me, his eyes glazing over, one hand still clutching the railing. "My lover has been to jail before; he's told me what happens to child fuckers there." His breathing was raspy and labored, but I still couldn't make myself stop. "I hope somebody takes pictures."

His grip loosened, and he crumpled to the dock. He was still breathing, great, rattling gasps, and his eyes were still open. But it was obvious he couldn't hear me anymore.

I just stood there staring for what could have been ten seconds or an hour. I was paralyzed, a character in a film that had frozen in the projector. The Dane was twitching slightly, gape-mouthed like a fish, his glassy eyes fixed on my face.

The door burst open between us. "Sorry," said the Scarecrow who had given me my award as he plunged out into the night, a cigarette already in his hand. "Must have a fag." He saw the Dane and froze for what I was sure was no more than three seconds. "Bloody hell." He closed the door completely but quietly and squatted down beside the Dane, sticking his cigarette behind his ear, and touched the pulse at the side of the Dane's neck, concentrating

"What's wrong with him?" I said.

"No idea." He stood up. "Heart attack, maybe, or stroke." He looked back at me and grinned. "Unless you shot him?"

"No!" I said, appalled. "I just...we were just talking, and he...he just fell over." The sound of my own voice was bringing me out of my trance, and not in a good way. I felt like I might pass out.

"Steady on, love," the Scarecrow said, standing up and catching me firmly by both arms. "You didn't do anything wrong." His bright blue eyes took in my face, the Dane, my vomit on the pavement, all in a series of camera-like clicks that again took no more than a few seconds. "Far from it is my guess." He kissed my forehead, and I smelled soap, whiskey, and tobacco. "There now, run along inside." Keeping a firm but gentle grip on my arm above the elbow, he opened the door and steered me back inside.

The backstage area hadn't changed at all. We might have just that moment stepped outside. The last few minutes might not ever have happened.

"There's a good girl," the Scarecrow said softly just behind my ear. I turned to him, and he smiled, a charming grin that completely transformed his gaunt and slightly horsy face, making him quite handsome. "I'll sort it out," he promised.

"Scarlett!" Miss Golden Globes was rushing toward me, surefooted in her heels. "Your dad just won!"

The Scarecrow let me go as she grabbed hold of me. I looked back over my shoulder as she hauled me toward the wings, and he waved, still grinning as I rounded the corner and stopped at the edge of the light.

Calvin was standing at the podium, his golden hair glowing in the spotlight. He was obviously giving a kick-ass speech; the actress who had presented to him was crying, her hands clasped as in prayer between her tits, ready to burst into applause. I realized I was crying, too; I had tears running down my cheeks. Without letting myself stop to think another moment, I turned away from the stage and started pushing through the gathering crowd, headed for the exit.

I found a side door that by-passed the press and opened on a mostly deserted alley. I knew it was likely that any minute now, Calvin would realize I wasn't in the press room, or worse, the Dane would be discovered. But I didn't know how to escape. I had nothing, no money, no clue what to do next. My purse was still hanging on the back of my chair in the ballroom.

A small knot of security guards was gathered in the alley smoking, but they barely seemed to notice me. A barricade had been set up at the end of the alley, blocking it off from the street. Just beyond that was a seething tide of photographers waiting for the show to be over. If I tried to go that way, I'd be overrun.

Just as I was starting to panic, I heard the door behind me open. "Miss Cross?" It was the Scarecrow again, the actor who had presented me with the award I was still carrying. "The paramedics have been called, and my agent has informed me that I need to not be on the scene when they arrive." He seemed to notice my panicked expression. "Are you all right now?" he asked. "Do I need to find your father?"

"No!" I made myself calm down. "I mean, yes, I'm fine." That wasn't technically true, but we had just met. "I'm sorry; I'm a little freaked out. I can't remember your name."

"Simon Price." He made a little bow that only an English actor could have pulled off without looking ridiculous. "So what's the plan, Scarlett? Are we hiding out until the heat blows over?"

I couldn't help but smile, scared as I was. "Something like that. I need to get to the Sunset Strip. I have to find someone."

"Lucky someone." Simon said.

"I'm not so sure about that." He was being so nice. "You keep rescuing me tonight."

Simon just smiled. "My pleasure. How can I help?"

"Well…I feel horrible asking, but I don't have anything but this stupid award." I couldn't believe I was asking a stranger for money. "Could you maybe lend me cab fare?"

"I'm not sure you can be trusted on your own," he said, but I could see from his face he was teasing. "Before I abduct you, how old are you, Scarlett?"

"Eighteen," I lied without a moment's hesitation. "Perfectly legal, I swear."

"Well, not perfectly," he said with another grin. "But I'll risk it. Come on, let's go."

CHAPTER 29

It took us a couple of hours, and we ended up having to pay the cover at four different clubs. But in the end, we found Romeo.

He was standing on the wall behind the bandstand, talking to a guy with an electric guitar. Fiona was standing beside him, dressed now in jeans and a tee-shirt, drinking from a bottle of beer she had just taken from Romeo's hand. She saw me before he did, and her eyes widened. Romeo saw her expression change and turned. He saw me, and his face lit up, and every little fucked up thing was fine.

"Baby," he said, coming to meet me. I threw my arms around his neck and held on tight. He crushed me close, and I could feel his heart beating just as hard as mine.

"I ran away," I told him. "I couldn't stay." In that moment, I almost told him everything, all about Berlin and the Dane and Italy and why I couldn't go there and why I was so scared and how I was pretty sure I had just murdered him on the loading dock outside the Golden Globes. But those weren't the words that came out. "I couldn't give you up."

"It's okay," he promised. He cradled the back of my head in his hand, holding me to him. "It'll be fine."

Simon had finally made it through the crowd. "I'll take it this is the person we were looking for," he said as Romeo kissed me again.

"She sucked you in, too?" I heard Fiona say. "You poor bastard."

"Romeo, this is Simon Price," I said, ignoring her. "Simon, yes, this is exactly who I wanted. Meet Romeo Kidd."

"Delighted," Simon said, smiling.

"Simon helped me get here," I explained. "I didn't have my purse, so I didn't have any money."

"I believe Scarlett was forced to make an unplanned escape," Simon said.

"Are you all right?" Romeo asked me.

"Yes, I'm fine now." That wasn't true; we were still fucked, but I felt safer with him. "He rescued me."

"It wasn't quite that dramatic," Simon said.

"Still, thanks," Romeo said, kissing the top of my head.

"Let's hope it doesn't come back to bite you in the ass," Fiona said.

"Shouldn't you be back at Castle Asshole chewing on my father's tongue or something?" I said.

Simon looked over at her like he was noticing her for the first time and found her fascinating. "I'm not worried." He was looking at all of us like we were a particularly interesting play. "Scarlett, if you're safe now, I'll leave you with your friends."

"Thanks, Simon." I let go of Romeo just long enough to hug him. "I'll pay you back, I promise."

"It was my pleasure." He hugged me back then shook Romeo's hand. "Good luck."

"Scarlett, what happened?" Fiona put a hand on my bare arm.

"Go find Sebastian," Romeo told her. He drew back from me enough to look at her, but his arm was still around me. "Tell him Scarlett's safe with me and to meet us at my sister's house as quick as he can get there."

"I'm sure Sebastian's still at the after party," I said. Romeo sounded so calm, I could already feel my heart rate coming back to normal. "I would have thought Fiona would be, too."

"She left when you disappeared," Romeo said. "She was looking for you."

"This is crazy," Fiona said, but she wasn't talking to me. "Don't do this."

"Are you going to help us or not?" he asked. I smelled whiskey on his breath, but his voice was perfectly steady.

"Of course I'm going to help you." She looked at me. "And you, whether you deserve it or not."

I rode with Romeo on his motorcycle through a misting, steamy rain to his sister's McMansion in the valley. By the time we got there, my teeth were chattering with cold. I had never seen the house before. He had always come to me. It was big and brick, kind of pink; it looked like a Suburban Barbie Dream House. Every window was blazing with lights, and there were two valets out front, parking cars. A pair of stretch limos, one white and one black, were pulled up at the front door, which was standing open, showing people standing in a cloud of smoke inside.

We drove around back and into the garage. "Come on," he said, helping me climb down, my party dress now soaked and hiked up past my ass. I wobbled a little on my heels, clinging to him with both my hands as he led me through the kitchen door into the house.

We made our way past the caterers and down a short hallway to the stairs. Hip-hop was throbbing so loud, I could feel it in my teeth, and a red-haired girl with perfect make-up was on the landing doing coke off a hand mirror held by a pudgy, middle-aged man I recognized from brunch at my father's. He actually nodded to me as we passed. We went up two floors to a door at the very top of the stairs. Romeo took a key out of his pocket and unlocked it. "This is my room." Still holding my hand, he led me inside. "Wait for me in here." He kissed me, and I clung to him. "I'll go see if Amy has something dry you can put on." I didn't want to let him go. "It's okay," he promised again, touching his cheek to mine. "I'll be right back."

His bedroom looked like it belonged in a completely different house. It was the attic, with a sloping ceiling on either side. The walls at either end were lined completely with cheap plywood bookshelves.

One side was all books, hardcovers, paperbacks, magazines, and comics, all lined up neatly but stuffed in so tightly they looked ready to explode. The other side was record albums, most so old the edges of the covers were worn white. These shelves were labeled with neat black plastic label-maker strips, A-C, D-F, etc.

I sat down on the bed, tarnished brass, neatly made with a navy blue duvet decorated with what looked little red, white, and yellow sailing flags. Three unframed posters hung above the headboard—the Allman Brothers Band and Jean-Paul Belmondo in a close-up from *Breathless* were hanging side by side; above them was a naked fairy princess with light brown hair and gossamer lavender wings. There were two more white doors in the wall across from the bed, one open to a tacky gold-and-salmon-colored bathroom, the other closed. Between the doors was a battered dresser with a mirror half-obscured with taped up photographs.

I went and used the bathroom and wrapped up in a flannel shirt Romeo had left on the floor. The music from downstairs had changed. I could hear it better in the bathroom, and I heard the throbbing bass fade out. I went back out and looked at the photos on the mirror. One was recent, Romeo before he got his hair cut, standing with some other young dude, their arms around each other's shoulders, cigarettes hanging from the corners of their mouths. I smiled, barely touching the image of Romeo's face.

The others were obviously older, snapshots of a gorgeous little boy with Romeo's eyes sitting on some woman's lap on an ugly plaid couch and of a pretty brunette girl in short shorts posing beside a muscle car. Then there was a really old one, a battered sepia portrait of a Civil War soldier. Under his cap, I thought he had Romeo's eyes, too. Then taped at the very edge of the mirror were three photographs of me. One was a paparazzi shot, obviously torn out of a tabloid, of me and Calvin coming out of a restaurant in Beverly Hills a year or so before. Then there was a smaller publicity still from *Match Girl* that had been carefully cut out of a glossy magazine. Finally, there was a Polaroid of me and Romeo together in a club. "Look sexy!" Sebastian had said before he snapped it. I had my chin tilted up and my lips pouted out. Romeo was kissing my throat, his eyes closed like he was praying.

Just as I was taking it down to look at it more closely, the door opened, and he came back in. "Hey," he said, smiling and kissing me quickly on the mouth. "I got you some of Amy's jeans." He handed them to me and opened a dresser drawer. "This will swallow you, but at least it's dry." He handed me a soft, black tee-shirt with a cracked logo for the Ramones on it.

"Thanks." I held it to my face, breathing in his smell. He kept rummaging through the drawer, coming out with a thick, tight roll of cash. "What is that?"

He pulled out two more. "Road money." He lined them up on the dresser top. "We don't have much time." He took my hands and kissed me again, deeper this time, and I slumped against him. I needed his warmth and his kiss and most of all his certainty.

"I'm so sorry, baby," I said, wrapping my arms around him. "What are we going to do?" I started shaking, thinking about Ranhosky's threats and the Dane touching me like I belonged to him then slumping to the ground. "I won't let them arrest you, I swear."

"Nobody's going to arrest me." He held me tighter for a moment, kissing the top of my head, then pulled away to look at me. "They're bluffing, I promise."

No, they're not, I thought. "We have to get married." The thought didn't even form inside my head; it just fell out of my mouth. "If we're married, Calvin won't dare let anyone arrest you."

He looked stunned. "Scarlett…"

"People get married for stupider reasons all the time." For a second, I thought about Stella, but I pushed the thought away. "I love you," I said, touching his cheek. "I want to be with you."

He smiled, the sweet and dreamy smile that always made me melt. "I love you, too."

"Then marry me." I smiled back. "You want me to get down on my knees?"

"Not just now." He kissed me. "You're crazy." He kissed me again. "I will have a crazy wife."

Once we decided to do it, things started moving really fast. Romeo took me back downstairs and got his sister, Amy, to call her lawyer, who showed up within about ten minutes. Amy didn't talk to me or even really look at me, but she made us sandwiches in the kitchen. The lawyer sat at the bar talking to his office on the phone until he found out the closest place we could get married without my father's permission—Texas. By that time, Sebastian and Fiona had shown up. Fiona and Amy hugged, and Sebastian took me outside.

"Did she tell him? I asked him. "Did Fiona tell Calvin where I am?"

"Of course not," he said. "Sissy, listen to me." The last of Amy's male guests were driving away, and some of the girls from the party were gathering on the deck, kicking off their shoes, opening a bottle of wine. A guy in a white uniform was cleaning the hot tub with a long-handled brush. "Are you sure about this?" he asked.

"I'm sure," I said. "I love him." *Will we live here after?* I thought. *Will Daddy let me bring my husband home?* "It will be okay."

Romeo and the lawyer decided driving would be safer than flying. Sebastian said that Calvin had gone to the hospital with the Dane, so we were pretty sure he wouldn't miss me before morning. "I'm coming with you," Sebastian said. "He won't miss me, either, and you might need me."

"Great," Amy's lawyer said, shaking Romeo's hand. "I'll see you in El Paso." He was planning to fly out overnight and get things set up for us, and Amy had hired us a limo.

"I'm scared for you," Amy told Romeo as she hugged him good-bye at the front door. She was scary beautiful, a Barbie come to life, with long, platinum blonde hair and the same huge brown eyes as her brother, and she had the soft Southern accent he had worked so hard to lose.

"Don't be scared," he told her, hugging her back. She closed her eyes and leaned her head on his shoulder. Suddenly, I recognized her from her photo on his dresser mirror. She was the brunette posed on the muscle car. "I'll be back in a couple of days."

Sebastian came out of the house carrying a bottle of champagne in one hand and a bag of taco chips in the other. "Let's hit it."

"We better get going," Romeo agreed. He let go of Amy and took my hand. "Are you ready?"

"Absolutely." Fiona was leaning on the railing of the steps. "Thanks for your help," I said. "When you see my dad, tell him I'm sorry."

"I'm going with you, too." Her eyes were on Romeo. "If this thing goes to shit, you'll need all the help you can get."

Sitting on the plush leather seat of the limo, watching the lights of Los Angeles slide past the windows like stars, I pushed all the scary bits about what I was doing—Calvin's reaction, where we would live, what would happen to Romeo if we got caught before the deed was done—into the iron closet in my mind where I had learned to lock up demons long ago. Sebastian was sitting across from me, crunching down his taco chips, and I smiled at him. Holding Romeo's hand, I closed my eyes, and five minutes later, I was sound asleep.

CLIPPING 10

from *The Los Angeles Times*

Famed Danish director Aksel Jorgen, 61, suffered a massive stroke on Sunday night backstage at this year's Golden Globe Awards just after being presented with the award for Best Director. The Hollywood Foreign Press honored Jorgen for his film The Little Match Girl, *based in part on the director's own experiences in Europe before and after WWII. The film garnered awards for stars Calvin Cross (Best Actor in a Drama) and his fourteen-year-old daughter, Scarlett Cross (Best Supporting Actress).*

Jorgen was alone at the time of his attack but was discovered within minutes. He remains in what doctors describe as 'stable but uncommunicative' condition at St. Joseph's Hospital in Beverly Hills.

CHAPTER 30

When my eyes opened, it was daylight. "Where are we?" I had slumped over with my head in Romeo's lap.

He brushed the hair back from my face. "Arizona."

Fiona was stretched out alone on her back on the seat across from us, covered with Sebastian and Romeo's jackets. "Where's Sebastian?" I said, sitting up.

"Up front with the driver." He smiled at me. "They hit it off at the last pit stop."

"We stopped?" I looked out the window. We were in the desert, blinding bright, with telephone poles whipping past.

"Twice." He put his arm around me, and I snuggled up against him. "You were sleeping so hard, we decided not to wake you." I was shivering. "Are you cold?"

"No." I laced my fingers with his, drawing his arm more tightly around me. "Just waking up." I felt weird, watching the desert go by; all my serenity seemed to be bleeding away in the light. I had a sudden, crazy urge to start screaming, to lunge past Fiona and start banging on the glass to tell the driver to stop and turn around.

"Hey, come here." Romeo pulled me into his lap, and I turned to face him, to face away from the window, straddling him as he kissed me. "I love you," he said.

"I love you." Fiona muttered something vaguely pissy and rolled over, putting her back to us. "I love you," I repeated, framing his face in my hands as I kissed him again.

"Baby," he mumbled low against my mouth, his hands on my hips to shift me closer. "My baby."

I moved my mouth to his throat, biting and sucking, his stubble prickling my lips. He smelled so good, I wanted to breathe him in forever. He dipped his head to catch my mouth with his again, and he tasted as good as he smelled, so good I felt dizzy. *I could have lost him*, I thought, the inexplicable fear I'd felt a few moments before refocusing on him. He turned to lie back on the seat, and I scrambled to keep up, to keep my mouth feeding on his. I was laying full length on top of him, my crotch pressed to his, and I felt him swell hard between us through our jeans. His hands slipped underneath my loose T-shirt, caressing my bare back, and my breath caught short. The hard denim seam of my jeans was driving me crazy. My hand came down with a crunch on what was left of Sebastian's chips as I tried to brace on the floor to change positions. We both laughed; I put my head down on his shoulder, trying to hold back the giggles.

"Hang on," he said, kissing my cheek. He sat up, shifting me to his lap, and leaned forward to rap on the glass. "Dude, we need to stop."

"Like this," I said, reaching over him to press the intercom button. "Excuse me, driver. We need to stop." He nuzzled my ear, and I bit back a giggle. "It's an emergency."

"Scarlett, are you sick?" Sebastian's voice came back, concerned.

"No." Romeo slid a hand under my shirt again to cup my breast over my bra, the same lacy underwire I had worn to the awards. I closed my eyes, light-headed. "I just need to pee."

"God, shut up!" Fiona moaned, pulling Romeo's jacket up over her head.

"You shut up," I said, nudging her ass with my foot. She flipped me off, one hand emerging from her cocoon, and Romeo and I both laughed, wrapped around each other.

We stopped at a dusty little two-pump gas station in the middle of nowhere. There was literally nothing but road, rocks, and cacti as far as you could see in every direction. The heat was like walking into a wall. It knocked the breath out of me as soon as I stepped out of the car, and for a second, I was scared again. Then Romeo took me in his arms and kissed me, and the demon that was trying to escape the box in my head retreated. I wasn't a scared little girl; I was a woman in love.

We went into the gas station, and he followed me into the ladies' room, ignoring the shocked expression of the woman stocking shelves with canned goods on the way. "Hey, wait," I said, laughing, planting a palm in the middle of his chest. "I really do have to pee."

"So go ahead," he asked with a grin of pure mischief. "I'll wait."

"Well, yeah, but…"

"We're going to be married, remember?" He took my hands and kissed me. "This will be good practice."

"Practice, huh?" Feeling very reckless and wicked, I backed into a stall, dropped my pants, and peed. I didn't even close and lock the door. "Okay," I said again when I was done and wiped. "Let's do it." I kicked out of my shoes and pants as I came out of the stall, and he grabbed me up and kissed me. He lifted me off of my feet to swing me up on the edge of the sink. "I love you," I sighed into his ear as I ground myself against him, and his kiss at my throat became a bite, his breathing hot and labored. I didn't help him with his jeans, just held on, caressing his hair. His mouth caught mine again as I heard his belt buckle fall on the dirty tile floor, and I caught a glimpse that barely registered of a security camera in the corner pointed straight at us at the sink before I closed my eyes.

When we came out of the ladies' room, we could see Sebastian and Fiona through the window, already back in the parking lot. Fiona was talking to the driver, and Sebastian was coming around the corner of the building. "Go on back out," Romeo said, kissing the corner of my mouth. "I'll get us something to eat."

He came out a few minutes later with a box full of white bags and

Styrofoam cups. "They have a grill," he explained, setting it down on the hood of the limo.

"Thank God," Fiona said, reaching past me to grab a red-and-white checked tray of fries. "I'm starving."

"You kids better eat in the car," the driver said, taking a soda. "We're supposed to be in El Paso by two."

"We'll make it," Romeo said. Sebastian was drinking beer from a longneck bottle, and Romeo put a burger in his hand. "You better slow down, Sunshine."

"Fuck you," Sebastian said, but he was smiling.

"Can't do it," Romeo answered, smiling at me. "I'm engaged." He reached into his pocket and pulled out a little crumpled brown bag. "I got you a present."

"What is it?" I said, but I already knew. The Mexican police detective who had come to see me every day after Stella was killed had always brought me the exact same kind of bag. I took it and opened it. "Oo, look." A wave of love for him swept over me and relief so strong I could easily have cried. "I've got candy." Inside the bag were a handful of skull-shaped lollipops, red and orange and purple with the faces frosted white.

"They're for the Day of the Dead," Romeo explained. "I think the idea is that you eat them and devour all your ghosts." He fished a purple one out of the bag. "Eat this, and you don't have to be scared anymore."

"That sounds good." I kissed him. "Actually, that sounds perfect."

We were only a few minutes late pulling into El Paso. Romeo had the driver pull over at a pay phone so he could call the local lawyer Amy's lawyer had hooked us up with from L.A. "I'll be right back," he said, kissing me on the mouth.

I stared out the window, sucking on one of my skull pops, and watched him cross the street. We were in an ugly freeway neighborhood surrounded by billboards in Spanish and a rat's nest of power lines. Behind the phone stand was a motel or apartment block with a mural painted on it of a big, fat, orange Aztec god reclining on his side. The driver had turned on the radio for traffic reports, and

Michael Stipe was singing "It's the end of the world as we know it, and I feel fine."

"This looks like Mexico," I said.

"Does it?" Sebastian said. He moved to sit beside me. "We're close."

"Really close," the driver said; Sebastian had opened the glass. "Like, one block over there."

I looked the direction he was pointing and saw a high, cinder block wall. "I'm surprised you even remember Mexico," Sebastian said, taking my hand.

"When were you in Mexico?" Fiona asked. She had been watching Romeo, too, in a kind of sleepy trance, but this seemed to perk her up.

"When she was really small," Sebastian explained before I could answer. "Her mother was murdered there."

"Don't tell her that," I said. "I don't want to talk about that."

Fiona shook her head. "You know, I don't know why you feel like you have to be such a bitch to me, Scarlett." She took the last of Sebastian's longnecks out of the refrigerator. "I didn't steal your boyfriend; you stole mine."

"He wasn't your boyfriend," I pointed out, looking out the window again. "You just wanted to fuck him." Romeo was on the phone now. He looked like an unmade bed in ratty jeans and a T-shirt. But the old *mamacita* ladies walking past him on the sidewalk still turned around to look at him and smiled at one another—he was so beautiful. *He doesn't look real,* I thought.

"You don't know that," Fiona said.

"So what?" I said, looking back at her. "You love him?" She didn't answer. "If that's true, why are you with my father? What are you really doing here?"

"Hey, cut it out," Sebastian said. "He's coming back."

The local lawyer's office was right down the street from the courthouse. One of the secretaries took me and Fiona over to the mall to buy a dress so I didn't have to get married in Amy's hootchie mama jeans and Romeo's tee-shirt. I bought a white dress with spaghetti straps and lots of filmy layers with some of the Romeo's road money. Romeo and Sebastian went with the lawyer to a jewelry store to buy a ring. We met back up at the law firm, ate take-out Chinese they had ordered in, and I changed my clothes. Then we went over to the courthouse: me, Romeo, Sebastian, Loki, Amy's lawyer (who pretended to be Romeo's uncle), the local lawyer, and the local lawyer's secretary, who had all of our paperwork in a manila folder.

The judge was a pretty lady who looked to be in her fifties with a thick, Dale Evans accent. She was wearing a pink linen suit with short sleeves and a pink and green floral print blouse with a big, floppy bow. I was carrying the white Bible my grandmother had sent me because Amy's lawyer thought it would add a nice touch, so Fiona was carrying my flowers, a little white bouquet someone at the law firm had gotten from somewhere.

The local lawyer talked to the judge, telling her some story about who we were and why we were in Texas getting married. I didn't really pay attention. "You look beautiful," Romeo whispered in my ear. "I love you."

"I love you, too." It was hot, even with the air conditioning. I remember bars of sunlight falling on us through the venetian blinds like in a film noir. The judge had a beautifully carved wooden desk and a rolling office chair so old and busted the yellow foam had worn through the upholstery.

We signed our application for a marriage license with the same blue ballpoint pen. The judge's clerk made photocopies of my birth certificate and Romeo's driver's license, then the judge gave us a little talk about the sanctity of marriage. I halfway expected her to start in on the birds and the bees. She asked us if we were sure we were ready to be married, and I suppose I must have told her yes. I really don't remember. I do remember Romeo saying he was and taking my hand, and she smiled. I was holding the Bible in my other hand like a clutch purse. The air conditioning kicked in again, and goose flesh broke out on my bare back.

Then the ceremony started. It only took five minutes, if that. I was surprised to hear it was exactly the same words from every wedding I had ever seen in a movie or TV show. I said, "I do," when I was supposed to, and Romeo did, too. When he put the ring on my finger, our eyes met, and we both smiled at the same moment, and I realized I was happy.

"I now pronounce you man and wife," the judge said. "So go on and give her a kiss."

We kissed like people in a movie, and everybody applauded. "Congratulations, honey," the judge said to me when Romeo let me go, taking my hand in both of hers.

"Thank you." I turned back to Romeo and kissed him again, throwing my arms around his neck. Sebastian and the secretary cried.

CHAPTER 31

We checked into a nice hotel, all of us staggering and stupid, we were so tired. Standing at the front desk with Sebastian and Fiona while Amy's lawyer checked us in, Romeo and I both got the giggles and couldn't stop. I'm sure the desk clerk thought we were drunk out of our minds. My new husband tried to kiss my mouth and missed, catching my cheek instead. "Hey, Scarlett, guess what?" he said, making me break up again. "We're married."

"Holy crow, you're kidding!" I said, making Sebastian and Fiona bust up, too. The desk clerk and Amy's lawyer exchanged weary smiles. "That's Mrs. Kidd to you, buddy," I said, poking Romeo in the chest.

"Oo, sorry."

"Mr. Kidd."

Fiona and Sebastian broke down in giggles again, but we were kissing. That time, he didn't miss.

As soon as we made it to the room, I dropped my purse and the shopping bag I was carrying and went into the bathroom. I turned on the cold water and used hotel soap to start taking off the thick layer of make-up I'd put on back at the lawyer's office to make myself look like a marriageable person. From where I was standing, I could see Romeo in the mirror, putting the rest of our shopping bags on the bed. "Do you need to get in here?" I asked him.

"No," he said. "I'm good." He opened my purse and took out the white Bible. "I didn't realize you had kept this."

"Yeah, I've been carrying it around in my purse since we found it." My eyes were still smeared with mascara. I looked like a raccoon. "I'm not sure why."

"I think it's nice." He put the Bible down on the dresser and started emptying his pockets.

"I guess." I put hotel toothpaste on my hotel toothbrush. "My grandmother is a fine, God-fearing woman."

He was taking off his shirt, but I could hear his muffled snicker. "You don't have to sound so snarky about it." He came into the bathroom. "God, you're such a brat."

"Yeah, well," I said through a mouthful of toothpaste before spitting it out in the sink. "You knew what I was when you married me, pal."

"I did." He came up behind me as I wiped my mouth on a towel and put his hands on my hips. It felt strange, being together again after being apart for so long, sharing the same bathroom, strange but good. "It must be love." I giggled as he kissed my shoulder and nuzzled my neck. "You know what we should do?"

"Not absolutely," I said, pressing back against him. "But I can guess."

"Oh yeah, that too." He squeezed me tight for a moment, his arms wrapped around me. Exhausted as I was, I still shivered, wanting him. "But after that." He kissed my cheek. "After we get some sleep." He unzipped my dress. "We should go to Tupelo."

"What?" I wasn't really focusing on what he was saying. I thought I must have heard him wrong.

"We should go see your grandmamma." He slid my dress off my shoulders, brushing the backs of his fingers down my spine.

"Oh god, why?" I looked at our reflection in the bathroom mirror. We were as beautiful as made-up people from a movie, especially him.

"I want to meet your people." He traced the curve of my shoulder blade. "God, you're beautiful."

"Trust me, baby. They are not my people." The last thing I wanted to think about was my long-lost white trash grandparents in Tupelo, Mississippi. "I only met them once, and I barely remember them." I turned to face him. "You know Sebastian." I draped my arms around his neck. "He's my people."

"And your father." His eyes were serious. "Maybe I want to meet some more of your people who don't actually hate my guts."

"Calvin doesn't hate your guts." I didn't know that this was true, but I didn't want to think about Calvin, either. "But it doesn't matter." I kissed him, pressing close. "You're my people now."

"Yes." He held me tight, resting his chin on the top of my head. "I am."

"You're all the people I need."

We consummated our marriage in the traditional way on the hotel bed. By the big red numbers on the digital clock on the bedside table, it took about four minutes, and I was asleep before he'd finished rolling off of me.

I woke up a few hours later to the ringing of the phone. Romeo rolled over and made a sort of moaning, grunting sound, but it was on my side of the bed. "No, I'll get it," I said, pretty much instantly awake. "Hello?"

"Hey," Sebastian's voice answered.

"Go back to sleep," I told Romeo, who already had. "It's Sebastian." I sat up, propping a pillow behind me. "Hey," I said back to Sebastian. "What are you doing up?"

"Can you meet me in the lobby by yourself?" He sounded awful, I realized, as if he had been crying. "It's important."

"What's going on?" The terrible anxiety I had been pretending I didn't feel for the past thirty-six hours writhed in my belly like a snake.

"Just come down," he said. "It's fine; everything's cool. Just don't bring Romeo, okay?"

I pinched my lower lip, thinking about it. "Okay." He was my brother; I trusted him. "I'll be down in a minute."

I put on a hotel bathrobe over the slip I was still wearing from underneath my wedding dress and combed my fingers through my hair. *I should get dressed*, I thought, looking at my reflection in the mirror. But I looked so grown-up the way I was, older than I ever had before. I slipped the room key into the pocket of the robe. Romeo was snoring now, lying on his back. I thought about leaving him a note, but I didn't think I'd be gone more than a few minutes. I turned my pillow sideways beside him and left.

There were two leather club chairs that faced the elevator in the lobby. When the doors opened, Sebastian was sitting in the one on the right, and Ranhosky was sitting in the other, his briefcase on the floor between his feet. "Shit," I said, hitting the door close button, but Sebastian was faster. He jumped up and lunged between the sliding doors, making them open again.

"Scarlett, it's fine," he said, grabbing my hand and trying to pull me out of the elevator. "He just wants to talk to you."

"You called him?" I demanded. "How could you do that?"

"I didn't," he said, talking over me. "You think I would do that?"

"Then how did he get here?" Ranhosky stood up and picked up his briefcase. At four o'clock in the morning, he was wearing a suit and tie. "How did he know we were here?"

"Amy's lawyer called him," Sebastian said. I was so shocked, I stopped struggling, but he didn't let me go. He drew me out of the elevator, and the doors closed behind me. "He's been in El Paso all day."

I looked at Ranhosky for confirmation. "Come on, kiddo," he said with his weary, seen-it-all-in-Technicolor smile. "Let's talk."

"I'm not going back," I told him. "We're married; we slept together. You can't make me get it annulled."

"Oh, not to worry," he said. "We've gone way past that now."

He led us through the lobby, past the registration desk, and through a door marked "Staff Only, Please," into a short, bright service corridor that looked like its own separate planet from the plush taste of the lobby. "Sebastian," he said, stopping outside a metal door. "Wait here for a minute." There was an ugly orange chair already sitting beside the door. "You shouldn't see this."

I thought Sebastian would protest, but he didn't. He sat down in the chair, and Ranhosky took a key out of his pocket and unlocked the door. "What's going on?" I asked. Behind the door was an ugly little office. "What is this?" There were more orange chairs and a cheap-looking laminated wood grain desk. There was a calendar with a picture of a hunting dog hanging on the wall, and a photo of a blonde with two kids framed in silver on the desk. A television and VCR were set up on a rolling cart in the corner. Two of the orange chairs had been turned toward it, away from the desk.

"This is what we have to talk about," Ranhosky said, closing the door behind me. "Sit down, Scarlett." He set his briefcase on the desk, opened it up, and took out a big manila envelope marked URGENT and CONFIDENTIAL in bold red ink. It had already been torn open.

I sat down in one of the chairs as he took out a videotape. He pushed it into the VCR and turned on the television. "What are we watching?" I asked, trying to sound nonplussed but starting to freak out. I couldn't imagine what was on the tape, but I knew it couldn't possibly be good.

"Brace yourself," was all he said, sitting down beside me, remote control in hand.

The tape started. At first I couldn't tell what it was, the quality was so bad, shades of gray in too dim light on dirty, scratched-up video. Then Ranhosky turned up the sound, and I heard my own voice, moaning. The image clicked like magic into place. Me and Romeo, having sex in the gas station toilet.

Ranhosky was turned in his chair to watch my face, not the tape. "Is that you?" he asked.

"Yes." *I look like an octopus*, I thought. In the movies, my new husband and I looked too perfect to be real. On this tape, we looked ugly and awkward and gross, too disgusting to be human.

"There was a note that said it was taped yesterday morning at a truck stop in New Mexico." You could see the toilet stall standing open behind us, the dirty commode I had been afraid to sit on. "Is that true?"

"Yes." Watching, listening, I felt sick to my stomach.

Ranhosky raised the remote and made the screen go black. "Jesus Christ," he swore, both of us just staring at it. "Jesus, Scarlett."

I was profoundly relieved that it had stopped; I doubt I could have stood much more. "How did you get that?" I asked.

"How do you think I got it?" He stood up and ejected the tape, snatching it out of the machine. The cool, calm lawyer he had been was gone; now he was furious.

I couldn't begin to imagine. "From the woman at the truck stop?" I wrapped my robe more tightly around me, covering up. "But how did she know where to send it?"

He just stared at me like he couldn't believe what he was hearing. "She didn't send it, Scarlett," he said, speaking to me like I was a child. "She gave it to your husband when he asked for it. I imagine he paid her quite a bit. His lawyer sent it to me."

For a long moment, I thought he must be joking. "Romeo?" I even had a stupid smile on my face. But he didn't smile back, and it faded. "I don't believe you." I felt like someone had punched me in the stomach. "Why would he do that?"

"To protect himself." He took a folded sheet of paper out of the envelope. "To blackmail your father." He unfolded it. "Shall I read aloud?"

"Romeo wouldn't blackmail anybody," I insisted. "You're just trying to scare me, like you did before. He loves me."

"So I noticed," he said, putting on his glasses.

"You don't know what he's like!" I said, jumping to my feet.

"No, Scarlett, you don't know what he's like!" he answered, looking up at me. "Your Romeo is a drug dealer and a gigolo who fucked you in the first place because your brother paid him to do it." He had barely raised his voice, but I froze as if he had slapped me. "You think you have this big romance—Jesus, Scarlett! What you have, my darling little girl, is a big, fat fucking mess that I'm trying to clean up." He was still sitting, peering up at me over his glasses. "What

Romeo has is a very pretty, very stupid golden ticket." I sat down very slowly, unable to speak. "Now listen closely. This is what he wants." He turned his attention to the paper in his shaking hands. "He wants to stay married to you—as you saw, he's prepared to prove that an annulment is out of the question." I bent my head and put my hands over my face. "He wants me fired from any part in the management of your career or your finances, me and anyone else connected to your father." He paused as if waiting for me to speak, but I still couldn't. Even if I could have, what could I have said? "He wants any money you were paid for the two movies you've done moved from the accounts I set up for you into an account you control completely on your own. Though as your husband, I would imagine he will expect to be made a fully-empowered signatory." He paused again. "Scarlett? Are you listening to me?"

I didn't look up or uncover my face. "Yes."

After a moment, he went on. "And finally, he wants to be left alone. He wants your father to make no attempt to contact you or—how does he put it?" He read from the paper. "'Fuck with you or try to control you ever again.'" I raised my head as he chuckled. "Charming. And if we refuse, he will release the tape. If we attempt to have him arrested, he will release the tape." He waited as if he expected me to respond, but I said nothing. After a moment, he went on. "His lawyer suggested I set up a meeting for him with your father's agent as a gesture of good faith," he said. "Is he any good?"

I raised my head, and the voice that came out of me sounded like somebody else. "As a piece of ass?" I asked. "Or as an actor?" The look of shock on Ranhosky's face was almost comical; if I hadn't felt so horrible, I might have even laughed. "It doesn't matter," I said, letting my head drop again. "He's phenomenal as both."

"Scarlett." The lawyer put a hand on my shoulder. "Honey, listen." His voice had changed again; he sounded like the vaguely uncomfortable but very nice man he had been before he ever heard of Romeo. "You don't have to do this," he promised. "We can put you into rehab, say you were on drugs, that you didn't know what you were doing."

"I wasn't on drugs." I didn't tell him that anytime anyone offered me so much as a cigarette, Romeo took it away from me, but I thought it.

"We'll call his bluff," he went on like he hadn't heard me. "If he releases this tape to the media, he'll never work in Hollywood again. In fact, he'll go to jail."

"Mr. Ranhosky, I don't want him to go to jail," I said. "I love him." I suddenly realized what I had to do. I could be a golden ticket, stupid, just like he had said. Or I could be Romeo's accomplice. "What else does he want?" I could feel myself taking on a character, just like when I was working. I was becoming the girl who could elope with her drug dealer boyfriend just because she thought it might be fun.

Ranhosky just stared at me. "My god," he said at last. "You look just like your mother." He smiled, but he didn't look happy. "Do you remember how we met, sweetheart?" he said. "Do you remember Mexico?"

I did. He had been the man with the briefcase, the lawyer in the limo. But I had never let myself think about it before. For years, I had met with him, talked with him, and never let myself remember him opening his briefcase there, my grandmother crying, my grandfather taking the pen to sign as soon as it was offered. He had helped my father buy me. "No," I lied. "I was just a baby, Mr. Ranhosky. I don't remember Mexico."

"Your father had chased your mother all over the world," he said. "He wanted you from the moment he knew she was pregnant. He had offered her anything she wanted, everything he had and more to give you up."

"My mother loved me," I said, gripping the arm of the chair with one hand, the other hand limp in my lap. "I'm sure she said no."

"Oh no, dear, she said yes." His expression was mild; his eyes and tone were gentle as he ripped my heart out of my chest. "Three different times before she died. Three times she told him he could have you. Three times she took his money, and three times, she took off."

"That's not true." I was amazed to hear how calm I sounded.

"Oh, I promise you it is true," he said, opening his briefcase again.

"Would you like to see the papers, the contracts that she signed?" He took out a folder. "The bills of sale, I've always thought they were." His eyes met mine as he waited for me to answer, and I made myself go cold so he wouldn't see the screaming wreck I was inside peering out at him through the mask. I didn't say anything at all, didn't reach for the folder, didn't do anything. "Do you know why she did it, Scarlett?" he finally went on, setting the folder aside, putting it under the envelope with the videotape still inside. "I think you do." He sat back in his chair. "I think you remember exactly."

I shook my head. "I don't."

"She was an addict, Scarlett." His dog-brown eyes were serious and sad. "She couldn't help herself. She had to have the drugs. She couldn't take care of you; she couldn't even love you."

"She loved me," I interrupted sharply.

"All she could love was heroin, Scarlett," he went on. "All she could care about was where she would get her next fix."

Then why didn't he help her? I wanted to scream in his face. *Why didn't he use some of that fucking money to fix her so we could all be together? She was his wife, not that bitch, Greta. Why couldn't he want us both? Why did she have to die?*

But I didn't say any of those things. "You know what, Mr. Ranhosky?" I said instead. "Whatever. I am not on drugs. If you don't believe me, I'll pee in a cup."

"Don't you even want to talk to your father?" he said. "Let's call him, honey, right now."

"If he wanted to talk to me, he would have come himself instead of sending you." *He doesn't want me anymore*, I thought. I was like Stella, a problem to be paid for. "Tell him not to worry: I won't embarrass him."

"Scarlett."

"That's what he's so scared of, isn't it?" It occurred to me that I could really, really use a drink. In my mind, I could see the glass of hotel ice I would have just as soon as this was over, see the bottle of whiskey I knew Romeo had stashed in his duffel bag. I knew the way it would feel going down my throat, the blissful, uncomplicated warmth of it. Maybe a drink would warm me up, melt the ice I felt all over, make me forget what Ranhosky had said. "He's afraid of what will happen to his precious fucking movie if it gets out that I'm all grown up and married."

Again, Ranhosky just stared at me for a long, blank beat, as if he wasn't quite sure what he was seeing. "This is all grown up?" he finally said, looking away. He took a fat cigar out of the breast pocket of his jacket.

"It's my precious fucking movie, too." I sound just like Fiona, I suddenly realized. That was just what she would say. "I have no interest in screwing it up." I knew how much *Match Girl* meant to my father. His last movie had done only mediocre business; the two before that had been disasters. *Match Girl* was his chance to be a major star again, an A-list leading man. "So we'll keep our wedding a secret until after Calvin gets his Oscar. I'll move back home, and Romeo will move into a hotel. But I won't leave Los Angeles."

"So you plan to keep working?" he said, lighting up. "While you finish high school?"

"Fuck high school," I said.

"Not a chance." He puffed his cigar. "There's still hope you might smarten up someday, and if you do, you'll need a real high school diploma."

I felt myself actually smile. "You still want to send me to Harvard, Mr. Ranhosky?"

He leaned towards me. "Kid, if you were mine, you bet your ass." He leaned back again. "If you and Sebastian were my kids, I'd spank the both of you until your butts turned blue, then slap you in the meanest, toughest therapy I could find until they had wrung every drop of poison and talked every ounce of crazy out of you. Then I'd put you in separate Catholic prep schools on a twenty-four-hour disciplinary watch until you each graduated with honors."

I couldn't quite believe he was serious, but he looked it. "I didn't realize you were so religious, Mr. Ranhosky."

"Then yeah, I would send you to Harvard," he went on as if I hadn't spoken. "Or Brown or whatever decent East Coast college would take you. I would make you have a real life if it killed you." His cigar was going out from neglect between his fingers. "And as for this little white trash shit you've somehow decided to marry, I'd let him show his dirty movies on a marquee in Times Square if he wanted, and I'd let his ass rot in jail for as long as they'd keep him, and I would die and be damned before he ever worked in Hollywood again." He stopped, slightly breathless, and took a long drag on the cigar, the tip glowing orange again. "But I'm just the hired help," he went on, opening his briefcase, the cigar clamped between his teeth. "It sounds like you and your father are pretty much on the same page." He put his folder and the envelope with the videotape into the briefcase.

"I want that," I said, holding out my hand. "I want the tape."

"You can't have it," he said in the same businesslike tone. "I'll book you and Romeo on separate flights back to Los Angeles later today, and I'll book him a place to stay." He flicked ashes onto the ugly carpet. "Will a bungalow at the Chateau Marmont be up to his usual standards?"

"That would be great," I answered, barely hearing him.

"Oh good." He stood up. "If you're serious about keeping this a secret, you'll have to learn to be discreet. No more sex in public, please." His voice wavered slightly, and I thought of all the things he'd said he'd do if I were his daughter and not Calvin's. *Was that a performance?* I wondered. *Or did he really mean it?*

"Don't worry, Mr. Ranhosky," I said, standing up. It didn't matter. I wasn't his daughter; I was Stella's and Calvin's, which meant that I was on my own and really always had been. He was the hired help. I smiled at him. "I'll be good."

CHAPTER 32

Sebastian was still sitting sprawled on the chair in the hallway when we came out. "Hey," he said, jumping up, his brown eyes wide with anxiety.

Looking at him, I felt my legs start to go, shaking and weak. "I'm not talking to you," I decided, walking past him.

"Scarlett! Sissy, wait!" He chased me down the hall, catching my arm just as I was breaking into a run. I stumbled, and he had to catch me to keep me from falling. "Scarlett, he just wants to help you," he said, holding on to me.

"Fuck him and his help!" I shouted straight into his face. This was Sebastian; I couldn't lie to him, couldn't pretend to be calm. "You're my brother, for fuck's sake! How can you be on his side?"

"I just want you to be safe," he was pleading, tears running down his face.

"And Romeo—did you want me to be safe when you paid him?" I was barely hearing him. "When you paid him to have sex with me? Why would you do that?"

"What?" He looked utterly confused. "What are you talking about?"

"You paid Romeo to sleep with me." In his shock, his hold on me had relaxed, and I shoved him away. "That first night, when I first met him—did you know him? Why didn't you tell me?" Just the sight of his shocked, tearful face made me so furious, I felt like I might burst into flames. "How could you do that?" I demanded.

"Scarlett, what is the big fucking deal?" He was looking at me like I'd lost my mind. "I thought you knew. I thought surely, he would have told you by now. And even if he hadn't, how could you not know?"

"How would I know that?" I said, nearly screaming.

"You saw where he was when you met him," he pointed out. When you met him, he said, not when we met him. Ranhosky was standing with his back to the door that led back to the lobby, watching us fight. When the night manager pushed his head in, obviously curious, Ranhosky pushed him out again.

"I could see you were really into him," Sebastian was saying. "And yeah, I knew he was in a bind, so I figured what the hell."

"Oh my god," I said, turning away. All I could think about was how starry-eyed and stupid I had been, how elated I was to think that this beautiful boy wanted me. And all the time, he'd been on the clock.

"Sissy, what did you think?" Sebastian asked as if reading my mind.

"I thought he wanted me, you stupid fuck!" I really was screaming now, and crying, too. I hadn't even noticed that until I heard myself; now I felt the hot tears on my face.

"I'm sure he did," my brother said, comforting me, placating me the same way he always did. "He said you were amazing."

"He said…you talked about it?" I felt like I was going to be sick. "You saw him after? Of course you did. You still had to pay him, didn't you?" I took a staggering step toward the wall, wanting to lean against it. Sebastian tried to take my arm again, but I slapped his hand away.

"Scarlett, stop it," he said, pleading again. "This is not a big deal."

"Don't you dare say that!" *Didn't he realize that was the worst part of the whole thing?* I thought. To me, it had been the whole world. To him and to Romeo, it was no big deal. "Did he give you a cut from the money he took from my purse?" I said, leaning on the wall, staring at the ugly neutral wallpaper. "Or was that just a bonus?"

'Oh my god, he stole from you?" he said, aghast. That was apparently a big deal. "Why didn't you tell me?"

"I thought he needed it," I said, talking over him again. "I loved him, idiot. I thought—fuck it; it doesn't matter." *It doesn't matter*, echoed the voice inside my head. *It's no big deal.*

"Scarlett, come on." He took hold of my arm. "Let's just go home, okay?" His hand was shaking. "Let's just let Ranhosky fix it."

"No." I turned to face him. "I've had all the help I can stand." He looked utterly miserable, but I had a weird, ugly desire to laugh. "I'm handling this one myself."

He couldn't have looked worse if I'd slapped him. "Sissy, I'm so sorry."

"I know you are." I touched his cheek. Sebastian had always seemed older than me, somehow, so much smarter and worldlier and more experienced. But just then, he looked like a child. "It will be okay." *It doesn't matter*, the voice inside my head repeated, soothing me. *The past is in the past.*

I went back upstairs.

Romeo was still sleeping, lying on his back, his arm thrown back over his head. I watched him for a long time, thinking about the night we had met. He had seemed so sweet, so helpless, but dangerous, too, with his dirty jeans and soft Savannah accent.

The drapes were open from the night before, and the sun was coming up the way it always does. Outside I could see the town of El Paso and the glittering ribbon of the Rio Grande. The dark, bare brown beyond it would be Mexico. *Three times she took his money,* Ranhosky's voice was saying in my head. *And three times, she took off.*

I crossed the room in three quick, silent strides and opened up Romeo's duffel. The bottle of whiskey was exactly where I had known it would be, sealed up in a plastic bag. I took it out, twisted off the cap, and drank down about a third of the bottle without stopping, the brown liquor burning my throat. I took the bottle from my lips, eyes watering, feeling dizzy. *I could see you really liked him,* Sebastian was repeating in my mind. *I knew that he was in a bind, so I figured what the hell.* My lower lip was trembling so badly that the next drink dribbled down my chin, and my hands were shaking so I could barely hold the bottle. Ranhosky's voice was back. *What Romeo has is a very pretty golden ticket.* A sob escaped me as I fumbled the bottle back into the plastic bag. I reached back into the duffel bag to put it back under the clothes and found a hidden pocket in the bottom.

Inside I found the gun.

I lifted it out, vaguely horrified by the weight of it hanging from my hand. I had never held a gun before. Careful to keep my finger off the trigger, I lifted it close to my face to examine it, the dawn light gleaming on the dull gray barrel. It was loaded. I could see the yellow ends of the brass bullets in the cylinder. I let my index finger creep down to the trigger. Ranhosky thought he had known Stella, that he had understood exactly what she must have been thinking, but I didn't think that was true. I didn't think he had ever understood her at all. The gun was perfectly clean. I had seen Romeo clean it, oiling the parts carefully, putting them back together, tucking it away. We had never discussed it, but he had never tried to hide from me the fact that it was there.

"Scarlett." Romeo's voice was very tense but soft. *He doesn't want to startle me,* I thought. I looked up at him. He was sitting up in bed. "Sweetheart," he said, and the gun in my hand swung around to point at him. He raised his hands to the level of his chest in surrender, but his expression didn't change. "What are we doing?"

"Tell me the truth," I said. I was shaking so much, the barrel of the gun was bouncing up and down. I put my other hand on it, too, to steady it.

"Always." He was wide awake and naked, looking me dead in the eye.

"No." I made a noise between a giggle and a sob. "Not always." I considered cocking the hammer back, but I wasn't really sure I could. "Did Sebastian pay you that first time to fuck me?"

"Yes." He didn't even hesitate. "The first time, yes." He stood up but didn't come closer. "Scarlett, put the gun down."

"So that was the only reason?" Writing about this now, I still don't know if I really wanted him to tell me the truth or if I wanted him to tell a better lie. I wanted things to be the way I had thought they were.

I wanted that great romance Ranhosky had mocked me about. "If he hadn't paid you, would you have even wanted me?"

"Of course I would have wanted you." Surely he knew I wouldn't really shoot him, but he still didn't try to move closer. "But I don't think I would have slept with you." He still sounded perfectly calm, but I could see tears in his eyes. "You were such a baby."

"So why are you here now?" I said with an angry catch in my voice, his words like a punch to the stomach. "Why not just take the money Ranhosky offered you in the first place to leave me alone?"

"Because I love you." He said this as calmly as everything else. "Because you need me." He did take a step toward me then. "Just give me the fucking gun."

"No way." My hands were sweating now as well as shaking; I had to hold the gun in one hand to wipe the other on my robe, then switch. "You don't love me." I wrapped both hands around the gun again. "I'm just your golden ticket."

He had moved steadily closer. "If you really believed that, you wouldn't be here." He was almost close enough to touch.

"Stay back!" I tried to wave the gun and almost dropped it, and my panic at that gave me a shot of adrenaline that made me steadier. "Why didn't you tell me?" I could smell him, he was so close, and his eyes made me want to drop the gun and run back to his arms. "You had to know they would tell me if you didn't."

"I wanted Ranhosky to tell you." He let his hands fall to his sides. "I wanted you to have the chance to leave me if you wanted."

"But if I had, you would have released that video." The memory of the ugly images on the TV screen made my stomach clench.

He did pause then, just for a beat. "Yes," he said at last. "I wouldn't have had any choice." He was completely still. "Lesson one, sweetheart. Never make a threat you can't back up."

He moved so fast, I barely saw it happen. One second, I was holding the gun pointed at him. The next second, he had wrenched it from my hand. He held it out from us, pointed away, as he pinned me to his chest with his other arm, my wrist still in his grip. "Watch me," he said, his voice still calm. "You have to take the safety off." He clicked the little lever with his thumb. "Then it will fire." He fired three shots, bang bang bang, at the plate glass window, filling the room with sound, drowning out my scream. The glass shattered, falling like water, and I was still screaming when he tossed the gun aside and gathered me into his arms.

"I'm sorry," I was chanting, not even sure why, as he kissed my face, kissing away my tears.

"I do love you," he was saying as if he couldn't hear me. "Scarlett, I love you so much." He kissed my mouth, and I kissed him back. But when he let me go, I slumped to the floor, head down to cry, not looking at him at all. "Baby, I will take care of you." He touched my cheek, but I didn't look up, still crying. "Jesus fucking Christ." He turned his back on me, took a cigarette out of the pack on the dresser and lit it with trembling hands. "It's over, right?" he said, an edge of ugly laughter in his tone. "You'll never trust me again."

"Yes, I will." He turned around to find me looking back at him, and I smiled. "I don't really have any choice."

CLIPPING 11

Excerpt from Rock and Rolling *cover story: "Calvin Cross: Midwestern Farm Boy Makes Good...Again."*

RR:When you were growing up on a dairy farm in Minnesota, did you ever envision yourself as the biggest movie star on the planet?

CC:I don't have that vision now. You can't think about that stuff. You can't compare yourself to other people. You can't worry about how famous you are or who likes you or who doesn't. You'll go crazy.

But no, back in Minnesota, I wasn't thinking about Hollywood. When I was a young kid, ten or eleven, I wanted to play football. I thought that might be a way out, a way to see some of the world. I thought I'd play ball for one of the big colleges, maybe even get a scholarship. [laughs] The only problem was, I stunk. I loved the game; I still love it as an old guy spectator. I just didn't play very well. So I ended up doing school plays for the same reason every other rotten athlete does, to get girls.

RR:I can't imagine that was ever a problem.

CC:Oh, you'd be amazed. Those Midwestern farm girls can be pretty picky.

RR:You mentioned getting out. No ambitions to be a farmer like your dad?

241

CC:Maybe when I was really young. I used to love helping him, getting up early, seeing the sunrise, feeding the cows. I've been a lot of places, and I can tell you, there's no place calmer and more zen than a cow barn before the sun comes up—a real cow barn, not one of these industrial warehouses where they torture the animals, of course. Especially in winter. You come in out of the snow, and it's warm and quiet. And there's life all around you, these incredibly peaceful female animals just waking up, doing their thing. I loved it. But the farm was the family, and the family just sort of fell apart.

RR:You've spoken before in interviews about the impact your younger sister's death from polio had on you.

CC:One of the two or three worst experiences of my life—no, honestly, the worst. The only thing I can imagine coming close to it would be if something happened to one of my kids. That would be worse. But yeah, after Liddy was gone, I just sort of checked out of the family, and I know my mom did, too. Dad had the farm, but it was never the same for any of us.

RR:Your parents are both gone now?

CC:Yeah, my mom died while I was in college. She had a massive stroke, very sudden. They said she probably never felt a thing. Dad was later. I was already working in New York. Cancer. The doctor told me later that he had been sick for more than a year before he told me. But that was my dad, very quiet, very reserved.

RR:Family—or rather, the lack of family—is a theme in a lot of your films, especially your latest, The Little Match Girl.

CC:Yeah, that's something Aksel [Jorgen, the director] and I talked about a lot when we first started thinking about working together. It's an idea that has always haunted both of us, this idea of a man who's been left completely alone, trying to build a family for himself, to forge those kinds of connections.

RR:But in the movie, that man fails.

CC:Yeah. [laughs] Thanks for blowing the ending.

RR:Do you feel you've been more successful?

CC:Obviously, yes. I have two beautiful children that I'm very close to. I'm very proud of the bond we have. Their lives haven't been perfect, but I hope they realize how much they've always been loved. I'm in a wonderful relationship now with an extremely gifted and intelligent young woman. I'm very happy with my domestic life at the moment. I've been very lucky, very blessed.

RR:Your daughter, Scarlett, is also in the movie, playing the child that you lose. How did that come about?

CC:That was not my idea; that was all Aksel. He met Scarlett while he was writing the script. He said she inspired him, this sweet, tough kid who's been through so much but still...[clears his throat, takes a sip of water]...she's still so kind, so open-hearted. He wrote the character of Josephine specifically for her without telling me a thing about it, then when the script was done, he sprung on me that he wanted to give her a screen test. And of course, she just blew us away.

RR:Was it hard, working with her on such a dark story?

CC:Most of the time it was sheer delight. Scarlett and my son, Sebastian, are both insanely talented actors. I just bust my buttons with pride watching them work. To see the commitment they have, the focus, it's just pure joy for me as a father. But there were moments, yeah. I couldn't actually film her death scene with her. I couldn't be there watching her and act; it was too painful. I just lost it. All of my reaction shots were filmed later after she was gone. Meanwhile, to her, it was nothing. She did it, nailed it, and danced away. [laughs] But that's Scarlett. Nothing gets her down.

CHAPTER 33

The next few weeks were like a whole new life, like it was all happening to a completely different person from the girl I had always been. I was back living in Castle Asshole with my father and Sebastian. A week after we got back, Fiona moved in, too. Somehow, she had become the new, official live-in girlfriend, Calvin's first since Greta had moved out. Calvin acted like this was the big event that had happened in our lives, like my eloping to Texas had never happened, and I let him. I didn't want to talk about it anyway. I didn't even know how to feel about it. I loved Romeo; I wanted to be with him. But the videotape still haunted me. Nothing he had asked for was anything I hadn't wanted for myself. But the idea that he would take that tape and use it to blackmail my father with it made me feel sick. Had he planned it that way? Had he taken me into that gas station toilet with the specific intention of having sex with me on tape so he had a bargaining chip? Every time I thought about it, I wanted to vomit, so I stopped thinking about it and waited. Like when Romeo and I had been apart before, I felt sick to my stomach pretty much all the time, But again, it was just like the last time, so I figured it was normal, that it made perfect sense.

Things felt even weirder when Calvin's big interview in *Rock and*

Rolling came out. It was a big deal, his getting it; it meant he was a big star again, and I was happy for him. But reading it, I didn't recognize the people he was talking about at all, particularly not the girl he said was me. Calvin sounded like Calvin, but the daughter he described sounded like a girl in a movie, not me. It was the same feeling of disconnection I had when my own interview with *Jeune Fille* had come out a month before. The writer had quoted me perfectly, but the girl talking couldn't possibly have been me. I was two people at once, the one the world had decided to care about and thought they knew, and the one I knew from inside my own head. Whenever I stopped to think about it, it was like the worst version of the moments of crazy I had been having since I was four, only bigger with the whole wide world watching. So I stopped thinking about that, too.

If I could have seen Romeo, I might have felt better. He had moved out of Amy's house and into a bungalow at the Chateau Marmont, less than two miles away. But he might as well have been on the moon. Right after we got back, the VHS of *The Funhouse* came out; my name was everywhere because of the Golden Globes, and *The Romantics*, the pilot Romeo had shot over Christmas, had been picked up by one of the basic cable networks, and they were already flogging the shit out of it. The show was set in nineteenth-century England with Romeo and his co-star, an Australian named Peter August, as ghost-and-ghoul-chasing poets who spent most of their time tumbling wenches and knocking back absinthe. Filming on the episodes had barely started, and already there was a huge billboard on Sunset Boulevard of Romeo and Peter both looking gothically gorgeous. So the paparazzi were on both of us like flies on a corpse. There was no way in hell I could sneak in to see him without being noticed. And anytime I tried to call him, he was always on the set. And of course, he couldn't call me.

Sebastian kept me up all night the night before the Oscar nominations were announced. We set up a TV-watching nest on the big leather couch in Calvin's living room the way we had in hotel rooms as kids. Calvin's cook made us Cuban sandwiches and big bowls of popcorn and movie candy. Then we watched movies on VHS tapes all night long, one of our father's old westerns, a Marx Brothers comedy, a period weepie I had missed in theaters in December, and finally *The Funhouse*.

Calvin and Fiona came downstairs around 4:30 a.m., and Bette and her fiancé showed up at 5, just in time for the movie's big finish. Romeo and I were both already dead; Fiona was unconscious; and Sebastian was confronting the evil stepmother in her lair.

"You're not young!" he was saying, advancing on her with his ancient, blessed sword. "You're not beautiful! You're ugly!" Bloodied and intense with his clear blue eyes and blond hair, he was the perfect hero. He raised the sword and shouted in the pure, clear tones of justice, "Die, you pathetic old crone!" He brought the sword down, and she screamed, and the screen exploded in blood.

"Holy Christ," our father said, watching, sleepy-eyed in his pajamas. "Cole is one sick fuck."

"No kidding," Fiona said. She was in pajamas, too, but she looked like a lingerie ad.

"Yay for Sebastian!" Bette said, giving my brother a kiss.

"You know Cole used to live with that woman," Daddy said as the Sebastian on the screen finished hacking off the witch's head. "He left his second wife for her back in the '70s." On screen, Sebastian raised the decapitated head in triumph.

"Did they part well?" Bette said with a snicker.

"Apparently not," Daddy said. He ruffled Sebastian's hair. "You're brilliant, kid."

Sebastian grinned. "Thanks, Dad."

I watched them, feeling distant and left out. Then Bette squeezed onto the sofa beside me. "I'm glad we missed Magenta dying," she said, snuggling under my blanket. "I hate that."

"So do I," Daddy agreed. He reached over and touched my cheek. "I could only watch it once." Then he sat down on the other couch with Fiona. Bette's fiancé, Tomas, sat on the arm of the couch beside Bette, hovering over all of us.

Sebastian checked his watch. "They're starting."

We flipped the TV to the local news channel, which was covering the announcement live. Standing at the podium were an actress from a TV drama and Simon Price, the English actor who had helped me get to Romeo the night I eloped. "Oh look, it's Simon," I said. "He's the one who gave me my Golden Globe."

"Oo, I love him," Bette said. "He has an enormous dong."

"Shhh," Tomas said, but Calvin burst out laughing.

"Well, he does," she whispered to me. "I've seen it in a movie."

"They're starting," Sebastian said.

I nodded off during the technical award nominations. Truth be told, I would have been just as glad to sleep through the whole thing. I wanted Calvin to get his nomination because he wanted it so much, and I thought Sebastian deserved one for his first movie of the year, *The House*. For myself, I really, honestly, completely didn't care.

"Scarlett, wake up," Sebastian said, poking me. "They're getting ready to do you and Bette."

"The nominations for best actress in a supporting role are," Simon was saying on the screen. He looked fresh as a daisy and better-looking than I remembered. The camera had a crush on him even at five in the morning. "Deidre Holt for *Rites of the Italian Spring*." This was the '60s siren I had beaten out at the Golden Globes. "Bette Haust for *The Little Match Girl*."

"Oh my god!" Bette and I screamed in unison.

"Congratulations!" Sebastian said as she and I hugged. My father didn't say anything.

"Augusta Franklin for *Where It Hurts*," Simon was going on. "Kelly Christie for *Swing*." The Oscars didn't have separate categories for dramas versus comedies and musicals like the Golden Globes. These two had been in the other category there. "Anna Sophia Strasberg for *Heist*." This one I had never heard of, and she was the last. I hadn't been nominated.

"Holy crap," Sebastian said. "I can't believe it."

"It's okay," I said, squeezing his arm. "Hush, they're doing yours."

TV Actress was reading now. "The nominees for Best Actor in a Supporting Role are." Bette put her arm around me, but I was more relieved than hurt. Everything would be so much easier now. "Sebastian Cross for *The House*."

"Yes!" I said as my brother's face went blank with shock.

"Congratulations, son," my father said, leaning over me and Bette to kiss him on the forehead.

"Thank you." He looked like he'd been shot. Then suddenly he smiled. "Thanks!" He hugged me, and Bette and Daddy were hugging us, and I was barely hearing what was being said on TV until she said, "Romeo Kidd for *The Funhouse*."

"What?" I said, turning back to the screen. "What did she say?"

"She said Romeo," Sebastian said. "Holy shit." He glanced over at our father, then broke into a laugh, and I laughed with him. "Holy shit!"

"I can't believe it," I said. I could see from my father's face that he was having trouble believing it, too. "Okay, here's best actress," I said. "I want to hear Simon say that Romanian woman's name." Daddy looked at me and smiled.

Simon sounded brilliant saying the Romanian name and the name of his own fiancée, Clare Tidwell, who was nominated for playing a Victorian poetess. But what really electrified his audience was when he paused, smiled, said, "Wow," and then said, "Scarlett Cross for *The Little Match Girl*."

Bette's scream was literally deafening; I couldn't hear anything else for several seconds, not even the names of the other two nominees. "It's a mistake," I said. "It has to be a mistake."

"Hang on," Sebastian said, clutching my hand. "This is Daddy."

The little audience of press at the ballroom where the announcements were being made were still buzzing when TV Actress started reading out the best actor nominees. The third name on the list was, "Calvin Cross for *The Little Match Girl*." Someone in the press hooted approval, and a smattering of applause broke out. At our place, the crowd went wild.

Match Girl and *The House* were both nominated for best picture, and Aksel Jorgen was nominated as both writer and director. The phone started ringing as soon as the last nomination was read, and

Calvin went off to answer it and be congratulated. Sebastian and Bette went to the kitchen for champagne.

I took the kitchen phone with a long cord into the bathroom and called Romeo.

"Chateau Marmont, how may I help you?"

"George Gordon's bungalow, please." Romeo was reading a lot of Byron to stay in character for *The Romantics*.

"Mr. Gordon has asked that we screen his calls after midnight," the clerk said, surprising me. I didn't think anybody but me, Amy, and Sebastian had his alias, and why would he screen out any of us? "May I ask who's calling?"

"This is Mrs. Gordon," I said. "Scarlett."

"I'll put you straight through, Mrs. Gordon." Now he sounded a little flustered. "So sorry for the delay." The phone was ringing before he finished his apology.

"Hello?" Romeo's voice mumbled—he had obviously been asleep.

"Romeo? It's me."

"Scarlett?" He was instantly awake. "What's wrong? Are you all right?"

"I'm fine; nothing's wrong," I said. "I'm great."

"Okay...great. Hang on a second." I heard him moving around, a small crash like something falling off the bedside table, him swearing. Then he was back. "Angel, it's five thirty in the morning."

"I know," I said, laughing. "They just announced the Oscar nominations."

"Oh." I heard his TV come on. "Did you get your nomination, sweetheart?"

"Sort of." I could hear Sebastian and Bette outside calling for me and Daddy. The champagne was ready. "They switched my category. I got nominated for best actress."

"That's fantastic, angel." He didn't sound all that surprised, but he was obviously genuinely happy for me. "Congratulations."

"Thanks, but that's not the best part."

"Did your dad get nominated?"

"Of course—best actor. Hang on a second." I put my hand over the phone. "I'm in here! I'll be out in a minute!"

"You're hiding in the toilet?" Romeo said, laughing.

"I didn't want to be disturbed. Baby, listen…"

"Holy shit," he interrupted. "I just saw my message light. It's blinking like crazy; are these all you? Why didn't they put you through?"

"Those aren't me; that's what I'm trying to tell you," I said, laughing. "You got nominated, too."

"Bullshit." I could hear him flipping channels and then heard the theme music for the news. "For what?"

"For *Funhouse*, of course." He didn't sound so much happy as pissed off. "Best supporting actor. You're up against Sebastian for *House*."

"Oh crap."

"I'm not going to know who to root for."

"Root for Sebastian, please. I can't believe this."

"Aren't you at least a little bit pleased?" I said. His reaction was more than just being sleepy, I could tell, but I didn't understand it.

"Of course," he said. "I guess."

"Scarlett?" My father was knocking on the door. "Are you all right."

"Yes, I'm fine," I said. "I'll be right out."

"Brian is on the phone." Brian was the main producer for *Match Girl*, the one who would keep the statue if it won for best picture. "He wants to speak to you."

"Okay, I'll be right there," I promised.

"You sound busy," Romeo said.

"I'm sorry."

"Angel, it's okay," he said.

"It isn't." I was speaking barely louder than a whisper, but I still heard my father linger for a moment outside the door before he went away. "I'm so happy for you and so proud. You were so good in *Funhouse*."

"If I was, it was because of you. I love you, angel."

"I love you." Now Bette was calling for me, laughing. "I guess I have to go."

"It's okay," he promised. "Maybe we can see one another later."

"Maybe." I wanted to see him. More than anything, I wanted to go off somewhere with him to celebrate, convince him that he totally deserved his nomination, bask in the moment. The odds were hugely against anything like this ever happening to us again. "I'll try to call you back when things calm down. You should answer your other calls."

"I will."

Sebastian pounded on the door. "Sissy, come on!"

"Just go," Romeo said. "I've got to get up and go to work anyway. I'll talk to you soon."

Outside in the living room, my father was talking on the phone, and Bette was pouring champagne. "Here she is," she said, holding out a glass to me.

"Thanks," I said, taking it, though I didn't feel so much like celebrating any more.

"Here, sweetpea," Daddy said, handing me the phone. "Talk to Brian."

CHAPTER 34

The rest of that day was a circus. After Brian and the champagne and a call from my agent and bacon and eggs, I went upstairs for a nap. By the time I came back down at mid-morning, the house was full of people. Walking through, I quickly realized it wasn't so much a celebration party as a war room. Everybody was working, and everybody had a plan.

"Scarlett, you're up," one of Calvin's assistants said, catching me. "Thank god." She consulted the clipboard in her hand. "Do you have a favorite stylist?"

I thought about the poor woman who had dealt with me as zombie girl before the Golden Globes. "I really liked Nora."

"Yeah." Miss Assistant didn't sound impressed. "Nora's more supporting actress material. Don't worry; I'll find you somebody." She gave me the dazzling smile of a cheerleader on her way to the playoffs. "And by the way, congratulations."

"Thanks." From where I was standing, I could see the back of my father's head as he sat on the couch in the living room, holding court. Fiona was beside him with her head on his shoulder. "Have you seen Sebastian?"

"He went out to the pool, I think."

"Thanks." She was flipping through her clipboard again, but I wasn't ready for a consult. "I'm just going to grab something to eat."

She didn't look happy, but she didn't look brave enough to tell me I had to listen to her, either. That moment, looking into her eyes, I got my first taste of being the 800-pound gorilla that is a real movie star. "You need me to get you something?" she asked.

"Of course not." She probably had an M.B.A., but she was offering to make me a sandwich. I put my hand on her shoulder and gave her my best approximation of the cheerleader grin. "Let me know about the stylist. I don't have a clue what I'm supposed to wear."

"Will do." She hustled off to attack the crisis of my wardrobe, and I slipped away to find food.

The kitchen was overflowing with caterers making the kinds of snacks that look really casual and homey but take a cast of pros to pull together for a crowd, cheeseburger sliders and cute little brownies and perfectly presented individual cones of popcorn and pretzels and homemade trail mix. As I was coming in from the living room, a delivery guy from the liquor store was coming in the back door, pushing a hand truck stacked high. "Holy crap," I said, stepping aside for a waiter in a golf shirt and khakis carrying an overloaded tray the size of a small dining table.

Ivy the Housekeeper was apparently the foreman of the operation. "Hi Scarlett," she said, looking and sounding frazzled. "What can we get you?"

"I was just going to grab some cereal or something." Another waiter was trying to stare at me without looking like he was staring at me. I winked at him, and he grinned and looked away. "Are we having a party?"

"Just friends of your father's dropping by to congratulate him." She reached back and got a cereal bowl out of the cabinet, but the refrigerator where the milk was and the pantry where we kept the cereal were both blocked by people working. "Why don't you go on out to the breakfast room, and I'll bring you something?"

"It's okay," I said. "I can just grab something off a tray." I grabbed a bottle of soda with a straw from Mister Stare and Smiley. "It's fine."

"Thanks, Scarlett." She turned away from me to sign the liquor store guy's invoice, and I made my escape.

Back out in the living room, someone had put on an advance tape of *Match Girl*. Daddy's character was having an argument with a guy in a military uniform.

"I can't just abandon this kid," Daddy was saying.

"Berlin is full of street kids," the colonel answered. "What's so special about this one? She's probably some Russian's bastard."

"She's not Russian."

"You can't know that."

"Yes, I do know that."

"How?"

"Because she's mine!" Watching Cal's face on the screen, I knew his Oscar was inevitable. "She's not just some street kid, Harry; she's my kid, and I'm not leaving her here."

"Listen to me," the colonel said. "A lot of guys fathered kids here before the war. How can you possibly know this one is yours?"

"Because I've seen her." The camera moved in slowly on his beautiful face, the heartbroken truth in his beautiful blue eyes. "I loved her mother, Harry—like a lunatic, I loved her. I begged her to come back to the States with me, to be my wife. But she wouldn't be persuaded. She wouldn't leave Berlin."

"Did you know she was pregnant?" the colonel asked.

"I didn't have a clue. If I had, I would have…I don't know what I would have done." The camera backed away again to a middle shot of both men. "As soon as I saw that kid, all I could see was Marina. Her eyes, her mannerisms…I asked her about her mother, who she was, how she died. She is Marina's child."

"Which begs the question—and I mean no disrespect, but…does that really mean she's yours?"

Cal answered without hesitation. "Yes. If she's Marina's, she's mine, and I won't leave her. Trust me, Harry; I'm not crazy."

In the real world of the living room, people were murmuring

about how awesome Daddy's performance was, and Fiona was giving him a kiss. But I had seen enough. Without speaking to anybody, I slipped out the patio door.

More people were gathered around the pool. This seemed to be where the serious business was going on. I saw Bette and Tomas sitting at one of the umbrella tables with a man wearing a suit and tie in spite of the sunshine. A stack of important-looking papers was spread out between them. Bette saw me, and I waved. She smiled and waved back.

Another group was huddled at the edge of the pool; one guy was squatting on his haunches. As I came around, I saw why. Sebastian was in the pool, treading water at the edge. I heard Haunches make a joke about holding up somebody for ten million—fifteen if they waited until after Sebastian won. Everybody laughed, including my brother. I couldn't help remembering the first time I had seen him in that same pool, the wild imp who had scared his mom half to death by leaping into the deep end just to make our father laugh. I waved at Sebastian, too, but again, I didn't stop.

I hadn't been back in the guesthouse since we'd left for Berlin before Christmas. Every stitch of clothing I owned, every book, every CD, every bottle of shampoo had been packed up by some mysterious someone and moved across the lawn to my new room at Castle Asshole. So when I used my key and slipped inside, I expected to find it empty.

It wasn't. The dishwasher was running, and there were books and newspapers scattered on the kitchen table. A pair of ancient-looking men's shoes were sitting on the mat beside the back door, and a neat line of half-full liquor bottles stood straight down the middle of the bar. From the living room, I could hear the TV playing—old school Bugs Bunny cartoons.

I was just about to sneak back out again when a voice I recognized called out, "Hello?"

"Hi," I called back. It was Wallace Cole, my director from *The Funhouse*. "It's me, Scarlett."

He was sitting on the sofa with his sock feet propped on the coffee table next to an empty plate and a half-drunk glass of brown liquor over melting ice. "I'm sorry to disturb you," I said. "I didn't know anybody was here."

"Hey cupcake," he said. "Come here." He opened his arms, and I hugged him. "How are you doing?"

"Okay, I guess." Suddenly for some strange reason, I felt like I was going to cry. "I got nominated for an Oscar; did you hear?"

"I did indeed." He patted the sofa beside him, and I sat down, kicking off my sandals. "Congratulations."

"Thanks." I put my bare feet on the coffee table, remembering how Greta used to rage at me and Sebastian for doing it when we were little, like little kid feet could somehow damage a marble tabletop. "Daddy, too, and Sebastian."

"Oh yeah," he said, sounding amused. "It will be one for the record books."

"And Romeo, too. Did you see they nominated Romeo for *Funhouse*? Isn't that great?"

"It's grand, cupcake." He patted my knee. "So how is Romeo, anyway?"

"I guess he's okay," I hedged. "I haven't really seen him."

"Save it, cupcake. I know all about it." He moved slightly away from me and lit a cigarette. Greta would have had a stroke. "Who do you think your dad blames for you two getting together?"

"I'm sorry."

"No, no, it's okay. I don't give a shit." He gave me an evil grin around the cigarette. "Your pappy's been bitching at me so long, I wouldn't know him any other way." He took a last big drag then stubbed it out barely smoked in his dirty plate. "How's he liking his circus?"

"He seems to like it." I couldn't resist a little truth telling; Cole brought it out in me. "He's got fucking caterers."

"Jesus wept." He laughed, not in a bitter, bitchy way but with genuine enjoyment. "Good for him. And that Bette Boop—she's a dish, ain't she? I can't believe he let that one go."

"A total dish. But you know, he's with Fiona now." He was a certifiable crazy person who had no filters who had put me through hell to get what he wanted on film. But I trusted him. I knew he'd only ever use me as an actress, that he'd never hit on me or lie to me or manipulate me to get at Calvin for good or for bad. He was just Cole, and all he'd ever care about was getting the shot.

"Yeah, I heard about that, too." He gave the dead cigarette a longing look. "Poor kid." He picked it up then dropped it in his drink. "Can a crazy old coot tell you something, cupcake?"

"Sure." My heart rate picked up.

"You were better in *Funhouse* than you were in *Match Girl*, and the Academy can kiss my ass." This was not what I was expecting. "Can I tell you why?"

"Because you were my director on *Funhouse*?"

He chuckled. "Cute, but no. In *Funhouse*, it was all you, and that's what made the difference. You were playing that girl; she wasn't you, but you understood her. You understood exactly what she wanted, and you put it on the screen. I didn't do that, not for you, not for Romeo, not for Sebastian or Fiona. I just got it all on film and stayed out of the way."

"Thanks." At least he wasn't telling me why he thought Fiona was a poor kid; I didn't want to hear it.

"In *Match Girl*, you're somebody else's vision of you, Jorgen's and your father's. You look amazing; you break my heart, but half of it is you giving them what you sense they want, and half of it is where that brilliant old pervert aims his camera." He sounded more serious than I had ever heard him sound. "You're a smart girl, and you can have a fine career just giving people what they want, playacting what you know they want you to be. But there's more to you than that."

"Are you sure?" I knew he was right about *Match Girl*. But in *Funhouse*, all I had wanted was Romeo.

"I'm positive. You don't have to be anybody's doll." He took another drag on his cigarette. "Or anybody's angel."

My eyes filled with tears, though I still couldn't have explained just why. "I love him, Cole," I said.

"I know, cupcake, and that's great stuff." He kissed my forehead. "Just don't try to make it everything."

"I'll try not." I didn't know how to answer him or what else to say. I wasn't even sure how I felt. "They'll be looking for me, I guess. I should head back." I hugged him again. "Thanks, Cole."

"Anytime." He grinned. "See you soon."

CHAPTER 35

After the Oscar nominations came out, the media frenzy around us got even more frantic. The producers of *The Romantics* had to send a different car and driver for Romeo every day to get him to the set on time for filming because of all the photographers staking out his hotel. And Castle Asshole had become an armed camp. We even had guards with dogs patrolling the walls around the perimeter to deal with the bastards trying to climb over and snap pictures of us at home. I stopped reading the papers after somebody tagged us "a great acting dynasty in the tradition of the Barrymores." The whole thing was just too much.

"Not to worry, kids," Daddy told us over breakfast the morning that quote came out. "A month after the Oscars, they'll have forgotten we exist."

"Until our next movie comes out, I hope," Sebastian said.

"God willing," our father agreed. Me, I was just looking forward to the being forgotten part and to hell with anything else. "It's okay, sweetpea," Daddy said, reading my thoughts in my face. "It will never be this bad again." He smiled and ruffled my hair. "Next time you won't be new meat."

The worst thing about all the attention was it made seeing Romeo face to face impossible. "When this is over, they're talking about moving the show back to Vancouver for filming," Romeo said on the phone when I called him that night. "We could both move there."

"God, yes," I said. "That sounds wonderful."

"You really hate it, don't you, angel?"

"I really do." I was flopped across my bed in my pajamas with a late-night talk show playing on the TV. "I mean, it's nice that people say nice things, and it's good to be wanted and noticed. I'm an actress, I get that." The talk show host was doing his monologue, and I barely caught Calvin's name. I picked up the remote and turned down the volume. "But I don't think I've done anything to deserve it. I've only played two parts, and I didn't work all that hard on either one."

"I don't think it's your work people care about," he said. "It's who you are."

"And that's wrong, right? That's crazy." I could see myself in the mirror on the dresser, a perfectly ordinary teenage girl with freckles and a truly revolting zit coming up on her chin. "It's not even me. This person they want pictures of doesn't even exist."

"She's a product," he said. "Just like that douche on that billboard." Romeo hated the billboard for *The Romantics* with the passion of a thousand burning suns.

"He's not a douche." I smiled, feeling a little better. "He's awesome. But he's not you."

"Definitely not." He sounded like he was smiling, too. "I love you, you know. Real you."

"I love real you, too."

"You're still my angel."

Something about the way he said this made me feel like crying. "I can't wait for this to be over," I said. "I just want to get away."

The one time I knew I would definitely get to see him was the Oscar nominees' luncheon. Every year the Academy gets all of the nominees together for a "casual" lunch to take a lot of pictures and drum up a little more last-minute publicity for the ceremony. It's a huge deal, and everybody who possibly can and isn't a conscientious objector shows up. I knew Romeo would be there, and even if I couldn't throw my arms around him and call him my husband, I could talk to him, touch him, give him one of those "Oh yeah, we've met; this will make a nice photo" hugs. We talked about it for days beforehand, promising to make a beeline for one another as soon as we got there, our publicists be damned.

But he never showed up. I slipped free of Sebastian as soon as we passed through the door and started searching the crowd, but Romeo was nowhere. I couldn't believe he was late; the Academy's invitation was blatantly bossy about wanting everybody there on time for pictures. And while my darling talked a good rebel game, he had a Southern boy's horror of being rude. But I couldn't find him anywhere.

I was considering going outside to watch for his car when Simon Price appeared out of the crowd. "Scarlett?" He touched my arm. "Are you all right?"

"Yes," I said, putting on a smile without thinking. I was becoming a natural. "I'm fine." I suddenly realized who he was. "Hey Scarecrow!" I turned and gave him a hug.

He laughed, hugging me back. "I suppose I ought to be insulted."

"Why?" I let him go. "I think you're awesome."

"That's very flattering, but that nickname is appalling."

"No, it's not." Running into him made me feel better. The Scarlett who was playing at flirting with him seemed to be a completely different girl from the one who'd eloped to Texas in a panic and pulled a pistol on her husband. I hadn't become self-aware enough yet to see the connections between them. "What should I call you instead?"

"Call me whatever you like," he said. "But Simon would seem to be the most conventional option."

"Booo-ring." I liked being this girl; it was easy and fun and new. He barely knew me, but he obviously liked me—I could still be whatever I wanted with him. "Hey Scarecrow, guess what? Don't tell anybody yet, but I got married."

"You never did," he scoffed. "You're just a baby."

"I'm not. I'm eighteen, remember? And I did so get married, the day after we met."

He just stared at me for a moment with a look I couldn't read on his face. "Of course you did," he said finally. "So who's the lucky fella?" He said this last in an exaggerated "American" accent.

"Romeo Kidd," I said. "You know, the guy I was looking for the night of the Golden Globes. The actor."

"I've never heard of such a person," he said. "I think you're making him up."

"I am not!" I protested, laughing. "You met him! He was in *The Funhouse* with me and Sebastian, my brother. He played my boyfriend. He was nominated for an Oscar, too; that's why I'm looking for him."

"Your brother played your boyfriend?" he said. "What sort of perverse film are we talking about here?"

"No, you swine, Romeo played my boyfriend," I cut him off. "And now he's nominated for an Oscar, and he's on a TV show, and I'm going to marry him."

"You're going to marry him because he's on television? What an absurd reason—I'm surprised at you, Scarlett, really."

"I'm going to marry him because I love him."

He frowned as if he were giving the matter grave thought. "What did you say his name was?"

"Romeo Kidd."

"And what's this television show?"

"*The Romantics*. It's coming out this summer, and it's going to be a big hit."

"Oh dear god—that thing? That hideous Lord Byron, Frankenstein thing?"

"See? You have heard of him."

"I've heard of that show, and it sounds absolutely appalling. Is he English?"

"He's not." I snickered. "He's from Savannah, Georgia, actually."

"Dear god in heaven!"

"But his accent is really, really good."

"I promise you it isn't."

A beautiful woman who had done her best to mask her beauty behind a double smear of black eyeliner and a shockingly ugly black tea gown walked up and took his hand, glaring at me like she meant to deliver a gypsy curse. I wondered what she'd charge to haunt a house. Then I remembered his fiancée. "This must be Miss Tidwell," I said.

"It is," he said. "Clare, meet Scarlett. Scarlett, Clare."

"Hi," I said, offering my hand. "I just saw your movie the other night. You're amazing."

She looked a little confused for a second, but she smiled and shook my hand. "Cheers."

"Scarlett looked a little lost," Simon said.

"Don't I always?" I said. "I'm looking for my husband. Simon helped me the last time I lost him."

"Oh, I've heard all about it," she said, her smile growing warmer. She really was a knockout, even though everything about her look and posture said she hated it.

"And I was just telling her she's much too young to have a husband at all," Simon said.

"Congratulations," Clare said, laughing. "Simon, darling, don't be a clot."

"We aren't telling people until after the Oscars," I said.

"So where is he?" Simon said.

"What's it to you, darling?" Clare said, echoing my thoughts.

"I'm just surprised." He gave me a one-armed hug, still holding Clare's hand, and I heard the click of digital cameras like the chattering of sparrows all around us. "Well done."

"Thanks very much." I looked back toward the entrance, hoping to see Romeo finally coming in, but no. Sebastian and Daddy were posing for pictures. They'd be calling for me soon.

"He's apparently in some television thing," Simon said. He was being a clot, I thought; that was the perfect word. "He plays a nineteenth-century English poet, and Scarlett is convinced his accent is quite good."

"I bet it is," Clare said. "He played that Russian in the mini-series with Angus and Evelyn, darling, remember? They said his accent in that was excellent." She smiled at me. "Friends of ours from London. They were very impressed with him."

"Russian isn't English," Simon said. "And they had other reasons for being impressed with him."

"He's an amazing actor," I said, smiling back at Clare and ignoring him. "But I'm still going to kick his ass."

Simon and Clare ended up sitting with me and Sebastian at the luncheon. Sebastian switched place cards to make it possible. He even went all around the room and found Romeo's and put it next to me for when he finally showed up. But he didn't show up. In between the four courses and all the speeches about the history and general awesomeness of the Academy, I excused myself twice to go to the pay phone to call him on his direct line, and as soon as it was over as I was waiting between photo ops, I tried to call again. But the front desk of the hotel kept telling me they didn't get an answer. As soon as we got home, I called the studio, ignoring my father's dirty look. But they hadn't seen him either. Principal photography was shut down for the day so he could go to the luncheon.

"It's okay, Sissy," Sebastian said, giving me a squeeze. "He'll call."

But he didn't. All through the rest of the day and into the night, I waited. I even tried calling Amy's house, thinking she might have had some emergency, and he might be there. But her housekeeper said she was in Baja shooting a new calendar, and she hadn't seen Romeo in a week. I kept telling myself that if he'd been in an accident, I would have heard. I watched the news all night. But again, there was nothing.

Finally, sometime after midnight, I'd had enough. Sebastian was out, so I went through his closet by myself and found a dark hoodie and a pair of old sweats that hadn't fit him in years. I pulled my hair back in a ponytail and grabbed a baseball cap off the rack as I went out the back door. In a moment of inspiration, I grabbed the keys to the gardener's truck, too. When I drove out the front gate, the one sleepy paparazzo still keeping vigil in his car across the street barely looked up.

CHAPTER 36

The sidewalk in front of the Chateau Marmont was virtually deserted. One long-haired, loud-voiced English dude in a silk scarf, short shorts, and fringed boots was pontificating for a group of girls who were capturing the moment on their video camera. Other than that, there was no one in sight.

Rather than pulling up to the front door, I drove around and parked in the service vehicle lot. I had never visited Romeo here, but I knew his number, and Sebastian and I had visited people in bungalows here with Greta when we were kids. With the key Romeo had given me in hand, I checked the rearview mirror one last time then headed for the courtyard.

From the outside, Romeo's bungalow was dark; the drapes were drawn. I let myself in.

The tiny living room was empty, lit by one lamp in the corner. It looked neater than I expected. The only clutter I could see was the usual scattering of books and magazines that followed Romeo wherever he went. But going in, I tripped over a little pile of shoes by the door. One pair I recognized as Romeo's, then there was a pair of scuffed motorcycle boots that could have been his, too. But the red high heels most definitely were not. I just stared at them for at least a minute, shocked. Amy's, I told myself. They've got to be Amy's.

Making no more effort to be quiet, I headed for the bedroom. "Romeo?" I said, opening the door. "Baby, are you here?"

The only light came from the muted TV playing a movie. Two people were obviously sleeping twined together on the bed. The one closest to me had her head and one bare leg out of the covers. It was Fiona's best friend, Stacy, the girl who had been in *The Funhouse*.

"You bastard!" I screamed, launching myself at the bed. I snatched off my sneaker and started beating every part of him I could reach, kneeling on the bed and bashing away at him through the covers.

"Scarlett!" Stacy said, grabbing for me. With my free left hand, I grabbed her by the face and shoved her out of the bed, loving the thump she made as her bare ass hit the floor.

A muffled stream of profanity was coming from under the blanket as I kept beating. "I should fucking kill you!" I screamed in response.

"Scarlett!" Romeo's voice said from behind me. "Baby, stop!" He was laughing so hard he could barely speak, but he managed to grab me and my shoe. "Stop!" The covers boiled, and a head I vaguely recognized popped out.

"Fuck me!" he said in an unmistakably Australian accent. "What the fuck?"

"You got off easy," Romeo said, still laughing and still holding on to me as I climbed down from the bed. "Last time she had a gun."

"Who is that?" I demanded. "What the fuck is going on?"

"Scarlett Kidd, meet Peter Thatcher," Romeo said. "Peter, meet the wife."

Suddenly I knew exactly who he was. "You're the other Romantic," I said. "The other guy from the show."

"I am." Now that I'd stopped trying to fracture his skull with a sneaker, he was smiling. "Lovely to meet you, Mrs. Kidd."

"I think I've sprained my ass," Stacy said from the floor. "Just in case anybody cares."

"Darling!" Peter said, rushing to help her. They were both naked as newborns. Romeo, at least, was dressed.

"Where were you? What were they doing in your bed?" I said. "And where the fuck have you been?"

"I was in the bathroom when you came in," he said. "And they came over here to console me."

"Restrain him, more like," Peter said, getting Stacy a robe. Even in my present state, I couldn't help noticing how nicely he was built. "Keep him from murdering your father."

"Can we please not go crazy again?" Stacy said. "My ass can't take it."

"Why are you murdering my father?" I said, turning my back while Peter put on pants. "And why weren't you at the luncheon?"

"Come on, angel," Romeo said, kissing my forehead. "Let's go in the other room and leave these two lovebirds to soothe Stacy's ass." He took my arm and steered me out to the living room, closing the door behind us.

"What is going on?" I said. "Where have you been? Why didn't you call me?"

"I needed to think, I guess." Now that we were alone, he wasn't smiling.

"Think about what?" I was losing some of my momentum, starting to lose adrenaline, starting to get scared. "Why are you mad at Da—at Calvin?"

He did smile at that, but not in a fun, happy way. "I'll show you." He unzipped my hoodie, exposing the lacy tank underneath.

"You're mad at Calvin because of my boobs?" I said, trying to lighten the mood.

"You just look hot." He helped me take the jacket off. "And hot." He kissed my bare shoulder. "Have a seat. I want to show you something."

"Okay." He was right; the jacket had been smothering me.

He got a manila envelope from the sideboard and handed it to me. "This was delivered today just as I was getting dressed for the luncheon."

As soon as I saw the return address, things started to make more sense—Ranhosky's law firm. "Oh for fuck's sake." Inside were freshly drafted divorce proceedings, no fault, with Romeo as the Plaintiff divorcing me.

"The big man brought those over himself," Romeo said. He was still standing across from me, watching me read.

"Not Daddy?"

"Oh no, of course not. He was busy being a movie star; he didn't have time to dirty his hands. Ranhosky." I suddenly realized he was shaking. "He said I had gotten everything I could from you. A TV series. An Oscar nomination."

"I had nothing to do with either of those things!"

"All I could do now was bring you down," he went on. "And eventually you'd end up being a drag on me."

I couldn't believe it. "He said that?"

"He said with the right people to take care of you, you could be a great actress," he said. "But if you stayed with me, you'd shatter inside of a year."

"That is so not true," I said. I was shaking now, too. "You know that's not true." But looking into his eyes, I could see he wasn't sure. "Romeo, there's nothing wrong with me. I'm not a child; I'm not fragile. You know that."

"You're perfect." He came to me now and gathered me up in his arms. "Absolutely perfect." I clung to him tight, fighting tears. He wasn't saying it; he didn't have to. The night we'd met, I'd been a fragile little girl living alone in her dollhouse. I'd finally taken him away from Fiona by freaking out over a lot of fake blood and almost killing myself, either by accident or on purpose; neither of us had ever decided which. We had eloped when I ran away from home. But that was then, I told myself. I was different now; I was going to be different.

"He's wrong, baby," I promised him. "Ranhosky is wrong."

"I know he is." He drew back and smiled at me. "I don't think Ranhosky has been right a moment in his life." He framed my face in his hands and kissed me. *I'll be strong,* I promised him inside my head. *Whatever happens, I will never shatter, never again.*

When the kiss broke, I smiled. "I still have to kick your ass. I can't believe you stood me up at that stupid luncheon."

"I'm sorry, angel." He hugged me close and kissed the top of my head, then got up. "By the time I threw Daddy's lawyer out, I was already late. I started getting dressed again, but I couldn't stop thinking." He went to the bar and poured himself a drink, whiskey neat. "How did I end up nominated for an Oscar for ten minutes in a horror movie?"

He had a point, but I wasn't going to admit it. "For one thing, you're really, really good," I said. "For another, your gorgeous face is plastered on billboards all over L.A. and on the front ad of every magazine anybody in this town bothers to read." He shrugged, taking a swallow of his drink. "And if you want to get all down and dirty about it…" I couldn't believe I was going to say this, but it was the one thing I was almost sure he'd believe. "Didn't you used to fuck some of the most powerful people in Hollywood?"

He laughed. "Good point." He drank some more. "But not so many as you might think." He finished his whiskey. "That night we met?" He wasn't looking at me. "That was my first time," he said. "I owed so much money, and Amy couldn't stop using and was making it worse. I knew I had to get her into rehab." I wanted to go to him and hug him, but I held back and let him finish. "He offered me this massive amount of money, half before, half after. We didn't even…" He shook his head, barely smiling. "Then you showed up and rescued me." I did get up then. "You really were my angel." I wrapped my arms around him and held him tight. "I love you so much."

"I love you." In my mind, I could see the whole world like an angry mob around us, but as long as we were together, we were safe. "It doesn't matter what anybody says or does or what happened before. And as for the Oscars." I drew back and looked him in the eye and told him the absolute truth. "Fuck the Oscars. You are the best actor I have ever seen. Better than Sebastian. Better than my father. And someday, everybody in the world is going to know it." I kissed him. "Now explain to me, please, why Stacy and this Peter person were naked in your bed?"

He laughed. "Peter was here with me when Ranhosky showed up," he said. "He's been seeing Stacy, sort of. They hooked up at the Rainbow one night."

"He's her new meat."

"Exactly." He let me go to pour himself another drink. "Peter is starting to sense that she might not love him for his brains and wanted to ask me what I thought he should do."

"Dump her and find somebody else?" I suggested.

"Actually, no," he said, laughing. "I think they may be perfect for one another."

"Yikes."

"So after Ranhosky left and I was freaking out, she was the one he knew to call. We talked and drank until I fell asleep over there on the couch. When I woke up, they were in the bed."

"Classy."

"No doubt. I went to the bathroom and was brushing my teeth when I heard you come in." He grinned. "By the time I could rinse and spit, my baby had gone kung fu."

"You laugh," I said. "I was going to literally kill you."

"And I would have deserved it." He smiled. "You don't have to worry." He kissed me. "I don't want anybody else."

"Good." I took the drink out of his hand and put it on the bar, then draped my arms around his waist. "Now kick those sluts out of our bed. I want to go to sleep."

"You're staying?" He put his arms around me, too. "Are you sure?"

"Oh yeah." I wasn't sure he was right about Daddy and Ranhosky. I thought the lawyer was perfectly capable of acting on his own. But either way, someone had broken our agreement, so I could, too. "I'm sure."

The morning of the Oscars, our entire weird little family relocated from Castle Asshole to a posh hotel three blocks from the Dorothy Chandler Pavilion. Sebastian and I shared a suite; Fiona, who was presenting, was right next door; and Calvin had the penthouse. We visited back and forth all morning long. A parade of professionals came and went to make us all beautiful while well-wishers, publicists, and studio executives dropped by to let us know how awesome we were and how happy they were to know us. It was like being royalty in a big-budget musical from the 1950s. I kept expecting a chorus of bellhops and hairdressers to break into song at any moment.

My biggest worry was fitting into my dress. My brilliant stylist, Cristofer, had found me the most gorgeous gown I had ever seen, but I had gained a few pounds since Texas. He had combed through stacks of magazines and fashion house catalogs and watched hours of runway videos until he found something close to what he wanted, a bridal gown from a French designer's spring line two years before. Then he called her up and begged, pleaded, and bullied her into making an updated, less bridal version just for me.

The underdress was a slightly A-line sheath of tissue-thin rose gold lamé, tight-fitting at the top then fuller from just below my breasts. Over that was an empire-waisted, sheer, intricately-beaded chiffon over-gown in a rosy shade of cream with cap sleeves and a rounded bodice. The subtle gold background made it dramatic enough for the Oscars, but the sweet simplicity of the design and the pinkish color of the overlay kept it from looking too flashy. I adored it at first sight; I never even tried on anything else. I had been having fittings every other day since it was completed, and one of the designer's own seamstresses was there at the hotel to make any last-minute adjustments. But I was still worried.

"You don't think it looks too much like a wedding dress, do you?" I asked Sebastian as we sat around in robes eating our lunch.

"I think the gold saves it," he said, smiling. He had been reassuring me for days and thought it was hilarious. I had never cared this much about anything I wore. "You'll look like Donald Trump's idea of an angel."

"Golly, thanks." I threw a cherry tomato at him. I was having a huge salad with strips of sirloin on it and a glass of milk. He was having toast and champagne. "Shouldn't you be eating real food?"

"My food is not imaginary." He poured himself another glass. "Just very dry."

Someone knocked at the door to the suite, and Sebastian's brand-new assistant, Carollee, answered it. "Scarlett," she said, coming back. "It's a package for you."

Swag had been showing up for both of us all day from various people and companies who wanted us to use their stuff, everything from designer cupcakes to videogames. But this was an actual wrapped package with a big pink bow on top. "Who's it from?" Sebastian asked as I opened the card that was taped to the top.

"Romeo." All it read was, "I love you. See you tonight," with his signature.

"Awwww," Sebastian said. "Open it up. Or do you want me to leave?"

"No, it's okay. Stay." I opened the box and found two smaller wrapped boxes. One was tiny and wrapped like the big one in white tissue with another pink bow. The other was wrapped in black with a tag that read, "Open me first."

I tore off the black wrapping. Inside was a scratched and battered videocassette. A sticker on the outside was stamped "Cammy's Quick Stop" and dated the day we had eloped. "Oh my god…it's the tape." Sebastian didn't seem to understand. "The tape from the gas station in New Mexico."

"Oh my god," he echoed.

A note was taped to the bottom. "Let's burn this together. You can even invite your dad." I showed it to Sebastian.

"Okay, don't you dare start crying over a sex tape," he said. "You'll ruin your face." He leaned over and gave my hand a squeeze. "Open the other box."

I tore off the tissue and found a tiny silver box. "Oh wow." Inside the box was a ring. When we'd gotten married in El Paso, Romeo and I had given one another plain, cheap gold bands, the kind of thing a pair of Texas teens in love might be able to afford. Romeo carried his in his pocket, and I usually kept mine in a jewelry box at home. That day I happened to have mine in my purse; I'd put it in for luck and with the idea I might put it on as soon as the ceremony was over.

This ring was very different. It looked like platinum lace, delicate filigree encrusted with tiny diamonds that each to my untrained eye looked perfectly shaped and flawless. "Bubba, look." I slipped it on, and it covered my ring finger to the first knuckle. But it was light in both look and feel. From a distance, it would show up as nothing but sparkle.

"It's beautiful," Sebastian said, barely looking. "He had it designed just for you. There's no other one exactly like it anywhere."

"He told you about it?" I couldn't stop looking at it. "You talked to him?"

"Yeah. Sissy, listen to me for a second." He moved to a closer chair and took my hands in his. "Stop being all girly and stupid for a second and think. He's giving you a choice. If you have that tape, you don't have to stay married to him."

"'Bastian, are you crazy? I want to stay married to him." I couldn't believe he was saying this.

"Are you sure?" He had started squeezing my hands tight; now he let me go. "It's all cool and romantic, eloping in the middle of the night with this gorgeous guy everybody wants, chucking it all for love. I get it; I do. But do you really think that's going to last? You are giving up so much. You could do so much, and you're trapping yourself in this marriage that's going to define you for the rest of your life."

"Define me? What are you talking about?"

"You and Romeo are both famous now, both actors. As soon as you go public, you're going to be a Hollywood couple. You won't be Scarlett Cross, the wonderful actress. You'll be the girl half of Romeo and Scarlett. It won't matter what else you do. All anybody is ever going to care about is that. Either your marriage will succeed, and you'll disappear when you stop working to keep it succeeding and another power couple turns up. Or it will fail, and you'll either be a pathetic victim or the bitch who dumped Romeo Kidd."

"I'm not 'Scarlett Cross, the wonderful actress' now," I said. "I'm Calvin Cross' daughter."

"No, but see, that's just it," he said. "You're not. Our father may be a shit parent, but he's been a fucking awesome career mentor, at least for you. He has steered you toward every possible opportunity to shine, and you've come through in aces without even trying. You've blown everybody away, knocked everybody's socks off. After tonight, win or lose, you'll have a window of opportunity where you could do whatever kind of parts you want. If you were smart, in a couple of years, you could have people calling him Scarlett Cross's father. But you aren't interested in any of that. You want to throw it all away to keep trying to live out this fairy tale."

"You think my life has been a fairy tale?" I said. "You think being in love with Romeo has been easy?"

"No, I think it's been hard as hell, and that's why it feels like finally getting to be with him is the prize."

"You've been thinking about this a lot, haven't you?"

"Yeah, I have. I'm so jealous of you, I could smother you in your sleep." The room had emptied, I noticed. I wondered how many people were listening at the door outside. "But I love you more than I love anybody or anything else on this earth. And as great as Romeo is, it kills me to think of you ending up like Mom."

I didn't know what to say to that. For a long moment, I mostly just wanted to punch him in the face. "I won't," I finally said. "Romeo isn't going to cheat on me."

"You don't know that," he said. "He's an actor. Hell, you're an actress. Maybe you'll cheat on him."

"I won't," I said. "I couldn't."

"You don't know that."

Cris came in, gently tapping on the door. "I'm so sorry to interrupt, honey, but we have got to get started on your hair."

"It's okay." I got up, then leaned over and kissed Sebastian. He hugged me fiercely tight for a moment, then I made him let me go. "Look what I got, Cris," I said, showing the stylist my ring. "Will it work with the dress?"

He looked stunned. "Oh yeah." He smiled. "That works."

After that, things started moving fast. All the same people who had been hanging out chatting and drinking champagne all day were suddenly very intense and very, very busy. Before I knew it, I was coiffed and manicured and made up to perfection. Then it was time for the dress.

I spritzed down one last time with deodorant and the lightest possible powder under my arms. Then two of Cris' assistants lifted the gold underdress over my head, careful as a bomb squad as they worked it over my hair and tugged it down into place. The designer's seamstress whipped up the side seams for the last time, sewing me in. If I ate an extra cookie, I was going to pop out.

The make-up artist brushed a last shimmer of highlighter across my cleavage. Then Cris himself stepped up on a footstool to lift the gauzy, sparkling overdress and drop it over my head.

"How is that?" he asked as the seamstress ran her fingertips over me, checking for loose beads. "Is it too heavy?"

"No, it feels great." I looked at myself in the mirror, trying as always to convince myself that the image I was seeing was the girl inside my head. "Do I look okay?"

Everybody laughed. "Uh huh," Cris said, beaming at me like he'd made me from scratch. "The fashion police can suck it."

Then Sebastian was there, and somebody was handing me sunglasses, and I could hear Daddy laughing in the hallway, and suddenly we were going. Daddy kissed me as we were waiting for the elevator. "You look so grown-up," Daddy said, wiping away a tear. "I can't believe it."

Then we were in the limo, moving at a crawl with people lining the sidewalks, waving and screaming. Then we were passing through security with our army of publicists banked around us. People in uniforms passed metal detecting wands over us and tried to look serious. "I love your dress," one security woman said.

"Thank you," I said, returning her smile.

Then we were on the red carpet. I didn't have a publicist of my own, so a woman named Susan from Daddy's publicist's office was walking behind me, just a few steps back, a lady-in-waiting with my purse. She steered me through the throng from one interview to another, avoiding any journalist who wasn't on her list. I stopped and spoke to other actors I knew, but I didn't really hear what they were saying, and they didn't really hear me either. It didn't matter. It was like a dream. We were improvising a weird performance for the people watching at home.

I turned around about halfway down the carpet, and suddenly there was Romeo. "Oh hi," I said, beaming, frozen in my tracks. "You look so beautiful." He did. He was wearing a perfectly fitted black tuxedo, classic and manly and gorgeous.

"So do you." The carpet was so crowded, we were pushed together until we were almost touching, both of us perfectly still.

"I love my present." I showed him I was wearing the ring. "It's perfect."

He smiled. "I'm glad you like it."

Then our publicists were pulling us apart and on to the next interview.

At the very end of the carpet was my last interview, a woman I had been dreading for weeks. She was a comedian who had made herself over as an entertainment journalist, and her whole schtick was flustering her subjects, asking just the right question to make them lose their cool. My cool was pretty shaky already, so I was pretty sure I was fucked. She had just finished interviewing my father when I walked up, and for a moment I had visions of just slipping by her with him. But she wasn't about to let me escape.

"Hey Scarlett!" she said, stepping in front of me. "God, what a stunning dress!"

"Thanks." I made myself smile, and together we went through the red carpet litany—who designed my dress, my shoes, my earrings. She seemed very nice, and I almost believed I'd dodged the bullet after all, that I'd been worried for nothing.

Then she pulled the trigger. "So Scar, a lot of people are saying your father is responsible for your nomination." I hadn't heard of anybody saying that, but whatever. "What do you say to that?"

"I say they're right." I wasn't poised like my father or Sebastian; my only defense was to blurt out the truth. "My father is responsible for every good thing that's ever happened to me. My mom was killed when I was four years old, and she left me by myself in a strange city where I didn't even speak the language. My father rescued me, and he's been taking care of me ever since." I could tell from the look on her face that her team hadn't prepped her for this. "The only reason I have ever achieved anything is that I have his support. He took care of me through *Match Girl* the way he always has; no actress ever had an easier first movie."

"That's really sweet," she said, looking at a loss.

"And besides, if it weren't for him, I would never have gotten the part." I smiled at her. "Have a great night!"

She smiled back for the camera. "You too!"

My father was waiting just out of camera range. "Hey you." He put his arm around my shoulders and kissed the top of my head. "Just in case I don't see you later, I think you're amazing."

"Thanks, Daddy." The next day, one of the major entertainment magazines put a picture on their cover of me kissing his cheek.

CHAPTER 38

The ceremony itself was kind of boring; everything was timed and staged for the TV broadcast. Nominees, movie stars, publicists, and seat fillers all milled around together between awards like extras waiting for the next set-up while techies worked feverishly around them. Daddy, Sebastian, and I were all seated in a line together about three rows back. Sebastian said this was a good sign. His whole attitude about awards had changed since the Golden Globes. That night, he had prayed out loud that he wouldn't win so he wouldn't have to make a speech. Tonight he was nervous in a completely different way. He had done twice as much publicity as I had over the past month; he really wanted to win. So I wanted him to win, too. I knew Romeo didn't care.

For myself, I wasn't sure what I wanted. Before that day, I had just been trying to get through it, to plow past tonight to get to what came after, being with Romeo. But now I couldn't stop thinking about all the things Sebastian had said at the hotel and the question that bitch on the red carpet had asked. If all I wanted was to be Mrs. Romeo Kidd, my nomination really was a scandal. I hadn't worked for it; I didn't need it; and I was taking a career boost away from another girl who did. I thought about Fiona who had always been so focused and had always worked so hard and who was so incredibly talented. She had been brilliant in *Funhouse*, and she hadn't been nominated, hadn't been nominated for anything since she was a little kid. Yet here I sat.

Bette's award was first, and she lost, and from what I could see, she couldn't have cared less. When the Sixties Siren won, she applauded more loudly than anybody else. Daddy leaned over from his seat behind her and whispered something in her ear. She laughed out loud and turned around and kissed him.

Then came an endless parade of categories I couldn't have cared less about. I'm sure the winner of best live action documentary short subject was a brilliant artist and that her mother, her agent, and her high school English teacher were all justifiably proud. But I just wanted her to get off the stage so we could move on.

Finally, it was time for Sebastian and Romeo. I had stood up earlier and shamelessly gawped until I'd found where Ro was sitting; more than halfway back but fairly close to the aisle. Amy was his date, and she and I had waved to one another. Romeo had been turned around talking to someone in the row behind him. Now I restrained myself from looking back again as his name was read, though Sebastian and I both hooted our support, getting a little laugh from the audience. When my brother's name was read, I took his hand in both of mine and held it tight.

The actress on stage opened the envelope. "And the award goes to…Sebastian Cross for *The House*."

I jumped to my feet and screamed, clapping like a crazy woman. Sebastian grabbed me and kissed me and hugged Daddy and Loki. Then he walked to the stage looking pleased and surprised and a little embarrassed with a camera on him every step of the way. Watching him at the podium, it was impossible to believe he had ever been afraid of making a speech. He was funny and self-deprecating and grateful; he thanked all the right people from the movie and the studio, even cracking an inside joke about one of his co-stars that got a huge response from a small knot of people near the back. He thanked Daddy and me for our support and said he loved us very much. I noticed he didn't thank his mother.

Aksel Jorgen won for Best Director, shocking no one. Bette had lost, but *Match Girl* had won two of the three tech awards for which it was nominated. Calvin went onstage and accepted the award on Jorgen's behalf and gave what I'm sure was a very touching speech wishing him a speedy recovery. I barely heard him; that was one of those things I just didn't allow myself to think about. Besides, I was starting to get nervous. Odds were excellent that all I'd have to do for the rest of the night was lose graciously and applaud for my father, but I couldn't help wondering what I would do if I won. What would I say? Would I feel more like an actress? Would my career suddenly become more important to me? *You're more than somebody's angel,* Cole had said. Was that what he had meant? *I'd hate to see you end up like Mom,* Sebastian had said. At the time, my feelings had been hurt, but if I won, would I suddenly know he was right?

Then suddenly it was time. The guy who'd won best actor the year before was reading off names, and they were showing clips, and there I was, a little girl in an ugly coat shouting in a German accent.

Then he was saying something that sounded familiar, and everyone around me was applauding, and Bette was turning around to grab my hands. I squeezed back then let her go, stood up, and reached for Daddy. "Go," he whispered in my ear, barely kissing my cheek. He steered me into the aisle, and I headed for the stage. Some nice man helped me up the slippery steps; I don't know if he was someone from the audience or someone whose job it was to keep me from breaking my neck. Either way, I was grateful for the help. I made my way to the podium and took possession of my incredibly heavy award.

"This would make a great weapon," I said into the mike, the first words that popped into my head. Everybody laughed, which made me feel a little better. This audience was at least ten times bigger than the one at the Globes had been and at least a hundred times scarier. I couldn't believe any of them thought I deserved this. I didn't believe it myself. I found myself scanning the crowd for Simon, my Scarecrow. He was sitting down front, beaming up at me.

"Thank you to the Academy." I could see Daddy and Bette both beaming, too; Sebastian hadn't come back from the press room. Fiona was smiling, but it was her actress smile. "And to my father and Bette and Aksel and everyone else on the movie who was so brilliant. You all made me look like I knew what I was doing, and I really appreciate it." Everyone laughed again. "I want to thank my brother, Sebastian, for loving me and trying to help me be smarter." Searching the crowd, I finally found what I was looking for, watching me, smiling his beautiful smile. "Finally, I want to thank my husband, Romeo Kidd. I love you very, very much."

In the three seconds of stunned silence that followed, I held up my award and started off the stage. Then the music kicked in from the orchestra, and the crowd broke into applause.

CHAPTER 39

The glamour girl who herded me off the stage handed me over to a guy in a tuxedo and a headset. "I've got Scarlett Cross," he said into the headset. "We're coming to you."

I had slipped past the press machine at the Golden Globes fairly easily. To get free at the Oscars, I would have needed a stealth assassin. My handler wove me down a narrow, crowded hallway at a brisk trot to a doorway where another guy just like him was waiting. "Are they ready for her?" One asked.

Two laughed and nodded. "Oh yeah."

Behind the doorway was a cavernous ballroom filled with light and sound and cameras and people shouting my name. "One at a time!" the publicist in charge was shouting as Two led me to the dais. "One at a time!" There was no podium, just a backdrop with the Oscar logo all over it. "Congratulations," the publicist said as Two backed off and the press subsided to a burbling roar.

"Thanks." A technician had just finished attaching a microphone to my dress, so this roared out over the room.

"Scarlett, were you surprised to win?" a woman called out.

"Hey, I was surprised to be nominated," I said. "I was freaking shocked to win. Honored, grateful, thrilled, but definitely shocked."

"Did your dad know you were married?" a man asked.

"Of course he did," I said. "We got married in January."

"Was your father at the wedding?" another guy asked.

"Dude, if I'd wanted people to know who was at my wedding, I'd have told people I was getting married." I had been terrified of these questions for weeks, but now it didn't matter. Answering was almost fun. "My dad was surprised, and he worries that we're so young, but he hasn't disowned me yet."

A little flurry of applause went up from the very back of the room. Just through another door were monitors still playing the broadcast. "Speaking of your dad, he just won," a journalist called from the back.

"Yes!" I said, making everybody laugh. "Yay Daddy!"

"Okay, we've got to move on," the boss publicist said. "Does anybody have one more question about Scarlett's work?"

"I do," a woman said. I recognized her; she was Alice Brown. I remembered her from the *Match Girl* premiere. She asked me the same thing now as she had asked me there. "Scarlett, what's next?"

"I don't know." I said. "I don't really…" My attention drifted to a noise at the door where we'd come in. Romeo was charming and pushing his way past Two. "I don't have any projects lined up." At a high sign from the publicist, Two let him in, and I smiled. "I'm so sorry. Will y'all excuse me, please?" I left the dais and met him halfway through the crowd. He kissed me, and the cameras clicked, and every media outlet in the world seemed to carry the picture.

I expected Calvin to be furious, but he was too high on the awards to even seem to notice what I'd done. In addition to our wins, *The Little Match Girl* had won Best Picture. It wasn't a record, but it was enough to distract my movie star father from the shame of my teenage wedding. At the Governor's Ball, he hugged me and shook Romeo's hand and acted like he'd been in on the reveal from the beginning.

After a suitable interval there, Calvin took us all to the party at

Swifty Lazar's, one of his regular Oscar night stops. Romeo and I got swept apart by the crowd thirty seconds after we walked in the door, but he and I together were all anybody really wanted to talk about. I must have posed for pictures showing off my new ring a dozen times in an hour. Then Calvin was ready to move on and sent out the publicists to gather us all up to head for the exit. Romeo was still out of reach, but he waved to me and pointed to the door, and I nodded—he would meet me there.

Simon and Clare had turned up at the same party a few minutes earlier. I had been watching Clare work the room since they walked in, stopping every few steps to speak to someone with the over-bright laughter of a serious actress trying to act like a starlet. My poor Scarecrow was trailing in her wake, looking handsome and bored and miserable, the two of them linked by their pinkie fingers alone, a gesture I decided was the most stupid thing I'd ever seen in my life. I felt bad for him; I knew what it was like, being an accessory. As we passed them headed the other way, I reached out and clasped his other hand. He turned, startled, to look, and I smiled and winked at him as I gave his hand a squeeze. His vague smile widened into the movie star grin, and I smiled back, but neither of us really stopped. After barely a moment, we let our hands fall apart, and he kept moving with his fiancée, and I hurried after Sebastian. Romeo was already standing on the sidewalk with a freshly-lit cigarette, and I kissed him—another picture for the papers.

Sometime after midnight and two more parties later, I was standing on another sidewalk. Sebastian was beside me; we were waiting for our car. Romeo had gone down the street to talk to Peter, who he'd spotted coming out of another restaurant with his agent. Calvin and Fiona were right behind me and Sebastian; they were talking to one of Calvin's old girlfriends, another actress, and her new husband, a Russian ballet dancer.

"Did Fiona tell you?" Sebastian said, lighting a cigarette.

"Tell me what?" Looking down the sidewalk, I saw a paparazzo taking a picture of Romeo and Peter.

"She's pregnant." I was so engrossed in watching Romeo, what my brother had said didn't register for a moment. Then I turned and looked at him, shocked, and he nodded, a wry grin on his face. "We're going to have a baby brother or sister," he said, taking a puff from his cigarette. "Isn't that just groovy?"

I didn't even answer him. I started walking toward Romeo. Peter and his agent were walking into the restaurant, but Romeo had leaned into the front passenger window of their car, talking to the driver. I put both hands on his back. "Come on." He turned around to find me so close I was almost tucked under his chin.

"Scarlett?"

"Take me home." I took his hand and climbed into the back seat of the limo, and he followed me in.

"Where's your dad?" he said, closing the door.

"With his pregnant girlfriend." I sat back in the plush leather seat. "Just go."

The driver was watching us in the rearview mirror with the bland expression Hollywood drivers learn before they learn to park. "Just drive," Romeo told him. He sat back beside me, still holding my hand. "She told you?"

"Sebastian told me." I looked past him out the window on his side. Sebastian was talking to Calvin and Fiona, smiling and gesturing. Calvin didn't look alarmed; my brother was fixing it for me. Fiona was watching us drive away. "Wait, she told you?" I asked Romeo.

"Yeah." He brushed a stray tendril of hair back from my face. "What did Sebastian say?"

"Just that Fiona was pregnant." I frowned. "When did she tell you?"

"Earlier tonight." He was looking down now at our joined hands on the seat. "I didn't want to say anything while we were out like this; I knew you'd be upset." He looked up again, into my eyes. "I love you very much."

"I love you." I pushed the button to raise the screen between us and the driver. "So much." I climbed into his lap and kissed him. "Take me home."

"If we go back to the hotel, we'll get mobbed," he said. "The sidewalks out front will be crawling with photographers tonight; you know that."

"I know." I slumped forward, curling against his chest. "Let's just drive around for a while, okay."

He kissed the top of my head. "Okay."

About a week after the Oscars, Romeo asked me to go with him to the set. I loved it. He and Peter were both great, and the atmosphere was fun and relaxed. It was one of those sets where everybody seemed to know they were making a hit.

They finished up for the day around mid-afternoon. We got in my little car with Ro at the wheel, and I thought we'd be heading back to town. But instead he drove out to the coast and turned north. "It's our highway," I said. "We drove this way the night we met, going the other direction."

"I remember you asked me if I wanted to be an actor," he said. "I couldn't believe it."

"But look at you now. I was totally right." I turned toward him and leaned into my seat, just watching him drive. "You should have listened to me."

"I should have." He looked over at me and smiled. "I loved you that first night."

I reached out and touched his arm. "I loved you, too."

He drove past Malibu, so far up the coast that I started to drift off. When I woke up, we were pulling into a sandy driveway through a jungle of overgrown trees. "Where are we?"

"We're here." He parked in front of a tiny, cedar-shingled cottage. "Come on. I'll show you."

Inside it was empty, swept clean. All the light fixtures and switches and doorknobs looked original to around the 1920s, and the paint was old, cracked on the ceiling and faded in big patches on the walls. But the hardwood floors were polished and gleaming, and the mantle on the green marble fireplace in the living room where we were standing had been stripped to its original glowing wood. "It's beauti-ful," I said, holding Romeo's hand, lacing my fingers with his. To the right was a dining room with a built-in, glass front cupboard. Dead in front of us was a staircase. "I love it."

"There are three bedrooms upstairs," he said. "And there's a den in the back that could be another bedroom. The kitchen needs work, and we'd have to put in at least one more bathroom."

"We?" I said. "It's ours?"

"If you want it." For a moment, I almost thought he was joking. It seemed too good to be true. But I could see from his smile and the look in his eyes that he was completely serious. "Do you?"

"Oh my god…yes!" I threw my arms around him. "Of course I want it!" *A home*, I thought, doing cartwheels in my head. *We have a home.* "I love it." I kissed him all over his face, making him laugh. "I love you."

"I love you." He squeezed me tight. "But come on; you haven't seen the best part."

He walked me through the kitchen—clean, but very much out-of-date—and out the back door. A long porch with a low-hanging roof stretched all the way across the back and looked over a tiny strip of grass with an old-fashioned clothesline and a spigot on a pipe sticking out of the ground. Beyond that was a thick, thorny hedge with a little rusted wrought iron arbor gate covered with roses gone wild. "So pretty," I said, thinking this must be what he meant.

"Hang on." We walked hand in hand through the gate and down a narrow, winding path through the trees like children in a fairy tale. We turned a corner, and the trees parted, and there was the Pacific Ocean.

"Romeo," I said, clutching his hand. We were standing at the top of a high rocky cliff looking down on the beach. Our path became steep stone steps that looked like they'd been there forever with an ugly but sturdy-looking railing of rusted steel pipe. There was a little village of tiny trailers off to the right in the distance, and to the left we could see the highway snaking along the cliff. But the little strip of rocks and sand directly in front of us looked completely deserted.

"So what do you think?" he asked.

The sun was starting to set, painting the ocean and the sky in shades of orange and pink. Tears stung my eyes, and I leaned into his side. "Can we stay here forever?"

"We can." He turned my face up to his and kissed me. "I promise we can."

CLIPPING 12

from *The National Outlook*: "Can Scarlett Be Happy at Last?"

Many in Hollywood are shocked and even appalled by the engagement of barely-16-year-old Scarlett Cross to bad boy TV actor Romeo Kidd. But at least one source close to the Cross family is thrilled.

"I am so happy for her," says Carolina Garcia, longtime housekeeper for Scarlett's father, mega-star Calvin Cross. "Finally she can be safe."

According to Garcia, Scarlett was barely more than an infant when her mother, doomed beauty Stella St. John, was brutally murdered. Garcia came to work for the family some years later, and she remembers Scarlett's night terrors connected to that horrible event. "I felt so sorry for her," she told TNO. "She would wake up screaming and screaming, and nothing could comfort her, sometimes not even her father."

Thing only got worse, Garcia says, when Calvin Cross split from long-time love Greta Strassman, the mother of Scarlett's half-brother, Sebastian, also an Oscar-winning actor and a Tony nominee. Garcia was in the family employ and a daily fixture in the home at that time, and she says Strassman had acted as a surrogate mother to Scarlett after her own mother's death. Losing her was a terrible shock to the already-fragile little girl. "That woman abandoned that child," Garcia says. "The poor kid was lost without Greta and her big brother. She couldn't even sleep in her own bed she was so afraid. I would come to work in the mornings and find her sleeping on the couch with the TV playing, and I would know she had been there all night." And where was Scarlett's father? "Mr. Cross did everything he could to take care of her," Garcia insists. "But a little girl needs a woman in her life, especially when her own mother has been taken from her so horribly. I tried to help—she was always such a sweet child. But I know it wasn't the same."

Garcia was still a primary caregiver for Scarlett when she first met Kidd on the set of the horror film The Funhouse. *"I had never seen her so happy," she says. "She thought the world began and ended with that boy. And I could tell he felt the same. He was very gentle with her, very respectful, but it was obvious he adored her."*

But what about the rumors surrounding Kidd's past, his days as a bouncer and possible drug dealer on the Sunset Strip, his connection to his sister, porn star Amy Kidd? "It isn't a bad thing that he used to be bad, a tough guy," Garcia says. "All that is behind him now; he's a star. But he knows how to take care of Scarlett, and she knows he knows. I think they will be very happy and be married a very long time."

The odds in Hollywood are stacked against them, but TNO hopes she's right.

CHAPTER 40

For the rest of the spring into summer, I worked on the renovation at the beach house, hiring a general contractor and picking finishes and having the time of my life. I even hired my very own assistant, Lisa, who was amazing and brilliant and hilarious. Romeo kept filming the TV show, and people kept asking me what I was going to do next. I told them I was reading scripts, and it was true, my agent sent me scripts all the time. They piled up on the coffee table in the bungalow at the hotel, and I never opened a single one.

The Romantics premiered in June on the brand-new Limbo network. At Fiona's suggestion, we all got together to watch the premiere episode on my dad's big TV at Castle Asshole, me, Romeo, Peter, Stacy, Sebastian, and Fiona. Calvin was in New York working, and Fiona was staying in his house, looking more pregnant every day. She had ordered a bunch of pizzas and a big cake and champagne; it was a real family party.

The show was awesome. Romeo was the wild, rakish one with the tragic reputation; Peter was the angelic innocent being corrupted. The pilot was them meeting for the first time and getting mixed up in the death of a local virgin. Both were suspected of murdering her, but really it was a demon that had possessed her oh-so-respectable fiancé, Romeo's character's cousin. At the end, our heroes manage to cast out the demon and see it for themselves, but it gets away. The fiancé gets arrested for the murder, and they promise to catch the demon and reveal the truth, which sets up the rest of the series.

"Yes!" Sebastian said as soon as the final credits rolled over a wailing, goth-metal soundtrack, and the other girls and I joined his applause. Peter was blushing furiously, and he dragged Stacy into his lap to kiss her. Romeo was smiling and looking embarrassed.

"It was great," I said, kissing his cheek as the others jumped up to crack open more champagne. "I loved it."

"Thanks." He gave me a one-armed hug. "Yeah, it was good. The story, I mean, and Peter was great."

"You were awesome." I climbed into his arms, facing him. "You're brilliant." I kissed him, and he crushed me close, holding me tight.

The phone rang. "There it is!" Sebastian said, pouring champagne.

"I'll get it," Fiona said, waddling over. She was still as rail thin as ever except for the rounded swell of her belly, and her eyes had the weird, slightly manic glow of a junkie's. "It's Ted," she said, holding out the phone. Ted was the writer/creator/producer of the show and one of her old boyfriends. "He wants Romeo first."

"Go ahead," I said, climbing off Romeo's lap.

"He's crying," Fiona said, smiling at him as she handed him the phone. "I think he's a little bit happy."

"Hey Ted," Romeo said into the phone. Sebastian hugged him and put a foaming glass of champagne into his free hand. "Yeah, of course. Yeah, it was great." His eyes met mine, and we both smiled. "We all loved it."

My father's housekeeper touched my arm. "Excuse me, Scarlett," she said quietly. "There's a call for you on the office line." Everyone else was watching Romeo, all of them smiling. "I think it's your agent," she went on. "He says he has to speak to you right now."

"Okay." I squeezed Sebastian's hand on my way out and murmured in his ear, "I'll be right back."

My father's office was where exercise equipment went to die. He hadn't put in an actual gym yet at that point, but it was coming. The desk was shoved into a corner to make room for a treadmill, a weight machine, and a state-of-the-art stationary bike that looked like a transport to Venus. The phone was mounted on the wall beside the bike. The housekeeper started to move the desk chair over, but I stopped her, shaking my head as I climbed on the bike and picked up. "This is Scarlett," I said. "Is it Tony?"

"Scarlett, thank God." He sounded out of breath, but that didn't surprise me. Tony has two modes of conversation, utter boredom or end of the world. "I've been calling all over."

"What's up?" I hit the power button on the bike's big electronic console, making all kinds of little red and blue lights start blinking. My father's latest stats twinkled before me. His last workout had been an hour long on absolute flat ground.

"A job," he said. "No, sunshine, THE job."

"Oh yeah?" I entered my weight.

"Lady Macbeth." He sounded like he was giving me the password to the gates of Paradise. "Simon Price, and half the Royal Shakespeare Company—every actress in L.A. and London is dying for this part."

"What?" I pedaled slowly, not really paying attention. "Lady Macbeth like Shakespeare?"

"Yes, of course." My reactions always disappoint Tony. When he's bored, he thinks I'm overwrought; when he's excited, he thinks I'm clueless. It isn't much of a business plan, but we make it work for us. "Scarlett, honey, this is huge. *Match Girl* huge. Bigger than *Match Girl* huge."

"Isn't Lady Macbeth like…old?" The Scarecrow's name had registered, of course, but I didn't quite make the last connection. "Why am I up for this?"

"Because Price wants you," he said. "A lot, apparently. Rumor has it he said he would only take the lead if he could cast you opposite him —rumor, fuck it, no—his agent called me himself, all right?"

"But what do the producers say?" *Match Girl* notwithstanding, it seemed ludicrous that I could be up for this part. I had seen the first half of a movie version of Macbeth in one of my longer stints in school. Lady Macbeth was a throaty-voiced, middle-aged woman with big tits.

"They want you to read," Tony said. "Actually, they want you to work with a coach for a couple of weeks and then read. But honey, you can do this."

"What's the money like?" I wasn't thinking about the Scarecrow. I was thinking of Fiona's baby coming in a few months and finishing the house, and then what would I do?

"Their number is ridiculous right now, but that's to be expected," he said. "Nail the reading, and Price will go to the mat for you. We can make it worth your while."

"Yeah." I stopped pedaling. "Yeah, okay. Tell them I want to try." Romeo and I had planned a trip to Vegas to celebrate his show. "But after next week, okay?"

"Done." He sounded thrilled. "Actually, it may be months before anything happens; you know how these big epics get dragged through development. But I'll call you tomorrow."

I went back out to the living room. Peter was on the phone now, laughing and crying and telling Ted he was a genius. Someone had turned off the television and turned on the stereo, and Sebastian and Stacy were dancing, my charming brother twirling her like a ballerina on a jewelry box. "Where's Romeo?" I asked.

"I think he went looking for you," Stacy said, giggling.

"Come dance with us, Sissy," Sebastian said, dipping her so deep she shrieked. "He'll be back in a minute."

"Yeah," I said. "In a minute." The drapes were billowing in front of the sliding glass doors to the pool. "I'll be right back."

The back yard was almost pitch-black dark, the only light coming from inside the pool. Romeo and Fiona were silhouettes, two darker shadows bleeding together at the water's far edge from the house. Fiona was sitting on the diving board, and Romeo was squatted in front of her, the tip of his cigarette glowing orange for a moment in the dark. They were very close together, very obviously engrossed in their conversation, and they didn't hear my bare feet on the slate as I moved closer.

"You don't have to want this," Fiona was saying, her voice barely louder than a whisper, distorted by the water. "This doesn't have to be you."

"You don't think?" he answered. "Should I just say, hey, Ted, dude, I'm sorry. I changed my mind? I fought for this, Fee."

"You never asked for this," she cut him off.

"I did," he answered. "I auditioned."

"You auditioned for a pilot," she said. "For the money, for the moment, to get out from under Calvin for five minutes."

"If I didn't want to do it, I should never have auditioned."

"Nobody expected it to even get picked up, much less become this…whatever this is going to be. If those numbers the network is feeding Ted are right, the studio is going to go crazy. You don't know what this shit is like; I do."

"I like the project, Fee. It's good."

"Are you ready for this kind of attention? Do you want to be a big, shiny face on every billboard on the freeway, every magazine cover? That's not what you trained to do."

"What I trained to do was sell dope and fuck people for money," he said in a bitter, vaguely amused tone I had never heard from him before. "I don't really see where I have any room to complain."

"I think Peter and Ted may be engaged," I said.

They both looked up, obviously startled. "Hey Scarlett," Fiona said, looking guilty.

"Hey baby," Romeo said, just smiling. He stood up and held out his hand. "Where did you go?"

"I had a phone call, Tony calling me about a job." I took his hand and moved close to kiss his jaw. "He said to tell you congratulations."

"What job?" Fiona said, sounding very interested and casual and like a completely different girl from the one I'd overheard talking to my husband.

"Nothing," I said. "Well, maybe something, but it's early yet." I took a drag from Romeo's cigarette and smiled at her. "I told him we'd talk more after Vegas." Sebastian was calling for us from the house—something about more pizza. "Come on, let's go in."

CHAPTER 41

Vegas was amazing. We stayed in one of the big, glitzy high-roller suites in the old MGM Grand—this was just before they tore it down. The devil lived there in Romeo's all-time favorite novel, so he had always wanted to stay there. Peter, Stacy, and Sebastian all went with us, with all our usual entourage, a group that seemed to be growing all the time, including my new assistant, Lisa. In Vegas, Sebastian kept calling her a New York snob and dragging her off to cheesy shows and attractions with my hair and make-up guy and his boyfriend—I did a photo shoot for a fashion magazine while we were there, so I had my whole team with me. Peter tried to convince Stacy to marry him every time they passed a wedding chapel, but she managed to resist. Peter's brother had joined us, and he was hilarious, a former professional rugby player with bad knees and an accent so thick when he drank we could barely understand him. I saw him slow dancing with Sebastian on the terrace one night when I got up to get more ice. Romeo and I had sex on top of or against every flat surface in the suite and two separate times in the pool.

And everywhere we went, people recognized us. The projected numbers for *The Romantics* had actually been too low. It was a monster hit. Romeo and Peter signed autographs for strippers and little kids and the bored wives of grizzled old men at the slot machines at four o'clock in the morning. We were happy; it was like a dream.

On our last night in Vegas, we went on a total bender with Peter and Stacy. Either Peter or Romeo, I forget which, had decided, as a method exercise, that because their characters on the show drank absinthe all the time, we all needed to experience it. We completely emptied a very expensive bottle of very strong stuff someone had gotten from somewhere and several other bottles of other stuff besides. I have no clear recollection of what happened immediately after that and should probably be grateful that I don't. But somehow, we ended up back at the suite, me and both guys on the bed and Stacy passed out on the bathroom floor.

At daybreak I dreamed about Stella. She and I were on the beach in Mexico, and I was asking her if we could stay, but I was an adult, the age I had grown to in real life. "I think we have to, baby," she was saying, holding my hands as the surf swirled around us, foaming crystal blue. Her face was just as I remembered it, but I had never noticed before how tired she looked, the deep, dark shadows under her beautiful eyes or the way her lips were chapped and raw. "I don't think there's any place else we can go."

A telephone was ringing in the distance, and I held on tighter to her hands. "It's okay, Mama," I promised as the phone rang on. It made me mad; I wanted someone else to answer it. "I want to stay."

"Hello?" I heard Romeo's voice, and my heart beat faster. It was like he was on the beach behind us, like if I turned around, I would see him, see my whole real life. I didn't want to see it; I wanted to stay with Stella. Her back was to the ocean, the waves rising higher as they crashed behind her, but she didn't see. "Yes?" Romeo was saying. "No..." His tone went from groggy to alert, and he sounded closer. "No, ma'am, you have the right number."

A wave so tall it was bound to drown us both swelled and peaked, and I tried to pull Stella back toward the beach. "Mama, come on!" I was trying to shout, but I didn't have a voice. My feet were buried in the sand; I couldn't move.

"This is Romeo Kidd." His accent had changed; he had fallen back into the slow, sweet cadences of Savannah. "I'm Scarlett's husband."

I blinked, and the bright Mexican beach dissolved, fading to a dim, stale-smelling hotel room. "Yes ma'am," I could hear Romeo saying; I could hear him smiling. "For a few months now." My back was to him; my head was cradled on Peter's shoulder, and his arm was around me as he snored, open-mouthed. "We've been wanting to come see you," Romeo was saying. I felt dizzy and sick, completely disoriented, and the inside of my mouth felt like it was lined with the fur of some dead animal. "I'm so glad you called."

I pushed Peter's arm off of me and rolled over. Romeo was sitting up, leaned back against the pillows. "Yes ma'am, she's right here," he said into the phone as he smiled down at me, looking fresh as a daisy. "She just woke up." He caressed my cheek. "Yes, ma'am, I love her very much."

I smiled back automatically, my brain slowly waking up, slowly realizing I should wonder who was he was talking to. It had almost been like he must have been talking to Stella; that's what had seemed to make sense. But waking up, I knew that was impossible.

"Yes ma'am," he said again. "Hold on one second." He put his hand over the mouthpiece and offered me the receiver. "It's your grand-mother," he said, shattering the dream completely. "Something must have happened; she sounds upset."

"My grandmother?" I repeated, or tried to—my voice came out as a croak. I struggled to sit up, reaching over him for the half-full bottle of soda on the nightstand. I took a long, hot swallow, the bubbles burning the fuzz out of my mouth.

"From Tupelo," he said like I might have had grandmothers scattered all over the country.

I slurped down more hot soda, then lowered the bottle, wiping my mouth with the back of my hand. "Bullshit," I said, clear as a bell. I looked down at the receiver like it might have been a rattlesnake. "Hang up."

"Scarlett, wake up," he said, giving me a shake, though I knew he knew I was awake already. "Your grandmother needs to talk to you."

"I'm not talking to her," I said. My mother's mother belonged to my old life, the one I wanted to forget had ever happened. It was one thing to talk to Mama in a dream, quite another to talk to my grandmother for real. "Hang up the phone."

"I will not." A dangerous light had come into his eyes, one that said he didn't give a shit if he made a scene or not. Peter stirred beside me, and from the bathroom, I heard Stacy groan. "And yes, you are."

For a moment, I didn't care either. It was on the tip of my tongue to tell him to fuck off. But he was my Romeo; I couldn't. "Fine." I took the receiver and spoke into it, glaring at him. "Hello?" I was gripping it so tightly my knuckles were white. "This is Scarlett Cross."

"Scarlett, honey, I'm so sorry to wake you up." The voice was like something from another dream, familiar and horrible. *She's still crying*, I thought, appalled. The last time I had seen her, she had been sobbing, and she still sounded just the same. "I never could keep straight what time it is out there."

"We're two hours ahead of you." I sounded perfectly calm, like a stranger. "It's just after six in the morning."

"Honey, I'm so sorry," she repeated. *They were always so sorry*, I thought. She and Stella both, rocking me tight in their arms and begging my forgiveness. I thought of the wave in my dream, and a shudder passed through me, making my teeth chatter. "Your grand-daddy is dead."

Romeo put his arm around me, and I slumped against his side. "Oh," I said, surprised I could say that.

"Yeah...it happened pretty quick." She didn't seem to need me to say anything. She rushed forward like a mediocre actress who has over-rehearsed her big speech. "He was out in the garden just as the sun was going down yesterday evening." She pronounced it "yes-tiddy," the way Stella had whenever she was really stoned. "He had wanted to go out earlier, but I wouldn't let him. It was just too hot." She paused to hiccup; I could all but see the snotty tissue wadded in her fist. "I was watching through the screen door when he fell."

"He fell?" I was lost without a script, saying anything to fill my cues.

"Yes, darling, a stroke. The neighbor called the ambulance when she saw me running across the yard, and we got him to the hospital. But it wasn't any use. He died just after midnight."

"Oh," I said again. I thought of the old man with his red, wrinkled skin and his white straw cowboy hat, his gray clothes that smelled like Camel cigarettes, and the squint he made to look at me, his granddaughter, in a Mexican orphanage. "She don't look nothing like Stella," he had said, like I might have been a midget imposter.

"Do you even remember us, honey?" She was still crying, but the question was sharp.

"Yes." I had clenched the hand that wasn't holding the phone so tightly, my nails were digging into the palm, but I didn't notice until Romeo took it, opening my fist. I looked up at him, looked into his eyes, and suddenly, I understood. I thought of how I would feel, looking out a screen door, watching Romeo fall in the deepening dusk, knowing he was dying as I stumbled down the steps. "Yeah, Mawmaw," I said, dissolving into tears. "Of course I remember you."

"Sweet baby girl," she said, and Romeo held me in his arms. "My pretty girl. He was so proud of you; both of us are."

"I'm sorry, Mawmaw." Peter was awake now, watching us, looking confused. "I'm so sorry this happened."

"His sister wants to go ahead and have the funeral on Thursday," she said. "But if you need more time to get here, we can wait."

"No," I said. "Don't wait on me."

"You talk to Romeo and see when you can get away," she said, rushing forward again. "I'll be just fine 'til y'all get here."

There was no way I was going to Tupelo, Mississippi, then or ever, but I couldn't tell her that. "All right." Romeo kissed my temple. *Lisa can call her later,* I thought, *and tell her we're not coming, that it was just impossible.* We'd send a lot of flowers or some money for the funeral. Mr. Ranhosky would know what would be best.

"You call me when you know when you're coming," she said, sounding calmer. The tears were almost gone. "Brenda's boy, Travis, can come pick y'all up at the airport." I had no idea who Brenda or Travis might be and didn't care enough to ask. "Y'all can stay here at the house; there's plenty of room. Don't even worry about a hotel."

"We won't." I leaned over Romeo and got a pen from the night-stand drawer, hidden underneath the Gideon Bible. "What's your number, Mawmaw?"

"Mawmaw?" Peter mouthed, a twinkle of amusement in his eyes as I wrote the number on my bare thigh.

"You got that, honey?" Mawmaw said.

"I got it." I wrote "Tupelo" above it in jagged letters. "I'll call you right back."

CHAPTER 42

So we went to Tupelo. After we had booked our flight, Romeo
had called and gently explained to my grandmother that it
might not be the best idea for a family member to pick us up
at the airport. So my first sight of the Tupelo house came from the
window of a limousine. It was mid-afternoon under a blazing Mississippi sun. The square, two-story frame house was painted blue, faded
to the soft shade of old blue jeans, with white trim darkened to a
dusty cream. There were shingles missing from the roof, and the attic
window was half-covered with brown cardboard. A rust-colored, late
model Buick, covered in yellow-white dust, was drowsing in the
shade of a massive, gnarly tree. The shrubs around the porch were
wildly overgrown, but the grass was neatly cut, and the rockers on the
porch were blinding white with floral-covered cushions. A massive
spray of waxy-looking white flowers was mounted on a peeling
column by the steps.

"It looks nice," Lisa said, sounding surprised. I had told her she
didn't have to come with us, but she had insisted.

"Please tell me you're joking," I said. *Where the devil goes to shit,* I
heard my mother say inside my head.

Romeo grinned, kissing my cheek. "Don't be such a snob." I made a face at him, and he took my hand. "Come on."

The driver had barely opened the car door when the black screen door slapped open and people started boiling out of the house. A chubby woman in pink surgical scrubs came first, followed by a skinny old woman who could have played a damned fine Wicked Witch of the West. A girl of maybe twenty-five with a massive poodle perm passed the old woman on the right. A redneck hunk with a mullet was bringing up the rear, looking amused. I shrank against Romeo, clinging to his arm with both hands.

"Scarlett!" the nurse said, coming down the steps. Her scrub shirt had teddy bears and big red hearts all over it. "Honey, I'm Brenda, your mama's first cousin. We are just so glad to meet you!" She swept me into a big, soft hug, and she smelled lovely, baby powder and some flowery perfume. Still clutching tightly to my husband's hand, I hugged her back.

"Hey Brenda." I drew back and smiled at her, my best red carpet smile. Close up, I could see she was very pretty, with round, hazel eyes ringed in black liner and mascara. "This is my husband, Romeo."

"Oh my god!" the girl with the big hair shrieked. "You're Romeo Kidd!"

"Angie, honey, hush," Brenda scolded her. "I'm sure he knows who he is." She was still smiling. "Angie is my daughter, your second—no, your third cousin, I guess. And this is her brother, Travis." The redneck stud muffin grinned, a flash of white teeth a camera would love, and held out a hand to Romeo, who shook it, smiling back. "Hey Romeo," Brenda said, hugging him the same way she had me. "We're so glad to meet you, too."

The old woman was just watching, a step or two behind the others. Her steel-blue hair was styled like a falcon in flight, and she was wearing a white, high-necked blouse in spite of the heat with a gold pin at the collar. "This is your Great-Aunt Leila," Brenda said, reaching back to touch her on her skinny arm. "She was your granddaddy's sister. And my daddy, Ross, was your grandmama's brother before he died."

"I'm still her granddaddy's sister, Brenda," Leila said. "I'm not dead just yet." I had no trouble believing this was the sister of the dried-up old cowboy I had met in Mexico; she sounded just like him. But looking her full in the face, I shivered. She had Stella's high cheekbones; Stella's wide, half-hooded blue eyes. Even with the wrinkles and the layer of powder, I could see my mother in her face.

"Where is Mawmaw?" I asked. Angie looked like she might explode, she wanted so bad to ask questions; Travis seemed more shy, but he was still smiling.

"She's upstairs," Brenda said. "She needed to lie down."

"No, I am not." The screen door opened again, and my grandmother came out. She looked so much the same, I almost fainted. She seemed smaller, thinner, and her bright orange hair had faded to a softer apricot pink. But her face and her voice and her arms as she opened them to me were just the same.

I let go of Romeo's hand and started up the steps, having to make myself move at first then moving faster, almost running as I fell into her arms. "Hey Mawmaw," I said, hugging her tight.

"Hey precious," she said, hugging back. "Welcome home."

Brenda and her kids stayed just long enough to get our luggage inside and my grandmother doped up with another in what was apparently a fairly long line of "mild" sedatives. "You get some rest, Aunt Jazz," Brenda said. She tucked a crocheted blanket—an afghan, they called it—around my grandmother's legs as she sat dwarfed in a huge reclining chair in the dark little den at the back of the house. We had walked through the formal living room on the way in, just long enough to catch a glance at the faux Greek podium and guest book left by the funeral home for visitors and lots of big plants in pots wrapped in green foil with white ribbons. But in the den, a pair of men's brown corduroy slippers were still sitting on the hearth of the electric fireplace. "You too, Miz Leila," Brenda said, giving me a smile.

"We'll be just fine," my grandmother said. "You go on back to work."

"I'll be back tonight," Brenda said. "If y'all need anything, you just call…" She looked at me, and her voice seemed to fail her, something I doubted happened very often. "My godfrey, honey," she went on after a moment. "You look so much like your mama."

I made myself smile at her. "My dad says I look like his sister." I was sitting in the middle of the brown plaid couch as close to Romeo as I could get without actually climbing into his lap. Leila was sitting on my other side, smoking a cigarette. Romeo had lit it for her with his silver lighter with the flames painted on it and won her heart completely.

"Oh, he would say that," Leila said now before Brenda could answer. "He'd like to think Stella and her people had nothing to do with you at all."

"Leila, hush," Mawmaw said. She reached out toward me and Romeo, and Romeo took her hand.

"We'll all go out and do something fun tomorrow," Angie said. She was still watching my husband with hungry eyes.

"Hush up," Brenda said, shooing her toward the door. "They didn't come all this way for that." Travis grinned at me from the doorway and winked.

"You call the house if you need anything, Aunt Jazz," he said. Like the rest of them, he pronounced the word "aunt" as "ain't."

"We will, darling," Mawmaw said, smiling at him. The sedative was taking effect; her eyes looked drowsy, and her speech was slightly slurred. "But Scarlett and Romeo can take care of us old birds." She had taken Romeo as hers on sight. Lisa was in the hallway on the phone, calling around to find us a decent hotel.

"Well, bye-bye then," Brenda said. "I'm sure there'll be folks from the church in and out."

"Oh goody," Leila muttered around her ciggy, and Romeo snickered. He had fallen in with these people like he had lived here all his life.

"Miz Leila, aren't you ashamed?" Brenda said, her smile not quite reaching her eyes. "We'll see y'all tonight."

As soon as they were gone, a hush fell over the house as if a storm had finally passed. I could hear Lisa in the hallway, talking about Jacuzzi tubs.

"Lord love a duck," Leila said, taking a drag.

"Now, Leila, she means well," Mawmaw said, knowing exactly what her sister-in-law meant. "She's just like her mama was, if you'll recall."

"I do recall," Leila said. "And that daughter of hers—you reckon there's any make-up left in the dime store?"

"I thought she looked right cute," Mawmaw said. She smiled at me, patting Romeo's hand that she still held. "Not pretty like Scarlett, but that's not her fault."

I smiled back at her because I didn't know what else to do. Part of me wanted to crawl straight out of my skin with revulsion and run for the airport on foot if I had to. But another part of me felt right at home, every bit as much at home as Romeo seemed to be. That part wanted to lay her head over on Romeo's shoulder and listen to the strange music of these two old women's talk forever, drowsing in a cloud of smoke and White Shoulders perfume. Romeo put his arm around me and drew me in close to his chest, kissing the top of my head.

"Romeo, where are you from?" Leila asked. "Not California, I know."

"No ma'am." His voice was a rumble just under my ear, and his heartbeat was steady and strong. "I grew up in Savannah, but I was born not far from here, in Memphis, Tennessee."

"I knew it," Mawmaw said. "I told Leila, just as soon as I heard your voice on the telephone, I knew you had to be from Memphis." Every trace of the hysteria and grief I had heard in her voice on the phone at home was gone.

"What do your people do?" Leila asked. "And what do they think of you getting married with you just a baby and Scarlett, too?"

"My father died in Vietnam when I was four years old," Romeo said. I tensed slightly, surprised. He had never told me this before. He took a cigarette from the pack in his breast pocket and lit it up one-handed, adding to the haze. "My mom and stepfather still live in Savannah, but I haven't seen or spoken to them in…five years, maybe?"

"Oh honey," Mawmaw said. I knew I should say something, too, but I couldn't seem to make my eyes stay open.

"But my sister, Amy, lives in Los Angeles," Romeo said. "And she loves Scarlett."

"Amy's great," I agreed, smiling at Mawmaw, who smiled back. "She's an actress, too."

"Angie was driving us all crazy last night talking about that movie y'all were in," Leila said.

"Lord, yes," Mawmaw agreed. "I knew about it, of course. Your granddaddy and I saw the ads on the TV." Stella had called it "the TV" when she was stoned out of her mind. "But I just couldn't see it."

"Don't," I said, thinking about *The Funhouse*, all that blood and death.

"Oh don't worry, honey, I could not," she said. "But your grand-daddy and I went to Jackson and saw the other one, the one you did with your daddy."

"She was good, wasn't she?" Romeo said.

"Oh dear heavens," she said. "We just couldn't believe it." Her voice caught with tears. "Your granddaddy was so proud of you."

"Now, Jasmine, that's enough," Leila said, her tone softening only slightly, and I frowned. As if Mawmaw couldn't cry if she wanted to; her husband was dead, for pity's sake.

Before I could say anything, Lisa leaned in from the hallway. "Hi folks," she said in the bright, friendly tone she used with reporters and interior designers. "Scarlett, can I borrow you for just a minute?"

"Sure," I said, blinking to wake myself up. Romeo lifted his arm, and I climbed out of the warm cocoon of the couch to follow her into the hall.

"Okay," she said in an undertone, her normal voice. "I've found us what sounds like semi-habitable suites downtown at the Hilton."

"No," Romeo said from behind me. I hadn't realized he had followed me. "No, we're staying here."

"Romeo, come on," Lisa said before I could answer. "I've been to these things before. Trust me, by nightfall, this place is going to be packed, and you are going to want to be as far away as you can get."

"My grandmamma is expecting us to stay," I said.

"I'll explain it to her," Lisa said. "The last thing you need is to be stuck here with a bunch of strangers gawking at you. I'll go call a cab to go over and check things out at the hotel while you two visit for a while, then I'll bring back a car to pick you up. You can come back in the morning before the funeral."

"No," I said, shaking my head. She was doing exactly what I had hired her to do, exactly what I would have asked her to do as soon as we arrived if I had been even that self-sufficient. But suddenly the idea that this woman I paid to handle my dry cleaning and plane tickets might explain to my grandmother that I was just too fabulous to sleep in her house was appalling. "No, Lisa, I want to stay."

"Scarlett." She had been with me while Romeo had made the flight arrangements; she knew how I had felt about coming here in the first place. "You don't have to do this."

Mawmaw came out into the hall. "Is everything all right?"

"Yes, ma'am," I said, turning to her. "Lisa just needs to go over to the hotel where she's staying."

Lisa never missed a beat. "I've got some work I need to get done," she agreed. "I'll just call a cab."

"Oh honey, don't do that," Mawmaw said. "If you know where you're going, I can write down the directions, and Romeo can drive you over in the Buick." She looked over at him. "You do have a license, don't you, son?"

"Yes, ma'am," he said, smiling.

"Romeo's a great driver, Mawmaw," I said. "He used to be a stuntman."

"Well, I don't know how much stunting you can do in Granddaddy's old Buick," she said. "But I think it will make it to town." She started toward the kitchen, and we followed. "I'm going to make you a list for the Kroger while you're out."

My eyes met Romeo's, and we both smiled. Even Lisa cracked up just a bit. "Yes, ma'am," Romeo said.

"Pick me up a carton of Virginia Slims," Leila called from the den. "And some orange sherbet."

"I'll put it on the list," Mawmaw said, writing on a notepad with pictures of puppies on the corners of each page. Her handwriting was just the same as it was on all my birthday cards. "You smoke too much."

"That may well be," Leila called back. "But I don't believe I want to quit today." I heard the TV come on in the den—a talk show, from the sound of it.

"Here you go, honey," Mawmaw said, handing Romeo the list. "Now here, let me give you some money."

"No, no," Romeo said. "I've got it covered."

"Honey, I don't know that they take credit cards."

"I've got plenty of cash money." He was smiling his soul-stealing smile, and she smiled back.

"All right then," she said, patting his cheek. "Scarlett, honey, are you going to ride along with them? Don't you want to stay here and have a nap? You look worn slap out."

At any other strange place in the universe, I would have clung to Romeo like a fungus. He reached out and took my hand, obviously expecting that I would. "Yeah, I think I will, if that's all right," I said, squeezing his hand. "I don't know why I'm so wiped out all of a sudden."

"It's that airplane," Mawmaw said. "I hate them; it tears up my nerves for a week every time I have to go on one."

Romeo was smiling at me now, but Lisa looked stunned. "I'll be right back," Romeo said.

"And I'll be right across town if you need me," Lisa added.

"I'll be fine." I hugged Romeo, and he brushed my lips with his, barely a kiss. "Bring me some ice cream, too," I said. "The most chocolate you can find."

"I will." He took the keys from Mawmaw. "See y'all in a bit."

CHAPTER 43

My grandmother and I watched out the kitchen window as they drove away. "Mawmaw," I said. "I love him so much."

"I can tell," she answered. "Does he deserve it?"

For a moment, I thought of Ranhosky in Texas and the videotape. "Yes, ma'am," I said, pushing that image away. "I think he does."

She took me up the dark back stairs to a broad open landing as big as a room on its own. Behind one open door was a bathroom so pink it glowed. Three more doors were closed. The last door before the front stairs was standing ajar. Through the crack I could see a white iron bed with a fluffy white chenille bedspread. My suitcase was sitting on the floor.

"It will be tight with you and Romeo both, I know," she said, leaning on the doorknob as she led me in—she was winded from the stairs.

"No, it's okay." The idea of climbing into the cozy little bed with Romeo was actually very appealing.

The walls were painted a faded cornflower blue with stark white moldings and trim. The one window had a broad white sill with a cheap metal ranch-style dollhouse sitting on it. Inside I could see the dolls still perfectly posed around the dining room table, mommy, daddy, little girl. A larger, fancier dolly was propped against the pillows on the bed. She had long black curls and wide green eyes and a lacy white dress with green trim. When I picked her up and tilted her back, her eyes closed. "Your namesake," Mawmaw said, sitting down on the bed. "Your mama's first Scarlett."

I almost dropped the doll like a poisonous snake. Then I pulled it close and cradled it against me. "This was Stella's room?" I could hardly imagine it. Suddenly it all looked like a movie set. There was a dusty set of red and white pompoms propped on top of the dresser mirror and a pennant for Tupelo High School on the wall. I thought of my bedroom set on *The Funhouse*. This dresser would have fit right in.

"Yes, it was." The bookshelves by the bed were mostly loaded up with tattered paperback novels, the thick kind that swell and curve when they get damp. One shelf had what looked like a full, untouched set of hardback Nancy Drew mysteries. On top were two framed photographs. One was a studio shot from the 60s, a pretty black-haired girl I barely recognized as Stella with wide blue eyes and a hugely poufy hairdo and a black drape that exposed her shoulders. "That was her senior picture," Mawmaw explained when I touched it. The other was a snapshot, also of Stella, too, propped up in the same bed we were sitting on. She was wearing a lacy white nightgown, holding a bundle of white lace in her arms. At first I thought she was holding the same doll I was holding now. Then I saw a tiny, red face.

"Oh my god." I picked the photo up.

"That's you and your mama," Mawmaw said. She put an arm around me. "Look at that precious baby girl. That's the day you came home from the hospital."

"Wow." In the picture, my mother was smiling, and she was beautiful, but she looked exhausted. Her hair was cut short and looked thin at the front where it was held back with a ribbon, and there were dark circles under her eyes. Looking closer, I saw a man's hand on the bundle, the baby, on me. "Is that my dad?"

"What?" Somehow I could tell from her voice that she knew just what I meant and had been waiting for me to ask. "Oh yeah, honey, that's him." She touched my hair, brushing it back from my cheek. "We saw him that one time, then one more time in Mexico. Then never again—or not yet, anyway." I could hear tears in her voice. "We never meant to give you up, you know. We would have loved to have had you here and raised you as our little girl." She made a soft sound between a chuckle and a sob, but I didn't look at her. I was completely hypnotized by the picture. "I know you must think we abandoned you."

"No, I don't." I shook my head, still not looking up. "I never thought that." She seemed so sweet, so different from anybody else I had ever met, fragile in a completely different way than I was used to. I wanted to protect her. "I remember you and Granddaddy coming to Mexico." I was crying, I suddenly realized. My tears were falling on the picture's glass. "I remember you crying when Daddy came to take me away."

"My poor darling girl." I looked at her then and saw her eyes were spilling over with tears, rimmed in red. "I always prayed you had forgotten all of that."

"Not all of it." She took my hand, and I let her. "I still remember you."

"I sent you letters," she said. "And every year on your birthday…"

"You sent me a card." I looked back at the picture. "I didn't know that until about a year ago when I found all the cards. My daddy's girlfriend kept them from me." I looked at Stella, so delicate and tired. Had she asked my father to stay with her? I thought of the things Ranhosky had said about her trying to sell me, but looking at this, I was even more sure he was a liar. "She always hated me."

"Now, honey, I'm sure not," Mawmaw said, but her grip tightened on my hand. "I'm sure she never hated you."

"Yes, ma'am, I promise you she did. She still does." I looked at her and almost smiled. "But it's okay. I hate her back."

"Scarlett, baby, we don't hate," she said as if she had been taking care of me all my life, teaching me right from wrong. "Hate hurts you, not anybody else."

"I can't help it." I thought of all the people I hated. Greta, Ranhosky, Fiona sometimes…the man who had cut up my mother, the man with the long, greasy hair.

"You need to pray about it." She smiled, putting her other hand over mine. "The Lord Jesus wants to help you help it."

She might just as well have been speaking Chinese. "I don't really do that." I thought the Lord Jesus must surely have better things to do, but I knew better than to say it.

"Jasmine!" Aunt Leila shouted from downstairs, her raspy voice carrying clear as an alarm. "The minister is here!"

Mawmaw smiled at me. "All right, precious girl." She patted my cheek. "You have your nap." She opened her arms, and I hugged her. "That's my girl." She stroked my hair. "I'm so glad to have you here."

When she was gone, I sat down on the bed, still holding the doll and the picture, baby me with my parents. My mother looked so scared. But she looked happy, too. She was looking down at the baby in her arms like it was a perfect, precious treasure.

"Scarlett?" The door was slightly ajar again, but Romeo knocked even so. "Are you all right?" I looked up at him, tears spilling down my cheeks. He crossed the room in two steps as I let the picture and the dolly fall so that I could fall into his arms.

"I love you," I said, holding on to him with all my might. "Thank you for bringing me here."

He kissed my hair, holding me close, and I could feel him smiling. "You're welcome, sweetheart." He squeezed me tight. "I love you, too."

CHAPTER 44

That night, Romeo and I went to the funeral home with Mawmaw and Leila while Lisa went to the mall to get me another black dress. All the people at the visitation were very nice; I think I met my mother's entire high school graduating class. Most people had either seen *The Funhouse* or *The Romantics* or had at least seen the ads on TV; a lot of them had read something about our being married or seen us on one of the late-night talk shows. So they knew who Romeo was in the world and thought they knew how we had met. These people knew what year I had been born; they knew how old I was.

One woman who said she had been in Mama's prom queen court held my hand in both of hers and said, "Honey, it gave me such a chill, that movie you were in—all that blood. How in the world did you stand it?" I might have been angry if I hadn't seen the true horror in her haunted eyes. But before I could answer her, her husband had hustled her on down the line.

Several people had seen Romeo's mini-series on cable; a couple had even seen *Match Girl*. All of them said something kind about the work or Calvin or Stella or some combination of the three then moved straight on to Mawmaw to offer their condolences. The funeral home had set up a line of folding chairs across the room from the coffin. My grandfather looked like a doll; I thought he looked very strange without his cowboy hat. I sat on one side of Mawmaw and Romeo sat on the other. A few times she teared up or broke down and reached for either my hand or his. Leila sat on the other side of me and never reached for anyone at all. But once I saw her thin lips start to quiver, and I handed her a tissue from the little pack Mawmaw had given me back at the house.

"Thanks, darling," she said, patting my leg.

Afterwards, we went back to the house and ate ham and potato salad and cake people had brought as more people came and went, some dressed up, some in jeans or even shorts and flip-flops. About eleven o'clock, the last group from the church was standing on the front porch telling Mawmaw good-bye, and Romeo took me by the hand and drew me into the kitchen to kiss me. "I'm going to drive Lisa back to her hotel," he said as I held him tight. "But I'll be right back."

"Okay." I smiled at him and kissed him again before heading upstairs. I could hear Leila in the shower as I passed by the hall bath. A little pink and crystal lamp beside the bed was the only light in Stella's old room. I took off my black dress and put on a tee-shirt and slid into bed. I heard the water turn off, heard Leila moving around the bathroom, talking to herself. I barely heard the bathroom door squeak...then I was asleep, the lamp still burning beside me. I woke up once in the middle of the night and found Romeo sleeping beside me. I snuggled closer to him and sank back into the bed.

I woke to the smell of coffee and frying bacon. I yawned and stretched, feeling almost supernaturally relaxed. I padded down the hall to the bathroom in my tee shirt, peed and brushed my teeth. The faded pink and bright white room was flooded with sunlight. Standing at the sink, I could hear Leila still snoring like a chainsaw in the guestroom across the hall, and I smiled at my reflection. I looked young and clean, with no shadow of fear in my eyes.

I started down the stairs, all but silent in my bare feet. Halfway down, I heard Romeo's voice, and I froze in shock. He was crying.

"I didn't even know," he was saying. "She never even told me. All the newspaper reports said she was in Los Angeles with Calvin."

"Hush now, honey," Mawmaw said. "You take too much on yourself…"

"I'm her husband," he interrupted her. "I love her…"

"That doesn't mean you can fix her," she said. "Or that she even needs fixing." There was a pause, and I heard her footsteps, heard a pot sliding on the burner on the stove. "I always thought if she was with her daddy, he could take care of her, get her some help or make her forget. She was such a little thing when it happened."

"He should have let her come here," he said. "At least here there would have been somebody to take care of her, to love her."

"Now, now." I heard the scraping of a spatula in the skillet. "Just because he doesn't like you doesn't mean he doesn't love her."

"He doesn't even try to take care of her, and from what Sebastian says, he never has," he answered. "That's all I want, Miz Jazz, to keep her safe."

"I know you want that, honey." I was clenching my fists so tight, my nails were digging into my palms, and I made my hands relax. "The Lord knows what He's doing, Romeo, I promise you. That was hard for me to think when Stella first died, and we lost Scarlett. I was so mad at her granddaddy for letting her go, I wouldn't even speak to him for weeks. And when I saw that movie…" Her voice trailed off into a sniff, and I heard Romeo's chair scrape on the floor. "But we would have babied her too much," she went on. "Lord knows we did her mama."

I couldn't listen any more. I turned my back on the kitchen, barely aware where I was going as I walked down the hall to the opposite end of the house, out of earshot, into the formal parlor.

I had barely noticed this room when we first arrived, and it had been dark when we had walked through it the night before. The minister from the church had been holding court in here after the funeral home; Romeo and I had stayed away. But now I was looking, searching out details to distract me from what I had just heard.

It looked like a completely different house. The furniture looked expensive but old, box-shaped with faded blue silk upholstery, all covered in shiny clear plastic. The coffee table and end tables were dark cherry topped with white marble with little china knickknacks and brass-framed pictures everywhere. The drapes were a slightly darker shade of blue, raw silk with a heavy lining that blocked out the sunlight, with huge, tasseled tie-backs hanging slack on either side. The drapes were closed. The little podium from the funeral home with the guest book was standing near the front door, and a few baskets of flowers and potted plants were scattered around the room. Hanging over the plain pink brick fireplace was a massive photograph of Stella.

This was no cheap studio shot from the department store, and Stella was no pretty girl from Tupelo. She was wearing a soft-looking peasant blouse over tight slacks, and her hair was long and loose on her shoulders. Her sapphire eyes looked huge, and her skin was luscious as a freshly picked peach. I sat down on the cold marble slab of the coffee table, my legs giving way underneath me. This was the Stella I remembered, this supernatural being, not the tired, happy, mortal woman from the little snapshot in her room upstairs.

"She was a beauty," Leila said from behind me, making me jump. "The man who took that picture wanted to marry her, you know." She was wearing a long, orange housecoat with a high collar and a zipper up the front, and her hair was as stiff and perfectly in place as it had been the night before. "Some English lord with more money than sense, I believe. Richard was his name, Richard Browning."

"No," I said. My brain flashed on an image of the Scarecrow, but I pushed the thought away. "I didn't know that."

"That was long before you came along," she said, patting my shoulder. "Come on, let's get us some breakfast."

The funeral was fine. I wore my new black dress Lisa had bought, and Romeo wore his same sport coat from the night before and a tie with a clean white shirt, and he acted as one of the pallbearers. I sat between Mawmaw and Leila during the service, holding my grandmother's hand. The church was very bright. The brass and crystal chandelier hanging over the altar was at least three times as big as it should have been for the space, and the walls were painted white. The back wall was painted the blue and white of the sky in a fairytale book, and Jesus was levitating over some darker blue water, his hands outstretched, his palms dotted with stars of dark red blood. The minister looked barely older than I was, and his skin was so pink, it looked scrubbed. He was perfectly fit, but his face made me think of a shiny piglet in a nursery rhyme.

We sang a hymn when the preacher was done, "Amazing Grace," which I recognized from TV. I shared a hymnbook with my grandmother and sang along. When they started to recite the Lord's Prayer, Leila reached over and flipped the book open to the front cover where it was printed to I could read aloud. "Forgive us our trespasses," I read, joining in the droning spell. "As we forgive those who trespass against us." I looked over to the pew at the front where Romeo and the other pallbearers were sitting. He was between Travis and Travis' father, and he wasn't reading. He was reciting; he knew the words. He must have felt me looking; he looked back at me and winked.

When it was over, they rolled the silver casket up the aisle, and Mawmaw finally broke down. A man from the funeral home came and stood at the end of our aisle, and we stood up, me with my arm around Mawmaw, supporting her against my shoulder. We followed the casket, and I could hear people murmuring around us as we went, kind of like walking a red carpet. "So sweet...Lord help, she looks like her daddy!"

The cemetery was on the other side of the asphalt parking lot. People were milling around on the porch and the lawn like at the intermission of a play. As soon as we cleared the door of the church, the minister came and took Mawmaw from me, smiling at me as he put his own arm around her, and Leila followed them off to the side. Romeo and the other pallbearers had gone on with the hearse, trailing behind it on foot as it navigated a gravel drive beyond a chain link fence.

Brenda appeared out of the crowd beside me. "How are you holding up, honeybun?" she asked as she hugged me.

"I'm fine." She was wearing a short-sleeved suit in a shade of pink probably visible from space. I thought of the judge who had married me and Romeo in Texas. "I'm kind of worried about Mawmaw." I sounded like one of them, I thought. My accent had already fallen back into that rhythm, back into sounding like Stella. "I think she must be in shock."

"Oh, you know she is," she agreed. "She would have to be." She held my hand in both of hers as she surveyed the crowd. "She and your granddaddy have a lot of friends."

"Yes." I could see Lisa in the distance, crisp and appropriate in her New York office girl's suit and heels, conferring with the driver of the funeral home limousine. "Brenda, can I ask you something?"

"Of course, darling." She returned her full attention to my face. "What?"

"Did my…did Mama have one of these?" I had thought that I was only clinically curious, but suddenly I was crying, and the question would barely come out.

"Oh honey." She gathered me up in one of her soft, sweet-smelling hugs. "Of course she did."

"Good." I hugged her back, trying not to picture it too much. "I'm glad."

"We loved your mama very much." She drew back to pat my cheek, and for a split second, I saw the lie behind her eyes, but I smiled anyway, not letting it register.

"Let's head on down, folks," the minister called like he was opening a picnic. Brenda let me go, and I went back to Mawmaw.

The graveside service was very brief; people were sweltering in the heat. As soon as it was over, they started wandering away, everyone promising to see one another "at the house." Lisa came up to me from the back of the crowd, carrying a bouquet of roses and lilies. "I don't know if you'll want this or not," she said, handing it to me. "But I thought I'd get some, just in case."

"They're nice," I said, mystified. "But I don't understand."

"For your mother's grave." My face must have changed because hers did, going pale in spite of the flush of the heat. "You don't have to," she said quickly. "Here, I'll take them."

"No." I clutched the heavy vase. "I should have thought of it. Thanks, Lisa."

Stella's grave was less than three steps beyond the fake grass carpet that made my grandfather's still-open vault look like an Easter basket. Her headstone was pink granite with roses carved into it, and I could picture my grandmother picking it out. "Stella St. John," it read with her dates. She had been twenty-six years old the day she died. *Stella Cross*, I thought. *Her name was really Stella Cross.* There were still Tupelo people lingering about, and several of them were watching me. Romeo was talking to Angie and Travis. I looked at him until he looked back, then I looked away, back at the headstone.

"Hey Mama," I whispered. I squatted down and set the vase of flowers in front of the stone. I didn't think about her body rotting in the ground. That came later, in the dark, before I went to sleep that night. All I could think was that she was trapped here forever and would never get away. I thought about the tired, scared-looking girl with the freckles who had held me as a newborn in her arms, and I thought about the goddess from the portrait. "I'm sorry, Mama." I was crouched the way a child might crouch at the rolling, fearsome edge of the surf. "I didn't know what else to do."

I saw Romeo's feet coming toward me, and I straightened up. "Hey, sweetheart," he said, drawing me into his arms. "Are you okay?"

"Oh yeah." I leaned against his shirtfront for a moment, blinking back my tears. "Can we go?"

"Yeah, I think we're ready." Brenda was already herding Mawmaw and Leila to the car. "Angie and Travis want to take us out tonight."

I drew his arm around my shoulders as we walked away from Stella's grave. "Okay." I leaned against him, my arm around his waist. "Sure, why not?"

CHAPTER 45

My cousins took us to a place that looked a lot like the places we were accustomed to hang out in on the Sunset Strip, sans irony and starlets. Travis' date was a curvy blonde cutie so short the top of her head barely reached his chest. She stared at me and Romeo in awe-struck silence until she had finished her first beer, then she talked pretty much non-stop for the next hour until Travis kissed her and told her to shut up. Angie was single, but she had deep and dark designs on the lead singer of the house band, a Michael Hutchence wannabe with long, flowing locks and an open white shirt hanging from his skinny frame. "He is so sexy," she breathed to us between songs, leaning in among the empty bottles on the table.

"He is," I admitted. "He's hot." A couple of people had recognized us, I could tell, but no one had approached us but some friends of Angie and Travis who acted like I was just their cousin from out of town. It's weird; Los Angeles is full of people who think the whole city is basically a theme park and the famous people are attractions. New York can be just as bad if the people who spot you are tourists. I can't really speak for the Midwest; I haven't been there much. But in the South and the Pacific Northwest and in Ireland, people hang back until they figure out if you want them to make a fuss. If you bridge that gap by smiling back at someone you catch staring or chatting up the waitress, they'll approach you, even mob you with attention. But if you act like you don't want to be bothered, they won't bother you.

"You should go talk to him," I told Angie. I had already had a drink or two myself.

"Come with me," she said, pouncing on the idea at once. The band was just that moment leaving the stage for their break; the crisis was imminent.

"Angie, no," Travis' date protested. "She doesn't want to do that."

"Sure, I will." I stood up and bent over Romeo, kissing him full on the mouth. "I'll be right back."

"Hang on," Angie said, alarmed. She must have expected me to say no. "Let me go put on some lip gloss at least and fix my hair."

"He won't give a shit about that stuff," I said from the peak of my lofty experience. "You look great; come on."

"She's right," Romeo said, giving her his sexiest grin. "You look beautiful."

She smiled, her sudden flush making it true. "Y'all are crazy."

"Come on," I repeated, pulling on her hand.

I had run this con with Fiona and Stacy a dozen times before back in L.A. I led her not to the bandstand but to a spot on the edge of the dance floor between the bandstand and the bar. "What are we doing?" she said as I turned back to face her.

"Dance with me," I ordered. There were other pairs of girls on the dance floor; I wasn't trying to shock the Confederacy. But I moved just a little closer to her than the norm, rolling my hips to the classic rock blues someone had just cranked up on the jukebox. "Trust me, all right?"

She grinned. "You are so bad." She fell into the rhythm with me, just a little bit more slutty and a little bit more accomplished a dancer than me. The band was filing past behind her. "Is he looking?"

"Oh hell yeah." In fact, the object of her lust had stopped dead in his tracks to stare at me, and I smiled. I leaned closer, whispering a secret under the veil of her hair. "Just keep dancing." One of the other band members touched our mark on the shoulder, and he followed his buddies to the bar. They all got bottles of beer; he ordered a shot, knocking it back in one gulp. "Here we go," I said as he started back in our direction. His gaze was focused on the bandstand, but I wasn't fooled one bit. "Hey!" I called out to him, just a little louder than my normal speaking voice. "You guys are really good."

He did a brief but perfectly executed take like I had caught him completely off guard. "Thanks." He took the last two steps up to us, and we stopped dancing. I took Angie's hand loosely in mine. "I'm sorry," he said. "Don't I recognize you?"

"Yeah, maybe," I said, dropping my voice and moving close to him. "But don't say anything." He smelled like brand new sweat and hair product, and he really was a pretty thing. "I'm just in town for my granddaddy's funeral, and I don't want to mess up anybody's night." I drew Angie's arm through mine. "Hey, do you know my cousin, Angie? Angie, have y'all met?"

"No, we haven't," she said. "I've seen y'all play a few times, though. Scarlett's right; you're great."

"Thank you," he said, turning his focus to her, his smile beaming brighter. Most people would always rather be a star than see one. "Where did you see us?"

"At Leo's two weeks ago, for one time," she said. She really was lovely, I realized. With my trainer and make-up artist, she would be stunning. "You played Elvis Costello, and that guy walked out."

"Oh yeah," he said, laughing. "He was a Lynyrd Skynyrd fan, I think." In unison, they both called out, "Free bird!" and we all laughed. Several people turned to look, and most smiled. Meanwhile, he studied Angie's face. "I swear, I think I remember you."

Romeo picked up his cue perfectly, just like I'd known he would. "Hey you," he said, touching my shoulder. "Dance with your date, why don't you?"

"Okay." I gave Angie's hand a squeeze, and she squeezed back. "It was nice to meet you."

"You too," the singer said. He shook my hand, but he barely glanced at me as I walked away with Romeo. Angie had him hooked.

"Smartly done," Romeo said softly in my ear as he pulled me into a slow dance. He kissed my cheek. "That was very nice."

"Hey, you know me." I pressed close to him, breathing in the smell of him, the smell of home. "What's the point of being a movie star if I can't get my cousin laid?"

He snickered. "Amen." His hands slid down to cradle my ass. "Travis is hilarious." I caught a woman staring at us from the edge of the dance floor, but as soon as my eyes met hers, she looked away. I turned my face to Romeo's throat, closing my eyes. "As soon as you left the table, he started going on and on about how beautiful you are. I don't think Susie liked it very much."

"Susie? Oh yeah." Susie was Travis' date. The song that was playing was old; I recognized it from lying by the swimming pool at Castle Asshole with Daddy and Greta when I was a kid. "What did you say?"

"I told him he was right." He kissed my hair, squeezing me tighter. "I'm pretty sure you're not going to date your cousin."

"You never know." With my eyes closed, we could just as easily have been home on the Strip. "White trash is in my blood, apparently." He laughed, a low, intimate rumble, and I wrapped my arms around his waist. "But I like it here."

"I like it, too." He bent his knees slightly, his hips coming forward, and I slid into place against his thigh. "Your grandmama is a sweetheart."

"Yeah, she is. And I think she loves you, too." I had only had a couple of drinks, but I felt safe, at peace. "I'm kind of worried about her, though. Leila goes back to Florida tomorrow, and we're leaving, too. What is she going to do?"

"Do you want to stay?"

This was so unexpected, I didn't know quite what to say. "God, no." I thought of what I'd overheard that morning, the way he had cried, the things my grandmother had said to him. "Even if I wanted to, we couldn't. What about your show?"

"They do have TV here, you know." He squeezed me tighter, and I nuzzled his cheek. "You really wouldn't want to stay?"

"Um, no." I could hear the tension in his voice, but I decided to ignore it. "I think I've had plenty of Tupelo already."

I could tell he wanted to say more; I heard him take a breath as if he were about to speak a couple of times before he finally did. "Yeah." He kissed my cheek. "But we should visit more often."

"Yeah, I guess we should." I laid my head on his shoulder, and we stopped talking, but my mind kept drifting forward. What if we did stay here? I tried to imagine what my life might have been like if Cal had never come for me. Would I look like Angie? Would I be in college? There was a college nearby, not the Ivy League, but perfectly nice; probably exactly what my grandparents would have been able to afford. I would be reading books and going to ballgames. I would be an English major, I thought, the only school subject I had ever really liked. I would come home to Tupelo every weekend and tell Mawmaw all about my week. She would do my laundry. This week would be hard because of Pawpaw dying. I would know him, miss him for real, I thought. It would just be me and Mawmaw now in the house. I would worry about going back to school. But maybe Romeo or some boy like him would be with me, not as my husband, but my boyfriend. I would see him on the weekends, too. He would work on cars and take classes at night. Or he would be an English major, too, a poet version of Romeo who studied with me late into the night. Everyone would know how old I was and that we were in love. In a couple of years when we had our degrees, we would get married at Mawmaw's church under that big, tacky, brass chandelier. I would wear a frothy white dress and a veil much too long for the room, and Romeo would rent a tuxedo. Just across the dance floor now, I could see Angie dancing with her rock star, neither of them talking. Her eyes were closed, her lips barely curved in a smile. Angie would be my maid of honor, I decided, and Travis would be Romeo's best man.

Then suddenly, looking through the crowded bar, I saw him. He was standing near the door, a man with long, black, greasy hair. His plain white tee-shirt was glowing in the blue light of the neon beer sign, but there were dark splotches all over it; his shirt was stained with blood. Why did no one else see how bloody he was? People were standing all around him, but no one seemed to notice. His face was in shadow, but I could see him; I could recognize him. He raised a bottle of beer to his lips, a bottle of Mexican beer. His flat black eyes snapped into focus, and my flesh went cold. He could see me, too.

"Scarlett?" I had stopped moving, had pushed Romeo away. My whole body had gone numb. He touched my cheek. "What is it?"

My eyes met his for barely a moment before I snapped my gaze back to the man by the door. He was leaving; he had turned his back. His shoulder blades were sharp as razors underneath his bloody shirt, and veins stood out like ropes along his arms. I heard myself making a noise, a buzzing little keening sound deep down in my throat, and I made myself stop; I put my hands over my mouth. He was leaving, thank God. If I could just be quiet, he would go. He disappeared behind a group of people coming through the door, another flash of white moving out into the night.

"Scarlett!" Romeo was holding me by the arms, and he gave me a shake.

"I'm sorry." I wanted to cry, to scream, to grab him and run out the back door dragging him behind me and keep running as far and as fast as I could. But I knew that wouldn't save us. "I'm okay." I made myself smile. "I just felt sort of weird for a minute."

"Scarlett, tell me," he demanded. "What did you see?"

"Nothing," I insisted. "I'm just drunk, I think. I didn't really eat anything after the funeral."

"Just tell me." He turned around to look behind him, still holding me by one arm. "Who was it? A photographer?"

"It was no one!" What if he sees Romeo? I thought. I grabbed him and turned him back around, turned his back on the door. I wasn't completely out of my mind; I knew it was possible that the man wasn't real, that this was just some crazy vision. But I couldn't risk it. "I just feel weird, baby," I said. "Please, let's just go home."

He was just looking at me with big, sad eyes. He knew I was lying, and he knew this moment was important. Heaven help us both, he knew me too well.

"Please," I repeated. People really were staring at us now. Travis had stood up, his beer still in his hand. "Please, baby." I touched Romeo's cheek.

He took my hand and held it for a moment. "Okay." He took a step back from me, holding me at arm's length. "Come on. Let's go home."

Mawmaw and Leila were both sleeping when we got home. Romeo and I got undressed and climbed in bed. "Sleep well, sweetheart," he said, giving me a quick kiss before he turned off the little light. He turned his back on me, and I let him, turning my back on him, too.

But I couldn't fall asleep. I tossed and turned and stared at the shadows on the ceiling, but every time I closed my eyes, my mind brought back the man I had seen in the bar. He couldn't be real, I decided, rolling over to stare at Stella's Scarlett doll on the shelf beside the bed. I had to be seeing things. Better to be crazy than to be scared.

I heard a noise from outside—the creak of the back screen door in the wind. Mawmaw had wind chimes hanging over the back steps. I heard them tinkle like someone had brushed them as he passed. My heart was beating so fast I felt dizzy, and my whole body went cold. "Just my imagination," I said softly. Leila's snores from the next room were like something in another world, too far away to reach. "He wasn't real."

"Who wasn't?" Romeo said.

My husband was awake. "I saw a man at the bar." I kept my back turned to him. "I don't think he was real, but I saw him. I think he was a Mexican. He had blood on his tee-shirt." I made myself laugh. "I told you, I was drunk, seeing things. You know me. I freak out for no reason."

"No. I don't think anybody really knows you, sweetheart." I felt him roll over toward me. He put his arms around me and took my hands in both of his, pressed between the palms like we were praying together. "Why did you marry me? The first time in Texas?" Tears spilled down my cheeks. "Tell me the truth."

"Because I love you, stupid." That was the truth, more true than almost anything else I knew in my whole stupid, screwed up life. But it wasn't the whole truth. Nothing I said ever was. "Because they were taking me away from you, and I couldn't stand it."

He kissed my shoulder. "And when your father's lawyer told you what I'd done, did you still love me?"

"Yes," I said defensively. "You know I did."

"When you pulled a gun on me, was that because you were so happy?" He sounded desperate, close to tears. "When you told me you would shoot me, was that because you love me so much?"

"Yes." I heard the wind chimes again; the wind was picking up. "I have never not loved you, ever, not since the night we met."

"Then why can't you trust me?"

I rolled over to face him. "I do trust you." He smiled the sad, sweet smile that killed so completely on camera. "Romeo, I swear to God, I do." He was so close to me, I could see every one of his eyelashes, dark and wet, his lips almost touching mine, his breath warm on my mouth. I couldn't turn away from him, couldn't hide. "I heard you talking to Mawmaw in the kitchen this morning."

"She told me you were with your mother in Mexico when she was murdered," he said. "How have you never told me that?"

"I never tell anybody that, ever," I said. "When it happened, the papers all said I was in California with Calvin and Greta. Nobody ever told me I was supposed to tell that lie; nobody ever admitted that it was a lie. They just pretended it was real and acted like I wouldn't know the difference."

"Jesus," he said, putting a hand on my head. "Your father…I don't even know what to think about your father."

"He just wanted me to be okay," I said. "Greta used to tell me that the past was past, that all that mattered was the now. I think that's what it was. I think they thought I would just forget about it, that it would be better for me if I could just forget."

"And now you see phantom Mexican murderers in bars," Romeo said. "You freak out so bad at the sight of blood, you hurt yourself and can't function. Yeah, that worked out well."

"I said it was Calvin's plan," I said with a little smile. "I never said it was a good plan." Just telling him this much, my heart was racing.

"So baby, what happened?" He was stroking my hair. "What did you see?"

I told him the story I told at the beginning of this book, about the beach and the tamales and the hippies in the bus. He stroked my hair and kissed my forehead and never said a word until I finished. "I don't even know if that man I remember is real or if I just made him up," I finished. "But I saw him tonight in the bar. I saw him watching."

He pulled me close, wrapping his arms around me. "You know that's not possible, right?"

"I know." I was shaking all over, and the storm outside was breaking with thunder and lightning and spatters of rain. "But I swear I saw him."

"I believe you." He kissed the top of my head. "Maybe coming here was a mistake. Maybe seeing your grandmamma and all those people was too much."

"No," I said. "No, I'm glad we came, so glad. I'm okay, Romeo, I swear. I'll be okay." *Just take me home,* I wanted to say. *Stop asking me questions and just love me. Just let me keep you safe.*

"Okay." He kissed me, and I clung to him, kissing him back. "I love you, you know."

"I love you." The thunder was getting softer, rumbling now, and the rain was soft and steady. "I'm sorry I'm such a freak."

"I love that you're a freak." He rolled over on his back, and I snuggled down into his shoulder. "Now go to sleep. We've got an early flight in the morning."

CLIPPING 13

From *The Tube*
  "Falling Hard for The Romantics"

Against all odds, the Limbo's new supernatural drama, The Romantics, *lives up to the hype. Leads Romeo Kidd (he of the dreamy gypsy eyes in last year's blockbuster gorefest,* The Funhouse*) and Australian newcomer Peter August make a fine and clever pair of absinthe-swilling heartthrobs—Butch Cassidy and the Moondance Kid. The pilot episode is sexy and genuinely scary with feature-film quality effects, and the setting, which could have been utterly ridiculous, is actually quite fresh. A pair of nineteenth-century poets (think rock star, not English 101) find themselves investigating horrors beyond even their own imaginations, tumbling more than one comely wench along the way. If they can maintain this fine balance of thrills and chills, the Limbo may finally have its first real hit. (Sunday nights at 9 p.m. – four stars)*

CHAPTER 46

We went back to L.A., and Romeo went back to work on the show and lined up other possible jobs for his upcoming hiatus. He was now one of the hottest properties in Hollywood, a term he loathed with the passion of a thousand burning suns. I was in demand in a pretty big way, too, though I was a lot less interested in working. *Macbeth* was still in development; I hadn't even been officially hired. But I considered myself locked in for that, and I was driving Tony crazy by refusing to even take a meeting about anything that might interfere with it until we knew when Simon and his director intended to shoot.

Meanwhile, Fiona got more pregnant every day. She was determined to get back to her working weight as soon as the baby was born. As a former child star who had been called "fat" by casting directors and critics alike when she had first started to develop into a grown woman, she was crazy sensitive on the whole issue. She had a nutritionist all but living in Castle Asshole, feeding her just exactly what she needed in precisely the smallest possible amounts to keep the baby healthy without adding an extra ounce to her own body underneath. Consequently, in her bikini, swimming her laps every day in the pool at Castle Asshole, she looked like some kind of alien creature, a near-skeletal frame with a swollen, vaguely human-shaped growth lurking just beneath the skin of her belly, ready to burst out. In the professionally-staged photographs taken of her for magazines during that period, she looked like a Renaissance Madonna. In person, she looked like a freak.

I went with her to her six-month ultrasound. I sat beside her and held her hand while the technician squirted ice cold jelly on her tummy, and I was actually the first one to catch sight of the baby on the screen. "Oh my god." Lurking like a ghost in the dark was a tiny, perfectly formed human being. "There it is!"

"She," the doctor said, smiling. "There she is."

"Delilah," Fiona said. She was squeezing my hand so tightly it hurt, but I didn't mind; I totally understood. I was squeezing hers back just as tightly. "We're going to name her Delilah." I had never seen her face look more beautiful, even in a movie. *Daddy should be here*, I thought, kissing her forehead. *He shouldn't be missing this.* "Do you like it?" she asked me. "The name Delilah?"

"I love it. It rocks out." She smiled at me, and I smiled back. "She looks like a Delilah."

"She's beautiful," the doctor said, drawing on the screen with her little light pencil while the technician took screen shots. "Absolutely perfect."

After they were done, I helped Fiona clean up and get dressed. "She really is gorgeous, isn't she?" she said.

"For a tiny black and white alien? Yeah, she's a knockout," I teased. "Of course she is."

She hugged me, catching me by surprise. "You know I really love you, right?"

"Yeah, of course." I drew back, a little embarrassed. "Why do you ask?"

"Nothing." She pulled on her ridiculously chic silk knit maternity pants. "Just promise me you'll love her, no matter what."

"Who? Delilah?" I helped her with her tee-shirt. "Just tell her not to cross me."

"Scar, I'm serious, please." She had that weird, intense light in her eyes again. "Nobody in the world is going to know how to help her better than you."

"You're talking like a crazy person," I said. "You do realize that, right?" I got her shoes and socks.

"You know what it was like for you growing up." I put her socks on her. By that point, no matter how much yoga she did, she couldn't reach her own feet. "Whatever happens, she's going to need you."

"I'm studying up on the whole big sister thing, I promise." I tied her sneakers. "You worry way too much."

"I know." She leaned back on the table and let me do it. "Just promise you won't ever let my mom and dad get their hands on her." Fiona's parents, hippie burnouts from the Haight-Asbury era, had worked out early that their one hope for riches was to turn out photogenic moppets, and they'd been mining that gold strike hard ever since Fiona was about three. Stella and Calvin had never been the Parents of the Year, but they beat the hell out of Fiona's folks.

"Never ever," I promised. "But you and Calvin will take care of that."

"I know." She was watching me as I stood up. "Your dad misses you, you know." She was crying. "He wants to be close to you and Sebastian, and he worries about you so much."

"God, would you stop it?" I had made peace with the fact that she was not only dating my father but was having his kid; why did she have to keep pushing? "Your hormones are starting to make me sick." I held out my hands to help her get up. "Come on; let's get out of here."

When I got home to the bungalow that night, Romeo was soaking in the tub. "Hey, you." I slid out of my shoes and jeans before I kissed him and sat down on the floor. "How was work?" He was holding a glass of whiskey on the rocks against his temple, and the open bottle was propped on the rim of the tub against the wall. "That bad?"

"Aw, it was all right." His speech was slightly slurred, and his accent was more pronounced than usual. He had apparently had a couple already. "How was your day?"

"I guess it was okay." The latest issue of *Rock and Rolling* was lying on the floor beside me, the cover pocked with wet spots. "I went with Fiona to her ultrasound." I picked it up.

"Oh yeah?" He put a hand on my head, pulling me toward him, and I smiled, leaning in to let him kiss my cheek. "How was that?"

"It was fine. It's a girl." I turned my head and kissed him on the mouth again before settling back on the floor, my back against the wall. "She says she's going to name her Delilah." I opened the magazine with one hand, holding his hand with the other. "That's pretty, don't you think?" I smiled, seeing a picture of Sebastian with some random rock star in the "On the Scene" column, looking slightly drunk, very happy, and much too cool for school.

"Yeah." His fingers were laced with mine. "That'll be great." He kissed my hand. "So is everything okay with the baby?"

"Oh yeah; healthy and beautiful." I flipped the page to an article on the Scarecrow. "Oh wow, look at this. Remember Simon, the guy who's playing Macbeth in my movie?" I showed him the picture.

"How about that?" He barely looked, but he smiled. "So is Fiona okay?"

"Sure, I guess." I was skimming through the article. "Hey Ro, what's the IRA?" My haphazard approach to high school had left gaping holes in my education. But my husband the tenth-grade dropout had apparently read every book ever printed and subscribed to three different daily papers. "They're like terrorists, right?"

"Right," he said, unruffled by the question. I asked him weird shit all the time. "Well, it depends on who you ask. The Irish Republican Army—they've been around most of the century, trying to run Great Britain out of Ireland."

"But they blow people up, right?" I remembered seeing news reports in Europe.

"Yeah, they do. Innocent people, sometimes." He refilled his whiskey glass. "You going to join up?"

"Yeah, I thought I might." I took the glass and took a sip before I gave it back to him. "No, it's Simon. I thought he was English, but it says here that he's Irish, from Belfast, and that his brother is reported to be a member of the IRA."

"If he is, I feel bad for your friend, Simon." He lay back in the tub, soapy water sloshing up to the edge. "Those dudes are bad news, and most of them end up dead or in prison, I think." He tugged on my hand. "Hey pretty…how about you get in here and let me soap you up?"

I laughed. "Now why would I want to do that?" I tossed the magazine aside. "You're too drunk to do anything but wash."

He glanced down at the water, then back up at me with a grin. "My friend here thinks you might be mistaken," he said as I stood up.

"He does, does he?" I pulled my shirt over my head and tossed it away, then slid out of my underpants before stepping into the tub. "I think you and your friend might be hoping for a miracle."

He grinned up at me, purely wicked. "We're praying hard, baby." I unhooked my bra and let it drop into the water before going to my knees, crouched over him. "Praying real hard."

I let my eyes go wide, pretending to be shocked. "Praise the Lord." Laughing, we kissed and made love in the tub, and for that night, I forgot about Fiona and Simon and everything else.

That same summer I filmed a guest spot on Romeo's show for the season finale. I played both the dead soulmate of Romeo's character and the evil witchcraft-using con artist pretending to be her ghost. I still think it's the best piece of film the two of us have ever done together. We had an absolute ball filming it, running around in period costumes, making out and shouting at one another dramatically. We shot the exteriors on location in the Lake District of England. It was hugely expensive for a show in its first season on a baby network, but it was totally worth it. We left everybody else at home and had the closest thing to a honeymoon we would ever have.

Because they had spent so much money, the network wanted to promote the bejesus out of the finale. No one had ever done a summer start to a TV season before, so they wanted to go out with a bang. Romeo had a movie lined up for the hiatus, and I was scheduled to film a small part in the latest Andy Weissman movie. The part had been Fiona's originally, but she had been forced to drop out because she was pregnant. Plus, the producers of *Macbeth* were closing in on a studio deal for that. So some bright spark decided Romeo and I needed to do an interview as a couple for *Popcorn*.

Alice Brown did the interview. I still remembered her from the *Match Girl* premiere, and I still liked her. Most of it was light and breezy, talking about Hollywood. Romeo skimmed over his past like a pro, distracting her with funny stories about being the world's skinniest bouncer on the Sunset Strip. But when she asked about Amy and the porn, he was very candid, saying that he was proud of his sister for taking charge of her own career instead of letting herself be exploited. He even admitted to running lights and working as a production assistant on a couple of her films.

I talked a lot about Calvin and Sebastian. We talked about meeting at a party then seeing one another again several months later on the set of *Funhouse*. We said we really had been just friends for a long time before we started dating. We told her we were very much in love.

I told her about Stella. She asked, very gently, her eyes soft with sympathy, about Stella's murder. I told her the story I had told Romeo. Romeo sat beside me with his arm around me, and when I cried, he drew me close against his chest and told her we were done on that topic, to ask me something else. She agreed, bringing the subject back to my childhood and brunches at Castle Asshole with the Hollywood elite. When she left, we were all smiling, and we thought it had gone well.

For the pictures, they gave us a whole list of possible photographers and asked us whom we'd prefer. Reading through it, I recognized a name—Richard Browning. It took me a minute to place him, then I remembered. Leila had told me about him, the photographer who had taken Stella's picture that was hanging in Mawmaw's living room, the one who had wanted to marry her. I didn't mention any of this to Romeo, but I told him I had heard of Browning's work and wanted to use him, and he didn't object. Truth be told, he couldn't have cared less. But to me it felt like fate.

The day of the shoot, Romeo had meetings with his agent, so he was supposed to meet me at Browning's rented studio. I got there first, and as soon as I walked in, I saw the set—a big, white marble bathtub. I laughed, but Lisa immediately got on the phone to Ranhosky to check the details of the contract and release on the subject of nudity. I looked around, hoping to catch a glimpse of Browning, but he either hadn't arrived yet or was somewhere else. One of his assistants hustled me into the dressing room. I stripped down to my underpants and put on a robe, and the stylists went to work. They put me in a chair in front of the mirror, and a hair wizard went to work spritzing and rolling my hair while a make-up assistant gave me a pedicure. A production assistant brought me some iced lemonade and a little plate of cookies to nibble, and Browning's own assistant pulled out a crate of CDs and started going through them with me, letting me pick music Romeo and I would like for the actual shoot.

When we were done, I leaned back in the chair and closed my eyes. The make-up artist started on my face, and I had almost drifted off to sleep when I heard someone else come in. "Hey baby," I said without opening my eyes. "How was lunch?"

"Sorry, Miss Cross," a pleasant English accent said. "I can't imagine you mean me."

I opened my eyes and saw Richard for the first time, standing over me. "No," I said. "Hi…call me Scarlett."

"Scarlett," he said, smiling. He was my father's age, maybe a little older, maybe just not so well-preserved, with a handsome, freckled face and bright blue eyes. His hair was pale red, touched with silver. "Call me Richard." He offered me his hand. "I'm Richard Browning."

"Hi Richard." I smiled back, pleased. He wasn't at all what I had expected from a great artist. He looked like he spent a lot of time outside, like he might climb Mt. Everest for fun. I sat up and shook his hand. "It's great to meet you."

"Likewise." He moved back out of the make-up artist's way, and leaned against the counter. "I've wanted to meet you for some time now, actually." He handed me a small, framed, black and white photograph. It was my mother, a small print of the same portrait that hung up over the mantelpiece at Mawmaw's house in Tupelo. "I shot that four years before you were born," he said. "If my calculations are correct, she wouldn't have been much older than you are now."

"Oh wow." I thought about what Leila had said about him wanting to marry Mama and how she had turned him down. "You were in love with her."

His eyes widened for a moment, and he sounded a little shaken when he spoke again. "I was very much in love with her." The woman painting my toenails had frozen, her mouth a perfect O of shock. Richard and I caught sight of her at the same moment, and both of us laughed. She blushed and went back to work. "But that was a very long time ago," he finished. "Before she met your father."

"Did you know her after…?" I blinked back tears that caught me by surprise. "After I was born?"

"Know her? No, not really," he said. "I wish I had." He reached out and barely touched the back of my hand for just a second. "I wish she had felt she could come to me for help." His eyes looked a little wet, too, at least to me. "I'm so dreadfully sorry, Scarlett."

I smiled, liking him a lot. "Thanks."

He stood up. "I'll just be outside." He seemed a little embarrassed suddenly, a little bit abrupt. "Just wanted to say hello." Romeo came in as he was bending over me, giving me the standard Hollywood cheek kiss. Richard smiled at him as he straightened up. "And here's the groom."

"Hey." Romeo shook the hand he offered, but he looked wary. He could see I was on the point of tears in spite of my smile.

"I'll see you both out there," Richard said brightly. He squeezed his assistant's shoulder and murmured something in his ear, then he was gone.

"What's going on?" Romeo said, sitting in the chair by mine. "Who was that?"

"The photographer, Richard." I reached out and took his hand. "He knew my mom; can you believe it?"

"Wow." One of the wardrobe girls was pulling off his jacket, undressing him, but he barely seemed to notice. "Are you okay?"

"Yeah, it's just weird." The hair wizard was done with the curling iron for the moment. Now he was gathering the curls he'd made into a Grecian-style cascade on the back of my head.

"Get me something to fill this out," he told his assistant. "Nothing major, just a bump. And make sure the color is a match."

"They used to date," I told Romeo. "You know that big picture in Mawmaw's living room? He took that."

"He told you that just now?" They had him stripped down to his jeans, and a make-up artist was masking out a patch of zits on his shoulder.

"Leila had told me before." The hair wizard clipped a hairpiece the size of a newborn kitten at the back of my head under my own hair.

"So why did they break up?" He waved off the dresser who was reaching for his pants and shucked out of them himself, then sat back down and dropped a towel in his lap.

"He didn't say." I stood up to let the pedicurist smear baby oil up my legs. I had been waxed the week before. "But he acted like it wasn't his idea." I could see Richard's assistant pretending hard not to listen. "It's so strange." Another hairdresser was spritzing Romeo's hair with something shiny and running her fingers through it, making it stand up in artfully disheveled spikes. "Thinking of her like that, a girl with a boyfriend."

"Yeah, I guess it would be." He took my hand again and squeezed it. "You look really pretty, by the way."

"Thanks." The chief stylist handed my dresser a white silk robe dripping with lace. "I'm wearing that?" Lisa had come in and was sitting in the corner reading a magazine; when I said this, she looked up.

"Richard picked it out," the chief stylist said. "You're supposed to look like a princess."

"I like it," Romeo said as I shrugged out of the robe I was wearing and put it on.

"Really?" It felt heavy and slinky at the same time, gliding cool over my skin as the chief stylist tied the sash herself.

"Oh yeah." He put his jeans back on, ignoring the robe one of the dressers was holding open for him.

"Bandages," Lisa said, looking me up and down. "No nipples."

"Richard is well aware of the terms of Miss Cross' contract,"

Richard's assistant said, sounding very English. "He won't photograph her bare nipples."

"Then he won't notice the bandages," Lisa said, sounding very Manhattan.

"Lisa, it's okay," I said. "Bandages are going to look weird under the robe." I was still facing the mirror, and Romeo moved behind me, putting his hands on my shoulders.

"Jesus Christ," the hair wizard said, laughing. "You two are stupid, you're so gorgeous."

Romeo blushed, but I laughed. "Thanks." I turned my head to look at Romeo's real face. "Hey stupid," I said softly. "I love you."

He kissed me with no respect whatsoever for my perfectly glossed lips. "I love you, too."

Richard shot several rolls of film, most of it of us goofing around like lunatics covered in bubbles in the bathtub. He was funny and laid back and kind, putting both of us at ease almost as soon as we walked out. I've worked with a lot of photographers who make art by disappearing. Everything they do or say is designed to make you forget about the camera. I like that method; it works well for me as a model and as an actress. But Richard wasn't like that at all. His shoot was a lively conversation that included the three of us plus everyone else who passed across his line of sight as he peered through the camera. "Hannah just got married, too," he sang out, teasing a make-up assistant who was touching up my face. "Look at the rock on her hand. Scarlett, hold yours up; let's see whose is bigger." I did, smiling as Hannah blushed. Richard snapped a picture from an angle that cut her out of the frame entirely, me leaning back in Romeo's arms, seeming to admire my ring while Romeo kissed my hair, his eyes closed. It made it to the magazine in black and white opposite a page of text. "Revolting, Hannah, honestly," Richard said. "Scarlett is a movie star, for Christ's sake, and you have a bigger engagement ring. Your fiancé is a swine."

"A rich swine," she retorted with a grin. "He's going to take me away from all this."

"Tell him to call me," Romeo joked. "If he pulls that off, I want to know how he does it."

"Oh dear, Scarlett," Richard warned, still shooting. "It sounds to me like your husband means to keep you barefoot and pregnant."

"Of course," Romeo said. "It's the Southern way." I turned around to face him, and he caught me by the arms as I slipped. "Forget movie star." An assistant hurried forward to shovel in more bubbles until my tits and ass were covered. "Scar and I are just a pair of hicks, ain't we, baby?"

I braced on his shoulders, straddling his lap. "You know it, puddin' pop," I said in my deepest Stella drawl. He grinned, and I leaned forward to kiss him.

The moment just before our lips met made the first page of the article in color.

When Richard said we were done, Romeo got out of the tub first. He had already put on his jeans and lit a cigarette by the time I stood up. One assistant brushed the bubbles off of me as the other draped the lacy robe around my shoulders like a cape so it covered everything important but left my wet legs bare. Romeo turned and offered me his hand to help me out of the tub, and I took it, looking at Lisa as she asked me a question. Romeo was looking at me, squinting slightly, the cigarette hanging from his lip.

That one made the cover.

Romeo got called to the phone while we were still standing around in the studio, talking to Richard. As soon as he was gone, Richard said, "Scarlett, I want to get one more. Not for the magazine; just for me— and for you, of course."

"Sure," I said, flattered to be asked. "He should be back in a minute."

"Actually, I'd rather have just you." His blue eyes twinkled. "If that would be all right."

"Of course." I was a little taken aback, but not much. I trusted him. Besides, any photo he shot would be a Sir Richard Browning work of art. "Where do you want me?"

"Just here, in front of the drop." We had shot a few of me and

Romeo in front of the plain gray backdrop, lit for black and white, before we got in the tub. "And I'd love it if we could do it without the robe." He moved behind a larger, older-looking camera on a tripod. "If you're not comfortable with that, I entirely understand."

"No, it's okay." Lisa was shaking her head at me from behind him, but that just made me more determined to do it. Romeo's assistant, Kyle, went off to get him as I dropped the robe. "But don't show anything, okay?"

"I absolutely will not," he promised. "Hannah, someone, take down her hair." He was bent over the camera.

I started pulling out pins, and Hannah took them from me as a hair assistant took out the hairpiece. The assistant ran his fingers through my own damp hair and let it fall on my shoulders. "How's this?" he asked Richard. "Do I need to get the curling iron?"

"No, no, that's perfect," Richard said. "Don't do another thing, love; bugger off." He waved them off, and they moved away.

"What do you want me to do?" I said, starting to feel self-conscious.

"Absolutely nothing." He looked up from the camera so I could see his face and smiled. "I want you to look straight at me, but I don't want you to think about anything at all. Let your mind go totally blank."

"Okay," I said, laughing.

"It's not easy," he said, still smiling slightly. "Not everyone can do it." He looked back down through the camera. "Be absolutely still with absolutely no conscious expression and stop thinking."

I tried, then stopped. "For how long?"

"I don't know," he said, his tone perfectly patient. "I'll let you know when to stop."

"Okay." I crossed one arm over my breasts and let the other fall limp at my side. I tried not to think, but that seemed impossible, so I counted in my head, concentrating on letting my expression go absolutely slack. I kept counting, waiting, but I didn't hear the camera click, and he didn't say anything. The room had gone absolutely silent. I could hear water dripping in the sink in the dressing room. I forgot to count, forgot about my face. I listened to the steady dripping of the water in the sink…

"Great," Richard said after who knew how long. "That's lovely, Scarlett, thank you." My face was wet, I realized. Tears were streaming down my cheeks. Richard came out from behind the camera as Hannah helped me back into the robe. "You were perfect."

Romeo was standing in the shadows, just watching. "Hey," I said, going to him. "Is everything okay?"

He pulled me close and hugged me tight. "Yeah." He kissed my cheek. "Everything's fine."

CHAPTER 48

Not long after that, I went to New York to shoot the part for Andy Weissman. Sebastian was already there, working in another limited-run play, and Lisa was there, of course. They went through my scenes with me in the Weissman script (or the Weissman sides, I should say; I never saw a whole script, of course), and between them they were able to explain all the New York intellectual references that flew straight over my head so I sounded smarter on camera.

The actual job wasn't very memorable. Everyone always says it's such a privilege to work with Weissman, and I'm sure it is, but for me it was kind of like being in limbo. He never gave me any direction, never tried to explain my character to me, but I didn't really mind it. My process at that point mostly involved showing up on time and trying not to mispronounce any of my lines, so it worked out well for both of us. The one comment I heard him make in my general direction was "very pretty," but he might have just as easily meant my dress instead of me. In an interview later, I heard him say I was "unspoiled," which I took to mean kind of stupid. But again, it was okay. He didn't much impress me, either.

The Scarecrow called me once. It was the night of Sebastian's opening, so I didn't get back to the hotel until almost four in the morning. Lisa was still with me because she had wanted to see the play, and she hit the speaker button on the phone to play my messages while I poured myself a drink. "It must be Romeo," she said, and I smiled, dropping ice in the glass.

"Scarlett, this is Simon," the voice said through the crappy little speaker. "How can the Princess of Hollywood be in New York?" There was a pause, and Lisa reached for the button, but I shook my head, waving her off. "I can't stop thinking about you," he went on.

"Is that who I think it is?" Lisa said, her mouth and eyes like saucers.

"Shhh." I moved closer to the phone.

"I'm supposed to be married in a month," Simon's voice went on, interrupting us. "But somehow..." We could hear him moving, the clink of a bottle or glass. "I would like to speak with you again," he said, his voice suddenly more crisp, much more English. "Do ring me and tell me if you're well." He left his number and hung up.

"Scarlett?" Lisa was still gaping at me. "That can't really be him." She suddenly grabbed a pad and pen and jotted down the number. "Was it?"

"He's an actor, yeah." Her reaction was kind of annoying. I wasn't sure how I felt about him calling. "Simon Price, the guy I'm doing Macbeth with."

"Are you going to call him back?" Lisa asked.

I looked at the note in her hand. "No." I took a long swallow of Scotch. "Hell no." I drained my glass. "Please, just throw it away."

<hr>

The night after my last day of filming, I was supposed to have dinner with Sebastian, but he cancelled on me, saying he had a hot date. Lisa was busy, too, seeing some New York friends. My flight wasn't supposed to be until the next morning, but I decided I didn't want to wait. Leaving a message for Lisa at the hotel, I caught the red-eye back to Los Angeles.

I got back to the Chateau Marmont about seven the next morning, just as the sun was coming up. It was Saturday, so I knew Romeo wouldn't be working. There were a few people buzzing around the sidewalk outside the hotel, but no one seemed to notice me, just another skinny kid in jeans and a tee-shirt, as I ducked around the building to the bungalow.

The bungalow was dark, and I could hear Romeo snoring in the bedroom. I went into the bathroom, not bothering to be quiet, slipping out of my clothes, peeing, flushing, taking a shower, assuming some of this would wake him up. I wanted to talk to him; I had missed him terribly.

But when I came out, naked with wet hair, he was still snoring. "Romeo?" I said. Light was starting to show around the edges of the blinds. "Romeo?" I turned on the bedside lamp.

He was lying naked on his back on top of the covers. A zippered leather case was lying open on the bed beside him, and a rubber tourniquet was still half-draped around his upper arm. The needle was still held loosely in his hand.

For a long time, I just stood there, staring. I don't know if I remembered Stella or not; it was like I'd found a cobra in my bed. I knew exactly what the needle was, what it all meant. I had no confusion about that at all. He had been shooting up. He snorted once, coughing a little, and I stepped back, my hand flying to my mouth. But he settled, going back to snoring. "Romeo," I said again, my normal speaking voice. "Baby, wake up."

He didn't stir.

I took the needle from his hand very carefully, touching it as little as I could. I wrapped it in newspaper, one page at a time, round and round and round, three pages total. I threw it in the trashcan, shifting the trash to put it dead center between the top and the bottom so it would be covered up when the maid looked down into the can and still covered up when she emptied the trash. I went back to the bed and unwrapped the tourniquet from his arm, being very careful not to wake him, never looking at his face. I wound it up into a coil and tucked it away in the case, closed the case, and zipped it up. I took a tissue from the box beside the bed and wiped out the spoon. I put the spoon on the tray in the kitchenette with the dirty coffee cups and glasses from the day before. I put the case and the lighter on the dresser, lined up beside my husband's wallet and keys.

I took a spare blanket out of the closet, holding my breath as the closet door squeaked. I spread it carefully over my husband, draping it over the end of the bed. Still naked, I crawled underneath the blanket and curled up close beside him. He groaned once and mumbled, rolling over on his side. I drew his arm around me, pressing close, and closed my eyes, and I stayed perfectly still until I fell asleep.

When he woke up, he was glad to see me; he was fine; he never let on that anything was wrong at all, and neither did I. But he had to know that I knew. He had to know I was the one who had moved his stuff. We just didn't talk about it.

CLIPPING 14

from the New York Observer *movie page:* Paradise Watched

Andy Weissman's latest film is a surprisingly frothy comedy of manners called Paradise Watched. *Set in the Hamptons at the height of the summer season, it references works as serious and diverse as* The Great Gatsby *and* Smiles of a Summer Night. *But like all the best beach movies, all it really cares about are pretty girls and sunshine.*

. . . . . .

As Lisa, the oblivious object of Weissman's comic obsession, Oscar-winning teen-ager Scarlett Cross has little to do but be very pretty and look very young, both of which goals she achieves without effort. But she also brings an unexpected and refreshingly wry intelligence to the part, particularly in her scenes with Pamela Cary as her loving, rose-gardening mother. Playing a real kid of today in a film her character actually survives, she proves herself to be a talent of real wit and potential.

CHAPTER 49

B y the time the Weissman film came out that fall, Fiona was hugely pregnant, ready to pop. Romeo and Peter were back at work on the second season of *The Romantics*, set to premiere in the spring. Calvin was home with Fiona waiting for the baby and playing the proud papa; he seemed happier than I had seen him since Sebastian and I were little kids. Sebastian had a new secret boyfriend and had filmed three projects in the past six months. And I was deep in pre-production for *Macbeth* with the shoot set to begin in London right after Christmas.

The producers and director had gone along with Simon about casting me, but someone in the mix had insisted I get some Shakespeare coaching before filming began. So every day, I worked with Muriel. Unlike Romeo and Sebastian, I had never had any formal training as an actress. So it was really scary but also really fun. Everything she told me was like a light going on inside my head. Muriel was English with a perfect posh accent, more striking than beautiful with heavy, dark eyebrows and a long, strong jaw. Truth be told, she seemed to me to be exactly the person who ought to have been cast as Lady Macbeth. But instead of modeling the part for me, which was what had always been done for me in the past and what I expected,

354

she focused on teaching me the language of Shakespeare in general and the way I needed to carry my body, how to know what I was saying and look like someone who might say it.

"Simon and Roger have made a very specific choice in casting you," she said. Roger was the director, and I hadn't met him yet. "God only knows what they're thinking, so we'll have to take care not to make a mess of it." Instead of specifically addressing how I would play Lady Macbeth, we worked on ingénues, Juliet and Rosalind and the silly girls lost in the woods in *A Midsummer Night's Dream*. The first week, I felt like an idiot. The words all sounded fruity and foreign and dry as a bone, and I knew without Muriel saying it I stunk, which didn't deter her one bit from saying it anyway.

Then all of a sudden in the middle of a session in the middle of the second week, less than ten minutes after I had broken down and cried for half an hour and sworn I was going to quit, it clicked. I was doing Juliet, the bit where she's saying "give me my Romeo" and talking about how when he dies, she wants to cut him up in little bits and scatter them over the sky like stars. For whatever reason, that particular image slid into place inside my brain like a key fitting into a lock. I forgot about Muriel and the beige, empty room where we were working and the fact that I was starving for lunch, and I thought about my Romeo, the way his sad smile made me ache and the way his hands felt when he touched me. I thought of the morning in El Paso when he'd taken the gun away from me and shot out the hotel window and the way he had looked strung out unconscious the morning I came home early from New York, the rubber tourniquet still tied around his arm, still so beautiful. For once, Muriel didn't stop me until I had finished the monologue, and when I was done, she was smiling.

"You will very likely be a dreadful Lady Macbeth," she said. "But you could be the best Juliet I've ever seen."

"I agree." I turned around to find Simon standing in the doorway with his arms crossed and a satisfied smirk on his face. "About the Juliet part, I mean. I think your Lady Macbeth will be brilliant."

"Thanks." I suddenly realized I had never seen him dressed in anything but a suit and tie or a tuxedo before. He looked good in casual clothes, more solid and real. "I didn't know you'd be here today."

"I just got in from London," he said. "And I'm ravenous. Fancy some lunch?"

"I don't know," I said, looking to Muriel. "I'm not sure we're finished."

"It's all right," she said. She was smiling, but I got the impression she wasn't particularly pleased to see Simon show up. "We're done for the day. That was very good, Scarlett."

"Thanks." If she'd been a Hollywood person, I would have hugged her. As it was, I just got my purse.

I expected Simon to want some place private and quiet, but he took me to the Ivy. The photographers swarmed us as soon as we stepped out of the car, but we were both experts by then at ignoring them. Simon put his hand on the small of my back and steered me inside.

The maître d' found us a table in a corner—we each had an Oscar, after all—but we still got our fair share of gawking from our fellow lunchers. "You know we'll be all over the tabloids next week, right?" I said.

"I'm not worried," he said, smiling. "It won't be the first time, remember?"

"Oh yeah." The night he had trekked with me all over Hollywood looking for Romeo had made us an item for almost a week. "And hey, it's good for the movie, right?" He looked tired; he was pale, and his eyes were slightly bloodshot as if he hadn't slept. But I still couldn't get over how handsome he looked in jeans and a tee-shirt. "Will Clare be okay? It won't freak her out, will it?"

He laughed. "Trust me, darling. Clare could not care less." They had postponed their wedding so she could go on location for another project, but so far as I knew, they were still very much an engaged couple. He had ordered a bottle of wine, and he poured himself a second glass. "And yes, the publicity probably will be very helpful to the movie."

"And if Muriel's right, we'll need all the help we can get," I said.

"Muriel is an idiot."

"No, she's not." I drained the last swallow from my own first glass and poured myself a second, too. Simon raised an eyebrow. "Scarecrow, I'm almost twenty. It's fine."

"Almost twenty," he echoed, laughing again. "And by the way, I still find that nickname extremely insulting."

"Why?" I said. "I think it suits you."

"Oh thanks."

"Fine, you can call me something insulting, too." The waiter brought my cheeseburger and his fish. "How about Jailbait?"

"Best not," he said. "How about Princess?"

"Ugh, really?" I cut my burger in half.

"I think it's perfect," he said. "You are Hollywood royalty, after all."

"Please, I'm trying to eat." I took a big bite and wiped the ketchup from the corner of my mouth. "Seriously, though, I have to ask. What gives? Nobody in their right mind would cast me as Lady Macbeth."

"Probably not." He was barely touching his lunch; mostly he seemed to be watching me.

"So why did you do it?"

"I'm not in my right mind, obviously."

"Obviously." I raised an eyebrow, too, and he laughed. "So?"

"You mean why did we cast a beautiful young American girl instead of a middle-aged British harridan with the sex appeal of Margaret Thatcher?"

"Muriel is very sexy," I said. "And so is Clare."

"Ah," he said. "Yes, Clare is very sexy."

"So why not cast her?" I said. "Why cast me?"

"Does it matter?"

"It might." In most of the ways that mattered I was still a kid, but I wasn't stupid. I had been watching my father long enough to know about great actors who cast girls they wanted to fuck and to hell with the movie, and this had all the warning signs of that. Sometimes you got a Bette and an Oscar. But sometimes you got Dolci Guiliana, and your career went down the toilet and took hers right along with it. "If

I knew what you saw in me that made you think I was right for the part, I could probably play it better."

He looked stunned. "Has anyone ever told you how brilliant you are?" he said. "You're smart, Scarlett, not just beautiful. Do you realize that?"

"So you cast me because I'm smart?" I didn't believe him. Smart wasn't something we did in my family, not really. Talented, yes. But if any of us had ever had a lick of intelligence, could we have been as fucked up as we all were? It seemed unlikely. I thought Romeo was smart and Fiona and Simon himself, of course. But Sebastian and I were charming, talented liars, able to fake anything, just like our father. No one had ever suggested otherwise, not even Romeo. And I wasn't ready to hear it from Simon now.

"All right." He put down his fork and took my hand. "You've read the play by now, right?"

"Of course." Only because Muriel had insisted. I had intended to just read my own pages from the screenplay, but she had bullied me until I read the full Folger Library edition.

"So why does Macbeth go against everything he's ever known or believed to go bad and kill the king?"

"So he can be king."

"But why should he want to be king? He's been the king's cousin all his life, and he's obviously a kick-ass soldier. And Duncan is such a weakling, he can't even put down a rebellion unless Macbeth does it for him. So why hasn't Macbeth taken the crown from him before if he wants it?"

"Because the witches' prophecy makes him think for the first time that it's meant to be."

"But he says over and over again that he won't let that sway him—he says it to his best friend; he says it to his wife; he says it to himself. He thinks they're wrong or, if they're right, he doesn't have to do anything to make it happen. What changes his mind?"

"He says that, but he doesn't really believe it." Muriel and I had talked about this a little, but she had cut me off before the discussion had made it this far. "Roger will tell you what he thinks it means," she'd said. "Until then, you need to work out what you think on your own." So I had been thinking about it a lot. "I mean, he tells his best friend he's not worried about it, but then he stops in the middle of leading troops home from war to write a long letter home to his wife and tells her every detail," I said now.

"Exactly," Simon said. "His first thought is to tell his wife, to impress her with this great prophecy that's been made for him. But when the time comes to do the killing, he decides that he can't. Why does he change his mind?"

"She tells him if he doesn't do it, he's a pussy, and she doesn't want him anymore," I said. "But he really wants to do it; he just wants her to tell him to do it so he can tell himself it's all her fault." My real relationships with the men in my life contributed greatly to this interpretation, I suspect.

"No, he doesn't want to do it," Simon said. "Without the witches' prophecy, it never would have occurred to him to do it. And the only reason he goes through with it in the end is to keep his wife, not because she tells him to do it but because if he doesn't, he will lose her love. She won't want him anymore, just like you said."

"But like you said, he's this kick-ass soldier," I said. "This kick-ass Scottish medieval soldier. What does he care what some woman thinks of him?"

"Not some woman. His woman. And he's obsessed with her." He was still holding my hand. "And you, Princess, are the kind of woman who could inspire that level of obsession. You're the only woman I've ever met I can imagine a man killing his king to keep."

"Yeah, right." He was making me uncomfortable not because I wanted him to stop but because I wanted him to go on. Since I had met Romeo, I had never once entertained the notion that I could ever fall in love with anyone else. When my father had suggested it, trying to convince me to give up Romeo, I had taken it as sure proof of how little he understood how I felt and had loved Romeo even harder. But sitting here now with Simon holding my hand and saying these things, I could imagine falling in love with him very easily. I wanted him to keep telling me how smart I was, how beautiful. I wanted him to keep calling me Princess. I wanted to be the impossible golden goddess I saw reflected in his eyes. "Trust me," I said. "I'm not worth all that."

"You think not?" he said. "Ask Romeo."

I knew a cue when I heard one. *Who's Romeo?* I would have said in a romantic comedy, gazing up at him starry-eyed with love. *Please don't say his name; I can't stand it,* I would have said in a soap, closing my eyes as he leaned in to kiss me.

But there were no cameras rolling, and I had a real life. "Speaking of," I said, standing up. "I should call him." I squeezed his hand before I pulled free. "I'll be right back."

I borrowed the maître d's phone and called Romeo's dressing room, but he was on the set. I left a message with his assistant then called Lisa at home. "Hey gorgeous, guess who I'm having lunch with," I said when she answered.

"Sebastian?" she said.

"Nope. Simon Price. Shall I tell him you want to have his babies?"

"Yes, please."

"So why did you say Sebastian?" I said. "Did he call?"

"No, but Fiona did," she said. "Did she catch you at class?"

"No." The last person I wanted to talk to just then was Fiona. "What does she want?"

"She said if I talked to you first, I should ask you to go by the house and see her," she said. "She says she really needs to talk to you."

"Oh joy." From where I stood, I could see Simon. He looked keyed up and annoyed, drinking wine like water. He caught me watching, and I smiled and waved. He smiled and waved back. "On a scale of one to ten, how evil am I if I blow her off?"

"Ordinarily, I'd say no more than a two," she said. "But she sounded kind of upset, and she said it was important."

"Balls." Whatever Fiona wanted to say to me, I was pretty sure I didn't want to hear it. But getting away from Simon just then probably wasn't the worst idea. "Okay, I'll go as soon as we finish lunch. If Romeo calls, tell him that's where I went and that I'll see him at home." Suddenly the very idea that I could even think about another man made me feel like a monster. "And tell him I love him, okay?"

"He knows," she said. "But I'll tell him."

I went back to the table and rushed through the rest of lunch, and Simon let me. We talked about innocuous, gossipy stuff until we finished eating, and afterwards he drove me straight back to my car. But as I was getting out, he caught my hand. "It's going to be great," he said. "I promise you'll be brilliant."

"Thanks." I leaned in and kissed him lightly on the lips. "I'll see you soon."

CHAPTER 50

The first thing I noticed when I drove up the driveway at Castle Asshole was that all the lights were off even though the sun was almost down. Then I saw Fiona. She was lying on her side on the terrace, fully dressed, two feet from a cushioned chaise. She had one arm stretched above her head, and her eyes were closed.

"Oh shit." I threw the car into park and tried to get out, fighting free of the seatbelt before half-jumping, half-falling into the driveway. "Fiona!" I scrambled to my feet and ran to her, skirting the pool. She was wearing a long white sundress, and as I got closer I could see the skirt was soaked with blood. "Oh shit," I kept repeating, falling to my knees beside her. "Oh shit oh shit oh shit."

"Scarlett..." Her eyes popped open like a doll's, and she grabbed my arm, so fast and so hard I almost screamed. She smiled, but her eyes were too big and bright with pain. "Thank God." The walkaround phone from the kitchen was lying on the ground beside her, and I grabbed it, frantically punching in 911. "It's dead," she said. "Oh God..." Her eyes bulged, and both of us gasped as a fresh gout of blood soaked her skirt.

"It's okay," I heard myself saying like I meant it. "It will be okay." I took off my jacket and wadded it up behind her head, rolling her onto her back. "Lie still. I'll be right back."

"No," she said, clinging to me. "I have to tell you something."

"Tell me in a minute." I broke free of her, the bloody handprints she had left on my sleeves making me feel sick. "I have to call an ambulance." I stood up and ran into the house; luckily, I was wearing sneakers. I grabbed the phone from the living room and dialed 911. The voice on the other end was so calm and efficient, I could have cried. I gave her my name and address and told her what was happening. She said she was sending help and wanted me to stay on the line, but I hung up. I ran to the keypad for the security system and punched in the code to open the front gate. Castle Asshole was wide open. Then I grabbed a cashmere blanket and two pillows from the couch and ran back out to Fiona.

She was screaming, bowed in half with another contraction. I fell to my knees beside her again and let her grab my hand. "Where the fuck is the housekeeper?" I said. If I had any clear thought pattern at all, it was *Why for fuck's sake am I the one doing this? Why does it have to be me?*

She fell back again, subsiding, and I slid the pillows under her. "Gone." She was glassy-eyed, and the blood was now a fully-formed puddle on the ground between her legs. I covered her up with the blanket. "She had a family emergency."

"Fuck her emergency." I held both her hands in mine, and we were both wearing gloves of blood. "The ambulance is on its way." I could hear a siren in the distance and prayed it was for us. "It'll be okay."

"Oh God, it hurts." Her face contorted, but she didn't try to get up this time, and her grip on my hands was weaker now.

"I know." I wanted Romeo. I tried to think where exactly he could be, if there was any way to call him. "I know it hurts." Still holding her hands, I leaned down and kissed her cheek. "I'm here." The blanket was turning red, too. "It's going to be fine."

"I have to tell you," she whimpered. "I love you, Scarlett, swear to God...I'm so sorry."

"Whatever it is, it's okay," I said as the ambulance came screaming up the driveway, lights flashing, siren blaring. Right behind it was Sebastian in his convertible. He jumped out and ran towards us as the paramedics were unloading their stretcher.

"Scarlett!" he yelled. "What the fuck is going on?" He froze mid-step, seeing the blood. "Oh shit."

"Get out of the way!" The girl paramedic gave him a shove, and he jumped aside.

"Don't leave me," Fiona was begging.

"I won't." I squeezed her hands tight before I let her go. "I'll be right here." I stood up and let the paramedics get to her, and Sebastian put his arm around my shoulders.

"What happened?" he asked me.

"I don't know." A battered four-wheel drive clunker was driving slowly up the driveway. "She was like this when I got here." I saw the long lens of a camera poke out of the driver's side window. "Oh fuck."

"I'm on it," Sebastian said, starting down the driveway. The boy paramedic sprinted past him and dove into the back of the ambulance, coming out with a pair of plastic baggies full of blood.

"Miss, what happened?" the girl paramedic asked me. She looked back over her shoulder to look into my face for a second, and I saw her eyes widen as she recognized me. "Did she fall?"

"I'm sorry; I don't know." My stomach was starting to roll; I was pretty certain I was about to puke. *The pool,* I thought. *I'll puke into the pool.* "She was like this when I found her, about two minutes before I called 911." Sebastian was shouting at the photographer, blocking his lens, and a police car was coming up behind the four by four.

"Clear the driveway!" the boy paramedic shouted. They heaved Fiona onto the stretcher, the blood feeding into her arm, and she moaned. She was so white she looked dead, but her eyes were still open.

"Can I go with her?" I smiled at her, and she tried to smile back.

"Sure, honey," the girl paramedic said. The cops had put the photographer back into his car and had him backing it across the lawn to clear a path. His tires were digging thick black ruts in the grass, and the sprinklers were soaking him through his open window.

Sebastian turned to look at me, his blue eyes wide with shock and rimmed in red. Then they were hustling me into the back of the ambulance.

They put me at Fiona's head. "Stay there," the boy paramedic ordered. "Don't move, and don't touch her." The girl paramedic was driving. I hunkered on my knees and watched as he gave her a shot.

"You." She was looking up at me, her voice barely more than a rasp. "Not Calvin."

"What, honey?" I said. "What are you talking about?"

"Baby," she said, closing her eyes.

"It's okay, honey," the boy paramedic said, patting her. "Don't try to talk."

She frowned. "Take her." She was trying to reach out for something, and I took her hand. "Baby," she said, her eyes meeting mine, and suddenly I understood. "You…not Calvin. Not Romeo."

"I will." I squeezed her hand. "I'll take it, just like I promised. But you're going to be okay."

"Her," she corrected. Her eyes were clear and lucid, looking into mine. "Delilah."

"Delilah," I repeated. "Yes. I promise."

She moaned again, her head falling back, and the paramedic shoved me back out of the way as we roared up to the doors of the hospital.

I was beside her as they wheeled her inside; heaven only knows how I got out of the ambulance that fast. There were photographers already on the sidewalk; I barely noticed the flashbulbs, grabbing for her hand. We went through the sliding glass doors and down the hall, then someone else was grabbing me. A nurse held me by the shoulders as they pushed the stretcher through another set of doors, these heavy and silver, swinging open when someone punched a big red button. The nurse was asking me questions, calm but fast, as she steered me to the right. There was an open space with lines of chairs and people whose faces looked just like I felt. I was deciding if I had to answer her.

"Not there!" someone called out from behind us. "Private—no

public access!" Before I could turn around to see who had shouted, she had turned me back to the left and down another hallway to a wooden door with a window in it. A tiny brass plaque under the window read "Family."

The room beyond the door was empty. The furniture was plush, like an expensive hotel lobby. A TV in the corner was playing the news with the sound turned down. I got a glimpse of the gates of Castle Asshole on the screen before it went black, switched off by the nurse with a remote. *She's still talking*, I suddenly realized. She had asked me something else.

"Ranhosky," I said. "Jacob Ranhosky is our lawyer." I rattled off the number, and she wrote it down on her clipboard. "He'll tell you what you need to know." I sank into a chair. She asked me something else, but again, I barely heard her, didn't look at her. Then just as she was leaving, I turned. "Will Fiona be okay?"

She looked shocked by the question. "We're doing everything we can." I'm an actress; I know a line when I hear one. "Someone will be out to give you a progress report." I nodded, turning away, and she left.

CHAPTER 51

I don't know how long I just sat there, staring at nothing, thinking of nothing. Nobody came with a progress report. Sebastian came finally and sat down beside me. "I brought you some clothes."

I looked down and realized I was still soaked with Fiona's blood. "I'm fine." I looked at him. His face was deathly white; his lips were dark pink; and he was sweating. The hair on his forehead was damp. "Did they tell you anything outside?"

"Nothing. Just that you were in here." I was horrified by how calm we both sounded.

"I told them to call Ranhosky."

"I know." He took my hand, and I tried to make my fingers curl around his, but they wouldn't. "He's outside. I think he called Dad." He lifted my arm and started peeling off my sweater. "I tracked down Lisa, and she's finding Romeo." He dropped the sweater on the floor. "So they're probably all on their way."

"Okay." He pulled my tee-shirt over my head, and I let him. He dressed me like a doll, covering my bloody bra with a clean black blouse.

"We need to wash your face."

"I'm fine."

He went into the tiny attached bathroom I hadn't even noticed was there and came back with wet paper towels. "Just hold still." He wiped my face and throat down into my cleavage, then took each hand and scrubbed it back and forth until the blood was gone, even from around my nails. My jeans were a dark wash; the stains could have been an artful dye job. But I smelled. I could smell myself.

The door opened again. "Miss Cross?" This one was a man with a lab coat over his scrub suit—a doctor. "Scarlett?" Sebastian and I both stood up. "Who is this?" he asked, like he and I were friends and Sebastian was the outsider.

"I'm Scarlett's brother, Sebastian." He took my hand again.

"Of course." He looked down at his clipboard. "Is your father here?"

"Not yet," Sebastian said.

"What's going on?" I demanded.

He looked uncomfortable for another moment, then he started talking. He was reciting from the same script as the nurse had used, dialogue from a doctor show. I couldn't follow it. It was like I didn't really speak English any more. I picked out familiar phrases like "despite our best efforts" and "breach birth" and "traumatic hemorrhage." Blood, I thought. That's blood.

"She's dead," I said in that same horrible calm voice. "Fiona is dead."

Sebastian crumpled back down into his chair, sobbing, still holding my hand. He would have pulled me down with him, but I jerked free.

"She asked us to give you this," the doctor said, holding out a crumpled piece of paper.

I took it from him. It was a note scrawled in Fiona's handwriting. "Romeo's baby," it read. There was a bloody thumbprint on the corner. I just stared at it.

"What is it?" Sebastian said.

"Did you know?" I asked him. "No bullshit; tell me right now, and don't try to explain." I handed him the note. "Did you know?"

He looked at it and looked even sicker than he had before. "I wasn't sure," he said. "But I knew it was possible."

"You knew they were fucking."

"Yes."

"Since when?"

"Since always. They never stopped. Fiona wouldn't let him stop."

"And you didn't tell me." If at any point in the past I had imagined myself facing this moment, I would have expected to be a sobbing, suicidal, incoherent mess. But the weird calm that had come over me remained intact.

"I wanted to tell you," he said. My brother wasn't calm. Tears were pouring down his face. "I tried."

"The day of the Oscars when you said he would turn me into Greta," I said. "That's what you meant." *And he has,* I thought. *I never would have thought it was possible, but they've turned me into the survivor.* "Does Calvin know?"

"He knows it's not his baby," Sebastian said.

"She," I said. "Not it. She. Delilah."

"But he doesn't know Romeo is the father." He tried to take my hand again, and I jerked away from him.

"Don't touch me."

"For what it's worth, I don't think they've been together since you went public at the Oscars."

"It's not worth dick, Sebastian." Suddenly I knew I couldn't stay in that room another moment. Romeo and Calvin were both on their way, and I knew I couldn't see them, not yet. If I saw Calvin, I might start crying, and I might not ever stop, and Delilah needed me. And if I saw Romeo, I would kill him.

I went out in the hall and found Ranhosky. "How much do you know?" I asked him.

"The girl is dead, but the baby is fine," he said. "And your husband is the father."

"I want the baby," I said. "I'm going to London first thing in the morning, and I want to take Delilah with me."

Any other lawyer—any other reasonable person would have told me it was impossible, that there were too many obstacles, that a newborn baby couldn't fly, that Delilah didn't have a passport, that I had no legal right to take her anywhere. But this was Ranhosky. "I'll take care of it." He put his hand on my shoulder. "I've been taking care of you your whole life."

Down the hall, I saw Calvin coming in. Sebastian met him, spoke to him, and they both started bawling and hugging each other. "Where is Delilah now?" I said.

"Come on," Ranhosky said. "I'll show you."

He led me to the birthing room like he owned the hospital. Fiona's body was still lying on the bed, a cold, dead, bloody thing. Two nurses were cleaning up, and two more were across the room in an alcove under a blinding white light. They were the ones with the baby, cleaning her up, and I heard Delilah's voice for the first time.

One of the nurses working on the body saw us and came to block our path. "I'm sorry," she said. "You can't come in here."

"Miss Cross would like to see the baby," Ranhosky said.

Whether she recognized me or him or just the tone of his voice, she got out of the way.

They had just wrapped Delilah in a blanket. She was still wailing, and her little rosebud face was red. I held out my arms, and the nurse gave her to me.

She stopped crying. "It's okay," I told her. "You smell your mama on me, don't you?" Even toothless and red from crying, she looked exactly like Romeo. The arch of her brow line, the curve of her mouth, even her tiny fingers and fingernails were exactly like his. "You're going to be a knockout." She fit perfectly against me, a warm little weight in my arms. I thought again about Greta, how she must have felt when she held Sebastian for the first time, her own perfect little lump just like this, and how she must have felt later when she heard about me, another little lump out there with another mama. "I'm going to be your mama from now on, Delilah," I told the baby in my arms. "I will always love you and stay with you and keep you safe." She made a little cooing noise with her eyes turned on my face, and when I touched the tip of my finger to her tiny, wrinkled palm, she gripped it tight. I thought about my own mama running all over the world with me, trying to survive, trying to escape. I didn't want to be Greta, but I didn't want to be her, either. "I'm going to be strong and smart, and you and I are going to be okay."

"Miss Cross?" the nurse said. "We need to get the baby to the nursery."

"Delilah," I said, handing her over. "Her name is Delilah." The baby was still clutching my finger, and I kissed her little fist before I pulled free. "I'll be right here."

"That's so sweet," the nurse said, looking at me like she thought I was some kind of saint. "Thank God she has you."

I smiled the best version of my movie star smile I could muster. "Thank God I have her."

"Scarlett?" Ranhosky said as they put her in the plastic bassinet and rolled her away. "What exactly do you want to do?"

I turned back toward him and saw Fiona. The other nurses who had been blocking some of my view before had moved, and I could see everything, her beautiful face, her open eyes, the blood. I started shaking all over; I felt sick. I wanted to cover my eyes and fall on the floor and wail until someone came to take me in their arms and hide my eyes and tell me it wasn't real and didn't matter. If I had been with Romeo at that moment or Calvin or even Sebastian, that's probably exactly what I would have done. But I was with Ranhosky. And Delilah needed me.

"Fiona wanted me to take the baby," I said. "She made me promise I would, that I wouldn't let Calvin or her parents take her."

"That's a lot to ask," he said. "Are you sure?"

"Very sure." I looked him in the eye. "Are you going to try to stop me?"

"Me? No, not at all." He had that weird look on his face like he didn't know whether to be shocked or proud. "Like I said, if that's what you want, I'll take care of it. But what about Romeo?"

I made myself look at the dead girl on the bed. I wanted to be mad at her. If she had lived, and I had seen Delilah and known the truth, I probably would have hated her for the rest of our lives. But now I couldn't. "I'll take care of Romeo."

CHAPTER 52

When I walked back out into the hall, Calvin and Sebastian were still hugging and crying. Fiona's parents had shown up and were about to be escorted out by a pair of security guards as they screamed bloody hell at the doctor who wouldn't let them see Fiona's body.

And Romeo was standing at the window of the nursery looking at the babies. He was wearing jeans and his costume shirt from *The Romantics*, and he'd been crying, smearing black make-up down his cheeks, and I had never seen him look more beautiful, and I had never wanted him so much. I watched his face as he watched the nurse wheel in Delilah's bassinet, and I couldn't stop myself from crying. If I would let him, he would love the baby so much. I wanted to run to him and beat the hell out of him for cheating on me and let him beg my forgiveness and forgive him and hug him and be with him forever with Delilah as our little girl. But I couldn't pretend any more that a fairy tale like that could be real. I couldn't let myself not know about the drugs he was using. I couldn't pretend I didn't know he would cheat again. If I stayed with him and let Delilah stay with him and told the world she was his daughter, how would I protect her when the fairy tale fell apart? What would happen if the next Fiona pushed me out? I loved him like my own soul, but I couldn't trust him. I could pretend for myself. I could risk disaster when I was the one who might get hurt. But I wouldn't risk Delilah.

So I bit my lip and dried my eyes and went to meet him for the first time not as his broken girl but as Delilah's mama.

He was so wrapped up in watching the baby, he didn't hear me walk up behind him. "Did they tell you your girlfriend died?" I said. He turned around, and his eyes almost shattered me, but somehow, I held it together. "I'm sorry."

"Sweetheart." He tried to reach for me, and I backed away, holding up my hands to ward him off. "I am so sorry. Please, just let me…" He looked lost, wild-eyed—he looked like I had felt so many times, like he was on the razor's edge of losing it completely. "God, how can I ever explain?"

"I don't care, Ro." Such a lie. "I can't care. I'm sorry you're hurt, and I'm sorry Fee's dead, and I'm so mad at both of you I wish I could bring her back just so I could kill you both together. But none of that matters." He tried again to touch me, and I dodged him. "Please, don't." He let his hands fall to his sides. "All that matters is Delilah."

"Agreed." He looked back at her through the glass. "She's beautiful."

"Of course she is. She looks just like you." I swallowed the catch in my throat. "But you can't tell anybody she's your daughter." He turned back to me, shock on his face. "You weren't going to if Fiona had lived, were you? She hooked up with Calvin as a cover, right, so I wouldn't know? Wasn't that the plan?"

"She really loved your dad," he said. "But otherwise….yeah, she meant for you to think the baby was your sister." His eyes were still breaking my heart. "She made me promise not to tell you the truth."

"She made me promise to take the baby away from you and Calvin both," I said. "So that's what I'm going to do."

"Scarlett, stop."

"She made me promise I would love her, and I do," I went on. "I love her like she was my own baby girl." *Because she's yours,* I wanted to tell him, but I couldn't. "I'm going to take her to London as soon as the doctors will let her travel."

"No," he said.

"And you're going to let me," I cut him off. "You're going to keep your mouth shut and let us go because if you don't, I'll let Ranhosky destroy your life just like he's always wanted."

"If you leave me, my life is already destroyed." He didn't say it with any kind of drama or flourish; he just said it.

"Bullshit." He was a wonderful actor. It would have been so much easier to believe him than it was to doubt him. But I couldn't be stupid any more. "If that were true, you wouldn't have fucked Fiona."

"Sweetheart, you don't understand."

"I don't want to understand." I was an actor, too, maybe not as good as he was, but the lies were coming easier. "I don't want to hurt you, but for Delilah's sake, I will." I looked past him to the precious rosebud baby on the other side of the glass, and suddenly I could do exactly what I needed to do. "I will let them take you to prison. I will even testify against you if I have to. I'll tell then you forced me to marry you. I'll tell what I know about the dealing and the drugs. I'll tell them about the heroin." He had gone so pale, he looked sick, and his jaw was clenched so tightly, I could see the muscle twitching in his cheek. "Don't make me do it, baby," I said. "Just let me go."

"And what about you and me?" He sounded furious.

"I can't think about that now."

"You have to think about it, Scarlett. We're married, remember?"

"The way you thought about it when you were making a baby with my best friend?" *And she was,* I thought, a dawning realization that twisted in my gut. *She was, and now she's dead.* "Fine," I said. "I'll think about it just like that." I looked back and saw Ranhosky watching from the other end of the hall. "Bye, Romeo," I finished, walking away.

I found Sebastian and my father in the tiny private waiting room where the hospital had stashed me before. "Hey sweetpea," Calvin said as soon as he saw me. "Come here." He hugged me close, and I let him. He seemed calmer now like he'd been given a pill. Sebastian still looked like hell.

"Hey Daddy," I said, hugging him back.

"Where's Romeo?" Sebastian asked.

"Outside," I said. "Not with me."

"You guys are breaking up?" he said. "Over this?"

"For right now, I'm taking the baby and going to London," I said. "Mr. Ranhosky is helping me sort it out."

"No," Sebastian said. "That's crazy. Daddy, tell her that's crazy."

"Are you sure you're up to taking care of a baby by yourself?" Calvin said.

"I'll hire people to help me," I said. "I'm sure Mr. Ranhosky will help me with that, too."

"Of course he will," Calvin said. "He'll make sure you have whatever you need."

"I can't believe you're just running away," Sebastian said.

"Kiddo, your sister has to go to London anyway, remember?" Calvin said. "She has a job to do."

"I'm going to talk to Romeo," Sebastian said. "He can't let you do this." He walked out.

"Sebastian!" Calvin started to go after him.

"Let him go, Daddy," I said. "Ro will tell him he can't stop me."

My father looked very tired. "Yeah," he said. "I guess he will."

"You knew, didn't you?" I said. "You knew the baby was Romeo's."

"I knew the baby wasn't mine," he said. "Fiona never pretended it was." He was crying again. "That poor kid. I'm glad you were there with her at least, in spite of everything else."

"I'm glad I was, too." He hadn't really answered my question, but that didn't surprise me. "In spite of everything."

"This is going to sound weird, I know." He touched my cheek. "Your mom would be really proud of you."

I thought of the first time I had seen him. I had been the orphan then, and he had saved me. As fucked up as he was, as fucked up as he had helped make me, he had loved me all my life. "Thanks, Daddy." This time it was me who hugged him. "I love you very much."

By morning, Ranhosky had everything arranged. The hospital discharged Delilah into my care, and a nurse put her into my arms. "She'll need to be fed again in about an hour," she said. "And I know the doctor has already spoken to your lawyer, but I can't stress enough how much we advise against taking her on a transatlantic flight so soon."

"She'll be traveling with a certified nanny, an obstetrician and a nurse," Ranhosky said. "I'm sure she'll be fine."

All of those people were waiting for us at the airport when we arrived, along with my assistant, Lisa, who had packed my bags. "Oh, look at her," she said as I lifted Delilah in her rocket seat out of the car. "She's beautiful."

"Thanks," I said. "I mean, yes, she is." I'm sure all the runways they use for private jets look pretty much the same, but I could have sworn I had seen this one before. Looking at the plane, all I could think about was the night Fiona had helped Romeo escape to Canada, the night she had told me she meant to take him from me if she could. I had always thought she had failed, and I had won. But apparently, I had been wrong.

The nanny took the sleeping baby from me and got on board with the doctor and nurse following close behind. Ranhosky was conferring with the pilot and a customs agent. I couldn't even imagine how he'd gotten Delilah a passport so quickly. Probably the same way he'd gotten one to help Calvin bring me home from Mexico.

"Are you sure about this?" Lisa asked me. We had talked during the night, and I had told her everything.

I said, "Absolutely," but I wasn't. In a few minutes when the plane took off and left Ranhosky on the ground, I would be in charge. For the first time in my life, everything would be up to me. I had a place to go, an apartment booked, a staff, a nanny, Lisa. But I would be the one making all the decisions. I didn't know anybody in London, and I would have a newborn baby. I was terrified. But if I could do it, maybe I wasn't really so broken after all.

Just as I was having this exhilarating thought, a cab drove up, and Simon got out. "You're here already," he said as he came toward me. "I was hoping I'd be here first." He dropped his satchel and hugged me close. "You poor darling." He towered over me, and his arms around me felt so perfect, I couldn't help melting against him in relief. "I'm so sorry."

"What are you doing here?" The first time we'd met, I had fallen into his arms; now I was doing it again. "How did you know?"

"Mr. Ranhosky called me," he said. "He was worried about you and the baby traveling alone." A porter went by pushing a huge cart full of baby stuff. "Well, sort of alone." I hadn't realized I was crying until he wiped away a tear from my cheek. "I told him I'd take care of you."

"Thank you." I was a coward. I didn't want to be brave. "Thanks so much." I clung to him, burying my face in his shirtfront as I cried.

"It's all right, darling," he promised. "Everything will be fine."

End of Notebook 1

CHAPTER 53

Romeo closed the notebook and set it on the coffee table. "Are you finished?" Tracy the model/actress asked as he got up.

"Oh yeah." He went to the kitchen and poured himself a glass of juice.

"Can I read it?"

"If you want." He got some aspirin for his raging headache out of the cabinet. "I can save you some time, though." He took two, thought about it, then took a third. "My beautiful wife has had a hard, hard life, and most of it's my fault."

"Oh shut up," she said, laughing as she settled back on the couch with the notebook. "I bet she's wonderful. She's wonderful, isn't she?"

"Oh yeah, she's a peach." He sat back down beside her, tilted his head back and closed his eyes. "Why is it my destiny to fall in lust with women who are in love with my wife?"

"I could tell you, but I promised your therapist I wouldn't spoil the surprise."

"Wow," he said, laughing without opening his eyes. "Looks like that, and she's funny, too."

"What's this clipping?" she said

"Which one?"

"The one in Spanish." He opened his eyes and looked at her. "It was stuck down in the little pocket in the back of the notebook." She handed it to him. "It looks like a write-up from a Mexican newspaper," she said. "An obituary."

He didn't read Spanish, but he could read the date—five years ago, more than five years after Delilah's birth. "Tell me," he said, handing it back to her.

"My Spanish isn't perfect," she said. "But it's an obituary for a Mexican priest." She studied the clipping. "Apparently he was the parish priest in some little town and everybody loved him. He ministered to everybody, even...*los asasinos*. Murderers, killers. Apparently when he was younger, he used to give last rites to prisoners." She raised an eyebrow. "Why would Scarlett keep something like this with her memoirs?"

"Son of a bitch." His headache was turning into a monster that aspirin would never be able to handle. "She said she was in Mexico." He got up.

"What are you doing?"

"Calling my lawyer." He used the direct line to Anne's office. "Hey, it's Ro," he said when she answered. "Let her have the house. Just get me the rest of this book."

ACKNOWLEDGMENTS

Endless thanks as always to John Hartness and his asylum full of brilliant crazies at Falstaff Books for giving my most twisted psycho book baby to date a home and making her the best that she can be. Special thanks to Robyne Pomroy for giving me the exact cover I wanted, only better.

This particular novel has been with me in one form or another for a really long time. Much gratitude to the family and friends who have listened to me talk about it for decades and almost never begged me to shut up. I love y'all very much, and I know you're the reason I'm still writing. Your support has meant and will always mean the world.

ABOUT THE AUTHOR

Lucy Blue lives in a decrepit old house in a small town in South Carolina with her husband, artist and game designer Justin Glanville, and her dog, preternaturally brilliant and adorable Jack Russell terrier, Luke. She is a graduate of Winthrop University and the South Carolina Governor's School for the Arts.

9 781645 540076